CAPTAIN FLANDRY

DEFENDER OF THE TERRAN EMPIRE

CAPTAIN FLANDRY

DEFENDER OF THE TERRAN EMPIRE

THE TECHNIC CIVILIZATION SAGA

POUL ANDERSON

Captain Flandry: Defender of the Terran Empire

This is a work of fiction. All the characters and events portrayed in this book are fictional, and any resemblance to real people or incidents is purely coincidental.

"Introduction" copyright © 2009 by Hank Davis. "A Chronology of Technic Civilization" by Sandra Miesel copyright © 2008 by Sandra Miesel.

Acknowledgements
"Outpost of Empire"—originally published in *Galaxy*, December, 1967. Copyright © 1967, Galaxy Publishing Corp.
The Day of Their Return—originally published as a Signet Book by The New American Library, Inc. Copyright © 1975 by Poul Anderson.
"Tiger by the Tail"—originally published in *Planet Stories*, January, 1951. Copyright © 1951 by Love Romances Publishing Co., Inc.
"Honorable Enemies"—originally published in *Future* combined with *Science Fiction*, May, 1951. Copyright © 1951 by Columbia Publications, Inc.
"The Game of Glory"—originally published in *Venture Science Fiction*, March, 1958. Copyright © 1957 by Fantasy House, Inc.
"A Message in Secret"—originally published in *Fantastic*, December, 1959. Copyright © 1959 by Ziff-Davis Publications, Inc. Reprinted 1961 by Ace Books, Inc. under the title *Mayday Orbit*.

A Baen Book

Baen Publishing Enterprises
P.O. Box 1403
Riverdale, NY 10471
www.baen.com

ISBN 13: 978-1-4391-3333-0

Cover art by David Seeley

First Baen printing, February 2010

Distributed by Simon & Schuster
1230 Avenue of the Americas
New York, NY 10020

10 9 8 7 6 5 4 3 2 1

Pages by Joy Freeman (www.pagesbyjoy.com)
Printed in the United States of America

CONTENTS

❈ ACKNOWLEDGEMENT ❈

I'm indebted to Sandra Miesel for informing me, when I was still gathering the novels and stories of the Technic Civilization universe, that Poul Anderson had done revisions to the Flandry stories appearing in the Ace editions of the earlier collections, *Flandry of Terra* and *Agent of the Terran Empire*. Without that information, this book and the next in the series would have reprinted the original versions of the stories instead of Anderson's more polished and preferred later versions. That's in addition to my already being indebted to Sandra for her indispensible chronology of the Technic Civilization series. Take a bow, Sandra.

I'm also indebted to Karen Anderson for elucidating the pronunciation of Aycharaych, and to Geoffrey Kidd for catching a dumb factual mistake in my introduction, thereby making me look far more savvy than I am. Two more bows, if you will; and put your hands together, audience.

ENTER AN ADVERSARY, CHARISMATIC AND RUTHLESS

In fiction, not invariably but often, a resourceful and omnicompetent hero will be given a similarly formidable opponent. Sherlock Holmes had his Professor Moriarty, though for only one story, with a short mention in the final Holmes novel—after all, Sir Arthur Conan Doyle created him specifically for the purpose of killing off his detective so that he could write about something else. Nero Wolfe had his Arnold Zeck, at greater length (three novels), James Bond his Ernst Stavro Blofeld (two novels, and a somewhat longer run, though initially as a barely-seen presence, in the movie versions). In comic books, the presence of an adversary is almost mandatory: Batman vs. the Joker; Superman vs. Lex Luthor; Captain Marvel vs. Dr. Thaddeus Bodog Sivana; etc.

And Dominic Flandry has Aycharaych.

Working with the Merseians, the primary enemy of the Terran Empire, Aycharaych is a redoubtable antagonist, charming in both personality and physical appearance, brilliantly intelligent—and possessing the ability to read minds. Possibly descended from birdlike ancestors on his homeworld Chereion, a planet about which the Merseians know little and the Terrans less, his head is hairless, having instead eyebrows of tiny feathers and a crest of larger feathers atop his head. His feet, usually bare, are birdlike with spurs on the ankles. When the Terran official Desai meets him in *The Day of Their Return*, the Chereionite's appearance makes him think of a Byzantine saint. That particular description will quickly become ironic, and lethally so.

Saints also have causes for which they strive and even die. Aycharaych is working with the Merseians, but keeps a distant and amused attitude toward the Merseian-Terran conflict, as if it's all a game to him; certainly not a cause. He gives the impression that he's beyond causes, and seems to consider both Merseians and humans as his inferiors: clever animals, perhaps, and amusing ones, but nothing more.

Ironic detachment aside, he has more respect for Dominic Flandry than for most humans or Merseians, and at one point tells Flandry that the two of them are very much alike. In "Honorable Enemies," included in this volume, he even saves Flandry's life in a tight spot—but makes it clear that his motive was that Flandry was useful. Forget about hail fellow, well met.

In this fifth volume of the Technic Civilization saga, Aycharaych is active (mostly behind the scenes) in the novel *The Day of Their Return*, and personally makes Flandry's life more complicated in the aforementioned "Honorable Enemies." While the Chereionite is not involved in the other stories and novel contained herein, he will be an even more active nemesis to Flandry (and very much vice versa) in the sixth volume, *Sir Dominic Flandry: The Last Knight of Terra*. (Never let a good villain go to waste...)

The reader may be wondering about the pronunciation of "Aycharaych." Karen Anderson reports that Poul based it on the initials HRH, but pronounced the first and third syllables ('aych') with a Mexican "Ay!" followed by a guttural 'ch' like Scottish "loch."

Sandra Miesel, undisputed authority on most things Technic (and bordering on omnicompetent herself), has long kept track of its chronology and knows its cycles well.

✡   ✡   ✡

As I mentioned in the introduction to the previous volume, *Young Flandry*, Dominic Flandry is offstage for the earlier part of this book. The curtain raiser, "Outpost of Empire," tells of rebellion on a planet at the edge of the Empire's domain and how a far greater tragedy was averted. (Flandry is brilliant, but doesn't have an absolute monopoly on competence.)

That's followed by the novel *The Day of Their Return*, in which Flandry is briefly mentioned (his rank is still Commander), but remains offstage.

Then comes the first published (1951) Flandry story, "Tiger by the Tail," and Flandry, now a captain, is back in action, though most of the action consists of subtle manipulation. (I wonder if Poul Anderson read Dashiell Hammett's *Red Harvest* before writing this story.) There's more physical action in the second Flandry story to be published (also in 1951), "Honorable Enemies," and again the adversary is outfoxed, though Flandry this time has more than a little help from a very smart lady.

I should mention again that Anderson originally thought of Flandry as a science fiction counterpart to Leslie Charteris' Simon Templar, usually referred to as the Saint, and while Templar was a crack shot with a pistol, an artist with a knife, and usually came out on top in a fistfight, much of the time he outthought the bad guys. At the end of one Saintly tale, two gangsters were maneuvered into machine-gunning each other as the Saint walked away into the fog. Templar and Flandry are not only men of action, but adroit chess players as well.

A few years passed, and Flandry returned in 1957's novella "The Game of Glory." (Never let a good hero go to waste . . .) Then in 1959 came two Flandry novels. The earlier falls later in the overall Flandry timeline and will be in the next volume, but the other, *A Message in Secret*, concludes this book. In both, Flandry is once again a swash-buckler's swash-buckler and also adroitly outfoxes his enemies—and sometimes his allies as well.

Poul Anderson was a born writer from the beginning, but the passage of a few years had honed his skills, so the later Flandry stories were written with a surer hand and Flandry was becoming a more rounded character. However, Anderson did some tweaking of the present stories before they appeared in two collections from Ace books at the end of the 1970s. The Flandry of those first two stories as they originally appeared, upon learning that the humans on a planet have near-religious feelings about Terra, might not have mused:

> He didn't want to tell them what Terra was actually like these days. (Or perhaps had always been. He suspected men are only saints and heroes in retrospect.) Indeed, he dare not speak of sottish Emperors, venal nobles, faithless wives, servile commons, to this armed and burning reverence.

Or, elsewhere in the same yarn, might not have given voice to a complaining soliloquy:

> "This they call fun?" He tottered erect. Snow had gotten under his parka hood. It began to melt, trickling over his ribs in search of a really good place to refreeze. "Great greasy comets ... I might have been sitting in the Everest House with a bucket of champagne, lying to some beautiful wench about my exploits ... but no, I had to come out here and do 'em."

And while we do overhear his thoughts in the version of "Honorable Enemies" included in this volume:

> *... we're in the way of* [the Mersians'] *dream of galactic overlordship. We are the first ones they have to smash. Or so they believe. And so we believe. Never mind what the unascertainable objective truth of the matter may be. Belief is what brings on the killing.*

The more cynical of those thoughts, beginning with "*Or so they believe,*" was added by Poul Anderson at the end of the 1970s, adding a touch of humanizing tarnish to his hero's polish; a bit of tarnish which throws Flandry's undeniable valor into sharper relief.

No longer a cocky ensign, Flandry now has few illusions. (Mind, the cockiness isn't *completely* absent.) Yet he lacks any illusion that if the Terran Empire falls it will be replaced by anything that isn't much worse, including domination by the Merseians. And even if the Long Night is relentlessly approaching, he has no intention of going gentle into that Long Night. Instead, after donning the exceedingly colorful and flamboyant garb suitable to a decadent culture, he'll strap on a blaster, check to see that it's fully-charged, and prepare to go down fighting.

But he won't be going down in the pages which follow. His fight will continue in the next two volumes of the Technic Civilization saga. See you there.

—Hank Davis, 2009

OUTPOST OF EMPIRE

"No dragons are flying—"

Karlsarm looked up. The fog around him was as yet thin enough that he could glimpse the messenger. Its wings sickled across nightblue and those few stars—like diamond Spica and amber Betelgeuse—which were too bright and near to be veiled. So deep was the stillness that he heard the messenger's feathers rustle.

"Good," he murmured. "As I hoped." Louder: "Inform Mistress Jenith that she can get safely across open ground now. She is to advance her company to Gallows Wood on the double. There let someone keep watch from a treetop, but do not release the fire bees without my signal. Whatever happens."

The sweet, unhuman voice of the messenger trilled back his order.

"Correct," Karlsarm said. The messenger wheeled and flew northward.

"What was that?" Wolf asked.

"Enemy hasn't got anyone aloft, far as Rowlan's scouts can tell," Karlsarm replied. "I instructed—"

"Yes, yes," growled his lieutenant. "I do know Anglic, if not bird language. But are you sure you want to keep Jenith's little friends in reserve? We might have no casualties at all if they went in our van."

"But we'd have given away another secret. And we may very

1

badly want a surprise to spring, one of these times. You go tell
Mistress Randa the main body needs maximum cover. I'm after
a last personal look. When I get back, we'll charge."

Wolf nodded. He was a rangy man, harsh-faced, his yellow
hair braided. His fringed leather suit did not mark him off for
what he was, nor did his weapons; dirk and tomahawk were an
ordinary choice. But the two great hellhounds that padded black
at his heels could only have followed the Grand Packmaster of
the Windhook.

He vanished into fog and shadow. Karlsarm loped forward. He
saw none of his hundreds, but he sensed them in more primitive
ways. The mist patch that hid them grew tenuous with distance,
until it lay behind the captain. He stopped, shadow-roofed by a
lone sail tree, and peered before and around him.

They had had the coastal marshes to conceal them over most
of their route. The climb by night, however, straight up Onyx
Heights, had required full moonlight if men were not to fall and
shatter themselves. This meant virtually no moon on the second night, when they entered the cultivated part of the plateau.
But with a sidereal period of two and a third days, Selene rose
nearly full again, not long after the third sundown, and waxed
as it crossed the sky. At present it was hardly past maximum, a
dented disk flooding the land with iciness. Karlsarm felt naked
to the eyes of his enemies. None seemed aware of him, though.
Fields undulated away to a flat eastern horizon, kilometer after
kilometer. They were planted in rye, silvery and silent under the
moon, sweet-smelling where feet had crushed it. Far off bulked
a building, but it was dark; probably nothing slept within except
machines. The fact that agriculture took place entirely on robot-
ized latifundia made the countryside thinly populated. Hence the
possibility existed for Karlsarm of leading his people unobserved
across it after sunset—to a five-kilometer distance from Domkirk.

Even this near, the city looked small. It was the least of the Nine,
housing only about fifty thousand, and it was the second oldest,
buildings huddled close together and much construction underground in the manner of pioneer settlements. Aside from streets,
its mass was largely unilluminated. They were sober folk here who
went early to bed. In places windows gleamed yellow. A single
modern skyscraper sheened metallic beneath Selene, and it too had
wakeful rooms. Several upper facets of the cathedral were visible

above surrounding roofs. The moon was so brilliant that Karlsarm would have sworn he could see color in their reflection of it.

A faint murmur of machinery breathed across the fields. Alien it was, but Karlsarm almost welcomed the sound. The farmlands had oppressed him with their emptiness—their essential *lifelessness,* no matter how rich the crops and sleek the pastured animals—when he remembered his forests. He shivered in the chill. As if to seek comfort, he looked back westward. The fogbank that camouflaged the center of his army shimmered startlingly white. Surely it had been seen; but the phenomenon occurred naturally, this near the Lawrencian Ocean. Beyond the horizon, barely visible, as if disembodied, floated the three highest snowpeaks of the Windhoek. Home was a long march off: an eternal march for those who would die.

"Stop that, you," Karlsarm whispered to himself. He unshipped his crossbow, drew a quarrel from his quiver, loaded and cocked the piece. Hard pull on the crank, snick of the pawl were somehow steadying. He was not a man tonight but a weapon.

He trotted back to his people. The fog was thickening, swirling in cold wet drifts, as Mistress Randa sent ever more of her pets from their cages. He heard her croon a spell—

> *"Shining mist, flow and twist,*
> *fill this cup of amethyst.*
> *Buzzing dozens, brotherlings,*
> *sing your lullaby of wings.*
> *Ah! the moonlight flew and missed!"*

He wondered if it was really needed. Why must women with Skills be that secretive about their work? He heard likewise the tiny hum of the insects, and glimpsed a few when Selene sparked iridescence off them. They kept dropping down to the ryestalks after they had exuded all the droplets they could, filling up with dew and rising again. Soon the cloud was so dense that men were almost blind. They kept track of each other by signals—imitated bird calls, chirrs, cheeps, mews—and by odor, most of them having put on their distinctive war perfumes.

Karlsarm found Wolf near the red gleam of one hellhound's eyes. "All set?" he asked.

"Aye. If we can keep formation in this soup."

"We'll keep it close enough. Got a lot of practice in the tide-lands, didn't we? Very well, here we go." Karlsarm uttered a low, shuddering whistle.

The sound ran from man to man, squad to squad, and those who knew flutecat language heard it as: "We have stalked the prey down, let us leap."

The fog rolled swiftly toward Domkirk; and none in the city observed that there was no wind to drive it.

John Ridenour had arrived that day. But he had made planetfall a week earlier and before then had crammed himself with every piece of information about Freehold that was available to him—by any means necessary, from simple reading and conversation to the most arduous machine-forced mnemonics. His whole previous career taught him how little knowledge that was. It had amused as well as annoyed him that he ended his journey explaining things to a crewman of the ship that brought him thither.

The *Ottokar* was a merchantman, Germanian owned, as tautly run as most vessels from that world. Being short of bottom on the frontiers, the Imperial Terrestrial Navy must needs charter private craft when trouble broke loose. They carried only materiel; troops still went in regular transports, properly armed and escorted.

But Ridenour was a civilian: also on time charter, he thought wryly. His job was not considered urgent. They gave him a Crown ticket on Terra and said he could arrange his own passage. It turned out to involve several transfers from one ship to another, two of them with nonhuman crews. Traffic was sparse, here where the Empire faded away into a wilderness of suns unclaimed and largely unexplored. The Germanians were of his own species, of course. But since they were a bit standoffish by culture, and he by nature, he had rattled about rather alone on what was to be the final leg of his trip.

Now, when he would actually have preferred silence and soli-tude, the off-duty steward's mate joined him in the saloon and insisted on talking. That was the annoyance—with Freehold in the viewscope.

"I have never seen anything more...*prachtig*...more magnifi-cent," the steward's mate declared.

Then why not shut your mouth and watch it? grumbled Rid-enour to himself.

"But this is my first long voyage," the other went on shyly.

He was little more than a boy, little older than Ridenour's first son. No doubt the rest of the men kept him severely in his place. Certainly he had hitherto been mute as far as the passenger was concerned. Ridenour found he could not be ungracious to him. "Are you enjoying it...ah, I don't know your name?"

"Dietrich, sir. Dietrich Steinhauer. Yes, the time has been interesting. But I wish they would tell me more about the port planets we make on our circuit. They do not like me to question them."

"Well, don't take that to heart," Ridenour advised. He leaned back in his chair and got out his pipe—a tall, wiry, blond, hatchet-faced man, his gray tunic-and-trousers outfit more serviceable than fashionable. "With so much loneliness between the stars, so much awe, men have to erect defenses. Terrans are apt to get boisterous on a long voyage. But from what I've heard of Germanians, I could damn near predict they'd withdraw into routine and themselves. Once your shipmates grow used to you, decide you're a good reliable fellow, they'll thaw."

"Really? Are you an ethnologist, sir?"

"No, xenologist."

"But there are no nonhumans on Freehold, except the Arulians. Are there?"

"N-no. Presumably not. Biologically speaking, at any rate. But it is a strange planet, and such have been known to do strange things to their colonists."

Dietrich gulped and was quiet for a few blessed minutes.

The globe swelled, ever greater in its changing phases as the *Ottokar* swung down from parking orbit. Against starry blackness it shone blue, banded with blinding white cloudbanks, the continents hardly visible through the deep air. The violet border that may be seen from space on the rim of any terrestroid world was broader and more richly hued than Terra's. Across the whole orb flickered aurora, invisible on dayside but a pale sheet of fire on nightside. It would not show from the ground, being too diffuse; Freehold lacked the magnetic field to concentrate solar particles at the poles. Yet here it played lambent before the eye, through the thin upper layers of atmosphere. For the sun of Freehold was twice as luminous as Sol, a late type F. At a distance of 1.25 a.u., its disk was slightly smaller than that which Terra sees. But the illumination was almost a third again as great, more white than yellow; and through a glare filter one could watch flares and prominences leap millions of kilometers into space and shower fierily back.

The single moon hove into view. It was undistinguished, even in its name (how many satellites of human-settled worlds are known as Selene?), having just a quarter the mass of Luna. But it was sufficiently close in to show a fourth greater angular diameter. Because of this, and the sunlight, and a higher albedo—fewer mottlings—it gave better than twice the light. Ridenour spied it full on and was almost dazzled.

"Freehold is larger than Germania, I believe." Dietrich's attempt at pompousness struck Ridenour as pathetic.

"Or Terra," the xenologist said. "Equatorial diameter in excess of 16,000 kilometers. But the mean density is quite low, making surface gravity a bare ninety per cent of standard."

"Then why does it have such thick air, sir? Especially with an energetic sun and a nearby moon of good size."

Hm, Ridenour thought, you're a pretty bright boy after all. Brightness should be encouraged; there's precious little of it around. "Gravitational potential," he said. "Because of the great diameter, field strength decreases quite slowly. Also, even if the ferrous core is small, making for weaker tectonism and less outgassing of atmosphere than normal—still, the sheer pressure of mass on mass, in an object this size, was bound to produce respectable quantities of air and heights of mountains. These different factors work out to the result that the sea-level atmosphere is denser than Terran, but safely breathable at all altitudes of terrain." He stopped to catch his breath.

"If it has few heavy elements, the planet must be extremely old," Dietrich ventured.

"No, the early investigators found otherwise," Ridenour said. "The system's actually younger than Sol's. It evidently formed in some metal-poor region of the galaxy and wandered into this spiral arm afterward."

"But at least Freehold is old by historical standards. I have heard it was settled more than five centuries ago. And yet the population is small. I wonder why?"

"Small initial colony, and not many immigrants afterward, to this far edge of everything. High mortality rates, too—originally,

I mean, before men learned the ins and out of a world which they had never evolved on: a more violent and treacherous world than the one your ancestors found, Dietrich. That's why, for many generations, they tended to stay in their towns, where they could keep nature at bay. But they didn't have the economic base to enlarge the towns very fast. Therefore they practiced a lot of birth control. To this day, there are only nine cities on that whole enormous surface, and five of them are on the same continent. Their inhabitants total fourteen and a half megapeople."

"But I have heard about savages, sir. How many are they?"

"Nobody knows," Ridenour said. "That's one of the things I've been asked to find out."

He spoke too curtly, of a sudden, for Dietrich to dare question him further. It was unintentional. He had merely suffered an experience that came to him every once in a while, and shook him down to bedrock.

Momentarily, he confronted the sheer magnitude of the universe.

Good God, he thought, if You do not exist—terrible God, if You do—here we are, Homo sapiens, children of Earth, creators of bonfires and flint axes and proton converters and gravity generators and faster-than-light spaceships, explorers and conquerors, dominators of an Empire which we ourselves founded, whose sphere is estimated to include four million blazing suns... here we are, and what are we? What are four million stars, out on the fringe of one arm of the galaxy, among its hundred billion; and what is the one galaxy among so many?

Why, I shall tell you what we are and these are, John Ridenour. We are one more-or-less intelligent species in a universe that produces sophonts as casually as it produces snowflakes. We are not a hair better than our great, greenskinned, gatortailed Merseian rivals, not even considering that they have no hair; we are simply different in looks and language, similar in imperial appetites. The galaxy—what tiny part of it we can ever control—cares not one quantum whether their youthful greed and boldness overcome our wearied satiety and caution. (Which is a thought born of an aging civilization, by the way).

Our existing domain is already too big for us. We don't comprehend it. We can't.

Never mind the estimated four million suns inside our borders. Think just of the approximately one hundred thousand whose planets we do visit, occupy, order about, accept tribute from. Can you visualize the number? A hundred thousand; no more; you could count that high in about seven hours. But can you conjure up before you, in your mind, a wall with a hundred thousand bricks in it: and see all the bricks simultaneously?

Of course not. No human brain can go as high as ten.

Then consider a planet, a world, as big and diverse and old and mysterious as ever Terra was. Can you see the entire planet at once? Can you hope to understand the entire planet?

Next consider a hundred thousand of them.

No wonder Dietrich Steinhauer here is altogether ignorant about Freehold. I myself had never heard of the place before I was asked to take this job. And I am a specialist in worlds and the beings that inhabit them. I should be able to treat them lightly. Did I not, a few years ago, watch the total destruction of one?

Oh, no. Oh, no. The multiple millions of . . . of everything alive . . . bury the name Starkad, bury it forever. And yet it was a single living world that perished, a mere single world.

No wonder Imperial Terra let the facts about Freehold lie unheeded in the data banks. Freehold was nothing but an obscure frontier dominion, a unit in the statistics. As long as no complaint was registered worthy of the sector governor's attention, why inquire further? How could one inquire further? Something more urgent is always demanding attention elsewhere. The Navy, the intelligence services, the computers, the decision makers are stretched too ghastly thin across too many stars.

And today, when war ramps loose on Freehold and Imperial marines are dispatched to fight Merseia's Arulian cat's-paws—we still see nothing but a border action. It is most unlikely that anyone at His Majesty's court is more than vaguely aware of what is happening. Certainly our admiral's call for help took long to go through channels: "We're having worse and worse trouble with the hinterland savages. The city people are no use. They don't seem to know either what's going on. Please advise."

And the entire answer that can be given to this appeal thus far is me. One man. Not even a Naval officer—not even a specialist in human cultures—such cannot be gotten, except for tasks elsewhere that look more vital. One civilian xenologist, under contract to investigate, report, and recommend appropriate action. Which counsel may or may not be heeded.

If I die—and the battles grow hotter each month—Lissa will weep; so will our children, for a while. I like to think that a few friends will feel sorry, a few colleagues remark what a loss this is, a few libraries keep my books on micro for a few more generations. However, that is the most I can hope for.

And this big, beautiful planet Freehold can perhaps hope for much less. The news of my death will be slow to reach official eyes. The request for a replacement will move slower yet. It may quite easily get lost.

Then what, Freehold of the Nine Cities and the vast, mapless, wild-man-haunted outlands that encircle them? Then what?

Once the chief among the settlements was Sevenhouses; but battle had lately passed through it. Though the spaceport continued in use and the *Ottokar* set down there, Ridenour learned that Terran military headquarters had been shifted to Nordyke. He hitched a ride in a supply barge. Because of the war, its robopilot was given a human boss, a young lieutenant named Muhammad Sadik, who invited the xenologist to sit in the control turret with him. Thus Ridenour got a good look at the country.

Sevenhouses was almost as melancholy a sight from the air as from the ground. The original town stood intact at one edge; but that was a relic, a few stone-and-concrete buildings which piety preserved. Today's reality had been a complex of industries, dwelling places—mainly apartments—schools, parks, shops, recreation centers. The city was not large by standards of the inner Empire. But it had been neat, bright, bustling, more up-to-date than might have been expected of a community in the marshes.

Now most of it was rubble. What remained lay fire-scarred, crowded with refugees, the machinery silenced, the people sadly picking up bits and pieces of their lives. Among them moved Imperial marines, and warcraft patrolled overhead like eagles.

"Just what happened?" Ridenour asked.

Sadik shrugged. "Same as happened at Oldenstead. The Arulians made an air assault—airborne troops and armor, I mean. They knew we had a picayune garrison and hoped to seize the place before we could reinforce. Then they'd pretty well own it, you know, the way they've got Waterfleet and Startop. If the enemy occupies a townful of His Majesty's subjects, we can't scrub that town. At least, doctrine says we can't . . . thus far. But here, like at Oldenstead, our boys managed to hang on till we got help to them. We clobbered the blues pretty good, too. Not many escaped. Of course, the ground fighting was heavy and kind of bashed the town around."

He gestured. The barge was now well aloft, and a broad view could be gotten. "Harder on the countryside, I suppose," he added. "We felt free to use nukes there. They sure chew up a landscape, don't they?"

Ridenour scowled. The valley beneath him had been lovely, green and ordered, a checkerboard of mechanized agroenterprises run from the city. But the craters pocked it, and high-altitude bursts had set square kilometers afire, and radiation had turned sere most fields that were not ashen.

He felt relieved when the barge lumbered across a mountain range. The wilderness beyond was not entirely untouched. A blaze had run widely, and fallout appeared to have been heavy. But the reach of land was enormous, and presently nothing lay beneath except life. The forest that made a well-nigh solid roof was not quite like something from ancient Terra: those leaves, those meadows, those rivers and lakes had a curious brilliance; or was that due to sunlight; fierce and white out of a pale-blue sky where cumulus clouds towered intricately shadowed? The air was often darkened and clamorous with bird flocks which must number in the millions. And, as woodland gave way to prairie, Ridenour saw herds of grazers equally rich in size and variety.

"Not many planets this fertile," Sadik remarked. "Wonder why the colonists haven't done more with it?"

"Their society began in towns rather than smaller units like family homesteads," Ridenour answered. "That was unavoidable. Freehold isn't as friendly to man as you might believe."

"Oh, I've been through some of the storms. I know."

"And native diseases. And the fact that while native food is generally edible, it doesn't contain everything needed for human nutrition. In short, difficulties such as are normally encountered in settling a new world. They could be overcome, and were; but the process was slow, and the habit of living in a few centers became ingrained. Also, the Freeholders are under a special handicap. The planet is not quite without iron, copper and other heavy elements. But their ores occur too sparsely to support a modern industrial establishment, let alone permit it to expand. Thus Freehold has always depended on extraplanetary trade. And the system lies on the very fringe of human-dominated space. Traffic is slight and freight rates high."

"They could do better, though," Sadik declared. "Food as tasty as what they raise ought to go for fancy prices on places like Bonedry and Disaster Landing—planets not terribly far, lots of metals, but otherwise none too good a home for their colonists."

Ridenour wasn't sure if the pilot was patronizing him in revenge. He hadn't meant to be pedantic; it was his professional habit. "I understand that the Nine Cities were in fact developing such trade, with unlimited possibilities for the future," he said mildly. "They also hoped to attract immigrants. But then the war came."

"Yeh," Sadik grunted. "One always does, I guess."

Ridenour recollected that war was no stranger to Freehold. Conflict, at any rate, which occasionally erupted in violence. The Arulian insurgency was the worst incident to date—but perhaps nothing more than an incident, *sub specie aeternitatis*.

The threat from the savages was something else: less spectacular, but apt to be longer lasting, with more pervasive subtle effects on the long-range course of history here.

Nordyke made a pleasant change. The strife had not touched it, save to fill the airport with ships—and the seaport, as its factories drew hungrily on the produce of other continents—and the streets with young men from every corner of the Empire. The modern town, surrounding Catwick's bright turbulent waters, retained in its angular architecture some of the starkness of the old castle-like settlements on the heights above. But in the parks, roses and jasmine were abloom; and elsewhere the taverns brawled with merriment. The male citizens were happily acquiring the money that the Imperialists brought with them; the females were still more happily helping spend it.

Ridenour had no time for amusement, even had he been inclined. Plain to see, Admiral Fernando Cruz Manqual considered him one more nuisance wished on a long-suffering planetary command by a home government that did not know its mass from a Dirac hole. He had to swing more weight than he actually carried, to get billeted in a float-shelter on the bay and arrange his background-information interviews.

One of these was with an Arulian prisoner. He did not speak

any language of that world, and the slender, blue-feathered, sharp-snouted biped knew no Anglic. But both were fluent in the principal Merseian tongue, though the Arulian had difficulty with certain Eriau phonemes.

"Relax," said Ridenour, after the other had been conducted into the office he had borrowed, and the Terran marine had gone out. "I won't hurt you. I wear this blaster because regulations say I must. But you aren't so stupid as to attempt a break."

"No. Nor so disloyal as to give away what would hurt my people." The tone was more arrogant than defiant, as nearly as one could make comparisons with human emotions. The Arulian had already learned that captives were treated according to the Covenant. The reason was less moral than practical—the same reason why his own army did not try to annihilate Nordyke, though Terra's effort was concentrated here. Revenge would be total. As matters stood, the prisoners and towns they held, the other towns they could destroy, were bargaining counters. When they gave up the struggle (which surely they must, in a year or two), they could exchange these hostages for the right to go home unmolested.

"Agreed. I simply want to hear your side of the story." Ridenour offered a cigar. "Your species likes tobacco, does it not?"

"I thank." A seven-fingered hand took the gift with ill-concealed eagerness. "But you know why we fight. This is our home."

"Um-m-m ... Freehold was man-occupied before your race began space flight."

"True. Yet Arulian bones have strengthened this soil for more than two centuries. By longstanding agreement, the Arulians who lived and died here did so under the Law of the Sacred Horde. For what can your law mean to us, Terran—your law of property to us who do things mutually with our pheromonesharers; your law of marriage to us who have three sexes and a breeding cycle; your law of Imperial fealty to us who find truth's wellspring in Eternal Aruli? We might have compromised, after Freehold was incorporated into your domain. Indeed, we made every reasonable attempt to do so. But repeated and flagrant violation of our rights must in the end provoke secessive action."

Ridenour started his pipe. "Well, now, suppose you look at the matter as I do," he suggested. "Freehold is an old human colony, although it lies far from Terra. It was founded before the Empire and stayed sovereign after the Empire began. There was just no special reason why we should acquire it, take on responsibility for it, while the people remained friendly. But needing trade and not getting many human visitors, they looked elsewhere. The Merseians had lately brought modern technology to Aruli. Arulian mercantile associations were busy in this region. They had the reputation of being industrious and reliable, and they could use Freehold's produce. It was natural that trade should begin; it followed that numerous Arulians should come here to live; and, as you say, it was quite proper to grant them extraterritoriality.

"*But.*" He wagged his pipestem. "Relationships between the Terran and Merseian Empires grew more and more strained. Armed conflict became frequent in the marches. Freehold felt threatened. By now the planet had—if not a booming industry—at least enough to make it a military asset. A tempting target for anyone. Sovereign independence looked pretty lonely, not to say fictitious. So the Nine Cities applied for membership in the Empire and were accepted—as much to forestall Merseia as for any other reason. Of course the Arulian minority objected. But they were a small minority. And in any case, as you said, compromise should have been possible. Terra respects the rights of client species. We must; they are too many for suppression. In fact, no few nonhumans have Terran citizenship."

"Nevertheless," the prisoner said, "you violated what we hold hallowed."

"Let me finish," Ridenour said. "Your mother world Aruli, its sphere of influence, everything there has lately become a Merseian puppet. No, wait, I know you'll deny that indignantly; but think. Consider your race's recent history. Ask yourself what pronouncements have been made by the current Bearers of the Horns—as regards Merseia versus Terra—and remember that they succeeded by revolutionary overthrow of the legitimate heirs. Never mind what abuses they claim to be correcting; only recall that they are Merseian-sponsored revolutionaries.

"Reflect how your people here, on this planet, have always considered themselves Arulians rather than Freeholders. Reflect how they have, in fact, as tensions increased, supported the interests of Aruli rather than Terra. Maybe this would not have occurred, had the humans here treated you more fairly in the past. But we were confronted with your present hostility. What would you expect us to do—what would you do in our place—but decree some security regulations? Which is the prerogative of His Majesty's government, you know. The original treaty granting them extraterritoriality was signed by the Nine Cities, not by the Terran Empire.

"So you revolted, you resident aliens. And we discovered to our dismay that the rebellion was well prepared. Multiple tons of war supplies, multiple thousands of troops, had been smuggled beforehand into wilderness areas... from Aruli!"

"That is not true," the prisoner said. "Of course our mother world favors our righteous cause, but—"

"But we have census figures, remember. The registered Arulian-descended Freeholders do not add up to anything like the total in your 'Sacred Horde.' You yourself, my friend, whose ancestors supposedly lived here for generations, cannot speak the language! Oh, I understand Aruli's desire to avoid an open clash with Terra, and Terra's willingness to indulge this desire. But let us not waste our personal time with transparent hypocrisies, you and I."

The prisoner refused response.

Ridenour sighed. "Your sacrifices, what victories you have had, everything you have done is for nothing," he went on. "Suppose you did succeed. Suppose you actually did win your 'independent world in pheromone association with the Holy Ancestral Soil'—do you really think your species would benefit? No, no. The result would mean nothing more than a new weapon for Merseia to use against Terra... a rather cheaply acquired one." His smile was weary. "We're familiar with the process, we humans. We've employed it against each other often enough in our past."

"As you like," the Arulian said. By instinct he was less combative as an individual than a human is, though possibly more so in a collectivity. "Your opinions make scant difference. The great objective will be achieved before long."

Ridenour regarded him with pity. "Have your superiors really kept on telling you that?"

"Surely. What else?"

"Don't you understand the situation? The Empire is putting less effort into the campaign than it might, true. This *is* a distant frontier, however critical. Two hundred light-years make a long way from Terra. But our lack of energy doesn't matter in the long run, except to poor tormented Freehold.

"Because this system has in fact been taken by us. You aren't getting any more supplies from outside. You can't. Small fast courier boats might hope to run our blockade, I suppose, if they aren't too many and accept a high percentage of loss. But nothing except a full-sized task force would break it. Aruli cannot help you further. She hasn't that kind of fleet. Merseia isn't going to. The game isn't worth the candle to her. You are cut off. We'll grind you away to nothing if we must; but we hope you'll see reason, give up and depart.

"Think. You call it yaro fever, do you not—that disease which afflicts your species but not ours—for which the antibiotic must be grown on Aruli itself where the soil bacteria are right? We capture more and more of you who suffer from yaro. When did you last see a fresh lot of antibiotic?"

The prisoner screamed. He cast his cigar at Ridenour's feet, sprang from his chair and ran to the office door. "Take me back to the stockade!" he wept.

Ridenour's mouth twisted. Oh, well, he thought, I didn't really hope to learn anything new from any of those pathetic devils.

Besides, the savages are what I'm supposed to investigate. Though I've speculated if perhaps, in the two centuries they lived here, the Arulians had some influence on the outback people. Everybody knows they traded with them to some extent. Did ideas pass, as well as goods?

For certainly the savages have become troublesome.

The next day Ridenour was lucky and got a direct lead. The mayor of Domkirk arrived in Nordyke on official business. And word was that the Domkirk militia had taken prisoners after beating off a raid from the wilderness dwellers. Ridenour waited two days before he got to see the mayor; but that was about par for the course in a project like this, and he found things to do meanwhile.

Rikard Uriason proved to be a short, elegantly clad, fussy man. He was obviously self-conscious about coming from the smallest recognized community on the planet. He mentioned a visit he had once made to Terra and the fact that his daughter was studying on Ansa, twice in the first ten minutes after Ridenour entered his hotel room. He kept trying to talk the Emperor's Anglic and slipping back into Freeholder dialect. He fussed about, falling

between the stools of being a gracious host and a man of the
universe. Withal, he was competent and well informed where his
own job was concerned.

"Yes, sir, we of Domkirk live closer to the outback than anyone
else. For various reasons," he said, after they were finally seated
with drinks in their hands. A window stood open to the breeze
off Catwick—always slightly alien-scented, a hint of the smell that
wet iron has on Terra—and the noise of streets and freight-belts,
and the view of waters glittering out to the dunes of Longenhook.
"Our municipality does not yet have the manpower to keep a radius
of more than about two hundred kilometers under cultivation.
Remember, Terran crops are fragile on this planet. We can mutate
and breed selectively as much as we like. The native life forms
will nonetheless remain hardier, eh? And, while robotic machines
do most of the physical work, the requirement for supervision,
decision-making human personnel is inevitably greater than on
a more predictable world. This limits our range. Then too, we
are on a coastal plateau. Onyx Heights falls steeply to the ocean,
westward to the Windhoek, into marsh—unreclaimable—by us at
our present stage of development, at any rate."

Good Lord, Ridenour thought, I have found a man who can
out-lecture me. Aloud: "Are those tidelands inhabited by savages,
then?"

"No, sir, I do not believe so. Certainly not in any significant
degree. The raiders who plague our borders appear to be centered
in the Windhoek Range and the Upwoods beyond. That was where
the recent trouble occurred, on that particular margin. We have
been fortunate in that the war's desolation has passed us by. But
we feel, on this very account, our patriotic duty is all the more
pressing, to make up the agricultural losses caused elsewhere.
Some expansion is possible, now that refugees augment our
numbers. We set about clearing land in the foothills. A valley,
actually, potentially fertile once the weeds and other native pests
have been eradicated. Which, with modern methods, takes only
about one year. A Freehold year, I mean, circa about twenty-five
per cent longer than a Terran year. Ah...where was I?...yes. A
band of savages attacked our pioneers. They might have succeeded.
They did succeed in the past, on certain occasions, as you may
know, sir. By surprise, and numbers, and proximity—for their
weapons are crude. Necessarily so, iron and similar metals being

scarce. But they did manage, for instance, several years ago, to frustrate an attempt on settling on Moon Garnet Lake, in spite of the attempt being supplied by air and backed by militia with reasonably modern small arms. Ahem! This time we were forewarned. We had our guards disguised as workers, their weapons concealed. Not with any idea of entrapment. Please understand that, sir. Our wish is not to lure any heathen to their deaths, only to avoid conflict. But neither had we any wish for them to spy out our capabilities. Accordingly, when a gang attacked, our militiamen did themselves proud, I may say. They inflicted casualties and drove the bulk of the raiders back into the forest. A full twenty-seven prisoners were flitted to detention in our city jail. I expect the savages will think twice before they endeavor to halt progress again."

Even Uriason must stop for breath sometime. Ridenour took the opportunity to ask: "What do you plan to do with your prisoners?"

The mayor looked a little embarrassed. "That is a delicate question, sir. Technically they are criminals—one might say traitors, when Freehold is at war. However, one is almost obliged morally, is one not, to regard them as hostiles protected by the Covenant? They do by now, unfortunately, belong to a foreign culture; and they do not acknowledge our planetary government. Ah...in the past, rehabilitation was attempted. But it was rarely successful, short of outright brainscrub, which is not popular on Freehold. The problem is much discussed. Suggestions from Imperial experts will be welcomed, once the war is over and we can devote attention to sociodynamic matters."

"But isn't this a rather longstanding problem?" Ridenour said.

"Well, yes and no. On the one hand, it is true that for several centuries people have been leaving the cities for the outback. Their reasons varied. Some persons were mere failures; remember, the original colonists held an ideal of individualism and made scant provision for anyone who could not, ah, cut the mustard. Some were fugitive criminals. Some were disgruntled romantics, no doubt. But the process was quite gradual. Most of those who departed did not vanish overnight. They remained in periodic contact. They traded things like gems, furs, or their own itinerant labor for manufactured articles. But their sons and grandsons tended, more and more, to adopt a purely uncivilized way of life, one which denied any need for what the cities offered."

"Adaptation," Ridenour nodded. "It's happened on other planets. On olden Terra, even—like the American frontier." Seeing that Uriason had never heard of the American frontier, he went on a bit sorrowfully: "Not a good process, is it? The characteristic human way is to adapt the environment to oneself, not oneself to the environment."

"I quite agree, sir. But originally, no one was much concerned in the Nine Cities. They had enough else to think about. And, indeed, emigration to the wilderness was a safety valve. Thus, when the anti-Christian upheavals occurred three hundred years ago, many Christians departed. Hence the Mechanists came to power with relatively little bloodshed—including the blood of Hedonists, who also disappeared rather than suffer persecution. Afterward, when the Third Constitution decreed tolerance, the savages were included by implication. If they wished to skulk about in the woods, why not? I suppose we, our immediate ancestors, should have made ethnological studies on them. A thread of contact did exist, a few trading posts and the like. But . . . well, sir, our orientation on Freehold is pragmatic rather than academic. We are a busy folk."

"Especially nowadays," Ridenour observed.

"Yes. Very true. I presume you do not speak only of the war. Before it started, we had large plans in train. Our incorporation into His Majesty's domains augured well for the furtherance of civilization on Freehold. We hope that, when the war is over, those plans may be realized. But admittedly the savages are a growing obstacle."

"I understand they sent embassies telling this and that city not to enlarge its operations further."

"Yes. Our spokesman pointed out to them that the Third Constitution gave each city the right to exploit its own hinterland as its citizens desired—a right which our Imperial charter has not abrogated. We also pointed out that they, the savages, were fellow citizens by virtue of residence. They need only adopt the customs and habits of civilization—and we stood ready to lend them educational, financial, even psychotherapeutic assistance toward this end. They need only meet the simple, essential requirements for the franchise, and they too could vote on how to best develop the land. Uniformly they refused. They denied the authority of the mayors and laid claim to all unimproved territory."

Ridenour smiled, but with little mirth. "Cultures, like individuals, die hard," he said.

"True," Uriason nodded. "We civilized people are not unsympathetic. But after all! The outbacker population, their number, is unknown to us. However, it must be on the same order of magnitude as the cities', if not less. Whereas the potential population of a Freehold properly developed is—well, I leave that to your imagination, sir. Ten billion? Twenty? And not any huddled masses, either. Comfortable, well fed, productive, happy human beings. May a few million ignorant woodsrunners deny that many souls the right to be born?"

"None of my business," Ridenour said. "My contract just tells me to investigate."

"I might add," Uriason said, "that Terra's rivalry with Merseia bids fair to go on for long generations. A well populated highly industrialized large planet here on the Betelgeusean frontier would be of distinct value to the Empire. To the entire human species, I believe. Do you not agree?"

"Yes, of course," Ridenour said.

He readily got permission to return with Uriason and study the savage prisoners in depth. The mayor's car flitted back to Domkirk two days later—two of Freehold's twenty-one hour days. And thus it happened that John Ridenour was on hand when the city was destroyed.

Karlsarm loped well in among the buildings, with his staff and guards, before combat broke loose. He heard yells, crack of blasters, hiss of slugthrowers, snap of bowstrings, sharp bark of explosives, and grinned. For they came from the right direction, as did the sudden fire-flicker above the roofs. The airport was first struck. Could it be seized in time, no dragons would fly.

Selene light had drenched and drowned pavement luminosity. Now windows were springing to life throughout the town. Karlsarm's group broke into a run. The on-duty militiamen, barracked at the airport, were few.

Wolf's detachment should be able to handle them in the course of grabbing vehicles and that missile emplacement which Terran engineers had lately installed. But Domkirk was filled with other men, and some of them kept arms at home. Let them boil out and get organized, and the result would be slaughterous. But they couldn't organize without communications, and the electronic center of the municipality was in the new skyscraper.

A door opened, in the flat front of an apartment house. A citizen stood outlined against the lobby behind, pajama-clad, querulous at being roused. "What the hell d'you think—"

Light spilled across Karlsarm. The Domkirker saw: a man in bast and leather, crossbow in hands, crossbelts sagging with edged weapons; a big muscular body, weatherbeaten countenance, an emblem of authority which was not a decent insigne but the skull and skin of a catavray crowning that wild head. "*Savages!*" the Domkirker shrieked. His voice went eunuch high with panic.

Before he had finished the word, the score of invaders were gone from his sight. More and more keening lifted, under a gathering battle racket. It suited Karlsarm. Terrified folk were no danger to him.

When he emerged in the cathedral square, he found that not every mind in town had stampeded.

The church loomed opposite, overtopping the shops which otherwise ringed the plaza. For they were darkened and were, in any event, things that might have been seen anywhere in the Empire. But the bishop's seat was raised two centuries ago, in a style already ancient. It was all colored vitryl, panes that formed one enormous many-faceted jewel, so that by day the interior was nothing except radiances—and even by moonlight, the outside flashed and dim spectra played. Karlsarm had small chance to admire. Flames stabbed and bullets sang. He led a retreat back around the corner of another building.

"Somebody's got together," Link o' the Cragland muttered superfluously. "Think we can bypass them?"

Karlsarm squinted. The skyscraper poked above the cathedral, two blocks farther on. But whoever commanded this plaza would soon isolate the entire area, once enough men had rallied to him. "We'd better clean them out right away," he decided. "Quick, intelligencers!"

"Aye." Noach unslung the box on his shoulder, set it down, talked into its ventholes and opened the lid. Lithe little shapes jumped forth and ran soundlessly off among the shadows. They were soon back. Noach chittered with them and reported: "Two strong squads, one in the righthand street, one in the left. Door-ways, walls, plenty of cover. Radiocoms, I think. The commanders talk at their own wrists, anyhow, and we can't jam short-range transmissions, can we? If we have to handle long-range ones too? Other men keep coming to join them. A team just brought what I suppose must be a tripod blastgun."

Karlsarm rephrased the information in bird language and sent messengers off, one to a chief of infantry, one to the monitors.

The latter arrived first, as proper tactics dictated. The beasts— half a dozen of them, scaled and scuted crocodilian shapes, each as big as two buffalo—were not proof against Imperial-type guns. Nothing was. And being stupid, they were inflexible; you gave them their orders and hoped you had aimed them right, because that was that. But they were hard to kill...and terrifying if you had never met them before. The blast-gunners unleashed a single ill-directed thunderbolt and fled. About half the group barricaded themselves in a warehouse. The monitors battered down the wall, and the defenders yielded.

Meanwhile the Upwoods infantry dealt with the opposition in the other street. Knifemen could not very well rush riflemen. However, bowmen could pin them down until the monitors got around to them, after which a melee occurred, and everyone fought hand-to-hand anyway. A more elegant solution existed but doctrine stood, to hold secret weapons in reserve. The monitors were expendable, there being no way to evacuate creatures that long and heavy.

Karlsarm himself had already proceeded to capture the skyscraper and establish headquarters. From the top floor, he had an over-view of the entire town. It made him nervous to be enclosed in lifeless plastic, and he had a couple of the big windows knocked out. Grenades were needed to break the vitryl. So his technicians manning the communication panels, a few floors down, must endure being caged.

A messenger blew in from the night and fluted: "The field of dragons has been taken, likewise a fortress wherein our people were captive—"

Karlsarm's heart knocked. "Let Mistress Evagail come to me."

Waiting, he was greatly busied. Reports, queries, suggestions, crisis; directives, answers, decisions, actions. The streets were a phosphor web, out to the icy moonlands, but most of the build-ings hulked lightless again, terror drawn back into itself. Sporadic fire flared, the brief sounds of clash drifted faintly to him. The air grew colder.

When Evagail entered, he needed an instant to disengage his mind and recognize her. They had stripped her. They had stripped off her buckskins and gold furs, swathed the supple height of her in a shapeless prison gown; and a bandage still hid most of the ruddy-coiled hair. But then she laughed at him, eyes and mouth alive with an old joy, and he leaped across a desk to seize her.

"Did they hurt you?" he finally got the courage to ask.

"No, except for this battle wound, and it isn't much," she said. "They did threaten us with a . . . what's the thing called? . . . a hypnoprobe, when we wouldn't talk. Just as well you came when you did, loveling."

His tone shook: "Better than well. If that horror isn't used exactly right, it cracks apart both reason and soul."

"You forget I have my Skill," she said grimly.

He nodded. That was one reason why he had launched his campaign earlier than planned: not only for her sake, but for fear that the Cities would learn what she was. She might not have succeeded in escaping or in forcing her guards to slay her, before the hypnoprobe vibrations took over her brain.

She should never have accompanied that raid on Falconsward Valley. It was nothing but a demonstration, a test . . . militarily speaking. Emotionally, though, it had been a lashing back at an outrage committed upon the land. Evagail had insisted on practicing the combat use of her Skill; but her true reason was that she wanted to avenge the flowers. Karlsarm wielded no authority to stop her. He was a friend, occasionally a lover, some day perhaps to father her children; but was not any woman as free as any man? He was the war chief of Upwoods; but was not any Mistress of a Skill necessarily independent of chiefs?

Though a failure, the attack had not been a fiasco. Going into action for the first time, and meeting a cruel surprise, the outbackers had nonetheless conducted themselves well and retreated in good order. It was sheer evil fortune that Evagail was knocked out by a grazing bullet before she had summoned her powers.

"Well, we got you here in time," Karlsarm said. "I'm glad." Later he would make a ballad about his gladness.

"How stands your enterprise?"

"We grip the place, barring a few holdouts. I don't know if we managed to jam every outgoing message. Mistress Persa's buzzer-wave bugs could have missed a transmitter or two. And surely our folk now handling the comcenter can't long maintain the pretense of being ordinary, undisturbed Domkirkers. No aircraft have showed thus far. Better not delay any more than we must, though. So we ought to clear out the population—and nobody's stirred from their miserable dens!"

"Um-m, what are you doing to call them forth?"

"An all-phones announcement."

Evagail laughed anew. "I can imagine that scene, loveling! A poor, terrified family, whose idea of a wilderness trip is a picnic in Gallows Wood. Suddenly their town is occupied by hairy, skinclad savages—the same terrible people who burned the Moon Garnet camp and bushwhacked three punitive expeditions in succession and don't pay taxes or send their children to school or support the Arulian war or do *anything* civilized—but were supposed to be safe, cozy hundreds of kilometers to the west and never a match for regular troops on open ground—suddenly, here they are! They have taken Domkirk! They whoop and wave their tomahawks in the very streets! What can our families do but hide in their ... apartment, is that the word? ... the apartment, with furniture piled across the door? They can't even phone anywhere, the phone is dead, they can't call for help, can't learn what's become of Uncle Enry. Until the thing chimes. Hope leaps in Father's breast. Surely the Imperials, or the Nordyke militia, or somebody has come to the rescue! With shaking hand, he turns the instruments on. In the screen he sees—who'd you assign? Wolf, I'll wager. He sees a long-haired stone-jawed wild man, who barks in an alien dialect: 'Come out of hiding. We mean to demolish your city.'"

Evagail clicked her tongue. "Did you learn nothing about civilization while you were there, Karlsarm?" she finished.

"I was too busy learning something about its machines," he said. "I couldn't wait to be done and depart. What would you do here?"

"Let a more soothing image make reassuring noises for a while. Best a woman; may as well be me." Karlsarm's eyes widened before his head nodded agreement. "Meanwhile," Evagail continued, "you find the mayor. Have him issue the actual order to evacuate." She looked down at her dress, grimaced, pulled it off and threw it in a corner with a violent motion. "Can't stand that rag another heartbeat. Synthetic...dead. Which way is the telephone central?"

Karlsarm told her. Obviously she had already discovered how to use gravshifts and slideways. She departed, striding like a leontine, and he dispatched men on a search for city officialdom.

That didn't take long. Apparently the mayor had been trying to find the enemy leader. Toms led him and another in at the point of a captured blaster. The weapon was held so carelessly that Karlsarm took it and pitched it out the window. But then, Toms was from the Trollspike region—as could be told from his breechclout and painted skin—and had probably never seen a gun before he enlisted.

Karlsarm dismissed him and stood behind the desk, arms folded, against the dark broken pane, letting the prisoners assess him while he studied them. One looked almost comical, short, pot-bellied, red-faced and pop-eyed, as if the doom of his city were a personal insult. The fellow with him was more interesting, tall, yellow-haired, sharp-featured, neither his hastily donned clothes nor his bearing nor even his looks typical of any place on Freehold that Karlsarm had heard of.

"Who are you?" the little man sputtered. "What's the meaning of this? Do you realize what you have done?"

"I expect he does," said his companion dryly. "Permit introductions. The mayor, Honorable Rikard Uriason; myself, John Ridenour, from Terra."

An Imperialist! Karlsarm must fight to keep face impassive and muscles relaxed. He tried to match Ridenour's bow. "Welcome, sirs. May I ask why you, distinguished outworlder, are here?"

"I was in Domkirk to interview, ah, your people," Ridenour said. "In the hope of getting an understanding, with the aim of eventual reconciliation. As a house guest of Mayor Uriason, I felt perhaps I could assist him—and you—to make terms."

"Well, maybe." Karlsarm didn't bother to sound skeptical. The Empire wasn't going to like what the outbackers intended. He turned to Uriason. "I need your help quite urgently, Mayor. This city will be destroyed. Please tell everyone to move out immediately."

Uriason staggered. Ridenour saved him from falling. His cheeks went gray beneath a puce webwork. "What?" he strangled. "No. You are insane. Insane, I tell you. You cannot. Impossible."

"Can and will, Mayor. We hold your arsenal, your missile

emplacement—nuclear weapons, which some of us know how to touch off. At most, we have only a few hours till a large force arrives from another town or an Imperial garrison. Maybe less time than that, if word got out. We want to be gone before then; and so must your folk; and so must the city."

Uriason collapsed in a lounger and gasped for air. Ridenour seemed equally appalled, but controlled it better. "For your own sakes, don't," the Terran said in a voice that wavered. "I know a good bit of human history. I know what sort of revenge is pro-voked by wanton destruction."

"Not wanton," Karlsarm answered. "I'm quite sorry to lose the cathedral. A work of art. And museums, libraries, laboratories—But we haven't time for selective demolition." He drove sympathy out of his body and said like one of the machines he hated: "Nor do we have the foolishness to let this place continue as a base for military operations against us and civilian operations against our land. Whatever happens, it goes up before daybreak. Do you or do you not want the people spared? If you do, get busy and talk to them!"

Evacuation took longer than he had expected. Obedience was swift enough after Uriason's announcement. Citizens moved like cattle, streamed down the streets and out onto the airport expanse, where they milled and muttered, wept and whimpered under the bleak light of waning setting Selene. (With less luminescence to oppose, more stars had appeared, the stars of Empire, but one looked and understood how the gulf gaped between here and them, and shuddered in the pre-dawn wind.) Nevertheless people got in each other's way, didn't grasp the commands of their herders, shuffled, fainted, stalled the procession while they tried to find their kin. Besides, Karlsarm had forgotten there would be a hos-pital, with some patients who must be carried out and provided for in an outlying latifundium.

But, one by one, the aircraft filled with humans, and ran fifty kilometers upwind, and deposited their cargoes, and returned for more: until at last, when the first eastern paleness began to strengthen, Domkirk stood empty of everything save the wind.

Now the Upwoods army boarded and was flown west. Most of their pilots were city men, knives near to throats. Karlsarm and his few technicians saw the last shuttling vehicle off. It would return for them after they were through. (He was not unaware of the incongruity: skin-clad woodsrunners with dirks at their belts, proposing to sunder the atom!) Meanwhile it held Evagail, Wolf and Noach—his cadre—together with Uriason and Ridenour, who were helping control the crowds.

The mayor seemed to have crumpled after the pressure was off him. "You can't do this," he kept mumbling. "You can't do this." He was led up the gangway into the belly of the flyer.

Ridenour paused, a shadow in the door, and looked down. Was his glance quizzical? "I must admit to puzzlement about your method," he said. "How will you explode the town without exploding yourselves? I gather your followers have only the sketchiest notion of gadgetry. It isn't simple to jury-rig a timing device."

"No," Karlsarm said, "but it's simple to launch a missile at any angle you choose." He waved to unseen Evagail. "We'll join you shortly."

The bus took off and dwindled among the last stars. Karlsarm directed his crew in making preparations, then returned outside to watch the first part of the spectacle. Beyond the squat turret at his back, the airfield stretched barren gray to the ruined barracks. How hideous were the works of the Machine People!

But when the missiles departed, that was a heart-stopping sight.

They were solid-fuel rockets. There had been no reason to give expensive gravitic jobs to a minor colonial town so far from the battlefront that the Arulians couldn't possibly attack it in force. The weapons lifted out of their three launchers some distance away... with slow majesty, spouting sun-fire and white clouds, roaring their thundersong that clutched at the throat until Karlsarm gripped his crossbow and glared in defiance of the terror they roused... faster, though, streaking off at a steep slant, rising and rising until the flames flickered out... still rising, beyond his eyes, but drawing to a halt, caught now by the upper winds that twisted their noses downward, by the very rotation of the planet that aimed them at the place they should have defended—

And heavenward flew the second trio. And the third. Karlsarm judged he had better get into shelter.

He was at the bottom of the bunker with his men—tons of steel, concrete, force-screen generator shutting away the sky—when the rockets fell; and even so, he felt the room tremble around him.

Afterward, emerging, he saw a kilometers-high tree of dust and vapor. The command aircraft landed, hastily took on his group and fled the radioactivity. From the air he saw no church, no Domkirk, nothing but a wide, black, vitrified crater ringed in with burning fields.

He shook, as the bombproof had shaken, and said to no one and everyone: "This is what they would do to us!"

Running from the morning, they returned to a dusk before dawn. The other raiders were already there. This was in the eastern edge of wilderness, where hills lifted sharply toward the Windhoek Mountains.

Ridenour walked some distance off. He didn't actually wish to be alone; if anything, he wanted a companion for a shield between him and the knowledge that two hundred light-years reached from here to Lissa and the children, their home and Terra. But he must escape Uriason or commit violence. The man had babbled, gobbled, orated and gibbered through their entire time in the air. You couldn't blame him, maybe. His birthplace as well as his job had gone up in lethal smoke. But Ridenour's job was to gather information; and that big auburn-haired Evagail woman, whom he'd met not unamicably while she was still captive, had appeared willing to talk if she ever got a chance.

No one stopped Ridenour. Where could he flee? He climbed onto a crest and looked around.

The valley floor beneath him held only a few trees and they small, probably the result of a forest fire, though nature—incredibly vigorous when civilization has not sucked her dry—had covered all scars with a thick blanket of silvery-green trilobed "grass" and sapphire blossoms. No doubt this was why the area had been set for a rendezvous. Aircraft landed easily. Hundreds of assorted tools must have been stacked here beforehand or stolen from the city, for men were attacking the vehicles like ants. Clang, clatter, hails, cheerful oaths profaned the night's death-hush.

Otherwise there was great beauty in the scene. Eastward, the first color stole across a leaf-roof that ran oceanic to the edge of sight, moving and murmuring in the breeze. Westward, the last few stars glistened in a plum-dark sky, above the purity of Windhoek's snowpeaks. Everywhere dew sparkled.

Ridenour took out pipe and tobacco and lit up. It made him

hiccough a bit, on an empty stomach, but comforted him in his chilled weariness. And in his dismay. He had not imagined the outbackers were such threats. Neither had anyone else, apparently. He recalled remarks made about them in Nordyke and (only yesterday?) Domkirk. "Impoverished wretches... Well, yes, I'm told they eat well with little effort. But otherwise, just think, no fixed abodes, no books, no schools, no connection with the human mainstream, hardly any metal, hardly any energy source other than brute muscle. Wouldn't you call that an impoverished existence? Culturally as well as materially?"

"Surly, treacherous, arrogant. I tell you, I've dealt with them. In trading posts on the wilderness fringe. They do bring in furs, wild fruits, that sort of thing, to swap, mostly for steel tools—but only when they feel like taking the trouble, which isn't often, and then they treat you like dirt."

But a much younger man had had another story. "Sure, if one of us looks down on the woodsrunners, they'll look down right back at him. But I was interested and acted friendly, and they invited me to overnight in their camp.... Their songs are plain caterwauling, but I've never seen better dancing, not even on Imperial Ballet Corps tapes, and afterward, the girls—! I think I might get me some trade goods and return some day.

"Swinish. Lazy. Dangerous also, I agree. Look what they've done every time someone tried to start a real outpost of civilization in the mid-wilderness. We'll have to clean them out before we can expand. Once this damned Arulian war is over—No, don't get me wrong, I'm not vindictive. Let's treat them like any other criminal: rehabilitation, re-integration into society. I'll go further; I'll admit this is a case of cultural conflict rather than ordinary lawbreaking. So why not let the irreconcilables live out their lives peacefully on a reservation somewhere? As long as their children get raised civilized—

"If you ask me, I think heredity comes into the picture. It wasn't easy to establish the Cities, maintain and enlarge them, the first few centuries on an isolated, metal-poor world like this. Those who couldn't stand the gaff opted out. Once the disease and nutrition problems were licked, you could certainly live with less work in the forests—if you didn't mind turning into a savage and didn't feel any obligation toward the civilization that had made your survival possible. Later, through our whole history, the same thing continued. The lazy, the criminal, the mutinous, the eccentric, the lecherous, the irresponsible, sneaking off...to this very day. No wonder the outbackers haven't accomplished anything. They never will, either. I'm not hopeful about rehabilitating them, myself, not even any of their brats that we institutionalized at birth. Scrub stock!

"Well, yes, I did live with them a while. Ran away when I was sixteen. Mainly, I think now, my reason was—you know, girls—and that part was fine, if you don't wonder about finding some girl you can respect when you're ready to get married. And I thought it'd be romantic. Primitive hunter, that sort of thing. Oh, they were kind enough. But they set me to learning endless nonsense—stuff too silly and complicated to retain in my head—rituals, superstitions—and they don't really hunt much, they have some funny kind of herding—and no stereo, no cars, no air-conditioning—hiking for days on end, and have you ever been *out* in a Freehold rainstorm?—and homesickness, after a while; they don't talk or behave or think like us. So I came back: And mighty draggle-tailed, I don't mind admitting. No, they didn't forbid me. One man guided me to the nearest cultivated land."

"Definitely an Arulian influence, Professor Ridenour. I've observed the outbackers at trading posts, visited some of their camps, made multisensory tapes. Unscientific, no doubt. I'm strictly an amateur as an ethnologist. But I felt somebody must try. They are more numerous, more complicated, more important than Nine Cities generally realize. Here, I'll play some of my recordings for you. Pay special attention to the music and some of the artwork. Furthermore, what little I could find out about their system of reckoning kinship looks as if it's adopted key Arulian notions. And remember, too, the savages—not only on this continent, but on both others, where they seemed to have developed similarly. Everywhere on Freehold, the savages have grown more and more hostile in these past years. Not to our Arulian enemies, but to us! When the Arulians were marshalling in various wilderness regions, did they have savage help? I find it hard to believe they did not."

Ridenour drank smoke and shivered.

He grew peripherally aware of an approach and turned. Evagail joined him on panther feet. She hadn't yet bothered to dress, but the wetness and chill didn't seem to inconvenience her. Ridenour scolded himself for being aware of how good she looked. Grow up, he thought; you're a man with a task at hand.

"Figured I'd join you." Her husky voice used the Upwoods dialect, which was said to be more archaic than that of the Cities. The pronunciation was indeed different, slower and softer. But Ridenour had not observed that vocabulary and grammar had suffered much. Maybe not at all. "You look lonesome. Hungry, too, I'll bet. Here." She offered him a large gold-colored sphere.

"What's that?" he asked.

"Steak apple, we call it. Grows everywhere this time of year."

He lay down his pipe and bit. The fruit was delicious, sweet, slightly smoky, but with an underlying taste of solid protein. Ravenous, he bit again. "Thank you," he said around a mouthful. "This should be a meal by itself."

"Well, not quite. It'll do for breakfast, though."

"I, uh, understand the forests bear ample food the year around."

"Yes, if you know what to find and how. Was necessary to introduce plants and animals from offworld, mutated forms that could survive on Freehold, before humans could live here without any synthetics. Especially urgent to get organisms that concentrate what iron the soil has, and other essential trace minerals. Several vitamins were required as well."

Ridenour stopped chewing because his jaw had fallen. Savages weren't supposed to talk like that! Hastily, hoping to keep her in the right mood, he recovered his composure and said: "I believe the first few generations established such species to make it easier to move into the wilderness and exploit its resources. Why didn't they succeed?"

"Lots of reasons," Evagail said. "Including, I think, a pretty deep-rooted fear of ever being alone." She scowled. Her tone grew harsh. "But there was a practical reason, too. The new organisms upset the ecology. Had no natural enemies here, you see. They destroyed enormous areas of forest. That's how the desert south of Startop originated, did you know? *Our* first generations had a fiend's time restoring balance and fertility."

Again Ridenour gaped, not sure he had heard right.

"Of course, the sun helped," she went on more calmly.

"Beg pardon?"

"The sun." She pointed east. The early light was now like molten steel, and spears of radiance struck upward. Her hair was made copper, her body bronze. "F-type star. Actinic and ionizing radiation gets through in quantity, even with this dense an atmosphere. Biochemistry is founded on highly energetic compounds. Freehold life is more vigorous than Terran, evolves faster, finds more new ways to be what it wants." Her voice rang. "You learn how to become worthy of the forest, or you don't last long."

Ridenour looked away from her. She aroused too much within him.

The work of demolishing the aircraft went apace, despite the often primitive equipment used. He could understand why their metal was often desired. The outbackers were known to have mines of their own, but few and poor; they employed metal only where it was quite unfeasible to substitute stone, wood, glass, leather, bone, shell, fiber, glue.... But the vehicles were being stripped with unexpected care. Foremen who obviously knew what they were doing supervised the removal, intact, of articles like transceivers and power cells.

Evagail seemed to follow his thought. "Oh, yes, we'll use those gadgets while they last," she said. "They aren't vital, but they're handy. For certain purposes."

Ridenour finished his apple, picked up his pipe and rekindled it. She wrinkled her nose. Tobacco was not a vice of the woods-folk, though they were rumored to have many others, including some that would astonish a jaded Terran. "I never anticipated that much knowledgeability," he said. "Including, if I may make bold, your own."

"We're not all provincials," she answered, with a quirk of lips. "Quite a few, like Karlsarm, for instance, have studied offplanet. They'd be chosen, you see, as having the talent for it. Afterward they'd come back and teach others."

"But—how—"

She studied him for a moment, with disconcertingly steady hazel eyes, before saying: "No harm in telling you, I suppose. I believe you're an honest man, John Ridenour—intellectually honest—and we do need some communicators between us and the Empire.

"Our people took passage on Arulian ships. This was before the rebellion, of course. It began generations ago. The humans of the Nine Cities paid no attention. They'd always held rather aloof from the Arulians: partly from snobbishness, I suppose, and partly from lack of imagination. But the Arulians traded directly with us, too. That wasn't any secret. Nor was it a secret that we saw more of them more intimately, learned more from them, than the City men did. It was only that the City men weren't interested in details of that relationship. They didn't ask what their 'inferiors' were up to. Why should we or the Arulians volunteer lectures about it?"

"And what were you up to?" Ridenour asked softly.

"Nothing, at first, except that we wanted some of our people to have a look at galactic civilization—real civilization, not those smug, ingrown Nine—and the Arulians were willing to sell us berths on their regular cargo ships. In the nature of the case, our visits were mainly to planets outside the Empire, which is why Terra never heard what was going on. At last, though, some, like Karlsarm, did make their way to Imperial worlds, looked around, enrolled in schools and universities . . . By that time, however, relations on Freehold were becoming strained. There was no predicting what might happen. We thought it best to provide our students with cover identities. That wasn't hard. No one inquired closely. No one can remember all the folkways of all the colonies. This is such a big galaxy."

"It is that," Ridenour whispered. The sun climbed aloft, too brilliant for him to look anywhere near.

"What are you going to do now?" he asked.

"Fade into the woods before enemy flyers track us down. Cache our plunder and start for home."

"But what about your prisoners? The men who were forced to pilot and—"

"Why, they can stay here. We'll show them what they can eat and where a spring is. And we'll leave plenty of debris. A searcher's bound to spot them before long. Of course, I hope some will join us. We don't have as many men with civilized training as we could use."

"Join you?" Ridenour choked. "After what you have done?"

Again she regarded him closely and gravely. "What did we do that was unforgivable? Killed some men, yes—but in honest battle, in the course of war. Then we risked everything to spare the lives of everybody else."

"But what about their livelihoods? Their homes? Their possessions, their—"

"What about ours?" Evagail shrugged. "Never mind. I suspect

we will get three or four recruits. Young men who've felt vaguely restless and unfulfilled. I had hopes about you. But maybe I'd better go talk with someone more promising."

She turned, not brusquely or hostilely, and rippled back downhill. Ridenour stared after her.

He stood long alone, thinking, while the sun lifted and the sky filled with birds and the work neared an end below him. It was becoming more and more clear that the outbackers—the Free People, as they seemed to call themselves—were not savages.

Neither Miserable Degraded Savages nor Noble Happy Savages. All their generations, shaped by these boundless shadowy whispering woodlands and by what they learned from beings whose species and mode of life were not human: that alchemy had transmuted them into something so strange that their very compatriots in the Nine Cities had failed to identify it.

But what was it?

Not a civilization, Ridenour felt sure. You could not have a true civilization without... libraries, scientific and artistic apparatus, tradition-drenched buildings, reliable transportation and communication... the cumbersome necessary impedimenta of high culture. But you could have a barbarism that was subtle, powerful and deathly dangerous. He harked back to ages of history, forgotten save by a few scholars. Hyksos in Egypt, Dorians in Achaea, Lombards in Italy, Vikings in England, Crusaders in Syria, Mongols in China, Aztecs in Mexico. Barbarians, to whom the malcontents of civilization often deserted—who gained such skills that incomparably more sophisticated societies fell before them.

Granted, in the long run the barbarian was either absorbed by his conquests or was himself overcome. Toward the end of the pre-space travel era, civilization had been the aggressor, crushing and devouring the last pathetic remnants of barbarism. It was hard to see how Karlsarm's folk could hold out against atomic weapons and earthmoving machinery, let alone prevail over them.

And yet the outbackers had destroyed Domkirk.

And they had no immediate fear of punitive expeditions from Cities or Empire. Why should they? The wilderness was theirs, roadless, townless, mapped only from above and desultorily at that—three-fourths of Freehold's land surface! How could an avenger *find* them?

Well, the entire wilderness could be destroyed. High-altitude multimegaton bursts can set a whole continent ablaze. Or, less messily, disease organisms can be synthesized that attack vegetation and soon create a desert.

But no. Such measures would ruin the Nine Cities too. Though they might be protected from direct effects, the planetary climate would be changed, agriculture become impossible, the economy crumble and the people perforce abandon their world. And the Cities were the sole thing that made Freehold valuable, to Terra or Merseia. They formed a center of population and industry on a disputed frontier. Without them, this was simply one more undeveloped globe: because of its metal poverty, not worth anyone's trouble.

Doubtless Karlsarm and his fellow chiefs understood this. The barbarians could only be obliterated gradually, by the piecemeal conquest, clearing and cultivation of their forests. Doubtless they understood that, too, and were determined to forestall the process. Today there remained just eight Cities, of which two were in the hands of their Arulian friends (?) and two others crippled by the chances of war. Whatever the barbarians planned next, and whether they succeeded or not, they might well bring catastrophe on civilized Freeholder man.

Ridenour's mouth tightened. He started down the hill.

Halfway, he met Uriason coming up. He had heard the mayor some distance off, raving over his shoulder while several listening outbackers grinned:

"—treason! I say the three of you are traitors! Oh, yes, you talk about 'attempted rapprochement' and 'working for a detente.' The fact remains you are going over to the monsters who destroyed your own home! And why! Because you aren't fit to be human. Because you would rather loaf in the sun, and play with unwashed sluts, and pretend that a few superstitious ceremonies are 'autochthonous' than take the trouble to cope with this universe. It won't last, gentlemen. Believe me, the glamor will soon wear off. You will come skulking back like many other runaways, and expect to be received as indulgently as they were. But I warn you. This is war. You have collaborated with the enemy. If you dare return, I, your mayor, will do my best to see you prosecuted for treason!"

Puffing hard, he stopped Ridenour. "Ah, sir." His voice was abruptly low. "A word, if you please."

The xenologist suppressed a groan and waited.

Uriason looked back. No one was paying attention. "I really am indignant," he said after he had his breath. "Three of them! Saying they had long found their work dull and felt like trying something new.... But no matter. My performance was merely in character."

"What?" Ridenour almost dropped his pipe from his jaws.

"Calm, sir, be calm, I beg you." The little eyes were turned up, unblinking, and would not release the Terran's. "I took for granted that you also will accompany the savages from here."

"Why—why—"

"An excellent opportunity to fulfill your mission, really to learn something about them. Eh?"

"But I hadn't—Well, uh, the idea did cross my mind. But I'm no actor. I'd never convince them I was suddenly converted to their cause. They might believe that of a bored young provincial who isn't very bright to begin with. Even in those cases, I'll bet they'll keep a wary eye out for quite some time. But me, a Terran, a scientist, a middle-aged paterfamilias? The outbackers aren't stupid, Mayor."

"I know, I know," Uriason said impatiently. "Nevertheless, if you offer to go with them—telling them quite frankly that your aim is to collect information—they will take you. I am sure of it. I kept my ears open down yonder, sir, as well as my mouth. The savages are anxious to develop a liaison with the Empire. They will let you return whenever you say. Why should they fear you? By the time you, on foot, reach any of the cities, whatever military intelligence you can offer will be obsolete. *Or so they think.*"

Ridenour gulped. The round red face was no longer comical. It pleaded. After a while, it commanded.

"Listen, Professor," Uriason said. "I played the buffoon in order to be discounted and ignored. Your own best role is probably that of the impractical academician. But you may thus gain a chance for an immortal name. If you have the manhood!

"Listen, I say. I listened to them. And I weighed in my mind what I overheard. The annihilation of Domkirk was part of some larger scheme. It was advanced ahead of schedule in order to rescue those prisoners we held. What comes next, I do not know. I am only certain that the plan is bold, large-scale and diabolical. It seems reasonable, therefore, that forces must be massed somewhere. Does it not? Likewise, it seems reasonable that these murderers will join that force. Does it not? Perhaps I am wrong. If so, you have lost nothing. You can simply continue to be the absent-minded scientist, until you decide to go home. And that will be of service per se. You will bring useful data.

"However, if I am right, you will accompany this gang to some key point. And when you arrive...Sir, warcraft of the Imperial Navy are in blockading orbit. When I reach Nordyke, I shall speak to Admiral Cruz. I shall urge that he adopt my plan—the plan that came to me when I saw—here." Uriason reached under his cloak. Snake swift, he thrust a small object into Ridenour's hand. "Hide that. If anyone notices and asks you about it, dissemble. Call it a souvenir or something."

"But...but what—" Like an automaton, Ridenour pocketed the hemicylinder. He felt a pair of supercontacts on either end and a grille on the flat side and assumed that complex microcircuitry was packed into the plastic case.

"A communication converter. Have you heard of them?"

"I—yes. I've heard."

"Good. I doubt that any of the savages have, although they are surprisingly well informed in certain respects. The device is not new or secret, but with galactic information flow as inadequate as it is, especially here on what was a sleepy backwater...Let me refresh your memory, sir. Substitute this device for the primary modulator in any energy weapon of the third or fourth class. The weapon will thereupon become a maser communicator, projecting the human voice to a considerable distance. I shall ask Admiral Cruz to order at least one of his orbital ships brought low and illuminated for the next several weeks, so that you may have a target to aim at. If you find yourself in an important concentration of the enemy's—where surely stolen energy weapons will be kept—and if you get an opportunity to call down a warcraft... Do you follow me?"

"But," Ridenour stammered. "But. How?"

"As mayor, I knew that such devices were included in the last consignment of defensive materials that the Navy sent to Domkirk. I knew that one was carried on every military aircraft of ours. And several military aircraft were among those stolen last night. I watched my chance, I made myself ridiculous, and—" Uriason threw out his chest, thereby also throwing out his belly—"at the appropriate moment, I palmed this one from beneath the noses of the wrecking crew."

Ridenour wet his lips. They felt sandpapery. "I could've guessed that much," he got out. "But me—I—how—"

"It would not be in character for me to accompany the savages into their wilderness," Uriason said.

"They would be entirely too suspicious. Can I, can Freehold, can His Majesty and the entire human species rely upon you, sir?"

The man was short and fat. His words rose like hot-air balloons. Nevertheless, had he dared under possible observation, Ridenour would have bowed most deeply. As matters were, the Terran could just say, "Yes, Citizen Mayor, I'll try to do my best."

These were the stages of their journey:

Karlsarm walked beside Ridenour, amicably answering questions. But wariness crouched behind. He wasn't altogether convinced that this man's reasons for coming along were purely scientific and diplomatic. At least, he'd better not be, yet. Sometimes he thought that humans from the inner Empire were harder to fathom than most nonhumans. Being of the same species, talking much the same language, they ought to react in the same ways as your own people. And they didn't. The very facial expressions, a frown, a smile, were subtly foreign.

Ridenour, for immediate example, was courteous, helpful, even genial: but entirely on the surface. He showed nothing of his real self. No doubt he loved his family and was loyal to his Emperor and enjoyed his work and was interested in many other aspects of reality. He spoke of such things. But the emotion didn't come through. He made no effort to share his feelings, rather he kept them to himself with an ease too great to be conscious.

Karlsarm had encountered the type before, offplanet. He speculated that reserve was more than an aristocrat's idea of good manners; it was a defense. Jammed together with billions of others, wired from before birth into a network of communication, coordination, impersonal omnipotent social machinery, the human being could only protect his individuality by making his inner self a fortress. Here, in the outback of Freehold, you had room; neither people nor organizations pressed close upon you; if anything, you grew eager for intimacy. Karlsarm felt sorry for Terrans. But that did not help him understand or trust them.

"You surprise me pleasantly," he remarked. "I didn't expect you'd keep up with us the way you do."

"Well, I try to stay in condition," Ridenour said. "And remember, I'm used to somewhat higher gravity. But to be honest, I expected a far more difficult trip—narrow muddy trails and the like. You have a road here."

"Hm, I don't think a lot of it. We do better elsewhere. But then, this is a distant marchland for us."

Both men glanced around. The path crossed a high hillside, smoothly graded and switchbacked, surface planted in a mossy growth so tough and dense that no weeds could force themselves in. (It was a specially bred variety which, among other traits, required traces of manganese salt. Maintenance gangs supplied this from time to time, and thus automatically kept the moss within proper bounds.) The path was narrow, overarched by forest, a sun-speckled cool corridor where birds whistled and a nearby cataract rang. Because of its twistings, few other people were visible, though the party totalled hundreds.

Most of them were on different courses anyhow. Karlsarm had explained that the Free People laid out as many small, interconnected, more or less parallel ways as the traffic in a given area demanded, rather than a single broad highroad. It was easier to do, less damaging to ecology and scenery, more flexible to changing situations. Also, it was generally undetectable from above. He had not seen fit to mention the other mutant plant types, sown throughout this country, whose exudates masked those of human metabolism and thereby protected his men from airborne chemical sniffers.

"I've heard you use beasts of burden in a limited fashion," Ridenour said.

"Yes, horses and stathas have been naturalized here," Karlsarm said. "And actually, in our central regions, we keep many. City folk see just a few, because we don't often bring them to our thinly populated borderlands. No reason for it. You can go about as fast on foot, when you aren't overloaded with gear. But at home you'll see animals, wagons—boats and rafts, for that matter—in respectable totals."

"Your population must be larger than is guessed, then."

"I don't know what the current guess is in the Cities. And we don't bother with, uh, a census. But I'd estimate twenty million of us on this continent, and about the same for the others. Been stable for a long time. That's the proper human density. We don't crowd each other or press hard on natural resources. And so we've got abundant free food and stuff. No special effort involved in satisfying the basic needs. At the same time, there *are* enough of us for specialization, diversity, large-scale projects like road building. And, I might add, gifted people. You know, only about ten per cent of mankind are born to be leaders or creators in any degree. We'd stagnate if we were too few, same as we'd grow cramped and over-regulated if we became too many."

"How do you maintain a level population? You don't appear to have any strong compulsion mechanism."

"No, we haven't. Tradition, public opinion, the need to help your neighbor so he'll help you, the fact that out-and-out bastards get into quarrels and eventually get killed—such factors will do, when you have elbow room. The population-control device is simple. It wasn't planned, it evolved, but it works. Territory."

"Beg pardon?"

"A man claims a certain territory for his own, to support him and his family and retainers. He passes it on to one son. How he chooses the heir is his business. Anybody who kills the owner, or drives him off, takes over that parcel of land."

Ridenour actually registered a little shock, though he managed a smile. "Your society is less idyllic than some young City people told me," he said.

Karlsarm laughed. "We do all right—most of us. Can any civilization claim more? The landless don't starve, remember. They're taken on as servants, assistants, guards and the like. Or they become itinerant laborers, or entrepreneurs, or something. Let me remind you, we don't practice marriage. Nobody needs to go celibate. It's only that few women care to have children by a landless man." He paused. "Territorial battles aren't common any more, either. The landholders have learned how to organize defenses. Besides, a decent man can count on help from his neighbors. So not many vagabonds try to reave an estate. Those that do, and succeed—well, haven't they proven they're especially fit to become fathers?"

The paths ranged above timberline. The land became boulder-strewn, chill and stark. Ridenour exclaimed, "But this road's been blasted from the cliff side!"

"Why, of course," said Rowlan. "You didn't think we'd chip it out by hand, did you?"

"But what do you use for such jobs?"

"Organics. Like nitroglycerine. We compound that—doesn't take much apparatus, you know—and make dynamite from it. Some other explosives, and most fuels, we get from vegetables we've bred." Rowlan tugged his gray beard and regarded the Terran. "If you want to make a side trip," he offered, "I'll show you a hydro-electric plant. You'll call it ridiculously small, but it beams power to several mills and an instrument factory. We are not ignorant, John Ridenour. We adopt from your civilization what we can use. It simply doesn't happen to be a particularly large amount."

Even in this comparatively infertile country, food was plentiful. There were no more fruits for the plucking, but roots and berries were almost as easily gotten in the low brush, and animals—albeit of different species from the lowlands—continued to arrive near camp for slaughter. Ridenour asked scholarly little Noach how that was done, he being a beast operator himself. "Are they domesticated and conditioned?"

"No, I wouldn't call them that, exactly," Noach replied. "Not like horses or dogs. We use the proper stimuli on them. Those vary, depending on what you're after and where you are. For instance, in Brenning Dales you can unstopper a bottle of sex attractant, and every gruntleboar within ten kilometers rushes straight toward your bow. Around the Mare we've bred instincts into certain species to come when a sequence of notes is played on a trumpet. If nothing else, you can always stalk for yourself, any place. Hunting isn't difficult when critters are abundant. We don't want to take the time on this journey, though, so Mistress Jenith has been driving those cragbuck with her fire bees." He shrugged. "There are plenty of other ways. What you don't seem to realize, as yet, is that we're descended from people who applied scientific method to the problem of living in a wilderness."

For once, the night was clear above Foulweather Pass. Snow glistened on surrounding peaks, under Selene, until darkness lay drenched with an unreal brilliance. Not many stars shone through. But Karlsarm scowled at one, which was new and moved visibly, widdershins over his head.

"They've put up another satellite." The words puffed ghost white from his lips; sound was quickly lost, as if it froze and tinkled down onto the hoarfrosted road. "Or moved a big spaceship into near orbit without camouflage. Why?"

"The war?" Evagail shivered beside him and wrapped her fur cloak tighter about her. (It was not her property. Warm outfits were kept for travelers in a shed at the foot of the pass, to be returned on the other side, with a small rental paid to the servant of the landholder.) "What's been happening?"

"The news is obscure, what I get of it on that miniradio we took along," Karlsarm said. "A major fight's developing near Sluicegate. Nuclear weapons, the whole filthy works. By Oneness, if this goes on much longer we won't be left with a planet worth inhabiting!"

"Now don't exaggerate." She touched his hand. "I grant you, territory that's fought on, or suffers fallout, is laid waste. But not forever; and it isn't any big percentage of the total."

"You wouldn't say that if you were the owner. And what about the ecological consequences? The genetic? Let's not get overconfident about these plant and animal species we've modified to serve our needs while growing wild. They're still new and unstable. A spreading mutation could wipe them out. Or we might have to turn farmers to save them!"

"I know. I know. I do want you to see matters in perspective. But agreed, the sooner the war ends, the better." Evagail turned her gaze from that sinister, crawling spark in the sky. She looked down the slope on which they stood, to the camp. Oilwood fires were strewn along the way, each economically serving a few people. They twinkled like red and orange constellations. A burst of laughter, a drift of song came distantly to her ears.

Karlsarm could practically read her thought. "Very well, what about Ridenour?" he challenged.

"I can't say. I talk with him, but he's so locked into himself, I get no hint of what his real purpose may be. I could almost wish my Skill were of the love kind."

"Why yours?" Karlsarm demanded. "Why don't you simply wish, like me, that we had such a Mistress with us?"

Evagail paused before she chuckled. "Shall I admit the truth? He attracts me. He's thoroughly a man, in his quiet way; and he's exotic and mysterious to boot. Must you really sic an aphrodite onto him when we reach Moon Garnet?"

"I'll decide that at the time. Meanwhile, you can help me

decide and maybe catch forewarning of any plot against us. He can't hide that he's drawn to you. Use the fact."

"I don't like to. Men and women—of course, I mean women who don't have that special Skill—they should give to each other, not take. I don't even know if I could deceive him."

"You can try. If he realizes and gets angry, what of it?" Beneath the shadowing carnivore headpiece, Karlsarm's features turned glacier stern. "You have your duty."

"Well..." Briefly, her voice was forlorn. "I suppose." Then the wide smooth shoulders straightened. Moonfrost sparkled on a mane lifted high. "It could be fun, too, couldn't it?" She turned and walked from him.

Ridenour sat at one campfire, watching a dance. The steps were as intricate as the music that an improvised orchestra made. He seemed not only glad but relieved when Evagail seated herself beside him.

"Hullo," she greeted. "Are you enjoying the spectacle?"

"Yes," he said, "but largely in my professional capacity. I'm sure it's high art, but the conventions are too alien for me."

"Isn't your business to unravel alien symbolisms?"

"In part. Trouble is, what you have here is not merely different from anything I've ever seen before. It's extraordinarily subtle—obviously the product of a long and rigorous tradition. I've discovered, for instance, that your musical scale employs smaller intervals than any other human music I know of. Thus you make and use and appreciate distinctions and combinations that I'm not trained to hear."

"I think you'll find that's typical," Evagail said. "We aren't innocent children of nature, we Free People. I suspect we elaborate our lives more, we're fonder of complication, ingenuity, ceremoniousness, than Terra herself."

"Yes, I've talked to would-be runaways from the Cities."

She laughed. "Well, the custom is that we give recruits a tough apprenticeship. If they can't get through that, we don't want them. Probably they wouldn't survive long. Not that life's harder among us than in the Cities. In fact, we have more leisure. But life is altogether different here."

"I've scarcely begun to grasp how different," Ridenour said. "The questions are so many, I don't know where to start." A dancer leaped, his feather bonnet streaming in Selene light, flame light, and shadow. A flute twittered, a drum thuttered, a harp trilled, a bell rang, chords intertwining like ripple patterns on water. "What arts do you have besides...this?"

"Not architecture, or monumental sculpture, or murals, or multi-sense taping." Evagail smiled. "Nothing that requires awkward masses. But we do have schools of—oh, scrimshaw, jewelry, weaving, painting and carvings, that sort of thing—and they are genuine, serious arts. Then drama, literature, cuisine... and things you don't have—to call them contemplation, conversation, integration—but those are poor words."

"What I can't understand is how you can manage without those awkward masses," Ridenour said. "For example, everyone seems to be literate. But what's the use? What is there to read?"

"Why, we probably have more books and periodicals than you do. No electronics competing with them. One of the first things our ancestors did, when they started colonizing the outback in earnest, was develop plants with leaves that dry into paper and juice that makes ink. Many landholders keep a little printing press in the same shed as their other heavy equipment. It doesn't need much metal, and wind or water can power it. Don't forget, each area maintains schools. The demand for reading matter is a source of income—yes, we use iron and copper slugs for currency—and the transporters carry mail as well as goods."

"How about records, though? Libraries? Computers? Information exchange?"

"I've never met anybody who collects books, the way some do in the Cities. If you want to look at a piece again, copies are cheap." (Ridenour thought that this ruled out something he had always considered essential to a cultivated man—the ability to browse, to re-read on impulse, to be serendipitous among the shelves. However, no doubt these outbackers thought he was uncouth because he didn't know how to dance or to arrange a meteor-watching festival.) "Messages go speedily enough for our purposes. We don't keep records like you. Our mode of life doesn't require it. Likewise, we have quite a live technology, still developing. Yes, and a pure science. But they concentrate on areas of work that need no elaborate apparatus: the study of animals, for instance, and ways to control them."

Evagail leaned closer to Ridenour. No one else paid attention;

they were watching the performance. "But do me a favor tonight, will you?" she asked.

"What? Why, certainly." His gaze drifted across the ruddy lights in her hair, the shadows under her cloak, and hastily away. "If I can."

"It's easy." She laid a hand over his. "Just for tonight, stop being a research machine. Make small talk. Tell me a joke or two. Sing me a Terran song, when they finish here. Or walk with me to look at the moon. Be human, John Ridenour...only a man... this little while."

West of the pass, the land became a rolling plateau. Again it was forested, but less thickly and with other trees than in the warm eastern valleys. The travelers met folk more often, as population grew denser; and these were apt to be mounted. Karlsarm didn't bother with animals. A human in good condition can log fifty kilometers a day across favorable terrain, without difficulty. Ridenour remarked, highly centralized empires were held together on ancient Terra with communication no faster than this.

Besides, the outbackers possessed them: not merely an occasional aircar for emergency use, but a functioning web. He broke into uncontrollable laughter when Evagail first explained the system to him.

"What's so funny?" She cocked her head. Though they were much together, to the exclusion of others, they still lacked mutual predictability. He might now be wearing outbacker garb and be darkened by Freehold's harsh sunlight and have let his beard grow because he found a diamond-edge razor too much trouble. But he remained a stranger.

"I'm sorry. Old saying." He looked around the glen where they stood. Trees were stately above blossom-starred grasses; leaves murmured in a cool breeze and smelled like spice. He touched a green tendril that curled over one trunk and looped to the next. "Grapevine telegraph!"

"But...well, I don't recognize your phrase, John, but that kind of plant does carry signals. Our ancestors went to a vast amount of work to create the type and sow and train it, over the entire mid-continent. I confess the signals don't go at light speed, only neural speed; and the channel isn't awfully broad—but it suffices for us."

"How do you, uh, activate it?"

"That requires a Skill. To send something, you'd go to the nearest node and pay the woman who lives there. She'd transmit."

Ridenour nodded. "I see. Actually, I've met setups on nonhuman planets that aren't too different from this." He hesitated. "What do you mean by a Skill?"

"A special ability, inborn, cultivated, disciplined. You've watched Skills in action on our route, haven't you?"

"I'm not certain. You see, I'm barely starting to grasp the pattern of your society. Before, everything was a jumble of new impressions. Now I observe meaningful differences between this and that. Take our friend Noach, for one, with his spying quasi-weasels; or Karlsarm and the rest, who use birds for couriers. Do they have Skills?"

"Of course not. I suppose you might say their animals do. That is, the creatures have been bred to semi-intelligence. They have the special abilities and instincts, the *desire,* built into their chromosomes. But as for the men who use them, no, all they have is training in language and handling. Anybody could be taught the same."

Ridenour looked at her, where she stood like a lioness in the filtered green light, stillness and strange odors at her back. "Only women have Skills, then," he said finally.

She nodded. "Yes."

"Why? Were they bred too?"

"No." Astonishingly, she colored. "Whatever we may do with other men, we seldom become pregnant by anyone but a landholder. We want our children to have a claim on him. But somehow, women seem able to do more with hormones and pheromones. A biologist tried to explain why, but I couldn't follow him terribly well. Let's say the female has a more complex biochemistry, more closely involved with her psyche, than a male. Not that any woman can handle any materials. In fact, those who can do something with them are rare. When identified, in girlhood, they're carefully trained to use what substances they can."

"How?"

"It depends. A course of drugs may change the body secretions... delicately; you wouldn't perceive any difference; but someone like Mistress Jenith will never be stung by her fire bees. Rather, they'll always live near her. And she has ways to control them, make them go where she commands and—No, I don't know how. Each Skill keeps its secrets. But you must know how. Each few parts per million in the air will lure insects for kilometers around, to come and mate. Other insects, social ones, use odor signals to coordinate their communities. Man himself lives more by trace chemicals than he realizes. Think how little of some drugs is needed to change his metabolism, even his personality. Think how some smells recall a past scene to you, so vividly you might be there again. Think how it was proven, long ago, that like, dislike, appetite, fear, anger . . . every emotion . . . are conditioned by just such faint cues. Now imagine what can be done, as between a woman who knows precisely how to use those stimuli—some taken from bottles, some created at will by her own glands—between her and an organism bred to respond."

"An Arulian concept?"

"Yes, we learned a lot from the Arulians," Evagail said.

"They call you Mistress, I've heard. What's your Skill?"

She lost gravity. Her grin was impudent. "You may find out one day. Come, let's rejoin the march." She took his hand. "Though we needn't hurry," she added.

As far as could be ascertained, Freehold had never been glaciated. The average climate was milder than Terra's, which was one reason the outbackers didn't need fixed houses. They moved about within their territories, following the game and the fruits of the earth, content with shelters erected here and there, or with bedrolls. By Ridenour's standards, it was an austere life.

Or it had been. He found his canon gradually changing. The million sights, sounds, smells, less definable sensations of the wilderness, made a city apartment seem dead by contrast, no matter how many electronic entertainers you installed.

(Admittedly, the human kinds of fun were limited. A minstrel, a ball game, a chess game, a local legend, a poetry reading, were a little pallid to a man used to living at the heart of Empire. And while the outbackers could apparently do whatever they chose with drugs and hypnotism, so could the Terrans. Lickerish rumor had actually underrated their uninhibited inventiveness in other departments of pleasure. But you had only a finite number of possibilities there too, didn't you? And he wasn't exactly a young man any more, was he? And damn, but he missed Lissa! Also the children, of course, the tobacco he'd exhausted, friends, tall towers, the gentler daylight of Sol and familiar constellations after dark, the sane joys of scholarship and teaching: everything, everything.)

But life could not be strictly nomadic. Some gear was not portable, or needed protection. Thus, in each territory, at least one true house and several outbuildings had been erected, where the people lived from time to time.

Humans needed protection too. Ridenour found that out when he and Evagail were caught in a storm.

She had led him off the line of march to show him such a center. They had been en-route for an hour or two when she began casting uneasy glances at the sky. Clouds rose in the north, unbelievably high thunderheads with lightning in their blue-black depths. A breeze chilled and stiffened; the forest moaned. "We'd better speed up," she said at length. "Rainstorm headed this way."

"Well?" He no longer minded getting wet.

"I don't mean those showers we've had. I mean the real thing."

Ridenour gulped and matched her trot. He knew what kind of violence a deep, intensely irradiated atmosphere can breed. Karl-sarm's folk must be hard at work, racing to chop branches and make rough roofs and walls for themselves. Two alone couldn't do it in time. They'd normally have sought refuge under a windfall or in a hollow trunk or anything else they found. But a house was obviously preferable.

The wind worsened. Being denser than Terra's, air never got to hurricane velocity; but it thrust remorselessly, a quasi-solid, well-nigh unbreathable mass. Torn-off leaves and boughs started to fly overhead, under a galloping black cloud wrack. Darkness thickened, save when lightning split the sky. Thunder, keenings, breakings and crashings, resounded through Ridenour's skull.

He had believed himself in good shape, but presently he was staggering. Any man must soon be exhausted, pushing against that horrible wind. Evagail, though, continued, easy of breath. *How?* he wondered numbly, before he lost all wonder in the cruel combat to keep running.

The first raindrops fell, enormous, driven by the tempest, sting-ing like gravel when they struck. You could be drowned in a flash flood, if you were not literally flayed by the hail that would soon come. Ridenour reeled toward unconsciousness—no, he was helped, Evagail upbore him, he leaned on her and—

And they reached the hilltop homestead.

It consisted of low, massive log-and-stone buildings, whose overgrown sod roofs would hardly be visible from above. Everything stood unlighted, empty. But the door to the main house opened at Evagail's touch; no place in the woodlands had a lock. She dragged Ridenour across the threshold and closed the door again. He lay in gloom and gasped his way back to consciousness. As if across light-years, he heard her say, "We didn't arrive any too soon, did we?" There followed the cannonade of the hail.

After a while he was on his feet. She had stimulated the lamps, which were microcultures in glass globes, to their bright phosphorescence and had started a fire on the hearth. The principal heat source, however, was fuel oil, a system antique but adequate. "We might as well figure on spending the night," she said from the kitchen. "This weather will last for hours, and the roads will be rivers for hours after that. Why don't you find yourself a hot bath and some dry clothes? I'll have dinner ready soon."

Ridenour swallowed a sense of inadequacy. He wasn't an outbacker and couldn't be expected to cope with their country. How well would they do on Terra? Exploring, he saw the house to be spacious, many-roomed, beautifully paneled, draped and furnished. Evagail's advice was sound. He returned to her as if reborn.

She had prepared an excellent meal out of what was in the larder, including a heady red wine. White tablecloth, crystal goblets, candlelight were almost a renaissance of a Terra which had been more gracious than today's. (Almost. The utensils were horn, the knifeblades obsidian. The paintings on the walls were of a stylized, unearthly school; looking closely, you could identify Arulian influence. No music lilted from a taper; instead came the muffled brawling of the storm. And the woman who sat across from him wore a natural-fiber kilt, a fringed leather bolero, a dagger and tomahawk.)

They talked in animated and friendly wise, though since they belonged to alien cultures they had little more than question-and-answer conversation. The bottle passed freely back and forth. Being tired and having long abstained, Ridenour was quickly affected by the alcohol. When he noticed that, he thought, what the hell, why not? It glowed within him. "I owe you an apology," he said. "I classed your people as barbarians. I see now you have a true civilization."

"You needed this much time to see that?" she laughed. "Well, I'll forgive you. The Cities haven't realized it yet."

"That's natural. You're altogether strange to them. And, isolated as they are from the galactic mainstream, they . . . haven't the habit of thinking something different . . . can be equal or superior to what they take for granted is the civilized way."

"My, that was a sentence! Do you acknowledge, then, we are superior?"

He shook his head with care.

"No. I can't say that. I'm a city boy myself. A lot of what you do shocks me. Your ruthlessness. Your unwillingness to compromise."

She grew grave. "The Cities never tried to compromise with us, John. I don't know if they can. Our wise men, those who've studied history, say an industrial society must keep expanding or go under. We've got to stop them before they grow too strong. The war's given us a chance."

"You can't rebel against the Empire!" he protested.

"Can't we? We're a goodly ways from Terra. And we are rebelling. No one consulted us about incorporation." Evagail shrugged. "Not that we care about that in itself. What difference to us who claims the overlordship of Freehold, if he lets us alone? But the Cities have not let us alone. They cut down our woods, dam our rivers, dig holes in our soil, and get involved in a war that may wreck the whole planet."

"M-m, you could help end the war if you mobilized against the Arulians."

"To whose benefit? The Cities'!"

"But when you attack the Cities, aren't you aiding the Arulians?"

"No. Not in the long run. They belong to the Cities also. We don't want to fight them—our relationship with them was mostly pleasant, and they taught us a great deal—but eventually we want them off this world."

"You can't expect me to agree that's right."

"Certainly not." Her tone softened. "What we want from you is nothing but an honest report to your leaders. You don't know how happy I am that you admit we are civilized. Or post-civilized. At any rate, we aren't degenerate, we are progressing on our own trail. I can hope you'll go between us and the Empire, as a friend of both, and help work out a settlement. If you do that, you'll live in centuries of ballads: the Peacebringer."

"I'd like that better than anything," he said gladly.

She raised her brows. "Anything?"

"Oh, some things equally, no doubt. I am getting homesick."

"You needn't stay lonely while you're with us," she murmured.

Somehow, their hands joined across the table. The wine sang in Ridenour's veins. "I've wondered why you stood apart from me," she said. "Surely you could see I want to make love with you."

"Y-yes." His heart knocked.

"Why not? You have a . . . a wife, yes. But I can't imagine an Imperial Terran worries about that, two hundred light-years from home. And what harm would be done her?"

"None."

She laughed anew, rose and circled the table to stand beside him and rumpled his hair. The odor of her was sweet around him. "All right, then, silly," she said, "what have you been waiting for?"

He remembered. She saw his fists clench and stepped back. He looked at the candle flames, not her, and mumbled: "I'm sorry. It mustn't be."

"Why not?" The wind raved louder, nearly obliterating her words.

"Let's say I do have idiotic medieval scruples."

She regarded him for a space. "Is that the truth?"

"Yes." But not the whole truth, he thought. I am not an observer, not an emissary, I am he who will call down destruction upon you if I can. The thing in my pocket sunders us, dear. You are my enemy, and I will not betray you with a kiss.

"I'm not offended," she said at last, slowly. "Disappointed and puzzled, though."

"We probably don't understand each other as well as we believed," he ventured.

"Might be. Well, let's let the dishes wait and turn in, shall we?" Her tone was less cold than wary.

Next day she was polite but aloof, and after they had rejoined the army she conferred long with Karlsarm.

Moon Garnet Lake was the heart of the Upwoods: more than fifty kilometers across, walled on three sides by forest and on the fourth by soaring snowpeaks. At every season it was charged with life, fish in argent swarms, birds rising by thousands when a bulligator bellowed in a white-plumed stand of cockatoo reed, wildkine everywhere among the trees. At full summer, microphytons multiplied until the waters glowed deep red, and the food chain which they started grew past belief in size and diversity. As yet, the year was too new for that. Wavelets sparkled clear to the escarpments, where mountaintops floated dim blue against heaven.

"I see why you reacted violently against the attempt to found a town here," Ridenour said to Karlsarm. They stood on a beach, watching most of the expedition frolic in the lake. Those boisterous shouts and lithe brown bodies did not seem out of place; a cruising flock of fowl overhead was larger and made more clangor. The Terran drew a pure breath. "And it would have been a pity, aesthetically speaking. Who owns this region?"

"None," Karlsarm answered. "It's too basic to the whole country. Anyone may use it. The numbers that do aren't great enough to strain the resources, similar things being available all over. So it's a natural site for our periodic head-of-household gatherings." He glanced sideways at the other man and added: "Or for an army to rendezvous."

"You are not disbanding, then?"

"Certainly not. Domkirk was a commencement. We don't intend to stop till we control the planet."

"But you're daydreaming! No other City's as vulnerably located as Domkirk was. Some are on other continents—"

"Where Free People also live. We're in touch."

"What do you plan?"

Karlsarm chuckled. "Do you really expect me to tell you?"

Ridenour made a rueful grin, but his eyes were troubled. "I don't ask for military secrets. In general terms, however, what do you foresee?"

"A war of attrition," Karlsarm said. "We don't like that prospect either. It'll taste especially sour to use biologicals against their damned agriculture. But if we must, we must. We have more land, more resources of the kind that count, more determination. And they can't get at us. We'll outgrind them."

"Are you quite sure? Suppose you provoke them—or the Imperial Navy—into making a real effort. Imagine, say, one atomic bomb dropped into this lake."

Anger laid tight bands around Karlsarm's throat and chest, but he managed to answer levelly: "We have defenses. And means of retaliation. This is a keystone area for us. We won't lose it without exacting a price—which I think they'll find too heavy. Tell them that when you go home!"

"I shall. I don't know if I'll be believed. You appear to have no concept of the power that a single, minor-class spaceship can bring to bear. I beg you to make terms before it's too late."

"Do you aim to convince a thousand leaders like me and the entire society that elected us? I wish you luck, John Ridenour." Karlsarm turned from the pleading gaze. "I'd better get busy. We're still several kilometers short of our campsite."

His brusqueness was caused mainly by doubt of his ability to dissemble much longer. What he, with some experience of Imperialists, sensed in this one's manner, lent strong support to the intuitive suspicions that Evagail had voiced. Ridenour had more on his mind than the Terran admitted. It was unwise to try getting the truth out of him with drugs. He might be immunized or counter-conditioned. Or his secret might turn out to be something harmless. In either case, a potentially valuable spokesman would have been antagonized for nothing.

An aphrodite? She'd boil the ice water in his veins, for certain! And, while possessors of that Skill were rare, several were standing by at present in case they should be needed on some intelligence mission.

It might not work, either. But the odds were high that it would. Damned few men cared for anything but the girl—the woman—the hag—whatever her age, whatever her looks—once she had turned her pheromones loose on him. She could ask what she would as the price of her company. But Ridenour might belong to that small percentage who, otherwise normal, were so intensely inner-directed that it didn't matter how far in love they fell; they'd stick by their duty. Should this prove the case he could not be allowed to leave and reveal the existence of that powerful a weapon. He must be killed, which was repugnant, or detained, which was a nuisance.

Karlsarm's brain labored on, while he issued his orders and led the final march. Ridenour probably did not suspect that he was suspected. He likeliest interpreted Evagail's avoidance of him as due to pique, despite what she had claimed. (And in some degree it no doubt is, Karlsarm snickered to himself.) Chances were he attributed the chief's recent gruffness to preoccupation. He had circulated freely among the other men and women of the force; but not having been told to doubt his good faith, they did not and he must realize it.

Hard to imagine what he might do. He surely did not plan on

access to an aircar or a long-range radio transmitter! Doubtless he'd report anything he had seen or heard that might have military significance. But he wouldn't be reporting anything that made any difference. Well before he was conducted to the agrolands, the army would have left Moon Garnet again; and it would not return, because the lake was too precious to use for a permanent base. And all this had been made explicit to Ridenour at the outset.

Well, then, why not give him free rein and see what he did? Karlsarm weighed risks and gains for some time before he nodded to himself.

The encampment was large. A mere fraction of the Upwoods men had gone to Domkirk. Thousands stayed behind, training. They greeted their comrades with envious hilarity. Fires burned high that night, song and dance and clinking goblets alarmed the forest.

At sunset, Karlsarm and Evagail stood atop a rocky bluff, overlooking water and trees and a northward rise to the camp. Behind them was a cave, from which projected an Arulian howitzer. Several other heavy-duty weapons were placed about the area, and a rickety old war boat patrolled overhead. Here and there, a man flitted into view, bow or blade on shoulder, and vanished again into the brake. Voices could be heard, muted by leaves, and smoke drifted upward. But the signs of man were few, virtually lost in that enormous landscape. With the enemy hundreds of kilometers off, guns as well as picketposts were untended; trees divided the little groups of men from each other and hid them from shore or sky; the evening was mostly remote bird cries and long golden light.

"I wonder what our Terran thinks of this," Karlsarm said. "We must look pretty sloppy to him."

"He's no fool. He doesn't underrate us much. Maybe not at all." Evagail shivered, though the air was yet warm. Her hand crept into his, her voice grew thin. "Could he be right? Could we really be foredoomed?"

"I don't know," Karlsarm said.

She started. The hazel eyes widened. "Loveling! You are always—"

"I can be honest with you," he said. "Ridenour accused me today of not understanding what power the Imperialists command in a single combat unit. He was wrong. I've seen them and I do understand. We can't force terms on them. If they decide the Cities must prevail, well, we'll give them a hard guerrilla war, but we'll be hunted down in the end. Our aim has to be to convince them it isn't worthwhile—that, at the least, their cheapest course of action is to arrange and enforce a status quo settlement between us and the Cities." He laughed. "Whether or not they'll agree remains to be seen. But we've got to try, don't we?"

"Do we?"

"Either that or stop being the Free People."

She leaned her head on his shoulder. "Let's not spend the night in this hole," she begged. "Not with that big ugly gun looming over us. Let's take our bedrolls into the forest."

"I'm sorry. I must stay here."

"Why?"

"So Noach can find me...if his animals report anything."

Karlsarm woke before the fingers had closed on his arm to shake him. He sat up. The cave was a murk, relieved by a faint sheen off the howitzer; but the entrance cut a blue-black starry circle in it. Noach crouched silhouetted. "He lay awake the whole night," the handler breathed. "Now he's sneaked off to one of the blaster cannon. He's fooling around with it."

Karlsarm heard Evagail gasp at his side. He slipped weapon belts and quiver strap over the clothes he had slept in, took his crossbow and glided forth. "We'll see about that," he said. Anger stood bleak within him. "Lead on." Silent though they were, slipping from shadow, he became aware of the woman at his back.

Selene was down, sunrise not far off, but the world still lay nighted, sky powdered with stars and lake gleaming like a mirror. An uhu wailed, off in the bulk of the forest. The air was cold. Karlsarm glanced aloft. Among the constellations crept that spark which had often haunted his thoughts. The orbit he estimated from angular speed was considerable. Therefore the thing was big. And if the Imperialists had erected some kind of space station, the grapevine would have brought news from the Free People's spies inside the Cities; therefore the thing was a spaceship—huge. Probably the light cruiser *Isis*: largest man-of-war the Terrans admitted keeping in this system. (Quite enough for their purposes. A heavier craft couldn't land if needed. This one could handle any probable combination of lesser vessels. If Aruli sent something more formidable, the far-flung scoutboats would detect that in time to arrange reinforcements from a Navy base before the enemy arrived. Which was ample reason to expect that Aruli would not "intervene in a civil conflict, though denouncing this injustice visited upon righteously struggling kinfolk.") Was it coincidence that she took her new station soon after Ridenour joined the raiders? Tonight we find out, Karlsarm vowed.

The blaster cannon stood on a bare ridge, barrel etched gaunt across the Milky Way. His group crouched under the last tree and peered. One of Noach's beasts could go unobserved among the scattered bushes, but not a man. And the beasts weren't able to describe what went on at the controls of a machine.

"Could he—"

Karlsarm chopped off Evagail's whisper with a hiss. The gun was in action. He saw the thing move through a slow arc and heard the purr of its motor. It was tracking. But what was it locked onto? And why had no energy bolt stabbed forth?

"He's not fixing to shoot up the camp," Karlsarm muttered. "That'd be ridiculous. He couldn't get off more than two shots before he was dead. But what else?"

"Should I rush?" Evagail asked.

"I think you'd better," Karlsarm said, "and let's hope the damage hasn't already been done."

He must endure the agony of a minute or two while she gathered the resources of her Skill—not partially, as she often did in everyday life, but totally. He heard a measured intake of breath, sensed rhythmic muscular contractions, smelled sharp adrenalin. Then she exploded.

She was across the open ground in a blur. Ridenour could not react before she was upon him. He cried out and ran. She overhauled him in two giantess bounds. Her hands closed. He struggled, and he was not a weak man. But she picked him up by the wrists and ankles and carried him like a rag doll. Her face was a white mask in the starlight. "Lie still," she said in a voice not her own, "or I will break you."

"Don't. Evagail, please." Noach dared stroke an iron-hard arm. "Do be careful," he said to Ridenour's aghast upside-down stare. "She's dangerous in this condition. It's akin to hysterical rage, you know—mobilization of the body's ultimate resources, which are quite astounding—but under conscious control. Nevertheless, the personality is affected. Think of her as an angry catavray."

"Amok," rattled in Ridenour's throat. "Berserk." He shivered.

"I don't recognize those words," Noach said, "but I repeat, her Skill consists in voluntary hysteria. At the moment, she could crush your skull between her hands. She might do it, too, if you provoke her."

They reached the gun. Evagail cast the Terran to earth, bone-rattlingly hard, and yanked him back on his feet by finger and thumb around his nape. He was taller than she, but she appeared to tower over him, over all three men. Starlight crackled in her coiled hair. Her eyes were bright and blind.

Noach leaned close to Ridenour, read the terror upon him, and said mildly, "Please tell us what you were doing."

In some incredible fashion, Ridenour got the nerve to yell, "Nothing! I couldn't sleep, I c-came here to pass the time—"

Karlsarm turned from his examination of the blaster. "You've got this thing tracking that ship in orbit," he said.

"Yes. I—foolish of me—I apologize—only for fun—"

"You had the trigger locked," Karlsarm said. "Energy was pouring out of the muzzle. But no flash, no light, no ozone smell." He gestured. "I turned it off. I also notice you've opened the chamber and replaced the primary modulator with this little gadget. Did you hear him talk, Evagail, before you charged?"

Her strange flat tone said: " '—entire strength of the outbacker army on this continent is concentrated here and plans to remain for several days at least. I don't suggest a multi-megatonner. It'd annihilate them, all right, but they *are* subjects of His Majesty and potentially more valuable than most. It'd also do great ecological damage—to Imperial territory—and City hinterlands would get fallout. Not to mention the effect on your humble servant, me. But a ship could land without danger. I suggest the *Isis* herself, loaded with marines, aircraft and auxiliary gear. If the descent is sudden, the guerrillas won't be able to flee far. Using defoliators, sonics, gas, stun-beam sweeps and the rest, you should be able to capture most of them inside a week or two. Repeat, capture, not kill, wherever possible. I'll explain after you land. Right now, I don't know how long I've got till I'm interrupted, so I'd better describe terrain. We're on the northeast verge of Moon Garnet Lake—' At that point," Evagail concluded, "I interrupted him." The most chilling thing was that she saw no humor.

"Her Skill heightens perceptions and data storage too," Noach said in a shocked, mechanical fashion.

"Well," Karlsarm sighed, "no real need to interrogate Ridenour, is there? He converted this gun into some kind of maser and called down the enemy on our heads."

"They may not respond, if they heard him cut off the way he was," Noach said with little hope.

"Wasn't much noise," Karlsarm answered. "They probably figure he did see somebody coming and had to stop in a hurry. If anything, they'll arrive as fast as may be, before we can disperse the stockpiles that'll give a scent to their metal detectors."

"We'd better start running," Noach said. Above the bristly beard, his nutcracker face had turned old.

"Maybe not." Excitement rose in Karlsarm. "I need at least an hour or two to think—and, yes, talk with you, Ridenour."

The Terran straightened. His tone rang. "I didn't betray you, really," he said. "I stayed loyal to my Emperor."

"You'll tell us a few things, though," Karlsarm said. "Like what procedure you expect a landing party to follow. No secrets to that, are there? Just tell us about newscasts you've seen, books you've read, inferences you've made."

"No!"

Roused by the noise, other men were drifting up the hill, lean leather-clad shapes with weapons to hand. But Karlsarm ignored them. "Evagail," he said.

Her cold, cold fingers closed on Ridenour. He shrieked. "Slack off," Karlsarm ordered. "Now—*slack off, woman!*—have you changed your mind? Or does she unscrew your ears, one by one, and other parts? I don't want you hurt, but my whole civilization's at stake, and I haven't much time."

Ridenour broke. Karlsarm did not despise him for that. Few men indeed could have defied Evagail in her present mood, and they would have had to be used to the Mistresses of War.

In fact, Karlsarm needed a lot of courage himself, later on, when he laid arms around her and mouth at her cheek and crooned, "Come back to us, loveling." How slowly softness, warmth and—in a chill dawnlight—color reentered her skin: until at last she sank down before him and wept.

He raised her and led her to their cave.

✧　　✧　　✧

At first the ship was a gleam, drowned in sun-glare. Then she was a cloud no bigger than a man's hand. But swiftly and swiftly did she grow. Within minutes, her shadow darkened the land. Men saw her from below as a tower that descended upon them, hundreds of meters in height, flanks reflecting with a metallic brilliance that blinded. Through light filters might be seen the boat housings, gun turrets and missile tubes that bristled from her. She was not heavily armored, save at a few key points, for she dealt in nuclear energies and nothing could withstand a direct hit. But the perceptors and effectors of her fire-control system could intercept virtually anything that a lesser mechanism might throw. And the full power of her own magazines, vomited forth at once, would have incinerated a continent.

The engines driving that enormous mass were deathly quiet. But where their countergravity fields touched the planet, trees snapped to kindling and the lake roiled white. Her advent was dancer graceful. But it went so fast that cloven air roared behind, one continuous thunderclap between stratosphere and surface. Echoes crashed from mountain to mountain; avalanches broke loose on the heights, throwing ice plumes into the sky; the risen winds smelled scorched.

Emblazoned upon her stood *HMS Isis* and the sunburst of chastising Empire.

Already she had discharged her auxiliaries, aircraft that buzzed across the lakeland in bright quick swarms, probing with instruments, firing random lightning bolts, shouting through amplifiers that turned human voices into an elemental force: "Surrender, surrender!"

At the nexus of the cruiser's multiple complexity, Captain Chang sat in his chair of command. The screens before him flickered with views, data, reports. A score of specialist officers held to their posts behind him. Their work—speech, tap on signal buttons, clickdown of switches—made a muted buzz. From time to time, something was passed up to Chang himself. He listened, decided and returned to studying the screens. Neither his inflection nor his expression varied. Lieutenant-Commander Hunyadi, his executive officer, punched an appropriate control on the communications board in front of him and relayed the order to the right place. The bridge might have been an engineering center on Terra, save for the uniforms and the straining concentration.

Until Chang scowled. "What's that. Citizen Hunyadi?" He pointed to a screen in which the water surface gleamed, amidst green woods and darkling cliffs. The view was dissolving.

"Fog rising, sir, I think." Hunyadi had already tapped out a query to the meteorological officer in his distant sanctum.

"No doubt, Citizen Hunyadi," Chang said. "I do not believe it was predicted. Nor do I believe it is precedented—such rapid condensation—even on this freak planet."

The M.O.'s voice came on. Yes, the entire target area was fogging at an unheard-of rate. No, it had not been forecast and, frankly, it was not understood. Possibly, at this altitude, given this pressure gradient, high insolation acted synergistically with the colloidogenic effect of countergravity beams on liquid. Should the question be addressed to a computer?

"No, don't tie facilities up on an academic problem," Chang said. "Will the stuff be troublesome?"

"Not very, sir. In fact, aircraft reports indicate it's forming a layer at about five hundred meters. An overcast, should be reasonably clear at ground level. Besides, we have instruments that can see through fog."

"I am aware of that latter fact, Citizen Nazarevsky. What concerns me is that an overcast will hide us from visual observation at satellite distance. You will recall that picket ships are supposed to keep an eye on us." Chang drummed fingers on the arm of his chair for a second before he said: "No matter. We will still have full communication, I trust. And it's necessary to exploit surprise, before the bandits have scattered over half this countryside. Carry on, gentlemen."

"Aye, aye, sir." Hunyadi returned to the subtle, engrossing ballet that was command operations.

After a while, Chang stirred himself and asked, "Has any evidence been reported of enemy willingness to surrender?"

"No, sir," the exec replied. "But they don't appear to be marshalling for resistance, either. I don't mean just that they haven't shot at us. The stockpiles of metallic stuff that we're zeroing in on haven't been moved. Terrain looks deserted. Every topographical and soni-probe indication is that it's normal, safe, not booby-trapped."

"I wish Ridenour had been able to transmit more," Chang complained. "Well, no doubt the bandits are simply running in panic. I wonder if they stopped to cut his throat."

Hunyadi understood that no answer was desired from him.

The ship passed through the new-born clouds. Uncompensated viewports showed thick, swirling gray formlessness. Infrared, ultra-violet and microwave scopes projected a peaceful scene beneath. It was true that an unholy number of tiny flying objects were registered in the area. Insects, no doubt, probably disturbed by the ship. Time was short in which to think about them, before *Isis* broke through. Ground was now immediately below: that slope on the forest edge, overlooking the lake and near the enemy weapon depots, which Chang had selected. It would have been a lovely sight, had the sky not been so low and gloomy, the tendrils and banks of fog drifting so many and stealthy among trees. But everyone on *Isis* was too busy to admire, from the master in his chair of command to the marines ranked before the sally locks.

Aircraft that had landed for final checks of the site flew away like autumn leaves. The cruiser hung until they were gone, extending her landing jacks, which were massive as cathedral buttresses. Then slowly she sank down upon them. For moments the engines loudened, ringing through her metal corridors. Words flew, quiet and tense: "—stability achieved . . . air cover complete . . . weapons crew standing by . . . detectors report negative . . . standing by . . . standing by . . . standing by . . ."

"Proceed with Phase Two," Chang ordered.

"*Now hear this,*" Hunyadi chanted to the all-points intercom. The engines growled into silence. The airlocks opened. Inhuman in helmets, body armor, flying harness, the weapons they clutched, the marine squadrons rushed forth. First they would seize the guerrilla arsenals, and next cast about for human spoor.

The bridge had not really fallen still. Data continued to flow in, commands to flow out; but by comparison, sound was now a mutter, eerie as the bodies of fog that moved out of undertree shadows and across the bouldery hillside. Hunyadi looked into the screens and grimaced. "Sir," he said uneasily, "if the enemy's as skilled in moving about through the woods as I've heard, someone could come near enough to fire a small nuclear missile at us."

"Have no worries on that score, Citizen Hunyadi," Chang said. "Nothing material, launched from a projector that one or two men might carry, could reach us before it was detected and intercepted. A blaster beam might scorch a hull plate or two. But upper and lower gun turrets would instantly triangulate on the source." His tone was indulgent: like most Navy men serving on capital ships, Hunyadi was quite new to ground operations. "Frankly, I could hope for a show of resistance. The alternative is a long, tedious airborne bushbeating."

Hunyadi winced. "Hunting men like animals. I don't like it."

"Nor I," Chang admitted. The iron came back into him. "But we have our orders."

"Yes, sir."

"Read your history, Citizen Hunyadi. Read your history. No empire which tolerated rebellion ever endured long thereafter. And we are the wall between humanity and Merseian—"

A scream broke through.

And suddenly war was no problem in logistics, search patterns, or games theory. It entered the ship with pain in one hand and blood on the other; and its footfalls thundered.

"*Bees, millions of things like bees, out of the woods—oh, God, coming inboard, the boys're doubled over, one sting hurts enough to knock you crazy—Yaaahhhh!*"

"Close all locks! Seal all compartments! All hands in spacesuits!"

"*Marine Colonel Deschamps to Prime Command. Detachments report small groups of women, unarmed, as they land. Women appear anxious to surrender. Request orders.*"

"Take them prisoners, of course. Stand around them. You may not be attacked then. But if a unit notes a dense insect swarm, the men are to seal their armor and discharge lethal gas at once."

"*Lock Watch Four to bridge! We can't shut the lock here! Some enormous animal—like a, a nightmare crocodile—burst in from the woods—blocking the valves with its body—*"

"Energy weapons, sweep the surrounding forest. All aircraft, return to bomb and strafe this same area."

Atomic warheads and poisons could not be used, when the ship would be caught in their blast or the gases pour in through three airlocks jammed open by slain monsters. But some gunners had buttoned up their turrets in advance of the bees. Their cannon hurled bolt after bolt, trees exploded and burned and fell, rocks fused...and fog poured in like an ocean. Simultaneously, the instrumentation and optical aids that should have pierced it failed. The crews must fire at random into horrible wet smoke, knowing they could not cover the whole ground about them.

"Radio dead. Radar dead. Electromagnetic 'scopes dead. Blanketed by interference. Appears to emanate from . . . from everywhere . . . different insects, clouds of them! What scanning stuff we've got that still works, sonics, that kind of thing, gives insufficient definition. We're deaf, dumb, and blind!"

Aircraft began to crash. Their instruments were likewise gone; and they were not meant to collide with entire flocks of birds.

"Marine Colonel Deschamps—reporting—reports received—catastrophe. I don't know what, except . . . those women . . . they turned on our men and—"

Troopers who escaped flew wildly through fog. Birds found them and betrayed them to snipers in treetops. They landed, seeking cover. Arrows whistled from brush, or hellhounds fell upon them.

"Stand by to raise ship."

"Lock Watch Four reporting—they've got in through the fog, under our fire—swarming in, wild men and animals—good-by, Maria, good-by, universe—"

Most aircraft pilots managed to break free. They got above the clouds and ran from that lake. But they were not equipped to evade ground fire of energy weapons with which there was no electronic interference such as continued to plague them. It had been assumed that the marines would take those emplacements. The marines were now dead, or disabled, or fleeing, or captured. The women called their men back to the guns. Stars blossomed and fell through the daylight sky.

"This is Wolf, commanding the Free People group assigned to HMS Isis. A prisoner tells me this thing communicates with the bridge. Better give up, Captain. We're inside. We hold the engine room. We can take your whole ship at our leisure—or plant a nuclear bomb. Your auxiliary forces are rapidly being destroyed. I hope you'll see reason and give up. We don't want to harm you. It's no discredit to you, sir, this defeat. Your intelligence service let you down. You met weapons you didn't know about, uniquely suited to very special circumstances. Tell your men to lay down their arms. We'll lift the interference blanket if you agree—not skyward, but on ground level, anyhow, so you can call them. Let's stop spilling lives and begin talking terms."

Chang felt he had no choice.

Soon afterward, he and his principal officers stood outside. The men who guarded them were clad and equipped like savages; but they spoke with courtesy. "I would like you gentlemen to meet some friends," said the one named Karlsarm. From the forest, toward the captured flying tower, walked a number of women. They were more beautiful than could be imagined.

Ridenour was among the last to go aboard. Not that there were many—a skeleton staff of chosen Imperialist officers, for the aphrodites could not make captives of more in the short time available, those women themselves, whoever of the army possessed abilities even slightly useful in space warship. But perhaps the measure of Karlsarm's audacity was his drafting of a known spy.

Whose loyalties had not been altered.

Standing in cold, blowing fogbanks, Ridenour shuddered. The cruiser was dim to his eyes, her upper sections lost. Water soaked the earth and dripped from a thousand unseen trees; the insects that made this weather flitted ceaselessly between lake and air, in such myriads that their wingbeats raised an underlying sussuration; a wild beast bellowed, a wild bird shrilled—tones of the wilderness. But the outback reaches were not untamed nature. Like some great animal, they had been harnessed for man, and in turn, something of theirs had entered the human heart.

A Terran went up a gangway, into the ship. His uniform was still neat blue, emblemmed with insignia and sunburst. He still walked with precision. But his eyes scarcely left the weather-beaten, leather-kilted woman at his side, though she must be twenty years his senior.

"There but for the grace of God," Ridenour whispered.

Evagail, who had appeared mutely a few minutes ago, gave him a serious look. "Is their treatment so dreadful?" she asked.

"What about their people at home? Their home itself? Their own shame and self-hate for weakness—" Ridenour broke off.

"They'll be released . . . against their wills, I'm sure; they'll plead to stay with us. You can make it part of your job to see that their superiors understand they couldn't help themselves. Afterward, you have reconditioning techniques, don't you? Though I expect most cases will recover naturally. They'll have had just a short exposure."

"And the, the women?"

"Why, what of them? They don't want to be saddled with a bunch of citymen. This is their wartime duty. Otherwise they have their private affairs."

"Their Skills." Ridenour edged away from her.

Her smile was curiously timid. "John," she said, "we're not monsters. We're only the Free People. An aphrodite doesn't use her Skill for unfair gain. It has therapeutic applications. Or I—I don't like raising my strength against fellow humans. I want to use it for their good again."

He fumbled out the tobacco he had begged from a Terran and began to stuff his pipe. It would give some consolation.

Her shoulders slumped. "Well," she said in a tired voice, "I think we'd better go aboard now."

"You're coming too?" he said. "What for? To guard me?"

"No. Perhaps we'll need my reaction speed. Though Karlsarm did hope I'd persuade you—Come along, please."

She led him to the bridge. Terran officers were already posted among the gleaming machines, the glittering dials. Hunyadi sat in the chair of command. But Karlsarm stood beside him, the catavray head gaping across his brow; and other men of the forest darkened that scene.

"Stand by for liftoff." Hunyadi must recite the orders himself. "Close airlocks. All detector stations report."

Evagail padded over to Karlsarm. Ridenour could not help thinking that her ruddy hair, deep curves, bare bronze, were yet more an invasion of this metal-and-plastic cosmos than the men were. A faint odor of woman lingered behind her on the sterile air.

"What's our situation with the enemy?" she asked.

"Fair, as near as we can learn," Karlsarm said. "You haven't followed events since the last fight?"

"No. I was too busy making arrangements for prisoners. Like medical care for the injured, shelter for everyone. They were too wretched, out in this mist."

"Can't say I've enjoyed it either. I'll be glad when we can let it up. . . . Well. We didn't try an aphrodite on old Chang. Instead, we had him call the Terran chief, Admiral Cruz, and report the capture of his ship. Naturally, having no idea we'd be able to raise her, he didn't give that fact away. Supposedly we'll hold vessel and personnel for bargaining counters. The stratosphere's full of aircraft above us, but they won't do anything as long as they think we're sitting with our hostages. Only one spaceship has moved to anything like immediate striking range of us."

"Are you certain?"

"About as certain as you can be in war, whatever that means. We gave the chief communications officer to an aphrodite, of course. He listened in and decoded orders for the main fleet to stand out to space. That was a logical command for Cruz to issue, once the evacuation notice went out."

"Evacuation—?"

"Loveling, you didn't think I'd vaporize the Cities *and* their people, did you? The instant I foresaw a chance to grab this boat, I got in touch with the Grand Council—by radio, for the other continents, because time was short, so short that it didn't matter the Terrans would hear. They're good codebreakers, but I think the languages we used must've puzzled them!" Karlsarm grinned. "As soon as we'd made this haul, orders went out to our agents in every City, whether Terran- or Arulian-occupied. They were to serve notice that in one rotation period, the Cities would be erased. But they were to imply the job will be· done from space."

Fright touched Evagail. "The people did evacuate, didn't they?" she breathed.

"Yes. We've monitored communications. The threat's convincing, when there's been so much fear of intervention from Aruli or from Merseia herself. An invading fleet can't get past the blockade. But a certain percentage of fast little courier boats can. Likewise a flight of robot craft with nuclear weapons aboard: which wouldn't be guaranteed to distinguish between friendly and unfriendly target areas."

"But has no one thought that we, in this ship, might—"

"I trust not, or we're dead," Karlsarm stated. "Our timing was phased with care. The fog, and interference, and our ground fire, kept the Terrans from finding out what had happened to their cruiser. We informed them immediately that she was disabled, and they doubtless supposed it was logical. How could anyone take an undamaged Imperial warcraft, without equipment they know we don't have? In fact, they probably took for granted we'd had outside technical assistance in rigging a trap. Remember, the City warning was already preoccupying their thoughts. Chang's call was a precaution against their growing frantic and bombing us in the hope of getting our supposed Merseian or Arulian allies. He made it a few hours ago; and I made certain that he didn't say the ship was captured *intact*."

"They'll know better now," Hunyadi said. His face was white, his voice tormented.

"Correct. Lift as soon as you're able," Karlsarm said. "If we're hit, your woman will die too."

The executive officer jerked his head. "I know! Bridge to all stations. Lift at full power. Be prepared for attack."

Engines growled. The deck quivered with their force. *Isis* climbed, and the sun blazed about her.

"Communications to bridge," said the intercom. "Calls picked up from Imperialists."

"I expected that," Karlsarm said dryly. "Broadcast a warning. We don't want to hurt them, but if they bother us, we'll swat."

Sickly, Ridenour saw the planet recede beneath him.

Flame blossomed a long way off. "Missile barrage from one air squadron stopped," said the intercom. "Shall fire be returned?"

"No," Karlsarm said. "Not unless we absolutely must."

"Thank you, sir! Those are...my people yonder." After a moment: "They were my people."

"They will be again," Evagail murmured to Ridenour. "If you help."

"What can I do?" he choked.

She touched him. He winced aside. "You can speak for us," she said. "You're respected. Your loyalty is not in doubt. You proved it afresh, that night when—We don't belong to your civilization. We don't understand how it thinks, what it will compromise on and what it will die for, the nuances, the symbols, the meanings it finds in the universe. And it doesn't understand us. I think you know us a little, though, John. Enough to see that we're no menace."

"Except to the Cities," he said. "And now the Empire."

"No, they threatened us. They wouldn't leave our forests alone. As for the Empire, can't it contain one more way of living? Won't mankind be the richer for that?"

They looked at each other, and a thrumming aloneness enclosed them. A screen showed space and stars on the rim of the world.

"I suppose," he said finally, "no one can compromise on the basics of his culture. They're the larger part of his identity. To give them up is a kind of death. Many people would rather die in the body. You won't stop fighting until you're utterly crushed."

"And must that be?" Her speech fell gently on his ears. "Don't you Terrans want an end of war?"

An earthquake rumble went through the ship. Reports and orders seethed on the bridge. She was in long-range combat with a destroyer.

Undermanned, *Isis* could not stand off Cruz's whole fleet. But those units were scattered, would not reach Freehold for hours. Meanwhile, a solitary Imperial craft went against her with forlorn gallantry. Her fire-control men wept as they lashed back. But they must, to save the women who held them.

"What can I do?" Ridenour said.

"We'll call as soon as we're finished, and ask for a parley," Evagail told him. "We want you to urge that the Terrans agree. Afterward we want you to—no, not help plead our cause. Help explain it."

"Opposition attack parried," said a speaker. "Limited return broadside as per orders appears to have inflicted some damage. Opposition sheering off. Shall she be annihilated?"

"No, let her go," Karlsarm said.

Ridenour nodded at Evagail. "I'll do what I can," he said.

She took his hands, gladness bursting through her own tears, and this time he did not pull away.

Isis swung back into atmosphere. Her turrets cut loose. A doomed, empty City went skyward in flame.

Admiral Fernando Cruz Manqual stood high in the councils of this Imperial frontier; but he was a Terran merely by citizenship and remote ancestry. Military men have gone forth from Nuevo Mexico since that stark planet first was colonized. His manner toward Ridenour was at once curt and courteous.

"And so, Professor, you recommend that we accept their terms?" He puffed hard on a crooked black cigar. "I am afraid that that is quite impossible."

Ridenour made a production of starting his pipe. He needed time to find words. Awareness pressed in on him of his surroundings.

The negotiating commissions (to use a Terran phrase; the Free People called them mind-wrestlers) had met on neutral ground, an island in the Lawrencian Ocean. Though uninhabited thus far, it was beautiful with its full feathery trees, blossoming vines, deep cane-brakes, wide white beaches where surf played and roared. But there was little chance to enjoy what the place offered. Perhaps later, if talks were promising and tension relaxed, a young Terran spaceman might encounter a lightfoot outbacker girl in some glen.

But discussion had not yet even begun. It might well never begin. The two camps were armed, separated by three kilometers of forest and, on the Terran side, a wall of guns. Ridenour was the first who crossed from one to another.

Cruz's reception had been so cold that the xenologist half expected arrest. However, the admiral appeared to comprehend why he was there and invited him into his dome for private, unofficial conversation.

The dome was open to a mild, sea-scented breeze, but also to the view of other domes, vehicles, marines on sentry-go, aircraft at hover. Wine stood on the table between the two men, but except for a formal initial toast it had not been poured. Ridenour had stated the facts, and his words had struck unresponding silence. Now:

"I think it's best sir," Ridenour ventured. "They can be conquered, if the Empire makes the effort. But that war would be long, costly, tying up forces we need elsewhere, devastating the planet, maybe making it unfit for human habitation; they'll retaliate with some pretty horrible biological capabilities. The prisoners they hold will not be returned. Likewise the *Isis*. You'll be compelled to order her knocked out, an operation that won't come cheap."

He looked straight into the hard, mustached face. "And for what? They're quite willing to remain Terran subjects."

"They rebelled," Cruz bit off; "they collaborated with an enemy; they resisted commands given in His Majesty's name; they occasioned loss to His Majesty's Navy; they destroyed nine Imperial communities; thereby they wrecked the economy of an entire Imperial world. If this sort of behavior is let go unpunished, how long before the whole Empire breaks apart? And they aren't satisfied with asking for amnesty. No, they demand the globe be turned over to them!"

He shook his head. "I do not question your honesty, Professor— someone had to be messenger boy, I suppose—but if you believe an official in my position can possibly give a minute's consideration to those woodrunners' fantasy, I must question your judgment."

"They are not savages, sir," Ridenour said. "I've tried to explain to you something of their level of culture. My eventual written report should convince everyone."

"That is beside the point." His faded, open-throated undress uniform made Cruz look more terrible than any amount of braid and medals. The blaster at his hip had seen much use in its day.

"Not precisely, sir." Ridenour shifted in his chair. Sweat prickled his skin. "I've had a chance to think a lot about these issues, and a death-strong motivation for doing so and a career that's trained me to think in impersonal, long-range terms. What's the real good of the Empire? Isn't it the solidarity of many civilized planets? Isn't it, also, the stimulus of diversity between those planets? Suppose we did crush the Free—the outbackers. How could the Cities be rebuilt, except at enormous cost? They needed centuries to reach their modern level unaided, on this isolated, metal-impoverished world. If we poured in treasure, we could recreate them, more or less, in a few years. But what then would we have? Nine feeble mediocrities, just productive enough to require guarding, because Merseia considers them a potential threat on her Arulian flank. Whereas if we let the *real* Freeholders, the ones who've adapted until they can properly use this environment, if we let them flourish...we'll get, at no cost, a strong, self-supporting, self-defending outpost of Empire."

That may not be strictly true, he thought. The outbackers don't mind acknowledging Terran suzerainty, if they can have a charter that lets them run their planet the way they want. They're too sensible to revive the nationalistic fallacy. They'll pay a bit of tribute, conduct a bit of trade. On the whole, however, we will be irrelevant to them.

They may not always be so to us, of course. We may learn much from them. If we ever fall, they'll carry on something of what was ours. But I'd better not emphasize this.

"Even if I wanted to accommodate them," Cruz said, "I have no power. My authority is broad, yes. And I can go well beyond its formal limits, in that a central government with thousands of other worries will accept any reasonable recommendation I make. But do not exaggerate my latitude, I beg you. If I suggested that the City people, loyal subjects of His Majesty, be moved off the world of their ancestors, and that rebels, no matter how cultivated, be rewarded with its sole possession...why, I should be recalled for psychiatric examination, no?"

He sounds regretful, leaped within Ridenour. *He doesn't want a butcher's campaign. If I can convince him there is a reasonable and honorable way out—*

The xenologist smiled carefully around his pipestem. "True, Admiral," he said. "If the matter were put in those words. But need they be? I'm no lawyer. Still, I know a little about the subject, enough that I can sketch out an acceptable formula."

Cruz raised one eyebrow and puffed harder on his cigar.

"The point is," Ridenour said, "that juridically we have not been at war. Everybody knows Aruli sent arms and troops to aid the original revolt, no doubt at Merseian instigation. But to avoid a direct collision with Aruli and so possibly with Merseia, we haven't taken official cognizance of this. We were content to choke off further influx and reduce the enemy piecemeal. In short, Admiral, your task here has been to quell an internal, civil disturbance."

"Hm."

"The outbackers did not collaborate with an external enemy, because legally there was none."

Cruz flushed. "Treason smells no sweeter by any other name."

"It wasn't treason, sir," Ridenour argued. "The outbackers were not trying to undermine the Empire. They certainly had no wish to become Arulian or Merseian vassals!

"Put it this way: Freehold contained three factions, the human City dwellers, the Arulian City dwellers, and the outbackers. The charter of Imperial incorporation was negotiated by the first of these parties exclusively. Thus it was unfair to the other two. When amendment was refused, social difficulties resulted. The outbackers had some cooperation with the Arulians, as a matter of expediency. But it was sporadic and never affected their own simple wish for justice. Furthermore, and more important, it was not cooperation with outsiders, but rather with some other Imperial subjects.

"Actually," he added, "when one stops to think about it, the Nine Cities have not at all been innocent martyrs. Their discrimination against the Arulians, their territorial aggressions against the outbackers, were what really brought on the trouble. Merseia then exploited the opportunity—but didn't create it in the first place. Why then should the heedlessness of the Cities, that proved so costly to the Empire, not be penalized?"

Cruz looked disappointed. "I suppose the Policy Board could adopt some such formula," he said. "But only if it wanted to. And it won't want to. Because what formula can disguise the fact of major physical harm inflicted in sheer contumacy?"

"The formula of overzealousness to serve His Majesty's interests," Ridenour cast back. He lifted one palm. "Wait! Please! I don't ask you, sir, to propose an official falsehood. The zeal was not greatly misguided. And it did serve Terra's best interest."

"What? How?"

"Don't you see?" Tensely, Ridenour leaned across the table. Here we go, he thought, either we fly or we crash in the fire. "*The outbackers ended the war for us.*"

Cruz fell altogether quiet.

"Between you and me alone, I won't insult your intelligence by claiming this outcome was planned in detail," Ridenour hurried on. "But that is the effect. It was Nine Cities, their manufacturing and outworld commerce, their growth potential, that attracted the original Arulian settlers, and that lately made Freehold such a bait. With the Cities gone, what's left to fight about? The enemy has no more bases. I'm sure he'll accept repatriation to Aruli, including those of him who were born here. The alternative is to be milled to atoms between you and the outbackers.

"In return for this service, this removal of a bleeding wound on the Empire, a wound which might have turned into a cancer—surely the outbackers deserve the modest reward they ask. Amnesty for whatever errors they made, in seizing a chance that would never come again; a charter giving them the right to occupy and develop Freehold as they wish, though always as loyal subjects of His Majesty."

Cruz was unmoving for a long time. When he spoke, he was hard to hear under the military noise outside. "What of the City humans?"

"They can be compensated for their losses and resettled elsewhere," Ridenour said. "The cost will be less than for one year of continued war, I imagine; and you might well have gotten more than that. Many will complain, no doubt. But the interest of the Empire demands it. Quite apart from the problems in having two irreconcilable cultures on one planet, there's the wish to keep any frontier peaceful. The outbackers are unprofitably tough to invade; I rather believe their next generation will furnish some of our hardiest marine volunteers; but at the same time, they don't support the kind of industrial concentration—spaceships, nuclear devices—that makes our opposition worried or greedy."

"Hm." Cruz streamed smoke from his lips. His eyes half closed. "Hm. This would imply that my command, for one, can be shifted to a region where we might lean more usefully on Merseia ... yes-s-s."

Ridenour thought in a moment that was desolate: Is that why I'm so anxious to save these people? Because I hope one day they'll find a way out of the blind alley that is power politics?

Cruz slammed a fist on the table. The bottle jumped. "By the Crown, Professor, you might have something here!" he exclaimed. "Let me pour. Let us drink together."

Nothing would happen overnight, of course. Cruz must ponder, and consult, and feel out the other side's representatives. Both groups must haggle, stall, quibble, orate, grow calculatedly angry, grow honestly weary. And from those weeks of monkey chatter would emerge nothing more than a "protocol." This must pass up through a dozen layers of bureaucrats and politicians, each of whom must assert his own immortal importance by some altogether needless and exasperating change. Finally, on Terra, the experts would confer; the computers spin out reels of results that nobody quite understood or very much heeded; the members of the Policy Board and the different interests that had put them there use this issue as one more area in which to jockey for a bit more power; the news media make inane inflammatory statements (but not many—Freehold was remote—the latest orgy given by some nobleman's latest mistress was more interesting) ... and a document would arrive here, and maybe it would be signed but maybe it would be returned for "further study as recommended...."

I won't be leaving soon, Ridenour thought. They'll need me for months. Final agreement may not be ratified for a year or worse.

Some hours passed before he left the Terran camp and walked toward the other. He'd doubtless best stay with the outbackers for a while. Evagail had been waiting for him. She ran down the path. "How did it go?"

"Very well, I'd say," he said.

She cast herself into his arms, laughing and weeping. He soothed her, affectionately but just a little impatiently. His prime desire at the moment was to find a place by himself, that he might write a letter home. ✳

To
Marion Zimmer Bradley,
my lady of Darkover

THE DAY OF THEIR RETURN

Now a thing was secretly brought to me, and mine ear received a little thereof. In thoughts from the visions of the night, when deep sleep falleth on men, fear came upon me, and trembling, which made all my bones to shake. Then a spirit passed before my face; the hair of my flesh stood up; it stood still, but I could not discern the form thereof; an image was before mine eyes, there was silence, and I heard a voice....
—JOB, iv, 12–16

☼ **1** ☼

On the third day he arose, and ascended again to the light.

Dawn gleamed across a sea which had once been an ocean. To north, cliffs lifted blue from the steel gray of its horizon; and down them went a streak which was the falls, whose thunder beat dim through a windless cold. The sky stood violet in the west, purple overhead, white in the east where the sun came climbing. But still the morning star shone there, the planet of the First Chosen.

I am the first of the Second Chosen, Jaan knew: *and the voice of those who choose. To be man is to be radiance.*

His nostrils drank air, his muscles exulted. Never had he been this aware. From the brightness of his face to the grit below his feet, he was real.

—O glory upon glory, said that which within him was Caruith.

—It overwhelms this poor body, said Jaan. I am new to resurrection. Do you not feel yourself a stranger in chains?

—Six million years have blown by in the night, said Caruith. I remember waves besparkled and a shout of surf, where now stones lie gaunt beneath us; I remember pride in walls and columns, where ruin huddles above the mouth of the tomb whence we have come; I remember how clouds walked clad in rainbows. Before all, I seek to remember—and fail, because the flesh I am cannot bear the fire I was—I seek to remember the fullness of existence.

Jaan lifted hands to the crown engirdling his brows.—For you, this is a heavy burden, he said.

—No, sang Caruith. I share the opening that it has made for you and your race. I will grow with you, and you with me, and they with us, until mankind is not only worthy to be received into Oneness, it will bring thereunto what is wholly its own. And at last sentience will create God. Now come, let us proclaim it to the people.

He/they went up the mountain toward the Arena. Above them paled Dido, the morning star.

✧ 2 ✧

East of Windhome the country rolled low for a while, then lifted in the Hesperian Hills. Early summer had gentled their starkness with leaves. Blue-green, gray-green, here and there the intense green-green of oak or cedar, purple of rasmin, spread in single trees, bushes, widely spaced groves, across an onyx tinged red and yellow which was the land's living mantle, fire trava.

A draught blew from sunset. Ivar Frederiksen shivered. Even his gunstock felt cold beneath his hand. The sward he lay on had started to curl up for the night, turning into a springy mat. Its daytime odor of flint and sparks was almost gone. A delphi overarched him: gnarled low trunk, grotto of branches and foliage. Multitudinous rustlings went through it, like whispers in an unknown tongue. His vision ranged over a slope bestrewn with shrubs and boulders, to a valley full of shadow. The riverside road was lost in that dusk, the water a wan gleam. His heart knocked, louder than the sound of the Wildfoss flowing.

Nobody. Will they never come?

A flash caught his eye and breath. An aircraft out of the west?

No. The leaves in their restlessness had confused him. What rose above Hornbeck Ridge was just Creusa. Laughter snapped forth, a sign of how taut were his nerves. As if to seek companionship, he followed the moon. It glimmered ever more bright, waxing while it climbed eastward. A pair of wings likewise caught rays from the hidden sun and shone gold against indigo heaven.

Easy! he tried to scold himself. *You're nigh on disminded. What if this will be your first battle? No excuse. You're ringleader, aren't you?*

Though born to the thin dry air of Aeneas, he felt his nasal passages hurt, his tongue leather. He reached for a canteen. Filled at yonder stream, it gave him a taste of iron.

"Aah—" he began. And then the Imperials were come.

They appeared like that, sudden as a blow. A part of him knew how. Later than awaited, they had been concealed by twilight and a coppice in his line of sight, until their progress brought them into unmistakable view. But had none of his followers seen them earlier? The guerrillas covered three kilometers on both sides of the gorge. This didn't speak well for their readiness.

Otherwise Ivar was caught in a torrent. He didn't know what roared through him, fear, anger, insanity, nor had he time to wonder. He did observe, in a flicker of amazement, no heroic joy or stern determination. His body obeyed plans while something wailed, *How did I get into this? How do I get out?*

He was on his feet. He gave the hunting cry of a spider wolf, and heard it echoed and passed on. He pulled the hood of his jacket over his head, the nightmask over his face. He snatched his rifle off the ground and sprang from the shelter of the delphi.

Every sense was fever-brilliant. He saw each coiled blade of the fire trava whereon he ran, felt how it gave beneath his boots and rebounded, caught a last warmth radiated from a giant rock, drank in the sweetness of a cedar, brushed the roughness of an oak, could have counted the petals a rasmin spread above him or measured the speed at which a stand of plume trava folded against the gathering cold—but that was all on the edge of awareness, as was the play inside of muscles, nerves, blood, lungs, pulse—his being was aimed at his enemies.

They were human, a platoon of marines, afoot save for the driver of a field gun. It hummed along on a gravsled, two meters off the road. Though helmeted, the men were in loose order and walked rather than marched, expecting no trouble on a routine patrol. Most had connected the powerpacks on their shoulders to the heating threads in their baggy green coveralls.

The infrascope on Ivar's rifle told him that. His eyes told of comrades who rose from bush and leaped down the hillsides, masked and armed like him. His ears caught raw young voices, war-calls and wordless yells. Shots crackled. The Aeneans had double the number of their prey, advantage of surprise, will to be free.

They lacked energy weapons; but a sleet of bullets converged on the artillery piece. Ivar saw its driver cast from his seat, a red rag. *We've got them!* He sent a burst himself, then continued his charge, low and zigzag. The plan, the need was to break the platoon and carry their equipment into the wilderness.

The cannon descended. Ivar knew, too late: *Some kind of dead-man switch.* The marines, who had thrown their bodies flat, got up and sought it. A few lay wounded or slain; the rest reached its shelter. Blaster bolts flared and boomed, slugthrowers raved. The Aenean closest to Ivar tumbled, rolled over and over, came to a halt and screamed. Screamed. Screamed. His blood on the turf was outrageously bright, spread impossibly wide.

A new Imperial took the big gun's controls. Lightning flew across the river, which threw its blue-whiteness back like molten metal. Thunder hammered. Where that beam passed were no more trees or shrubs or warriors. Smoke roiled above ash.

Blind and deaf, Ivar fell. He clawed at the soil, because he thought the planet was trying to whirl him off.

After a fraction of eternity, the delirium passed. His head still tolled, tatters of light drifted before his vision, but he could hear, see, almost think.

A daggerbush partly screened him. He had ripped his right sleeve and arm on it, but was otherwise unhurt. Nearby sprawled a corpse. Entrails spilled forth. The mask hid which friend this had been. How wrong, how obscene to expose the guts without the face.

Ivar strained through gloom. The enemy had not turned their fieldpiece on this bank of the river. Instead, they used small arms as precision tools. Against their skill and discipline, the guerrillas were glass tossed at armor plate.

Guerrillas? We children? And I *led us.* Ivar fought not to vomit, not to weep.

He must sneak off. Idiot luck, nothing else, had kept him alive and unnoticed. But the marines were taking prisoners. He saw them bring in several who were lightly injured. Several more, outgunned, raised their hands.

Nobody keeps a secret from a hypnoprobe.

Virgil slipped beneath an unseen horizon. Night burst forth.

Aeneas rotates in twenty hours, nineteen minutes, and a few seconds. Dawn was not far when Ivar Frederiksen reached Windhome.

Gray granite walled the ancestral seat of the Firstman of Ilion. It stood near the edge of an ancient cape. In tiers and scarps, crags and cliffs, thinly brush-grown or naked rock, the continental shelf dropped down three kilometers to the Antonine Seabed. So did the river, a flash by the castle, a clangor of cataracts.

The portal stood closed, a statement that the occupation troops were considered bandits. Ivar stumbled to press the scanner plate. Chimes echoed emptily.

Weariness was an ache which rose in his marrow and seeped through bones and flesh till blood ran thick with it. His knees shook, his jaws clattered. The dried sweat that he could taste and smell on himself stung the cracks in his lips. Afraid to use roads, he had fled a long and rough way.

He leaned on the high steel door and sucked air through a mummy mouth. A breeze sheathed him in iciness. Yet somehow he had never been as aware of the beauty of this land, now when it was lost to him.

The sky soared crystalline black, wild with stars. Through the thin air they shone steadily, in diamond hues; and the Milky Way was a white torrent, and a kindred cloud in the Ula was our sister galaxy spied across a million and a half light-years. Creusa had set; but slower Lavinia rode aloft in her second quarter. Light fell argent on hoarfrost.

Eastward reached fields, meadows, woodlots, bulks that were sleeping farmsteads, and at last the hills. Ivar's gaze fared west. There the rich bottomlands ran in orchards, plantations, canals night-frozen into mirrors, the burnished shield of a salt marsh, to the world's rim. He thought he saw lights move. Were folk abroad already? No, he couldn't make out lamps over such a distance...lanterns on ghost ships, sailing an ocean that vanished three million years ago....

The portal swung wide. Sergeant Astaff stood behind. In defiance of Imperial decree, his stocky frame bore Ilian uniform. He had left off hood and mask, though. In the unreal luminance, his head was not grizzled, it was as white as the words which puffed from him.

"Firstlin' Ivar! Where you been? What's gone on? Your mother's gnawed fear for you this whole past five-day."

The heir to the house lurched by him. Beyond the gateway, the courtyard was crisscrossed with moon-shadows from towers, battlements, main keep, and lesser buildings. A hound, of the lean heavy-jawed Hesperian breed, was the only other life in sight. Its claws clicked on flagstones, unnaturally loud.

Astaff pushed a button to close the door. For a time he squinted until he said slowly, "Better give me that rifle, Firstlin'. I know places where Terrans won't poke."

"Me too," sighed from Ivar.

"Didn't do you a lot o' good, stashed away till you were ready for—whatever you've done—hey?" Astaff held out his hand.

"Trouble I'm in, it makes no difference if they catch me with this." Ivar took hold of the firearm. "Except I'd make them pay for me."

Something kindled in the old man. He, like his fathers before him, had served the Firstmen of Ilion for a lifetime. Nevertheless, or else for that same reason, pain was in his tone. "Why'd you not ask me for help?"

"You'd have talked me out of it," Ivar said. "You'd have been right," he added.

"What did you try?"

"Ambushin' local patrol. To start stockpilin' weapons. I don't know how many of us escaped. Probably most didn't."

Astaff regarded him.

Ivar Frederiksen was tall, 185 centimeters, slender save for wide shoulders and the Aenean depth of chest. Exhaustion weighted down his normal agility and hoarsened the tenor voice. Snub-nosed, square-jawed, freckled, his face looked still younger than it was; no noticeable beard had grown during the past hours. His hair, cut short at nape and ears in the nord manner, was yellow, seldom free of a cowlick or a stray lock across the forehead. Beneath dark brows, his eyes were large and green. Under his jacket he wore the high-collared shirt, pouched belt, heavy-bladed sheath knife, thick trousers tucked into half-boots, of ordinary outdoor dress. There was, in truth, little to mark him off from any other upper-class lad of his planet.

That little was enough.

"What caveheads you were," the sergeant said at last.

A twitch of anger: "We should sit clay-soft for Terrans to mold, fire, and use however they see fit?"

"Well," Astaff replied, "I would've planned my strike better, and drilled longer beforetime."

He took Ivar by the elbow. "You're spent like a cartridge," he said. "Go to my quarters. You remember where I bunk, no? Thank Lord, my wife's off visitin' our daughter's family. Grab shower, food, sleep. I've sentry-go till oh-five-hundred. Can't call substitute without drawin' questions; but nobody'll snuff at you."

Ivar blinked. "What do you mean? My own rooms—"

"Yah!" Astaff snorted. "Go on. Rouse your mother, your kid sister. Get 'em involved. Sure. They'll be interrogated, you know, soon's Impies've found you were in that broil. They'll be narco-quizzed, or even 'probed, if any reason develops to think they got clue to your whereabouts. That what you want? Okay. Go bid 'em fond farewell."

Ivar took a backward step, lifted his hands in appeal. "No. I, I, I never thought—"

"Right."

"Of course I'll—What do you have in mind?" Ivar asked humbly.

"Get you off before Impies arrive. Good thing your dad's been whole while in Nova Roma; clear-cut innocent, and got influence to protect family *if* Terrans find no sign you were ever here after fight. Hey? You'll leave soon. Wear servant's livery I'll filch for you, snoutmask like you're sneezewort allergic, weapon under cloak. Walk like you got hurry-up errand. This is big household; nobody ought to notice you especially. I'll've found some yeoman who'll take you in, Sam Hedin, Frank Vance, whoever, loyal and livin' offside. You go there."

"And then?"

Astaff shrugged. "Who knows? When zoosny's died down, I'll slip your folks word you're alive and loose. Maybe later your dad can wangle pardon for you. But if Terrans catch you while their dead are fresh—son, they'll make example. I know Empire. Traveled through it more than once with Admiral McCormac." As he spoke the name, he saluted. The average Imperial agent who saw would have arrested him on the spot.

Ivar swallowed and stammered, "I...I can't thank—"

"You're next Firstman of Ilion," the sergeant snapped. "Maybe last hope we got, this side of Elders returnin'. Now, before somebody comes, haul your butt out of here—and don't forget the rest of you!"

✿ 3 ✿

Chunderban Desai's previous assignment had been to the delegation which negotiated an end of the Jihannath crisis. That wasn't the change of pace in his career which it seemed. His Majesty's administrators must forever be dickering, compromising, feeling their way, balancing conflicts of individuals, organizations, societies, races, sentient species. The need for skill—quickly to grasp facts, comprehend a situation, brazen out a bluff when in spite of everything the unknown erupted into one's calculations—was greatest at the intermediate level of bureaucracy which he had reached. A resident might deal with a single culture, and have no more to do than keep an eye on affairs. A sector governor oversaw such vastness that to him it became a set of abstractions. But the various ranks of commissioner were expected to handle personally large and difficult territories.

Desai had worked in regions that faced Betelgeuse and, across an unclaimed and ill-explored buffer zone, the Roidhunate of Merseia. Thus he was a natural choice for the special diplomatic team. In his quiet style, he backstopped the head of it, Lord Advisor Chardon, so well that afterward he received a raise in grade, and was appointed High Commissioner of the Virgilian System, at the opposite end of the Empire.

But this was due to an equally natural association of ideas. The mutiny in Sector Alpha Crucis had been possible because most of the Navy was tied up around Jihannath, where full-scale war looked far too likely. After Terra nevertheless, brilliantly, put the rebels down, Merseia announced that its wish all along had been to avoid a major clash and it was prepared to bargain.

When presently the Policy Board looked about for able people to reconstruct Sector Alpha Crucis, Lord Chardon recommended Desai with an enthusiasm that got him put in charge of Virgil, whose human-colonized planet Aeneas had been the spearhead of the revolt.

Perhaps that was why Desai often harked back to the Merseians, however remote from him they seemed these days.

In a rare moment of idleness, while he waited in his Nova Roma office for the next visitor, he remembered his final conversation with Uldwyr.

They had played corresponding roles on behalf of their respective sovereigns, and in a wry way had become friends. When the protocol had, at weary last, been drawn, the two of them supplemented the dull official celebration with a dinner of their own.

Desai recalled their private room in a restaurant. The wall animations were poor; but a place which catered to a variety of sophonts couldn't be expected to understand everybody's art, and the meal was an inspired combination of human and Merseian dishes.

"Have a refill," Uldwyr invited, and raised a crock of his people's pungent ale.

"No, thank you," Desai said. "I prefer tea. That dessert filled me to the scuppers."

"The what?—Never mind, I seize the idea, if not the idiom." Though each was fluent in the other's principal language, and their vocal organs were not very different, it was easiest for Desai to speak Anglic and Uldwyr Eriau. "You've tucked in plenty of food, for certain."

"My particular vice, I fear," Desai smiled. "Besides, more alcohol would muddle me. I haven't your mass to assimilate it."

"What matter if you get drunk? I plan to. Our job is done." And then Uldwyr added: "For now."

Shocked, Desai stared across the table.

Uldwyr gave him back a quizzical glance. The Merseian's face was almost human, if one overlooked thick bones and countless details of the flesh. But his finely scaled green skin had no hair whatsoever, he lacked earflaps, a low serration ran from the top of his skull, down his back to the end of the crocodilian tail which counterbalanced his big, forward-leaning body. Arms and hands were, again, nearly manlike; legs and clawed splay feet could have belonged to a biped dinosaur. He wore black, silver-trimmed military tunic and trousers, colorful emblems of rank and of the Vach Hallen into which he was born. A blaster hung on his hip.

"What's the matter?" he asked.

"Oh . . . nothing." In Desai's mind went: *He didn't mean it hostilely—hostilely to me as a person—his remark. He, his whole civilization, minces words less small than we do. Struggle against Terra is just a fact. The Roidhunate will compromise disputes when expediency dictates, but never the principle that eventually the Empire must be destroyed. Because we—old, sated, desirous only of maintaining a peace which lets us pursue our pleasures—we stand in the way of their ambitions for the Race. Lest the balance of power be upset, we block them, we thwart them, wherever we can; and they seek to undermine us, grind us down, wear us out. But this is nothing personal. I am Uldwyr's honorable enemy, therefore his friend. By giving him opposition, I give meaning to his life.*

The other divined his thoughts and uttered the harsh Merseian chuckle. "If you want to pretend tonight that matters have been settled for aye, do. I'd really rather we both got drunk and traded war songs."

"I am not a man of war," Desai said.

Beneath a shelf of brow ridge, Uldwyr's eyelids expressed skepticism while his mouth grinned. "You mean you don't like physical violence. It was quite an effective war you waged at the conference table."

He swigged from his tankard. Desai saw that he was already a little tipsy. "I imagine the next phase will also be quiet," he went on. "Ungloved force hasn't worked too well lately. Starkad, Jihannath—no, I'd look for us to try something more crafty and long-range. Which ought to suit your Empire, *khraich?* You've made a good thing for your Naval Intelligence out of the joint commission on Talwin." Desai, who knew that, kept silence. "Maybe our turn is coming."

Hating his duty, Desai asked in his most casual voice, "Where?"

"Who knows?" Uldwyr gestured the equivalent of a shrug. "I have no doubt, and neither do you, we've a swarm of agents in Sector Alpha Crucis, for instance. Besides the recent insurrection, it's close to the Domain of Ythri, which has enjoyed better relations with us than with you—" His hand chopped the air. "No, I'm distressing you, am I not? And with what can only be guesswork. Apologies. See here, if you don't care for more ale, why not arthberry brandy? I guarantee a first-class drunk and— You may suppose you're a peaceful fellow, Chunderban, but I know an atom or two about your people, your specific people, I mean. What's that old, old book I've heard you mention and quote from? Rixway?"

"Rig-Veda," Desai told him.

"You said it includes war chants. Do you know any well enough to put into Anglic? There's a computer terminal." He pointed to a corner. "You can patch right into our main translator, now that official business is over. I'd like to hear a bit of your special tradition, Chunderban. So many traditions, works, mysteries—so tiny a lifespan to taste them—"

It became a memorable evening.

Restless, Desai stirred in his chair.

He was a short man with a dark-brown moon face and a paunch. At fifty-five standard years of age, his hair remained black but had receded from the top of his head. The full lips were usually curved slightly upward, which joined the liquid eyes to give him a wistful look. As was his custom, today he wore plain, loosely fitted white shirt and trousers, on his feet slippers a size large for comfort.

Save for the communication and data-retrieval consoles that occupied one wall, his office was similarly unpretentious. It did have a spectacular holograph, a view of Mount Gandhi on his home planet, Ramanujan. But otherwise the pictures were of his wife, their seven children, the families of those four who were grown and settled on as many different globes. A bookshelf held codices as well as reels; some were much-used reference works, the rest for refreshment, poetry, history, essays, most of their authors centuries dust. His desk was less neat than his person.

I shouldn't go taking vacations in the past, he thought. *God knows the present needs more of me than I have to give.*

Or does it? Spare me the ultimate madness of ever considering myself indispensable.

Well, but somebody must man this post. He happens to be me.

Must somebody? How much really occurs because of me, how much in spite of or regardless of? How much, and what, should occur? God! I dared accept the job of ruling, remaking an entire world—when I knew nothing more about it than its name, and that simply because it was the planet of Hugh McCormac, the man who would be Emperor. After two years, what else have I learned?

Ordinarily he could sit quiet, but the Hesperian episode had been too shocking, less in itself than in its implications. Whatever they were. How could he plan against the effect on these people, once the news got out, when he, the foreigner, had no intuition of what that effect might be?

He put a cigarette into a long, elaborately carved holder of land-whale ivory. (He thought it was in atrocious taste, but it had been given him for a birthday present by a ten-year-old daughter who died soon afterward.) The tobacco was an expensive self-indulgence, grown on Esperance, the closest thing to Terran he could obtain hereabouts while shipping remained sparse.

The smoke-bite didn't soothe him. He jumped up and prowled. He hadn't yet adapted so fully to the low gravity of Aeneas, 63 percent standard, that he didn't consciously enjoy movement. The drawback was the dismal exercises he must go through each morning, if he didn't want to turn completely into lard. Unfair, that the Aeneans tended to be such excellent physical specimens without effort. No, not really unfair. On this niggard sphere, few could afford a large panoply of machines; even today, more travel was on foot or animal back than in vehicles, more work done by hand than by automatons or cybernets. Also, in earlier periods— the initial colonization, the Troubles, the slow climb back from chaos—death had winnowed the unfit out of their bloodlines.

Desai halted at the north wall, activated its transparency, and gazed forth across Nova Roma.

Though itself two hundred Terran years old, Imperial House jutted awkwardly from the middle of a city founded seven centuries ago. Most buildings in this district were at least half that age, and architecture had varied little through time. In a climate where it seldom rained and never snowed; where the enemies were drought, cold, hurricane winds, drifting dust, scouring sand; where water for bricks and concrete, forests for timber, organics for synthesis were rare and precious, one quarried the stone which Aeneas did have in abundance, and used its colors and textures.

The typical structure was a block, two or three stories tall, topped by a flat deck which was half garden—the view from above made a charming motley—and half solar-energy collector. Narrow windows carried shutters ornamented with brass or iron arabesques; the heavy doors were of similar appearance. In most cases, the gray ashlars bore a veneer of carefully chosen and integrated slabs, marble, agate, chalcedony, jasper, nephrite, materials more exotic than that; and often there were carvings besides, friezes, armorial bearings, grotesques; and erosion had mellowed it all, to make the old part of town one subtle harmony. The wealthier homes, shops, and offices surrounded cloister courts, vitryl-roofed to conserve heat and water, where statues and plants stood among fishponds and fountains.

The streets were cramped and twisted, riddled with alleys, continually opening on small irrational plazas. Traffic was thin, mainly pedestrian, otherwise groundcars, trucks, and countryfolk on soft-gaited Aenean horses or six-legged green stathas (likewise foreign, though Desai couldn't offhand remember where they had originated). A capital city—population here a third of a million, much the largest—would inevitably hurt more and recover slower from a war than its hinterland.

He lifted his eyes to look onward. Being to south, the University wasn't visible through this wall. What he saw was the broad bright sweep of the River Flone, and ancient high-arched bridges across it; beyond, the Julian Canal, its tributaries, verdant parks along them, barges and pleasure boats upon their surfaces; farther still, the intricacy of many lesser but newer canals, the upthrust of modern buildings in garish colors, a tinge of industrial haze—the Web.

However petty by Terran standards, he thought, that youngest section was the seedbed of his hopes: in the manufacturing, mercantile, and managerial classes which had arisen during the past few generations, whose interests lay less with the scholars and squirearchs than with the Imperium and its Pax.

Or can I call on them? he wondered. *I've been doing it; but how reliable are they?*

A single planet is too big for single me to understand.

Right and left he spied the edge of wilderness. Life lay emerald on either side of the Flone, where it ran majestically down from the north polar cap. He could see hamlets, manors, water traffic; he knew that the banks were croplands and pasture. But the belt was only a few kilometers wide.

Elsewhere reared worn yellow cliffs, black basalt ridges, ocherous dunes, on and on beneath a sky almost purple. Shadows were sharper-edged than on Terra or Ramanujan, for the sun was half again as far away, its disc shrunken. He knew that now, in summer at a middle latitude, the air was chill; he observed on the tossing tendrils of a rahab tree in a roof garden how strongly the wind blew. Come sunset, temperatures would plunge below freezing. And yet Virgil was brighter than Sol, an F7; one could not look near it without heavy eye protection, and Desai marveled that light-skinned humans had ever settled in lands this cruelly irradiated.

Well, planets where unarmored men could live at all were none too common; and there had been the lure of Dido. In the beginning, this was a scientific base, nothing else. No, the second beginning, ages after the unknown builders of what stood in unknowable ruins. . . .

A world, a history like that; and I am supposed to tame them?

His receptionist said through the intercom, "Aycharaych," pronouncing the lilting diphthongs and guttural *ch*'s well. It was programmed to mimic languages the instant it heard them. That gratified visitors, especially nonhumans.

"What?" Desai blinked. The tickler on his desk screened a notation of the appointment. "Oh. Oh, yes." He popped out of his reverie. *That being who arrived on the Llynathawr packet day before yesterday. Wants a permit to conduct studies.* "Send him in, please." (By extending verbal courtesy even to a subunit of a computer, the High Commissioner helped maintain an amicable atmosphere. Perhaps.) The screen noted that the newcomer was male, or at any rate referred to himself as such. Planet of origin was listed as Jean-Baptiste, wherever that might be: doubtless a name bestowed by humans because the autochthons had too many different ones of their own.

The door retracted while Aycharaych stepped through. Desai caught his breath. He had not expected someone this impressive.

Or was that the word? Was "disturbing" more accurate? Xenosophonts who resembled humans occasionally had that effect on the latter; and Aycharaych was more anthropoid than Uldwyr.

One might indeed call him beautiful. He stood tall and thin in a gray robe, broad-chested but wasp-waisted, a frame that ought to have moved gawkily but instead flowed. The bare feet each had four long claws, and spurs on the ankles. The hands were six-fingered, tapered, their nails suggestive of talons. The head arched high and narrow, bearing pointed ears, great rust-red eyes, curved blade of nose, delicate mouth, pointed chin and sharply angled jaws; Desai thought of a Byzantine saint. A crest of blue feathers rose above, and tiny plumes formed eyebrows. Otherwise his skin was wholly smooth across the prominent bones, a glowing golden color.

After an instant's hesitation, Desai said, "Ah...welcome, Honorable. I hope I can be of service." They shook hands. Aycharaych's was warmer than his. The palm had a hardness that wasn't calluses. *Avian,* the man guessed. *Descended from an analog of flightless birds.*

The other's Anglic was flawless; the musical overtone which his low voice gave sounded not like a mispronunciation but a perfection. "Thank you, Commissioner. You are kind to see me this promptly. I realize how busy you must be."

"Won't you be seated?" The chair in front of the desk didn't have to adjust itself much. Desai resumed his own. "Do you mind if I smoke? Would you care for one?" Aycharaych shook his head to both questions, and smiled; again Desai thought of antique images, archaic Grecian sculpture. "I'm very interested to meet you," he said. "I confess your people are new in my experience."

"We are few who travel off our world," Aycharaych replied. "Our sun is in Sector Aldebaran."

Desai nodded. "M-hm." His business had never involved any society in that region. No surprise. The vaguely bounded, roughly spherical volume over which Terra claimed suzerainty had a diameter of some 400 light-years; it held an estimated four million stars, whereof half were believed to have been visited at least once; approximately 100,000 planets had formalized relations with the Imperium, but for most of them it amounted to no more than acknowledgment of subordination and modest taxes, or merely the obligation to make labor and resources available should the Empire ever have need. In return they got the Pax; and they had a right to join in spatial commerce, though the majority lacked the capital, or the industrial base, or the appropriate kind of culture for that—*Too big, too big. If a single planet overwhelms the intellect, what then of our entire microscopic chip of the galaxy, away off toward the edge of a spiral arm, which we imagine we have begun to be a little acquainted with?*

"You are pensive, Commissioner," Aycharaych remarked.

"Did you notice?" Desai laughed. "You've known quite a few humans, then."

"Your race is ubiquitous," Aycharaych answered politely. "And fascinating. That is my heart reason for coming here."

"Ah ... pardon me, I've not had a chance to give your documents a proper review. I know only that you wish to travel about on Aeneas for scientific purposes."

"Consider me an anthropologist, if you will. My people have hitherto had scant outside contact, but they anticipate more. My mission for a number of years has been to go to and fro in the Empire, learning the ways of your species, the most numerous and widespread within those borders, so that we may deal wisely with you. I have observed a wonderful variety of life-manners, yes, of thinking, feeling, and perceiving. Your versatility approaches miracle."

"Thank you," said Desai, not altogether comfortably. "I don't believe, myself, we are unique. It merely happened we were the first into space—in our immediate volume and point in history—and our dominant civilization of the time happened to be dynamically expansive. So we spread into many different environments, often isolated, and underwent cultural radiation ... or fragmentation." He streamed smoke from his nose and peered through it. "Can you, alone, hope to discover much about us?"

"I am not the sole wanderer," Aycharaych said. "Besides, a measure of telepathic ability is helpful."

"Eh?" Desai noticed himself switch over to thinking in Hindi. But what was he afraid of? Sensitivity to neural emissions, talent at interpreting them, was fairly well understood, had been for centuries. Some species were better at it than others; man was among those that brought forth few good cases, none of them first-class. Nevertheless, human scientists had studied the phenomenon as they had studied the wavelengths wherein they were blind....

"You will see the fact mentioned in the data reel concerning me," Aycharaych said. "The staff of Sector Governor Muratori takes precautions against espionage. When I first approached them about my mission, as a matter of routine I was exposed to a telepathic agent, a Ryellian, who could sense that my brain pattern had similarities to hers."

Desai nodded. Ryellians were expert. Of course, this one could scarcely have read Aycharaych's mind on such superficial contact, nor mapped the scope of his capacities; patterns varied too greatly between species, languages, societies, individuals. "What can you do of this nature, if I may ask?"

Aycharaych made a denigrating gesture. "Less than I desire. For example, you need not have changed the verbal form of your interior dream. I felt you do it, but only because the pulses changed. I could never read your mind; that is impossible unless I have known a person long and well, and then I can merely translate surface thoughts, clearly formulated. I cannot project." He smiled. "Shall we say I have a minor gift of empathy?"

"Don't underrate that. I wish I had it in the degree you seem to." Inwardly: *I mustn't let myself fall under his spell. He's captivating, but my duty is to be cold and cautious.*

Desai leaned forward, elbows on desk. "Forgive me if I'm blunt, Honorable," he said. "You've come to a planet which two years ago was in armed rebellion against His Majesty, which hoped to put one of its own sons on the throne by force and violence or, failing that, lead a breakaway of this whole sector from the Empire. Mutinous spirit is still high. I'll tell you, because the fact can't be suppressed for any length of time, we lately had an actual attack on a body of occupation troops, for the purpose of stealing their weapons. Riots elsewhere are already matters of public knowledge.

"Law and order are very fragile here, Honorable. I hope to proceed firmly but humanely with the reintegration of the Virgilian System into Imperial life. At present, practically anything could touch off a further explosion. Were it a major one, the consequences would be disastrous for the Aeneans, evil for the Empire. We're not far from the border, from the Domain of Ythri and, worse, independent war lords, buccaneers, and weird fanatics who have space fleets. Aeneas bulwarked this flank of ours. We can ill afford to lose it.

"A number of hostile or criminal elements took advantage of unsettled conditions to debark. I doubt if my police have yet gotten rid of them all. I certainly don't propose to let in more. That's why ships and detector satellites are in orbit, and none but specific vessels may land—at this port, nowhere else—and persons from them must be registered and must stay inside Nova Roma unless they get specific permission to travel."

He realized how harsh he sounded, and began to beg pardon.

Aycharaych broke smoothly through his embarrassment. "Please do not think you give offense, Commissioner. I quite sympathize with your position. Besides, I sense your basic good will toward me. You fear I might, inadvertently, rouse emotions which would ignite mobs or outright revolutionaries."

"I must consider the possibility, Honorable. Even within a single species, the ghastliest blunders are all too easy to make. For instance, my own ancestors on Terra, before spaceflight, once rose against foreign rulers. The conflict took many thousand lives. Its proximate cause was a new type of cartridge which offended the religious sensibilities of native troops."

"A better example might be the Taiping Rebellion."

"What?"

"It happened in China, in the same century as the Indian Mutiny. A revolt against a dynasty of outlanders, though one which had governed for a considerable time, became a civil war that lasted for a generation and killed people in the millions. The leaders were inspired by a militant form of Christianity—scarcely what Jesus had in mind, no?"

Desai stared at Aycharaych. "You *have* studied us."

"A little, oh, a hauntingly little. Much of it in your esthetic works, Aeschylus, Li Po, Shakespeare, Goethe, Sturgeon, Mikhailov...the music of a Bach or Richard Strauss, the visual art of a Rembrandt or Hiroshige....Enough. I would love to discuss these matters for months, Commissioner, but you have not the time. I do hope to convince you I will not enter as a clumsy ignoramus."

"Why Aeneas?" Desai wondered.

"Precisely because of the circumstances in which it finds itself, Commissioner. How do humans of an especially proud, self-reliant type behave in defeat? We need that insight too on Jean-Baptiste, if we are not to risk aggrieving you in some future day of trouble. Furthermore, I understand Aeneas contains several cultures besides the dominant one. To make comparisons and observe interactions would teach me much."

"Well—"

Aycharaych waved a hand. "The results of my work will not be hoarded. Frequently an outsider perceives elements which those who live by them never do. Or they may take him into their confidence, or at least be less reserved in his presence than in that of a human who could possibly be an Imperial secret agent.

Indeed, Commissioner, by his very conspicuousness, an alien like me might serve as an efficient gatherer of intelligence for you."

Desai started. *Krishna! Does this uncanny being suspect—? No, how could he?*

Gently, almost apologetically, Aycharaych said, "I persuaded the Governor's staff, and at last had a talk with His Excellency. If you wish to examine my documents, you will find I already have permission to carry out my studies here. But of course I would never undertake anything you disapprove."

"Excuse me." Desai felt bewildered, rushed, boxed in. Why should he? Aycharaych was totally courteous, eager to please. "I ought to have checked through the data beforehand. I would have, but that wretched attempt at guerrilla action—Do you mind waiting a few minutes while I scan?"

"Not in the slightest," the other said, "especially if you will let me glance at those books I see over there." He smiled wider than before. His teeth were wholly nonhuman.

"Yes, by all means," Desai mumbled, and slapped fingers across the information-retriever panel.

Its screen lit up. An identifying holograph was followed by relevant correspondence and notations. (Fakery was out of the question. Besides carrying tagged molecules, the reel had been deposited aboard ship by an official courier, borne here in the captain's safe, and personally brought by him to the memory bank underneath Imperial House.) The check on Aycharaych's bona fides had been routine, since they were overworked on Llynathawr too, but competently executed.

He arrived on the sector capital planet by regular passenger liner, went straight to a hotel in Catawrayannis which possessed facilities for xenosophonts, registered with the police as required, and made no effort to evade the scanners which occupation authorities had planted throughout the city. He traveled nowhere, met nobody, and did nothing suspicious. In perfectly straightforward fashion, he applied for the permit he wanted, and submitted to every interview and examination demanded of him.

No one had heard of the planet Jean-Baptiste there, either, but it was in the files and matched Aycharaych's description. The information was meager; but who would keep full data in the libraries of a distant province about a backward world which had never given trouble?

The request of its representative was reasonable, seemed unlikely to cause damage, and might yield helpful results. Sector Governor Muratori got interested, saw the being himself, and granted him an okay.

Desai frowned. His superior was both able and conscientious: had to be, if the harm done by the rapacious and conscienceless predecessor who provoked McCormac's rebellion was to be mended. However, in a top position one is soon isolated from the day-to-day details which make up a body of politics. Muratori was too new in his office to appreciate its limitations. And he was, besides, a stern man, who in Desai's opinion interpreted too literally the axiom that government is legitimatized coercion. It was because of directives from above that, after the University riots, the Commissioner of Virgil reluctantly ordered the razing of the Memorial and the total disarmament of the great Landfolk houses—two actions which he felt had brought on more woes, including the lunacy in Hesperia.

Well, then, why am I worried if Muratori begins to show a trifle more flexibility than hitherto?

"I'm finished," Desai said. "Won't you sit down again?"

Aycharaych returned from the bookshelf, holding an Anglic volume of Tagore. "Have you reached a decision, Commissioner?" he asked.

"You know I haven't." Desai forced a smile. "The decision was made for me. I am to let you do your research and give you what help is feasible."

"I doubt if I need bother you much, Commissioner. I am evolved for a thin atmosphere, and accustomed to rough travel. My biochemistry is similar enough to yours that food will be no problem. I have ample funds; and surely the Aenean economy could use some more Imperial credits."

Aycharaych ruffled his crest, a peculiarly expressive motion. "But please don't suppose I wish to thrust myself on you, waving a gubernatorial license like a battle flag," he continued. "You are the one who knows most and who, besides, must strike on the consequences of any error of mine. That would be a poor way for Jean-Baptiste to enter the larger community, would it not? I intend to be guided by your advice, yes, your preferences. For example, before my first venture, I will be grateful if your staff could plan my route and behavior."

A thawing passed through Desai. "You make me happy, Honorable. I'm sure we can work well together. See here, if you'd care to join me in an early lunch—and later I can have a few appointments shuffled around—"

It became a memorable afternoon.

But toward evening, alone, Desai once more felt troubled.

He should go home, to a wife and children who saw him far too little. He should stop chain-smoking; his palate was chemically burnt. Why carry a world on his shoulders, twenty long Aenean hours a day? He couldn't do it, really, for a single minute. No mortal could.

Yet when he had taken oath of office a mortal must try, or know himself a perjurer.

The Frederiksen affair plagued him like a newly made wound. Suddenly he leaned across his desk and punched the retriever. This room made and stored holographs of everything that happened within it.

A screen kindled, throwing light into dusky corners; for Desai had left off the fluoros, and sundown was upon the city. He didn't enlarge the figures of Peter Jowett and himself, but he did amplify the audio. Voices boomed. He leaned back to listen.

Jowett, richly dressed, sporting a curled brown beard, was of the Web, a merchant and cosmopolite. However, he was no jackal. He had sincerely, if quietly, opposed the revolt; and now he collaborated with the occupation because he saw the good of his people in their return to the Empire.

He said: "—glad to offer you what ideas and information I'm able, Commissioner. Cut me off if I start tellin' you what you've heard *ad nauseam.*"

"I hardly think you can," Desai responded. "I've been on Aeneas for two years; your ancestors, seven hundred."

"Yes, men ranged far in the early days, didn't they? Spread themselves terribly thin, grew terribly vulnerable—Well. You wanted to consult me about Ivar Frederiksen, right?"

"And anything related." Desai put a fresh cigarette in his holder.

Jowett lit a cheroot. "I'm not sure what I have to give you. Remember, I belong to class which Landfolk regard with suspicion at best, contempt or hatred at worst. I've never been intimate of his family."

"You're in Parliament. A pretty important member, too. And Edward Frederiksen is Firstman of Ilion. You must have a fair amount to do with him, including socially; most political work goes on outside of formal conferences or debates. I know you knew Hugh McCormac well—Edward's brother-in-law, Ivar's uncle."

Jowett frowned at the red tip of his cigar before he answered slowly: "Matters are rather worse tangled than that, Commissioner. May I recapitulate elementary facts? I want to set things in perspective, for myself as much as you."

"Please."

"As I see it, there are three key facts about Aeneas. One, it began as scientific colony, mainly for purpose of studyin' natives of Dido—which isn't suitable environment for human children, you know. That's origin of University: community of scientists, scholars, and support personnel, around which mystique clusters to this very day. The most ignorant and stupid Aenean stands in some awe of those who are learned. And, of course, University under Empire has become quite distinguished, drawin' students both human and nonhuman from far around. Aeneans are proud of it. Furthermore, it's wealthy as well as respected, thus powerful.

"Fact two. To maintain humans, let alone research establishment, on planet as skimpy as this, you need huge land areas efficiently managed. Hence rise of Landfolk: squires, yeomen, tenants. When League broke down and Troubles came, Aeneas was cut off. It had to fight hard, sometimes right on its own soil, to survive. Landfolk bore brunt. They became quasi-feudal class. Even University caught somethin' of their spirit, givin' military trainin' as regular part of curriculum. You'll recall how Aeneas resisted—a bit bloodily—annexation by Empire, in *its* earlier days. But later we furnished undue share of its officers.

"Fact three. Meanwhile assorted immigrants were tricklin' in, lookin' for refuge or new start or whatever. They were ethnically different. Haughty nords used their labor but made no effort to integrate them. Piecewise, they found niches for themselves, and so drifted away from dominant civilization. Hence tinerans, Riverfolk, Orcans, Highlanders, et cetera. I suspect they're more influential, sociologically, than city dwellers or rural gentry care to believe."

Jowett halted and poured himself a cup of the tea which Desai had ordered brought in. He looked as if he would have preferred whiskey.

"Your account does interest me, as making clear how an intelligent Aenean analyzes the history of his world," Desai said. "But
what has it to do with my immediate problem?"

"A number of things, Commissioner, if I'm not mistaken,"
Jowett answered. "To begin, it emphasizes how essentially cut off
persons like me are from ... well, if not mainstream, then several
mainstreams of this planet's life.

"Oh, yes, we have our representatives in tricameral legislature.
But we—I mean our new, Imperium-oriented class of businessmen
and their employees—we're minor part of Townfolk. Rest belong
to age-old guilds and similar corporate bodies, which most times
feel closer to Landfolk and University than to us. Subcultures
might perhaps ally with us, but aren't represented; property quali-
fication for franchise, you know. And ... prior to this occupation,
Firstman of Ilion was, automatically, Speaker of all three Houses.
In effect, global President. His second was, and is, Chancellor
of University, his third elected by Townfolk delegates. Since you
have—wisely, I think—not dissolved Parliament, merely declared
yourself supreme authority—this same configuration works on.

"I? I'm nothin' but delegate from Townfolk, from one single
faction among them at that. I am not privy to councils of Frederiksens and their friends."

"Just the same, you can inform me, correct me where I'm
wrong," Desai insisted. "Now let me recite the obvious for a while.
My impressions may turn out to be false.

"The Firstman of Ilion is *primus inter pares* because Ilion is
the most important region and Hesperia its richest area. True?"

"Originally," Jowett said. "Production and population have
shifted. However, Aeneans are traditionalists."

"What horrible bad luck in the inheritance of that title—for
everybody," Desai said. And, seated alone, he remembered his
thoughts.

*Hugh McCormac was a career Navy officer, who had risen to
Fleet Admiral when his elder brother died childless in an accident
and thus made him Firstman. That wouldn't have mattered, except
for His Majesty (one dare not speculate why, aloud) appointing that
creature Snelund the Governor of Sector Alpha Crucis; and Snelund's
excesses finally striking McCormac so hard that he raised a rebel
banner and planet after planet hailed him Emperor.*

Well, Snelund is dead, McCormac is fled, and we are trying to reclaim the ruin they left. But the seeds they sowed still sprout strange growths.

McCormac's wife was (is?) the sister of Edward Frederiksen, who for lack of closer kin has thereby succeeded to the Firstmanship of Ilion. Edward himself is a mild, professorial type. I could bless his presence—except for the damned traditions. His own wife is a cousin of McCormac. (Curse the way those high families intermarry! It may make for better stock, a thousand years hence; but what about us who must cope meanwhile?) The Frederiksens themselves are old-established University leaders. Why, the single human settlement on Dido is named after their main ancestor.

Everybody on this resentful globe discounts Edward Frederiksen; but not what he symbolizes. Soon everybody will know what Ivar Frederiksen has done.

Potentially, he is their exiled prince, their liberator, their Anointed. Siva, have mercy.

"As I understand it," the image of Jowett said, "the boy raised gang of hotheads without his parents' knowledge. He's only eleven and a half, after all—uh, that's twenty years Terran, right? Their idea was to take to wilderness and be guerrillas until . . . what? Terra gave up? Ythri intervened, and took Aeneas under its wing like Avalon? It strikes me as pathetically romantic."

"Sometimes romantics do overcome realists," Desai said. "The consequences are always disastrous."

"Well, in this case, attempt failed. His associates who got caught identified their leader under hypnoprobe. Don't bother denyin'; of course your interrogators used hypnoprobes. Ivar's disappeared, but shouldn't be impossible to track down. What do you need my advice about?"

"The wisdom of chasing him in the first place," Desai said wearily.

"Oh. Positive. You dare not let him run loose. I do know him slightly. He has chance of becomin' kind of prophet, to people who're waitin' for exactly that."

"My impression too. But how should we go after him? How make the arrest? What kind of trial and penalty? How publicized? We can't create a martyr. Neither can we let a rebel, responsible for the deaths and injuries of Imperial personnel—and Aeneans, remember, Aeneans—we can't let him go scot-free. I don't know what to do," Desai nearly groaned. "Help me, Jowett. You don't want your planet ripped apart, do you?"

—He snapped off the playback. He had gotten nothing from it. Nor would he from the rest, which consisted of what-ifs and maybes. The only absolute was that Ivar Frederiksen must be hunted down fast.

Should I refer the problem of what to do after we catch him to Llynathawr, or directly to Terra? I have the right.

The legal right. No more. What do they know there?

Night had fallen. The room was altogether black, save for its glowboards and a shifty patch of moonlight which hurried Creusa cast through the still-active transparency. Desai got up, felt his way there, looked outward.

Beneath stars, moons, Milky Way, three sister planets, Nova Roma had gone elven. The houses were radiance and shadow, the streets dappled darkness, the river and canals mercury. Afar in the desert, a dust storm went like a ghost. Wind keened; Desai, in his warmed cubicle, shivered to think how its chill must cut.

His vision sought the brilliances overhead. Too many suns, too many.

He'd be sending a report Home by the next courier boat. (Home! He had visited Terra just once. When he stole a few hours from work to walk among relics, they proved curiously disappointing. Multisense tapes didn't include crowded airbuses, arrogant guides, tourist shops, or aching feet.) Such vessels traveled at close to the top hyperspeed: a pair of weeks between here and Sol. (But that was 200 light-years, a radius which swept over four million suns.) He could include a request for policy guidelines.

But half a month could stretch out, when he faced possible turmoil or, worse, terrorism. And then his petition must be processed, discussed, annotated, supplemented, passed from committee to committee, referred through layers of executive officialdom for decision; and the return message would take its own days to arrive, and probably need to be disputed on many points when it did—No, those occasional directives from Llynathawr were bad enough.

He, Chunderban Desai, stood alone to act.

Of course, he was required to report everything significant: which certainly included the Frederiksen affair. If nothing else, Terra was *the* data bank, as complete as flesh and atomistics could achieve.

In which case...why not insert a query about that Aycharaych?

Well, why?

I don't know, I don't know. He seems thoroughly legitimate; and he borrowed my Tagore. . . . No, I will ask for a complete informa-tion scan at Terra. Though I'll have to invent a plausible reason for it, when Muratori's approved his proposal. We bureaucrats aren't supposed to have hunches. Especially not when, in fact, I like Aycharaych as much as any nonhuman I've ever met. Far more than many of my fellow men.

Dangerously more?

❊ 4 ❊

The Hedin Freehold lay well east of Windhome, though close enough to the edge of Ilion that westerlies brought moisture off the canals, marshes, and salt lakes of the Antonine Seabed—actual rain two or three times a year. While not passing through the property, the Wildfoss helped maintain a water table that sup-plied a few wells. Thus the family carried on agriculture, besides ranching a larger area.

Generation by generation, their staff had become more like kinfolk than hirelings: kinfolk who looked to them for leadership but spoke their own minds and often saw a child married to a son or daughter of the house. In short, they stood in a relation-ship to their employers quite similar to that in which the Hedins, and other Hesperian yeomen, stood to Windhome.

The steading was considerable. A dozen cottages flanked the manse. Behind, barns, sheds, and workshops surrounded three sides of a paved courtyard. Except for size, at first glance the buildings seemed much alike, whitewashed rammed earth, their blockiness softened by erosion. Then one looked closer at the stone or glass mosaics which decorated them. Trees made a windbreak about the settlement: native delphi and rahab, Terran oak and acacia, Llynathawrian rasmin, Ythrian hammerbranch. Flowerbeds held only exotic species, painstakingly cultivated, eked out with rocks and gravel. True blossoms had never evolved on Aeneas, though a few kinds of leaf or stalk had bright hues.

It generally bustled here, overseers, housekeepers, smiths, masons, mechanics, hands come in from fields or range, children, dogs, horses, stathas, hawks, farm machinery, ground and air vehicles, talk, shouting, laughter, anger, tears, song, a clatter of feet and a whiff of beasts or smoke. Ivar ached to join in. His wait in the storeloft became an entombment.

Through a crack in the shutters he could look down at the daytime surging. His first night coincided with a birthday party for the oldest tenant. Not only the main house was full of glow, but floodlights illuminated the yard for the leaping, stamping dances of Ilion, to music whooped forth by a sonor, while flagons went from mouth to mouth. The next night had been moonlight and a pair of young sweethearts. Ivar did not watch them after he realized what they were; he had been taught to consider privacy among the rights no decent person would violate. Instead, he threshed about in his sleeping bag, desert-thirsty with memories of Tatiana Thane and—still more, he discovered in shame—certain others.

On the third night, as erstwhile, he roused to the cautious unlocking of the door. Sam Hedin brought him his food and water when nobody else was awake. He sat up. A pad protected him from the floor, but as his torso emerged from the sack, chill smote through his garments. He hardly noticed. The body of an Aenean perforce learned how to make efficient use of the shivering reflex. The dark oppressed him, however, and the smell of dust.

A flashbeam picked forth glimpses of seldom-used gear, boxes and loaded shelves. "Hs-s-s," went a whisper. "Get ready to travel. Fast."

"What?"

"Fast, I said. I'll explain when we're a-road."

Ivar scrambled to his feet, out of his nightsuit and into the clothes he wore when he arrived. The latter were begrimed and blood-spotted, but the parched air had sucked away stinks as it did for the slop jar. The other garment he tucked into a bedroll he slung on his back, together with his rifle. Hedin gave him a packet of sandwiches to stuff in his pouchbelt, a filled canteen to hang opposite his knife—well insulated against freezing—and guidance downstairs.

Though the man's manner was grim, eagerness leaped in Ivar. Regardless of the cause, his imprisonment was at an end.

Outside lay windless quiet, so deep that it was as if he could hear the planet creak from the cold. Both moons were up to whiten stone and sand, make treetops into glaciers above caverns, strike sparkles from rime. Larger but remoter Lavinia, rising over eastern hills, showed about half her ever-familiar face. Creusa, hurtling toward her, seemed bigger because of being near the full, and glittered as her spin threw light off crystal jaggedness. The Milky Way was a frozen cascade from horizon to horizon. Of fellow planets, Anchises remained aloft, lambent yellow. Among the uncountable stars, Alpha and Beta Crucis burned bright enough to join the moons in casting shadows.

A pair of stathas stood tethered, long necks and snouted heads silhouetted athwart the house. *We must have some ways to go,* Ivar thought, *sacrificin' horse-speed in pinch for endurance over long dry stretch. But then why not car?* He mounted. Despite the frigidity, he caught a scent of his beast, not unlike new-mown hay, before he adjusted hood and nightmask.

Sam Hedin led him onto the inland road, shortly afterward to a dirt track which angled off southerly through broken ground where starkwood bush and sword trava grew sparse. Dust puffed from the *plop-plop* of triple pads. Six legs gave a lulling rhythm. Before long the steading was lost to sight, the men rode by themselves under heaven. Afar, a catavale yowled.

Ivar cleared his throat. "Ah-um! Where're we bound, Yeoman Hedin?"

Vapor smoked from breath slot. "Best hidin' place for you I could think of quick, Firstlin'. Maybe none too good."

Fear jabbed. "What's happened?"

"Vid word went around this day, garth to garth," Hedin said. He was a stout man in his later middle years. "Impies out everywhere in Hesperia, ransackin' after you. Reward offered; and anybody who looks as if he or she might know somethin' gets quick narcoquiz. At rate they're workin', they'll reach my place before noon." He paused. "That's why I kept you tucked away, so nobody except me *would* know you were there. But not much use against biodetectors. I invented business which'll keep me from home several days, rode off with remount—plausible, considerin' power shortage—and slipped back after dark to fetch you." Another pause. "They have aircars aprowl, too. Motor vehicle could easily get spotted and overtaken. That's reason why we use stathas, and no heatin' units for our clothes."

Ivar glanced aloft, as if to see a metal teardrop pounce. An ula flapped by. Pride struggled with panic: "They want me mighty badly, huh?"

"Well, you're Firstlin' of Ilion."

Honesty awoke. Ivar bit his lip. "I . . . I'm no serious menace. I bungled my leadership. No doubt I was idiot to try."

"I don't know enough to gauge," Hedin replied judiciously. "Just that Feo Astaff asked if I could coalsack you from Terrans, because you and friends had had fight with marines. Since, you and I've gotten no proper chance to talk. I could just sneak you your rations at night, not dare linger. Nor have newscasts said more than there was unsuccessful assault on patrol. Never mentioned your name, though I suppose after this search they'll have to."

The mask muffled his features, but not the eyes he turned to his companion. "Want to tell me now?" he asked.

"W-well, I—"

"No secrets, mind. I'm pretty sure I've covered our spoor and won't be suspected, interrogated. Still, what can we rely on altogether?"

Ivar slumped. "I've nothin' important to hide, except foolishness. Yes, I'd like to tell you, Yeoman."

The story stumbled forth, for Hedin to join to what he already knew about his companion.

Edward Frederiksen had long been engaged in zoological research on Dido when he married Lisbet Borglund. She was of old University stock like him; they met when he came back to deliver a series of lectures. She followed him to the neighbor world. But even in Port Frederiksen, the heat and wetness of the thick air were too much for her.

She recovered when they returned to Aeneas, and bore her husband Ivar and Gerda. They lived in a modest home outside Nova Roma; both taught, and he found adequate if unspectacular subjects for original study. His son often came along on field trips. The boy's ambitions presently focused on planetology. Belike the austere comeliness of desert, steppe, hills, and dry ocean floors brought that about—besides the hope of exploring among those stars which glittered through their nights.

Hugh McCormac being their uncle by his second marriage, the children spent frequent vacations at Windhome. When the Fleet Admiral was on hand, it became like visiting a hero of the early days, an affable one, say Brian McCormac who cast out the nonhuman invaders and whose statue stood ever afterward on a high pillar near the main campus of the University.

Aeneas had circled Virgil eight times since Ivar's birth, when

Aaron Snelund became Governor of Sector Alpha Crucis. It circled twice more—three and a half Terran years—before the eruption. At first the developed worlds felt nothing worse than heightened taxes, for which they got semi-plausible explanations. (Given the size of the Empire, its ministers must necessarily have broad powers.) Then they got the venal appointees. Then they began to hear what had been going on among societies less able to resist and complain. Then they realized that their own petitions were being shunted aside. Then the arrests and confiscations for "treason" started. Then the secret police were everywhere, while mercenaries and officials freely committed outrages upon individuals. Then it became plain that Snelund was not an ordinary corrupt administrator, skimming off some cream for himself, but a favorite of the Emperor, laying grandiose political foundations.

All this came piecemeal, and folk were slow to believe. For most of them, life proceeded about as usual. If times were a bit hard, well, they would outlast it, and meanwhile they had work to do, households and communities to maintain, interests to pursue, pleasures to seek, love to make, errands to run, friends to invite, unfriends to snub, plans to consider, details, details, details like sand in an hourglass. Ivar did not enroll at the University, since it educated its hereditary members from infancy, but he began to specialize in his studies and to have off-planet classmates. Intellectual excitement outshouted indignation.

Then Kathryn McCormac, his father's sister, was taken away to Snelund's palace; and her husband was arrested, was rescued, and led the mutiny.

Ivar caught fire, like most Aenean youth. His military training, hitherto incidental, became nearly the whole. But he never got off the planet, and his drills ended when Imperial warcraft hove into the skies.

The insurrection was over. Hugh McCormac and his family had led the remnants of his fleet into the deeps outside of known space. Because the Jihannath crisis was resolved, the Navy available to guard the whole Empire, the rebels would not return unless they wanted immolation.

Sector Alpha Crucis in general, Aeneas in particular, was to be occupied and reconstructed.

Chaos, despair, shortages which in several areas approached famine, had grown throughout the latter half of the conflict. The

University was closed. Ivar and Gerda went to live with their parents in poverty-stricken grandeur at Windhome, since Edward Frederiksen was now Firstman of Ilion. The boy spent most of the time improving his desertcraft. And he gained identification with the Landfolk. *He* would be their next leader.

After a while conditions improved, the University reopened—under close observation—and he returned to Nova Roma. He was soon involved in underground activity. At first this amounted to no more than clandestine bitching sessions. However, he felt he should not embarrass his family or himself by staying at the suburban house, and moved into a cheap room in the least desirable part of the Web. That also led to formative experiences. Aeneas had never had a significant criminal class, but a petty one burgeoned during the war and its aftermath. Suddenly he met men who did not hold the law sacred.

(When McCormac rebelled, he did it in the name of rights and statutes violated. When Commissioner Desai arrived, he promised to restore the torn fabric.)

Given a conciliatory rule, complaints soon became demands. The favorite place for speeches, rallies, and demonstrations was beneath the memorial to Brian McCormac. The authorities conceded numerous points, reasonable in themselves—for example, resumption of regular mail service to and from the rest of the Empire. This led to further demands—for example, *no* government examination of mail, and a citizens' committee to assure this—which were refused. Riots broke out. Some property went up in smoke, some persons down in death.

The decrees came: No more assemblies. The monument to be razed. The Landfolk, who since the Troubles had served as police and military cadre, to disband all units and surrender all firearms, from a squire's ancestral cannon-equipped skyrover to a child's target pistol given last Founders' Day.

"We decided, our bunch, we'd better act before 'twas too late," Ivar said. "We'd smuggle out what weapons we could, ahead of seizure date, and use them to grab off heavier stuff. I had as much knowledge of back country as any, more than most; and, of course, I am Firstlin'. So they picked me to command our beginnin' operation, which'd be in this area. I joined my mother and sister at Windhome, pretendin' I needed break from study.

Others had different cover stories, like charterin' an airbus to leave them in Avernus Canyon for several days' campout. We rendezvoused at Helmet Butte and laid our ambush accordin' to what I knew about regular Impy patrol routes."

"What'd you have done next, if you'd succeeded?" Hedin asked.

"Oh, we had that planned. I know couple of oases off in Ironland that could support us, with trees, caves, ravines to hide us from air search. There aren't that many occupation troops to cover this entire world."

"You'd spend your lives as outlaws? I should think you'd soon become bandits."

"No, no. We'd carry on more raids, get more recruits and popular support, gather strength enemy must reckon with. Meanwhile we'd hope for sympathy elsewhere in Empire bringin' pressure on our behalf, or maybe fear of Ythri movin' in."

"Maybe," Hedin grunted. After a moment: "I've heard rumors. Great bein' with gold-bronze wings, a-flit in these parts. Ythrian agent? They don't necessarily want what we do, Firstlin'."

Ivar's shoulders slumped. "No matter. We failed anyhow. I did."

Hedin reached across to clap him on the back. "Don't take that attitude. First, military leaders are bound to lose men and suffer occasional disasters. Second, you never were one, really. You just happened to get thrown to top of cards that God was shufflin'." Softly: "For game of solitaire? I won't believe it." His tone briskened. "Firstlin', you've got no *right* to go off on conscience spin. You and your fellows together made bad mistake. Leave it at that, and carry on. Aeneas does need you."

"Me?" Ivar exclaimed. His self-importance had crumbled while he talked, until he could not admit he had ever seen himself as a Maccabee. "What in cosmos can I—"

Hedin lifted a gauntleted hand to quiet him. "Hoy. Follow me."

They brought their stathas off the trail, and did not rejoin it for ten kilometers. What they avoided was a herd belonging to Hedin: Terran-descended cattle, gene-modified and then adapted through centuries—like most introduced organisms—until they were a genus of their own. Watchfires glimmered around their mass. Hedin didn't doubt his men were loyal to him; but what they hadn't noticed, they couldn't reveal.

On the way, the riders passed a fragment of wall. Glass-black, seamless, it sheened above moonlit brush and sand. Near the top of what remained, four meters up, holes made an intricate pattern, its original purpose hard to guess. Now stars gleamed through.

Hedin reined in, drew a cross, and muttered before he went on.

Ivar had seen the ruin in the past, and rangehands paying it their respects. He had never thought he would see the yeoman—well-educated, well-traveled, hard-headed master and councilor—do likewise.

After a cold and silent while, Hedin said half defensively, "Kind of symbol back yonder."

"Well . . . yes," Ivar responded.

"Somebody was here before us, millions of years ago. And not extinct natives, either. Where did they come from? Why did they leave? Traces have been found on other planets too, remember. Unreasonable to suppose they died off, no? Lot of people wonder if they didn't go onward instead—out there."

Hedin waved at the stars. Of that knife-bright horde, some belonged to the Empire but most did not. For those the bare eye could see were mainly giants, shining across the light-years which engulfed vision of a Virgil or a Sol. Between Ivar and red Betelgeuse reached all the dominion of Terra, and more. Further on, Rigel flashed and the Pleiades veiled themselves in regions to which the Roidhunate of Merseia gave its name for a blink of time. Beyond these were Polaris, once man's lodestar, and the Orion Nebula, where new suns and worlds were being born even as he watched, and in billions of years life would look forth and wonder. . . .

Hedin's mask swung toward Ivar again. His voice was low but eerily intense. "That's why we need you, Firstlin'. You may be rash boy, yes, but four hundred years of man on Aeneas stand behind you. We'll need every root we've got when Elders return."

Startled, Ivar said, "You don't believe that, do you? I've heard talk; but you?"

"Well, I don't know." Hedin's words came dwindled through the darkness. "I don't know. Before war, I never thought about it. I'd go to church, and that was that.

"But since—Can so many people be entirely wrong? They are many, I'll tell you. Off in town, at school, you probably haven't any idea how wide hope is spreadin' that Elders will come back soon, bearin' Word of God. It's not crank, Ivar. Nigh everybody admits this is hope, no proof. But could Admiral McCormac have headed their way? And surely we hear rumors about new prophet in barrens—

"I don't know. I do think, and I tell you I'm not alone in it, all this grief here and all those stars there can't be for nothin'. If God is makin' ready His next revelation, why not through chosen race, more wise and good than we can now imagine? And if that's true, shouldn't prophet come first, who prepares us to be saved?"

He shook himself, as if the freeze had pierced his unheated garb. "You're our Firstlin'," he said. "We must keep you free. Four hundred years can't be for nothin' either."

Quite matter-of-factly, he continued: "Tinerans are passin' through, reported near Arroyo. I figure you can hide among them."

❊ 5 ❊

Each nomad train, a clan as well as a caravan, wandered a huge but strictly defined territory. Windhome belonged in that of the Brotherband. Ivar had occasionally seen its camps, witnessed raffish performances, and noticed odd jobs being done for local folk before it moved on, afterward heard the usual half-amused, half-indignant accusations of minor thefts and clever swindles, gossip about seductions, whispers about occult talents exercised. When he dipped into the literature, he found mostly anecdotes, picturesque descriptions, romantic fiction, nothing in depth. The Aenean intellectual community took little serious interest in the undercultures on its own planet. Despite the centuries, Dido still posed too many enigmas which were more fascinating and professionally rewarding.

Ivar did know that Trains varied in their laws and customs. Hedin led him across a frontier which had no guards nor any existence in the registries at Nova Roma, identified solely by landmarks. Thereafter they were in Waybreak country, and he was still less sure of what to expect than he would have been at home. The yeoman took a room in the single inn which Arroyo boasted. "I'll stay till you're gone, in case of trouble," he said. "But mainly, you're on your own from here." Roughly: "I wish 'twere otherwise. Fare always well, lad."

Ivar walked through the village to the camp. Its people were packing for departure. Fifty or so brilliantly painted carriages, and gaudy garb on the owners, made their bustle and clamor into a kind of rainbowed storm in an otherwise drab landscape. Arroyo stood on the eastern slope of the hills, where scrub grew sparse on dusty ground to feed some livestock. The soil became more dry and bare for every kilometer that it hunched on downward, until at the horizon began the Ironland desert.

Scuttling about in what looked like utter confusion, men, women, and children alike threw him glances and shouted remarks in their own language that he guessed were derisive. He felt awkward and wholly alone among them—this medium-sized, whip-slim race of the red-brown skins and straight blue-black hair. Their very vehicles hemmed him in alienness. Some were battered old trucks of city make; but fantastic designs swirled across them, pennons blew, amulets dangled, wind chimes rang. Most were wagons, drawn by four to eight stathas, and these were the living quarters. Stovepipes projected from their arched roofs and grimy curtains hung in their windows. Beneath paint, banners, and other accessories, their panels were elaborately carved; demon shapes leered, hex signs radiated, animals real and imaginary cavorted, male and female figures danced, hunted, worked, gambled, engendered, and performed acts more esoteric.

A man came by, carrying a bundle of knives and swords wrapped in a cloak. He bounded up into the stairless doorway of one wagon, gave his load to a person inside, sprang down again to confront Ivar. "Hey-ah, varsiteer," he said amicably enough. "What'd you like? The show's over."

"I . . . I'm lookin' for berth," Ivar faltered. He wet his lips, which felt caked with dust. It was a hot day, 25 degrees Celsius or so. Virgil glared in a sky which seemed to lack its usual depth, and instead was burnished.

"No dung? What can a townsitter do worth his keep? We're bound east, straight across the Dreary. Not exactly a Romeburg patio. We'd have to sweep you up after you crumbled." The other rubbed his pointed chin. "Of course," he added thoughtfully, "you might make pretty good nose powder for some girl."

Yet his mockery was not unkind. Ivar gave him closer regard. He was young, probably little older than the Firstling. Caught by a beaded fillet, his hair fell to his shoulders in the common style, brass earrings showing through. Like most tineran men, he kept shaved off what would have been a puny growth of beard. Bones and luminous gray eyes stood forth in a narrow face. He was nearly always grinning, and whether or not he stood still, there was a sense of quivering mobility about him. His clothes—fringed and varicolored shirt, scarlet sash, skin-tight leather trousers and buskins—were worn-out finery demoted to working dress. A golden torque encircled his neck, tawdry-jeweled rings his fingers, a spiral of herpetoid skin the left arm. A knife sat on either hip, one a tool, one a weapon, both delicate-looking compared to those miniature machetes the Landfolk carried.

"I'm not—well, yes, I am from Nova Roma, University family," Ivar admitted. "But, uh, how'd you know before I spoke?"

"O-ah, your walk, your whole way. Being geared like a granger, not a cityman, won't cover that." The Anglic was rapid-fire, a language coequal in the Trains with Haisun and its argots. But this was a special dialect, archaic from the nord viewpoint, one which, for instance, made excessive use of articles while harshly clipping the syllables. "That's a rifle to envy, yours, and relieve you of if you're uncareful. A ten-millimeter Valdemar convertible, right?"

"And I can use it," Ivar said in a rush. "I've spent plenty of time in outlands. You'll find me good pot hunter, if nothin' else. But I'm handy with apparatus too, especially electric. And strong, when you need plain muscle."

"Well-ah, let's go see King Samlo. By the way, I'm Mikkal of Redtop." The tineran nodded at his wagon, whose roof justified its name. A woman of about his age, doubtless his wife, poised in the doorway. She was as exotically pretty as girls of her type were supposed to be in the folklore of the sedentary people. A red-and-yellow-zigzagged gown clung to a sumptuous figure, though Ivar thought it a shame how she had loaded herself with junk ornaments. Catching his eye, she smiled, winked, and swung a hip at him. Her man didn't mind; it was a standard sort of greeting.

"You'll take me?" Ivar blurted.

Mikkal shrugged. Infinitely more expressive than a nord's, the gesture used his entire body. Sunlight went iridescent over the scales coiled around his left arm. "Sure-ah. An excuse not to work." To the woman: "You, Dulcy, go fetch the rest of my gear." She made a moue at him before she scampered off into the turmoil.

"Thanks ever so much," Ivar said. "I—I'm Rolf Mariner." He had given the alias considerable thought, and was proud of the result. It fitted the ethnic background he could not hope to disguise, while free of silly giveaways like his proper initials.

"If that's who you want to be, fine," Mikkal gibed, and led the way.

The racket grew as animals were brought in from pasture, stathas, mules, goats, neomoas. The dogs which herded them, efficiently at work in response to whistles and signals from children, kept silence. They were tall, ebon, and skeletally built except for the huge rib cages and water-storing humps on the shoulders.

Goldwheels was the largest wagon, the single motorized one. A small companion stood alongside, black save for a few symbols in red and silver, windowless. Above its roof, a purple banner bore two crescents. Mikkal sensed Ivar's curiosity and explained, "That's the shrine."

"Oh . . . yes." Ivar remembered what he had read. The king of a band was also its high priest, who besides presiding over public religious ceremonies conducted secret rites with a few fellow initiates. He was required to be of a certain family (evidently Goldwheels in the Waybreak Train) but need not be an eldest son. Most of a king's women were chosen with a view to breeding desired traits, and the likeliest boy became heir apparent, to serve apprenticeship in another Train. Thus the wanderers forged alliances between their often quarrelsome groups, more potent than the marriages among individuals which grew out of the periodic assemblies known as Fairs.

The men who were hitching white mules to the shrine seemed no more awed than Mikkal. They hailed him loudly. He gave them an answer which made laughter erupt. Youngsters milling nearby shrilled. A couple of girls tittered, and one made a statement which was doubtless bawdy. *At my expense,* Ivar knew.

It didn't matter. He smiled back, waved at her, saw her preen waist-long tresses and flutter her eyelids. *After all, to them—if I prove I'm no dumb clod, and I will, I will—to them I'm excitin' outsider.* He harked back to his half-desperate mood of minutes ago, and marveled. A buoyant confidence swelled in him, and actual merriment bubbled beneath. The whole carefree atmosphere had entered him, as it seemed to enter everybody who visited an encampment.

King Samlo returned from overseeing a job. Folk lifted hands in casual salute. When he cared to exercise it, his power was divine and total; but mostly he ruled by consensus.

He was a contrast to his people, large, blocky-boned, hooknosed. His mahogany features carried a fully developed beard and mustache. He limped. His garb was white, more clean than one would have thought possible here. Save for tooled-leather boots, crimson-plumed turban, and necklace of antique coins, it had little decoration.

His pale gaze fell on Ivar and remained as he lowered himself into an ornate armchair outside his wagon. "Hey-ah, stranger," he said. "What's your lay?"

Ivar bowed, not knowing what else to do. Mikkal took the word: "He tags himself Rolf Mariner, claims he's a hunter and jack-o'-hands as well as a varsiteer, and wants to come along."

The king didn't smile. His gravity marked him off yet more than did his appearance. Nonetheless, Ivar felt unafraid. Whether dreamy runaways, failed adults, or fugitives from justice, occasionally nords asked to join a Train. If they made a plausible case for themselves, or if a whim blew in their favor, they were accepted. They remained aliens, and probably none had lasted as much as a year before being dismissed. The usual reason given was that they lacked the ability to pull their freight in a hard and tricky life.

Surely that was true. Ivar expected that a journey with these people would stretch him to his limits. He did not expect he would snap. Who could await that, in this blithe tumult?

There passed through him: *In spite of everything they suffered, I've heard, I've read a little, about how those guests always hated to leave, always afterward mourned for lost high days—how those who'd lasted longest would try to get into different troop, or kill themselves—*But let him not fret when all his blood sang.

"Um-m-m-hm," Samlo said. "Why do you ask this?"

"I've tired of these parts, and have no readier way to leave them," Ivar replied.

Mikkal barked laughter. "He knows the formula, anyhow! Invoke the upper-class privacy fetish, plus a hint that if we don't know why he's running, we can't be blamed if the tentacles find him amongst us."

"Impie agents aren't city police or gentry housecarls," the king said. "They got special tricks. And . . . a few days back, a clutch of seethe-heads affrayed a marine patrol on the Wildfoss, remember? Several escaped. If you're on the flit, Mariner, why should we risk trouble to help you across Ironland?"

"I didn't say I was, sir," Ivar responded. "I told Mikkal, here, I can be useful to you. But supposin' I am in sabota with Terrans, is that bad? I heard tinerans cheer Emperor Hugh's men as they left for battle."

"Tinerans'll cheer anybody who's on hand with spending money," Mikkal said. "However, I'll 'fess most of us don't like the notion of the stars beswarmed by townsitters. It makes us feel like the universe is closing in." He turned to Samlo. "King, why not give this felly-oh a toss?"

"Will you be his keeper?" the seated man asked. Aside to Ivar: "We don't abandon people in the desert, no matter what. Your keeper has got to see you through."

"Sure-ah," Mikkal said. "He has a look of new songs and jokes in him."

"Your keeper won't have much to spare," Samlo warned. "If you use up supplies and give no return—well, maybe after we're back in the green and you dismissed, he'll track you down."

"He won't want to, sir . . . King," Ivar promised.

"Better make sure of that," Samlo said. "Mikkal, the shooting gallery's still assembled. Go see how many light-sweeps he can hit with that rifle of his. Find some broken-down equipment for him to repair; the gods know we have enough. Run him, and if he's breathing hard after half a dozen clicks, trade him back, because he'd never get across the Dreary alive." He rose, while telling Ivar: "If you pass, you'll have to leave that slugthrower with me. Only hunting parties carry firearms in a Train, and just one to a party. We'd lose too many people otherwise. Now I have to go see the animal acts get properly bedded down. You be off too."

✧ 6 ✧

In a long irregular line, herd strung out behind, the caravan departed. A few persons rode in the saddle, a few more in or on the vehicles; most walked. The long Aenean stride readily matched wagons bumping and groaning over roadless wrinkled hills. However, the going was stiff, and nobody talked without need. Perched on rooftops, musicians gave them plangent marches out of primitive instruments, drums, horns, gongs, bagpipes, many-stringed guitars. A number of these players were handicapped, Ivar saw: crippled, blind, deformed. He would have been shocked by so much curable or preventable woe had they not seemed as exhilarated as he was.

Near sundown, Waybreak was out on the undulant plain of Ironland. Coarse red soil reached between clumps of gray-green starkwood or sword trava, dried too hard for there to be a great deal of dust. Samlo cried halt by an eroded lava flow from which thrust a fluted volcanic plug. "The Devil's Tallywhacker," Mikkal told his protégé. "Traditional first-night stopping place out of Arroyo, said to be protection against hostile gods. I think the practice goes back to the Troubles, when wild gangs went around, starveling humans or stranded remnants of invader forces, and you might need a defensible site. Of course, nowadays we just laager the wagons in case a zoosny wind should blow up or something like that. But it's as well to maintain cautionary customs. The rebellion proved the Troubles can come again, and no doubt will . . . as if that'd ever 'needed proof."

"Uh, excuse me," Ivar said, "but you sound, uh, surprising sophisticated—" His voice trailed off.

Mikkal chuckled. "For an illiterate semi-savage? Well, matter o' fact, I'm not. Not illiterate, anyhow. A part of us have to read and write if we're to handle the outside world, let alone operate swittles like the Treasure Map. Besides, I like reading, when I can beg or steal a book."

"I can't understand why you—I mean, you're cut off from things like library banks, not to mention medical and genetic services, everything you could have—"

"At what price?" Mikkal made a spitting noise, though he did not waste the water. "We'd either have to take steady work to gain the jingle, or become welfare clients, which'd mean settling down as even meeker law-lickers. The end of the Trains, therefore the end of us. Didn't you know? A tineran can't quit. Stuff him into a town or nail him down on a farm, it's a mercy when death sets his corpse free to rot."

"I'd heard that," Ivar said slowly.

"But thought the tale must be an extravaganza, hey? No, it's true. It's happened. Tinerans jailed for any length of time sicken and die, if they don't suicide first. Even if for some reason like exile from the Train, they have to turn sitter, 'free workers' "—the tone spoke the quotation marks—"they can't breed and they don't live long. . . . That's why we have no death penalty. Twice I've seen the king order a really bad offender cast out, and word sent to the rest of the Trains so none would take him in. Both times, the felly begged for a hundred and one lashes instead." Mikkal shook himself. "C'mon, we've work to do. You unhitch the team, hobble them, and bring them to where the rest of the critters are. Dulcy'll answer your questions. Since I've got you for extra hands, I'll get my tools resharpened early, this trek." He performed as juggler and caster of edged weapons and, he added blandly, card sharp and dice artist.

Men erected a collapsible trough, filled it from a water truck, added the vitamin solutions necessary to supplement grazing upon purely native vegetation. Boys would spend the night watching over the small, communally owned herd and the draught animals. Besides spider wolves or a possible catavale, hazards included crevices, sand hells, a storm howling down with the suddenness and ferocity common anywhere on Aeneas. If the weather stayed mild, night chill would not be dangerous until the route entered the true barrens. These creatures were the product of long breeding, the quadrupeds and hexapods heavily haired, the big neomoas similarly well feathered.

Of course, all Ironland was not that bleak, or it would have been uncrossable. The Train would touch at oases where the tanks could be refilled with brackish water and the bins with forage.

Inside the wagon circle, women and girls prepared the evening meal. In this nearly fuelless land they cooked on glowers. Capacitors had lately been recharged at a power station. To have this done, and earn the wherewithal to pay, was a major reason why the migrations passed through civilized parts.

Virgil went down. Night came almost immediately after. A few lamps glowed on wagonsides, but mainly the troop saw by stars, moons, auroral flickers to northward. A gelid breeze flowed off the desert. As if to shelter each other, folk crowded around the kettles. Voices racketed, chatter, laughter, snatches of song.

Except for being ferociously spiced, the fare was simple, a thick stew scooped up on rounds of bread, a tarry-tasting tea for drink. Tinerans rarely used alcohol, never carried it along. Ivar supposed that was because of its dehydrating effect.

Who needed it, anyway? He had not been this happy in the most joyous beer hall of Nova Roma, and his mind stayed clear into the bargain.

He got his first helping and hunkered down, less easily than they, beside Mikkal and Dulcy. At once others joined them, more and more till he was in a ring of noise, faces, unwashed but crisp-smelling bodies. Questions, remarks, japes roiled over him. "Hey-ah, townboy, why've you gone walkabout?... Hoping for girls? Well, I hope you won't be too tired to oblige 'em, after a day's hike.... Give us a song, a story, a chunk o' gossip, how 'bout that?... Ay-uh, Banji, don't ride him hard, not yet. Be welcome, lad.... You got coin on you? Listen, come aside and I'll explain how you can double your money.... Here, don't move, I'll fetch you your seconds...."

Ivar responded as best he dared, in view of his incognito. He would be among these people for quite a while, and had better make himself popular. Besides, he liked them.

At length King Samlo boomed through the shadows: "Cleanup and curfew!" His followers bounced to obey the first part of the command. Ivar decided that the chaos earlier in the day, and now, was only apparent. Everyone knew his or her job. They simply didn't bother about military snap and polish.

Musicians gathered around the throne. "I thought we were ordered to bed," Ivar let fall.

"Not right away," Dulcy told him. "Whenever we can, we have a little fun first, songfest or dance or—" She squeezed his hand. "You think what you can do, like tell us news from your home. He'll call on you. Tonight, though, he wants—Yes. Fraina. Fraina of Jubilee. Mikkal's sister... half-sister, you'd say; their father can afford two wives. She's good. Watch."

The wanderers formed a ring before their wagons. Ivar had found he could neither sit indefinitely on his hams like them, nor crosslegged on the ground; after dark, his bottom would soon have been frozen. There was no energy to lavish on heated garments. He stood leaned against Redtop, hidden in darkness.

The center of the camp was bright silver, for Lavinia was high and Creusa hurrying toward the full. A young woman trod forth, genuflected to the king, stood erect and drew off her cloak. Beneath, she wore a pectoral, a broad brass girdle upholding filmy strips fore and aft, and incidental jewelry.

Ivar recognized her. Those delicate features and big gray eyes had caught his attention several times during the day. Virtually unclad, her figure seemed boy-slim save in the bosom. No, he decided, that wasn't right; her femaleness was just more subtle and supple than he had known among his own heavy folk.

The music wailed. She stamped her bare feet, once, twice, thrice, and broke into dance.

The wind gusted from Ivar. He had seen tineran girls perform before, and some were a wild equal of any ballerina—but none like this. *They save the best for their own,* he guessed; then thought vanished in the swirl of her.

She leaped, human muscles against Aenean gravity, rose flying, returned swimming. She flowed across ground, fountained upward again, landed to pirouette on a toe, a top that gyrated on and on and on, while it swung in ever wider precessions until she was a wheel, which abruptly became an arrow and at once the catavale which dodged the shaft and rent the hunter. She snapped her cloak, made wings of it, made a lover of it, danced with it and her floating hair and the plume of her breath. She banished cold; moonlight sheened on sweat, and she made the radiance ripple across her. She was the moonlight herself, the wind, the sound of pipes and drums and the rhythmic handclaps of the whole Train and of Ivar; and when she soared away into night and the music ended, men roared.

Inside, Mikkal's wagon was well laid out but had scant room because of the things that crowded it. At the forward end stood a potbellied stove, for use when fuel was available. Two double-width bunks, one above the other, occupied the left wall, a locker beneath and an extensible table between. The right wall was shelves, cupboard, racks, to hold an unholy number of items: the stores and equipment of everyday life, the costumes and paraphernalia of shows, a kaleidoscope of odd souvenirs and junk. From the ceiling dangled an oil lantern, several amulets, and bunches of dry food, sausages, onions, dragon apples, maufry, and more, which turned the air pungent.

Attached to the door was a cage. An animal within sat up on its hind legs as Mikkal, Dulcy, and Ivar entered. The Firstling wondered why anybody would keep so unprepossessing a creature. It was about 15 centimeters in length, quadrupedal though the forepaws came near resembling skinny hands. Coarse gray fur covered it beneath a leathery flap of skin which sprang from the shoulders and reached the hindquarters, a kind of natural mantle. The head was wedge-shaped, ears pointed and curved like horns, mouth needle-fanged. That it could not be a native Aenean organism was proved by the glittery little red eyes, three of them in a triangle.

"What's that?" Ivar asked.

"Why, our luck," Dulcy said. "Name of Larzo." She reached into the cage, which had no provision for closing. "C'mon out and say hey-ah, Larzo, sweet."

"Your, uh, mascot?"

"Our what?" Mikkal responded. "Oh. I grab you. A ju, like those?" He jerked his thumb at the hanging grotesques. "No. It's true, lucks're believed to help us, but mainly they're pets. I never heard of a wagon, not in any Train, that didn't keep one."

A vague memory of it came to Ivar from his reading. No author had done more than mention in passing a custom which was of no obvious attractiveness or significance.

Dulcy had brought the animal forth. She cuddled it on her lap when the three humans settled side by side onto the lower bunk, crooned and offered it bits of cheese. It accepted that, but gave no return of her affection.

"Where're they from, originally?" Ivar inquired.

Mikkal spread his hands. "Who knows? Some immigrant brought a pair or two along, I s'pose, 'way back in the early days. They never went off on their own, but tinerans got in the habit of keeping them and—" He yawned. "Let's doss. The trouble with morning is, it comes too damn early in the day."

Dulcy returned the luck to its cage. She leaned across Ivar's lap to do so. When her hand was free, she stroked him there, while her other fingers rumpled his hair. Mikkal blinked, then smiled. "Why not?" he said. "You'll be our companyo a spell, Rolf, and I think we'll both like you. Might as well start right off."

Unsure of himself, though immensely aware of the woman snuggled against him, the newcomer stammered, "Wh-what? I, I don't follow—"

"You take her first tonight," Mikkal invited.

"*Huh?* But, but, but—"

"You left your motor running," Mikkal said, while Dulcy giggled. After a pause: "Shy? You nords often are, till you get drunk. No need among friends."

Ivar's face felt ablaze.

"Aw, now," Dulcy said. "Poor boy, he's too unready." She kissed him lightly on the lips. "Never mind. We've time. Later, if you want. Only if you want."

"Sure, don't be afraid of us," Mikkal added. "I don't bite, and she doesn't very hard. Go on to your rest if you'd rather."

Their casualness was like a benediction. Ivar hadn't imagined himself getting over such an embarrassment, immediately at that. "No offense meant," he said. "I'm, well, engaged to be married, at home."

"If you change your mind, let me know," Dulcy murmured. "But if you don't, I'll not doubt you're a man. Different tribes have different ways, that's all." She kissed him again, more vigorously. "Goodnight, dear."

He scrambled into the upper bunk, where he undressed and crawled into his sleeping bag that she had laid out for him. Mikkal snuffed the lantern, and soon he heard the sounds and felt the quiverings below him, and thereafter were darkness, stillness, and the wind.

He was long about getting to sleep. The invitation given him had been too arousing. Or was it that simple? He'd known three or four sleazy women, on leaves from his military station. His friends had known them too. For a while he swaggered. Then he met star-clean Tatiana and was ashamed.

I'm no prig, he insisted to himself. Let them make what they would of their lives on distant, corrupted Terra, or in a near and not necessarily corrupted tineran wagon. A child of Firstmen and scholars had another destiny to follow. Man on Aeneas had survived because the leaders were dedicated to that survival: disciplined, constant men and women who ever demanded more of themselves than they did of their underlings. And self-command began in the inmost privacies of the soul.

A person stumbled, of course. He didn't think he had fallen too hard, upon those camp followers, in the weird atmosphere of wartime. But a . . . an orgy was something else again. Especially when he had no flimsiest excuse. Then why did he lie here, trying not to toss and turn, and regret so *very* greatly that he should stay faithful to his Tanya? Why, when he summoned her image to help him, did Fraina come instead?

✸ 7 ✸

Covering a hill in the middle of Nova Roma, the University of Virgil was a town within the city, and most of it older than most of the latter. The massive, crenelated wall around it still bore scars from the Troubles. *Older in truth than the Empire,* Desai thought. His glance passed over man-hewn red and gray stones to an incorporated section of glassy iridescence. A chill touched his spine. *That part is older than humanity.*

Beyond the main gateway, he entered a maze of courts, lanes, stairs, unexpected little gardens or trees, memorial plaques or statues, between the buildings. Architecture was different here from elsewhere. Even the newer structures—long, porticoed, ogive-windowed, until they rose in towers—preserved a tradition going back to the earliest settlers. *Or do they?* wondered Desai. *If these designs are from ancient Terra, they are crossbreeds that mutated. Gothic arches but Russko spires, except that in low gravity those vaultings soar while those domes bulge . . . and yet it isn't mismatched, it's strong and graceful in its own way, it belongs on Aeneas as . . . I do not.*

Chimes toned from a belfry which stood stark athwart darkling blue and a rusty streak of high-borne dustcloud. No doubt the melody was often heard. But it didn't sound academic to him; it rang almost martial.

Campus had not regained the crowded liveliness he had seen in holos taken before the revolt. In particular, there were few nonhumans, and perhaps still fewer humans from other colonies. But he passed among hundreds of Aeneans. Hardly a one failed to wear identification: the hooded, color-coded cloaks of teaching faculty, which might or might not overlay the smock of a researcher; student jackets bearing emblems of their colleges and, if they were Landfolk, their Firstmen. (Beneath were the tunics, trousers, and half-boots worn by both sexes—among nords, anyhow—except on full-dress occasions when women revived antique skirts.) Desai noticed, as well, the shoulder patches on many, remembrance of military or naval units now dissolved. *Should I make those illegal? . . . And what if my decree was generally disobeyed?*

He felt anger about him like a physical force. Oh, here a couple of young fellows laughed at a joke, there several were flying huge kites, yonder came a boy and girl hand in hand, near two older persons learnedly conversing; but the smiles were too few, the feet on flagstones rang too loud.

He had visited the area officially, first taking pains to learn about it. That hadn't thawed his hosts, but today it saved him asking for directions and thus risking recognition. Not that he feared violence; and he trusted he had the maturity to tolerate insult; however—His way took him past Rybnikov Laboratories, behind Pickens Library, across Adzel Square to Borglund Hall, which was residential.

The south tower, she had said. Desai paused to see where Virgil stood. After two years—more than one, Aenean—he had not developed an automatic sense of how he faced. The compass on a planet was always defined to make its sun rise in the east; and a 25-degree axial tilt wasn't excessive, shouldn't be confusing; and he ought to be used to alien constellations by now. *Getting old. Not very adaptable any longer.* Nor had he developed a reflex to keep him from ever looking straight at that small, savage disc. Blind for a minute, he worried about retinal burn. Probably none. Blue-eyed Aeneans kept their sight, didn't they? *Let's get on with business. Too much else is waiting back at the office as is, and more piling up every second.*

The circular stairway in the tower was gloomy enough to make him stumble, steep enough to make him pant and his heart flutter. Low gravity didn't really compensate for thin air, at his age. He rested for a time on the fourth-floor landing before he approached an oaken door and used a knocker which centuries of hands had worn shapeless.

Tatiana Thane let him in. "Good day," she said tonelessly.

Desai bowed. "Good day, my lady. You are kind to give me this interview."

"Do I have choice?"

"Certainly."

"I didn't when your Intelligence Corps hauled me in for questionin'." Her speech remained flat. A note of bitterness would at least have expressed some human relationship.

"That is why I wished to see you in your own apartment, Prosser Thane. To emphasize the voluntariness. Not that I believe you were arrested, were you? The officers merely assumed you would cooperate, as a law-abiding—citizen." Desai had barely checked himself from saying "subject of His Majesty."

"Well, I won't assault you, Commissioner. Have you truly come here unescorted as you claimed you would?"

"Oh, yes. Who'd pay attention to a chubby chocolate-colored man in a particularly thick mantle? Apropos which, where may I leave it?"

Tatiana indicated a peg in the entry. This layout was incredibly archaic. No doubt the original colonists hadn't had the economic surplus to automate residences, and there'd been sufficient pinch ever afterward to keep alive a scorn of "effete gadgetry." The place was chilly, too, though the young woman was rather lightly if plainly clad.

Desai's glance recorded her appearance for later study. She was tall and slim. The oval face bore a curved nose, arched brows above brown eyes, broad full mouth, ivory complexion, between shoulder-length wings of straight dark hair. *Old University family,* he recalled, *steeped in its lore, early destined for a scholarly career. Somewhat shy and bookish, but no indoor plant; she takes long walks or longer animalback rides, spends time in the desert, not to mention the jungles of Dido. Brilliant linguist, already responsible for advances in understanding certain languages on that planet. Her enthusiasm for the Terran classics doubtless kindled Ivar Frederiksen's interest in them and in history . . . though in his case, perhaps one might better say the vision of former freedom fighters inflamed him. She appears to have more sense than that: a serious girl, short on humor, but on the whole, as good a fiancée as any man could hope for.*

That was the approximate extent of the report on her. There were too many more conspicuous Aeneans to investigate. The Frederiksen boy hadn't seemed like anyone to worry about either, until he ran amok.

Tatiana led Desai into the main room of her small suite. Its stone was relieved by faded tapestries and scuffed rug, where bookshelves, a fine eidophonic player, and assorted apparatus for logico-semantic analysis did not occupy the walls. Furniture was equally shabby-comfortable, leather and battered wood. Upon a desk stood pictures he supposed were of her kin, and Ivar's defiant in the middle of them. Above hung two excellent views, one of a Didonian, one of Aeneas seen from space, tawny-red, green- and blue-mottled, north polar cap as white as the streamers of ice-cloud. Her work, her home.

A trill sounded. She walked to a perch whereon, tiny and fluffy, a native tadmouse sat. "Oh," she said. "I forgot it's his lunchtime." She gave the animal seeds and a caress. A sweet song responded.

"What is his name, if I may ask?" Desai inquired.

She was obviously surprised. "Why . . . Frumious Bandersnatch."

Desai sketched another bow. "Pardon me, my lady. I was given a wrong impression of you."

"What?"

"No matter. When I was a boy on Ramaujan, I had a local pet I called Mock Turtle.... Tell me, please, would a tadmouse be suitable for a household which includes young children?"

"Well, that depends on them. They mustn't get rough."

"They wouldn't. Our cat's tail went unpulled until, lately, the poor beast died. It couldn't adjust to this planet."

She stiffened. "Aeneas doesn't make every newcomer welcome, Commissioner. Sit down and describe what you want of me."

The chair he found was too high for his comfort. She lowered herself opposite him, easily because she topped him by centimeters. He wished he could smoke, but to ask if he might would be foolish.

"As for Ivar Frederiksen," Tatiana said, "I tell you what I told your Corpsmen: I was not involved in his alleged action and I've no idea where he may be."

"I have seen the record of that interview, Prosser Thane." Desai chose his words with care. "I believe you. The agents did too. None recommended a narcoquiz, let alone a hypnoprobing."

"No Aenean constable has right to so much as propose that."

"But Aeneas rebelled and is under occupation," Desai said in his mildest voice. "Let it re-establish its loyalty, and it will get back what autonomy it had before." Seeing how resentment congealed her eyes, he added low: "The loyalty I speak of does not involve more than a few outward tokens of respect for the throne, as mere essential symbols. It is loyalty to the Empire—above all, to its Pax, in an age when spacefleets can incinerate whole worlds and when the mutiny in fact took thousands of lives—it is that I mean, my lady. It is that I am here about, not Ivar Frederiksen."

Startled, she swallowed before retorting, "What do you imagine I can do?"

"Probably nothing, I fear. Yet the chance of a hint, a clue, any spark of enlightenment no matter how faint, led me to call you and request a confidential talk. I emphasize 'request.' You cannot help unless you do so freely."

"What do you want?" she whispered. "I repeat, I'm not in any revolutionary group—never was, unless you count me clerkin' in militia durin' independence fight—and I don't know zero about what may be goin' on." Pride returned. "If I did, I'd kill myself rather than betray him. Or his cause."

"Do you mind talking about them, though? Him and his cause."

"How—" Her answer faded out.

"My lady," Desai said, and wondered how honest his plea sounded to her, "I am a stranger to your people. I have met hundreds by now, myself, while my subordinates have met thousands. It has been of little use in gaining empathy. Your history, literature, arts are a bit more helpful, but the time I can devote to them is very limited, and summaries prepared by underlings assigned to the task are nearly valueless. One basic obstacle to understanding you is your pride, your ideal of discipline and self-reliance, your sense of privacy which makes you reluctant to bare the souls of even fictional characters. I know you have normal human emotions; but how, on Aeneas, do they normally work? How does it *feel* to be you?

"The only persons here with whom I can reach some approximation of common ground are certain upper-class Townfolk, entrepreneurs, executives, innovators—cosmopolites who have had a good deal to do with the most developed parts of the Empire."

"Squatters in Web," she sneered. "Yes, they're easy to fathom. Anything for profit."

"Now you are the one whose imagination fails," Desai reproved her. "True, no doubt a number of them are despicable opportunists. Are there absolutely none among Landfolk and University? Can you not conceive that an industrialist or financier may honestly believe cooperation with the Imperium is the best hope of his world? Can you not entertain the hypothesis that he may be right?"

He sighed. "At least recognize that, the better we Impies understand you, the more to your advantage it is. In fact, our empathy could be vital. Had— Well, to be frank, had I known for sure what I dimly suspected, the significance in your culture of the McCormac Memorial and the armed households, I might have been able to persuade the sector government to rescind its orders for dismantling them. Then we might not have provoked the kind of thing which has made your betrothed an outlaw."

Pain crossed her face. "Maybe," she said.

"My duty here," he told her, "is first to keep the Pax, including civil law and order; in the longer run, to assure that these will stay kept, when the Terran troops finally go home. But what must be done? How? Should we, for example, should we revise the basic structure altogether? Take power from the landed gentry especially, whose militarism may have been the root cause of the rebellion, and establish a parliament based on strict manhood suffrage?" Desai observed her expressions; she was becoming more open to him. "You are shocked? Indignant? Denying to yourself that so drastic a change is permanently possible?"

He leaned forward. "My lady," he said, "among the horrors with which I live is this knowledge, based on all the history I have studied and all the direct experience I have had. It is terrifyingly easy to swing a defeated and occupied nation in *any* direction. It has occurred over and over. Sometimes, two victors with different ideologies divided such a loser among them, for purposes of 'reform.' Afterward the loser stayed divided, its halves perhaps more fanatical than either original conqueror."

Dizziness assailed him. He must breathe deeply before he could go on: "Of course, an occupation may end too soon, or it may not carry out its reconstruction thoroughly enough. Then a version of the former society will revive, though probably a distorted version. Now how soon is too soon, how thoroughly is enough? And to what end?

"My lady, there are those in power who claim Sector Alpha Crucis will never be safe until Aeneas has been utterly transformed: into an imitation Terra, say most. I feel that that is not only wrong—you have something unique here, something basically good—but it is mortally dangerous. In spite of the pretensions of the psychodynamicists, I don't believe the consequences of radical surgery, on a proud and energetic people, are foreseeable.

"I want to make minimal, not maximal changes. They may amount to nothing more than strengthening trade relations with the heart stars of the Empire, to give you a larger stake in the Pax. Or whatever seems necessary. At present, however, I don't know. I flounder about in a sea of reports and statistics, and as I go down for the third time, I remember the old old saying, 'Let me write a nation's songs, and I care not who may write its laws.'

"Won't you help me understand your songs?"

Silence fell and lasted, save for a wind whittering outside, until the tadmouse offered a timid arpeggio. That seemed to draw Tatiana from her brown study. She shook herself and said, "What you're askin' for is closer acquaintance, Commissioner. Friendship."

His laugh was nervous. "I'll settle for an agreement to disagree. Of course, I haven't time for anywhere near as much frank discussion as I'd like—as I really need. But if, oh, you young Aeneans would fraternize with the young marines, technicians, spacehands—you'd find them quite decent, you might actually take a little pity on their loneliness, and they do have experiences to relate from worlds you've never heard of—"

"I don't know if it's possible," Tatiana said. "Certainly not on my sole recommendation. Not that I'd give any, when your dogs are after my man."

"I thought that was another thing we might discuss," Desai said. "Not where he may be or what his plans, no, no. But how to get him out of the trap he's closed on himself. Nothing would make me happier than to give him a free pardon. Can we figure out a method?"

She cast him an astonished look before saying slowly, "I do believe you mean that."

"Beyond question I do. I'll tell you why. We Impies have our agents and informers, after all, not to mention assorted spy devices. We are not totally blind and deaf to events and to the currents beneath them. The fact could not be kept secret from the people that Ivar Frederiksen, the heir to the Firstmanship of Ilion, has led the first open, calculated renewal of insurgency. His confederates who were killed, hurt, imprisoned are being looked on as martyrs. He, at large, is being whispered of as the rightful champion of freedom—the rightful king, if you will—who shall return." Desai's smile would have been grim were his plump features capable of it. "You note the absence of public statements by his relatives, aside from nominal expressions of regret at an 'unfortunate incident.' We authorities have been careful not to lean on them. Oh, but we have been careful!"

The tenuous atmosphere was like a perpetual muffler on his unaccustomed ears. He could barely hear her: "What might you do . . . for him?"

"If he, unmistakably of his own free will, should announce he's changed his mind—not toadying to the Imperium, no, merely admitting that through most of its history Aeneas didn't fare badly under it and this could be made true again—why, I think he could not only be pardoned, along with his associates, but the occupation government could yield on a number of points."

Wariness brought Tatiana upright. "If you intend this offer to lure him out of hidin'—"

"No!" Desai said, a touch impatiently. "It's not the kind of message that can be broadcast. Arrangements would have to be made beforehand in secret, or it would indeed look like a sellout. Anyhow, I repeat that I don't think you know how to find him, or that he'll try contacting you in the near future."

He sighed. "But perhaps—Well, as I told you, what I mainly want to learn, in my clumsy and tentative fashion, is what drives him. What drives all of you? What are the possibilities for compromise? How can Aeneas and the Imperium best struggle out of this mess they have created for each other?"

She regarded him for a second period of quiet, until she asked, "Would you care to have lunch?"

The sandwiches and coffee had been good; and seated in her kitchenette bay, which was vitryl supported on the backs of stone dragons, one had an unparalleled view across quads, halls, towers, battlements, down and on to Nova Roma, the River Flone and its belt of green, the ocherous wildernesses beyond.

Desai inhaled fragrance from his cup, in lieu of the cigarette he had not yet ventured to mention. "Then Ivar is paradoxical," he remarked. "By your account, he is a skeptic on his way to becoming the charismatic lord of a deeply religious people."

"What?" He'd lost count of how often today he had taken the girl aback. "Oh, no. We've never been such. We began as scientific base, remember, and in no age of piety." She ran fingers through her hair and said after a moment, "Well, true, there always were some believers, especially among Landfolk. And lately...m-m, I suppose tendency does go back beyond Snelund administration, maybe several lifetimes...reaction to general decadence of Empire?—but our woes in last several years have certainly accelerated it—more and more, people are turnin' to churches." She frowned. "They're not findin' what they seek, though. That's Ivar's problem. He underwent conversion in early adolescence, he tells me, then later found creed unbelievable in light of science— unless, he says, they dilute it to cluck of soothin' noises, which is not what he wants."

"Since I came here for information, I have no business telling you what you are," Desai said. "Nevertheless, I do have a rather varied background and—Well, how would this interpretation strike you? Aenean society has always had a strong *faith*. A faith in the value of knowledge, to plant this colony in the first place; a faith in, oh, in the sheer right and duty of survival, to carry it through the particularly severe impact of the Troubles which it suffered; a faith in service, honor, tradition, demonstrated by the fact that what is essentially paternalism continued to be viable in easier times. Now hard times have come back. Some Aeneans, like Ivar, react by making a still greater emotional commitment to the social system. Others look to the supernatural. But however he does it, the average Aenean must serve something which is greater than himself."

Tatiana frowned in thought. "That may be. That may be. Still, I don't think 'supernatural' is right word, except in highly special sense. 'Transcendental' might be better. For instance, I'd call Cosmenosis philosophy rather than religion." She smiled a trifle. "I ought to know, bein' Cosmenosist myself."

"I seem to recall—Isn't that an increasingly popular movement in the University community?"

"Which is large and ramified, don't forget. Yes, Commissioner, you're right. And I don't believe it's mere fad."

"What are the tenets?"

"Nothin' exact, really. It doesn't claim to be revealed truth, simply way of gropin' toward . . . insight, oneness. Work with Didonians inspired it, originally. You can guess why, can't you?"

Desai nodded. Through his mind passed the picture he had seen, and many more: in a red-brown rain forest, beneath an eternally clouded sky, stood a being which was triune. Upon the platformlike shoulders of a large monoceroid quadruped rested a feathered flyer and a furry brachiator with well-developed hands. Their faces ran out in tubes, which connected to the big animal to tap its bloodstream. It ate for all of them.

Yet they were not permanently linked. They belonged to their distinct genera, reproduced their separate kinds and carried out many functions independently.

That included a measure of thinking. But the Didonian was not truly intelligent until its—no, heesh's—three members were joined. Then not only did veins link; nervous systems did. The three brains together became more than the sum of the three apart.

How much more was not known, perhaps not definable in any language comprehensible to man. The next world sunward from Aeneas remained as wrapped in mystery as in mist. That

Didonian societies were technologically primitive proved nothing; human ones were, until a geologically infinitesimal moment ago, and Terra was an easier globe on which to find lawfulness in nature. That communication with Didonians was extraordinarily difficult, limited after seven hundred years to a set of pidgin dialects, proved nothing either, beyond the truism that their minds were alien beyond ready imagining.

What is a mind, when it is the temporary creation of three beings, each with its own individuality and memories, each able to have any number of different partners? What is personality—the soul, even—when these shifting linkages perpetuate those recollections, in a ghostly diminuendo that lasts for generations after the experiencing bodies have died? How many varieties of race and culture and self are possible, throughout the ages of an entire infinite-faceted world? What may we learn from them, or they from us?

Without Dido for lure, probably men would never have possessed Aeneas. It was so far from Terra, so poor and harsh—more habitable for them than its sister, but by no great margin. By the time that humans who lacked such incentive had filled more promising planets, no doubt the Ythrians would have occupied this one. It would have suited them far better than it did *Homo sapiens*.

How well had it suited the Builders, uncertain megayears in the past, when there were no Didonians and Aeneas had oceans—?

"Excuse me." Desai realized he had gone off into a reverie. "My mind wandered. Yes, I've meditated on the—the Neighbors, don't you call them?—quite a bit, in what odd moments fall to my lot. They must have influenced your society enormously, not just as an inexhaustible research objective, but by their, well, example."

"Especially of late, when we think we may be reachin' true communication in some few cases," Tatiana replied. Ardor touched her tone. "Think: such way of existence, on hand for us to witness and...and meditate on, you said. Maybe you're right, we do need transhumanness in our lives, here on this planet. But maybe, Commissioner, we're right in feelin' that need." She swept her hand in an arc at the sky. "What are we? Sparks, cast up from a burnin' universe whose creation was meanin'less accident? Or children of God? Or parts, masks of God? Or seed from which God will at last grow?" Quieter: "Most of us Cosmenosists think—yes, Didonians have inspired it, their strange unity, such little as we've learned of their beliefs, dedications, poetry, dreams—we think reality is

always growin' toward what is greater than itself, and first duty
of those that stand highest is to help raise those lower—"

Her gaze went out the window, to the fragment of what had
been ... something, ages ago ... and, in these latter centuries, had
never really been lost in the wall which used it. "Like Builders,"
she finished. "Or Elders, as Landfolk call them, or—oh, they've
many names. Those who came before us."

Desai stirred. "I don't want to be irreverent," he said uncom-
fortably, "but, well, while apparently a starfaring civilization did
exist in the distant past, leaving relics on a number of planets, I
can't quite, um-m, swallow this notion I've heard on Aeneas, that
it went onto a more exalted plane—rather than simply dying out."

"What would destroy it?" she challenged. "Don't you suppose we,
puny mankind, are already too widespread for extinction, this side
of cosmos itself endin'—or, if we perish on some worlds, we won't
leave tools, carvin's, synthetics, fossilized bones, traces enough to
identify us for millions of years to come? Why not Builders, then?"

"Well," he argued, "a brief period of expansion, perhaps scientific bases only, no true colonies, evacuated because of adverse
developments at home—"

"You're guessin'," Tatiana said. "In fact, you're whistlin' past
graveyard that isn't there. I think, and I'm far from alone, Builders never needed to do more than they did. They were already
beyond material gigantism, by time they reached here. I think they
outgrew these last vestiges we see, and left them. And Didonian
many-in-one gives us clue to what they became; yes, they may
have started that very line of evolution themselves. And on their
chosen day they will return, for all our sakes."

"I have heard talk about these ideas, Prosser Thane, but—"

Her look burned at him. "You assume it's crankery. Then consider
this. Right on Aeneas are completest set of Builder ruins known:
in Orcan region, on Mount Cronos. We've never investigated them
as we should, at first because of other concerns, later because
they'd become inhabited. But now ... oh, rumors yet, nothin' but
the kind of rumors that're forever driftin' in on desert wind ...
still, they whisper of a forerunner—"

She saw she might have spoken too freely, broke off and snapped
self-possession into place. "Please don't label me fanatic," she said.
"Call it hope, daydream, what you will. I agree we have no proof,
let alone divine revelation." He could not be sure how much or

how little malice dwelt in her smile. "Still, Commissioner, what if bein's five or ten million years ahead of us *should* decide Terran Empire is in need of reconstruction?"

Desai returned to his office so near the end of the posted working day that he planned to shove everything aside till tomorrow and get home early. It would be the first time in a couple of weeks he had seen his children before they were asleep.

But of course his phone told him he had an emergency call. Being a machine, it refrained from implying he ought to have left a number where he could be reached. The message had come from his chief of Intelligence.

Maybe it isn't crucial, went his tired thought. *Feinstein's a good man, but he's never quite learned how to delegate.*

He made the connection. The captain responded directly. After ritual salutations and apologies:

"—that Aycharaych of Jean-Baptiste, do you remember him? Well, sir, he's disappeared, under extremely suspicious circumstances.

"...No, as you yourself, and His Excellency, decided, we had no reasonable cause to doubt him. He actually arranged to travel with a patrol of ours, for his first look at the countryside.

"...As nearly as I can make out from bewildered reports, somehow he obtained the password. You know what precautions we've instituted since the Hesperian incident? The key guards don't know the passwords themselves, consciously. Those're implanted for posthypnotic recognition and quick re-forgetting. To prevent accidents, they're nonsense syllables, or phrases taken from obscure languages used at the far side of the Empire. If Aycharaych could read them in the minds of the men—remembering also his non-human brain structure—then he's more of a telepath, or knows more tricks, than is supposed to be possible.

"Anyhow, sir, with the passwords he commandeered a flyer, talked it past an aerial picket, and is flat-out gone.

"...Yes, sir, naturally I've had the file on him checked, cross-correlated, everything we can do with what we've got on this wretched dustball. No hint of motivation. Could be simple piracy, I imagine, but dare we assume that?"

"My friend," Desai answered, while exhaustion slumped his shoulders, "I cannot conceive of one thing in the universe which we truly dare assume."

✿ 8 ✿

"Hee-ah!" Mikkal lashed his statha into full wavelike gallop. The crag bull veered. Had it gone down the talus slope, the hunters could not have followed. Boots, or feet not evolved for this environment, would have been slashed open by the edges of the rocks. And the many cinnabar-colored needles which jutted along the canyon would have screened off a shot.

As was, the beast swung from the rim and clattered across the mountainside. Then, from behind an outcrop striped in mineral colors, Fraina appeared on her own mount.

The bull should have fled her too, uphill toward Ivar. Instead, it lowered its head and charged. The trident horns sheened like steel. Her statha reared in panic. The bull was almost as big as it, and stronger and faster.

Ivar had the only gun, his rifle; the others bore javelins. "*Yalawa!*" he commanded his steed: in Haisun, "Freeze!" He swung stock to cheek and sighted. Bare rock, red dust, scattered gray-green bushes, and a single rahab tree stood sharp in the light of noontide Virgil. Shadows were purple but the sky seemed almost black above raw peaks. The air lay hot, suckingly dry, soundless except for hoof-drum and human cries.

If I don't hit that creature, Fraina may die, went through Ivar. But *no use hittin' him in the hump. And anywhere else is wicked to try for, at this angle and speed, and her in line of fire*—The knowledge flashed by as a part of taking aim. He had no time to be afraid.

The rifle hissed. The bullet trailed a whipcrack. The crag bull leaped, bellowed, and toppled.

"Rolf, Rolf, Rolf!" Fraina caroled. He rode down to her with glory in him. When they dismounted, she threw arms around him, lips against his.

For all its enthusiasm, it was a chaste kiss; yet it made him a trifle giddy. By the time he recovered, Mikkal had arrived and was examining the catch.

"Good act, Rolf." His smile gleamed white in the thin face. "We'll feast tonight."

"We've earned it." Fraina laughed. "Not that folk always get paid what's owing them, or don't get it swittled from them afterward."

"The trick is to be the swittler," Mikkal said.

Fraina's gaze fell tenderly on Ivar. "Or to be smart enough to keep what you've been strong enough to earn," she murmured.

His heart knocked. She was more beautiful than she ought to be, now in this moment of his victory, and in the trunks and halter which clad her. Mikkal wore simply a loincloth and crossed shoulderbelts to support knives, pouch, canteen. Those coppery skins could stand a fair amount of exposure, and it was joy to feel warmth upon them again. Ivar stuck to loose, full desert garb, blouse, trousers, sun-visored burnoose.

That plateau known as the Dreary of Ironland was behind them. There would be no more struggle over stonefields or around crevasses of a country where nothing stirred save them and the wind, nothing lived save them alone; no more thirst when water must be rationed till food went uncooked and utensils were cleaned with sand; no more nights so cold that tents must be erected to keep the animals alive.

As always, the passage had frayed nerves thin. Ivar appreciated the wisdom of the king in sequestering firearms. At that, a couple of knife fights had come near ending fatally. The travelers needed more than easier conditions, they needed something to cheer them. This first successful hunt on the eastern slope of the Ferric Mountains ought to help mightily.

And, though the country here was gaunt, they were over the worst. The Waybreak Train was headed down toward the Flone Valley, to reach at last the river itself, its cool green banks and the merry little towns snuggled along it, south of Nova Roma. If now the hunters laughed overmuch and over-shrilly while they butchered the crag bull, Ivar thought it was not beneath a Firstling's dignity to join in.

Moreover, Fraina was with him, they were working together.... Their acquaintance was not deep. Time and energy had been lacking for that. Besides, despite her dancing, she behaved shyly for a tineran girl. But for the rest of his stay in the troop—*I hope I've honor not to seduce her and leave her cryin' behind, when at last I go. (I begin to understand why, no matter hardships, sharpest pain may be to leave.) And Tanya, of course, mustn't forget Tanya.*

Let me, though, enjoy Fraina's nearness while I can. She's so vivid. *Everything is. I never knew I could feel this fully and freely, till I joined wanderers.*

He forced his attention to the task on hand. His heavy sheath knife went through hide, flesh, gristle, even the thinner bones, much more quickly and easily than did the slender blades of his comrades. He wondered why they didn't adopt the nord model, or at least add it to their tool kit; then, watching how cunningly they worked, he decided it wouldn't fit their style. *Hm, yes, I begin to see for myself, cultures are unities, often in subtle ways.*

Finished, meat loaded on stathas, the three of them went to rest by the spring which had attracted their quarry. It made a deliciously chilly bowlful in the hollow of a rock, the shadow of a bluff. Plume trava nodded white above mossy chromabryon; spearflies darted silver-bright; the stream clinked away over stones till the desert swallowed it up. The humans drank deep, then leaned luxuriously back against the cliff, Fraina between the men.

"Ay-ah," Mikkal sighed. "No need for hurry. I make us barely ten clicks from the Train, if we set an intercept course. Let's relax before lunch."

"Good idea," Ivar said. He and Fraina exchanged smiles.

Mikkal reached across her. In his hand were three twists of paper enclosing brown shreds. "Smoke?" he invited.

"What?" Ivar said. "I thought you tinerans avoided tobacco. Dries mouth, doesn't it?"

"Oh, this's marwan." At the puzzled look he got, Mikkal explained: "Never heard of it? Well, I don't suppose your breed would use the stuff. It's a plant. You dry and smoke it. Has a similar effect to alcohol. Actually better, I'd say, though I admit the taste leaves a trifle to be desired alongside a fine whiskey."

"*Narcotic?*" Ivar was shocked.

"Not that fierce, Rolf. Hell-near to a necessity, in fact, when you're away from the Train, like on a hunting or scouting trip." Mikkal grimaced. "These wilds are too inhuman. With a lot of friends around, you're screened. But by yourself, you need to take the edge off how alone and mortal you are."

Never before had Ivar heard him confess to a weakness. Mikkal was normally cheerful. When his temper, too, flared in the Dreary, he had not gone for his steel but used an equally whetted tongue, as if he felt less pressure than most of his fellows to prove masculinity. Now—*Well, I reckon I can sympathize. It is oppressive, this size and silence. Unendin' memento mori. Never thought so before, out in back country, but I do now. If Fraina weren't here to keep me glad, I might be tempted to try his drug.*

"No, thank you," Ivar said.

Mikkal shrugged. On the way back, his hand paused before the girl. She made a refusing gesture. He arched his brows, whether in surprise or sardonicism, till she gave him a tiny frown and head-shake. Then he grinned, tucked away the extra cigarettes, put his between his lips and snapped a lighter to it. Ivar had scarcely noticed the byplay, and gave it no thought except to rejoice that in this, also, Fraina kept her innocence. Mostly he noticed the sweet odors of her, healthy flesh and sun-warmed hair and sweat that stood in beads on her half-covered breasts.

Mikkal drew smoke into his lungs, held it, let it out very slowly and drooped his lids. "Aaah," he said, "and again aah. I become able to think. Mainly about ways to treat these steaks and chops. The women'll make stew tonight, no doubt. I'll insist the rest of the meat be started in a proper marinade. Take the argument to the king if I must. I'm sure he'll support me. He may be a vinegar beak, our Samlo, but all kings are, and he's a sensible vinegar beak."

"He certainly doesn't behave like average tineran," Ivar said.

"Kings don't. That's why we have them. I can't deny we're a flighty race, indeed I boast of it. However, that means we must have somebody who'll tie us down to caution and foresight."

"I, yes, I do know about special trainin' kings get. Must be real discipline, to last through lifetime in your society."

Fraina giggled. Mikkal, who had taken another drag, kicked heels and whooped. "What'd I say?" Ivar asked.

The girl dropped her glance. He believed he saw her blush, though that was hard to tell on her complexion. "Please, Mikkal, don't be irrev'rent," she said.

"Well, no more'n I have to," her half-brother agreed. "Still, Rolf might's well know. It's not a secret, just a matter we don't talk about. Not to disillusion youngsters too early, et cetera." His eyes sparkled toward Ivar. "Only the lodge that kings belong to is supposed to know what goes on in the shrines, and in the holy caves and booths where Fairs are held. But the royal wives and concubines take part, and girls will pass on details to their friends. You think we common tinerans hold lively parties. We don't know what liveliness is!"

"But it's our religion," Fraina assured Ivar. "Not the godlings and jus and spells of everyday. This is to honor the powers of life."

Mikkal chuckled. "Aye-ah, officially these're fertility rites. Well, I've read some anthropology, talked to a mixed bag of people, even taken thought once in a while when I'd nothing better to do. I figure the cult developed because the king has to have all-stops-out orgies fairly often, if he's to stay the kind of sobersides we need for a leader."

Ivar stared before him, half in confusion, half in embarrassment. Wouldn't it make more sense for the tinerans as a whole to be more self-controlled? Why was this extreme emotionalism seemingly built into them? Or was that merely his own prejudices speaking? Hadn't he been becoming more and more like them, and savoring every minute of it?

Fraina laid a hand on his arm. Her breath touched his cheek. "Mikkal has to poke fun," she said. "I believe it's both holy and unholy, what the king does. Holy because we must have young—too many die small, human and animal—and the powers of life are real. Unholy because, oh, he takes on himself the committing of . . . excesses, is that the word? On behalf of the Train, he releases our beast side, that otherwise would tear the Train apart."

I don't understand, quite, Ivar thought. But, thrilled within him, *she's thoughtful, intelligent, grave, as well as sweet and blithe.*

"Yah, I should start Dulcy baby-popping," Mikkal said. "The wet stage isn't too ghastly a nuisance, I'm told." When weaned, children moved into dormitory wagons. "On the other hand," he added, "I've told a few whoppers myself, when I had me a mark with jingle in his pockets—"

A shape blotted out the sun. They bounded to their feet.

That which was descending passed the disc, and light blazed off the gold-bronze pinions of a six-meter wingspan. Air whistled and thundered. Fraina cried out. Mikkal poised his javelin. "Don't!" Ivar shouted. "*Ya-lawa!* He's Ythrian!"

"O-o-oh, ye-e-es," Mikkal said softly. He lowered the spear though he kept it ready. Fraina gripped Ivar's arm and leaned hard against him.

The being landed. Ivar had met Ythrians before, at the University and elsewhere. But his astonishment at this arrival was such that he gaped as if he were seeing one for the first time.

Grounded, the newcomer used those tremendous wings, folded downward, for legs, claws at the bend of them spreading out to serve as feet, the long rear-directed bones lending extra support when at rest. That brought his height to some 135 centimeters, mid-breast on Ivar, farther up on the tinerans; for his mass was a good 25 kilos. Beneath a prowlike keelbone were lean yellow-skinned arms whose hands, evolved from talons, each bore three sharp-clawed fingers flanked by two thumbs, and a dewclaw on the inner wrist. Above were a strong neck and a large head proudly held. The skull bulged backward to contain the brain, for there was scant brow, the face curving down in a ridged muzzle to a mouth whose sensitive lips contrasted curiously with the carnivore fangs behind. A stiff feather-crest rose over head and neck, white edged with black like the fan-shaped tail. Otherwise, apart from feet, arms, and huge eyes which burned gold and never seemed to waver or blink, the body was covered with plumage of lustrous brown.

He wore an apron whose pockets, loops, and straps supported what little equipment he needed. Knife, canteen, and pistol were the only conspicuous items. He could live off the country better than any human.

Mikkal inhaled smoke, relaxed, smiled, lifted and dipped his weapon in salute. "Hay-ah, wayfarer," he said formally, "be welcome among us in the Peace of Water, where none are enemies. We're Mikkal of Redtop and my sister Fraina of Jubilee, from the Waybreak Train; and our companyo is Rolf Mariner, varsiteer."

The Anglic which replied was sufficiently fluent that one couldn't be sure how much of the humming accent and sibilant overtones were due to Ythrian vocal organs, how much simply to this being an offplanet dialect the speaker had learned. "Thanks, greetings, and fair winds wished for you. I hight Erannath, of the Stormgate choth upon Avalon. Let me quench thirst and we can talk if you desire."

As awkward on the ground as he was graceful aloft, he stumped to the pool. When he bent over to drink, Ivar glimpsed the gill-like antlibranchs, three on either side of his body. They were closed now, but in flight the muscles would work them like bellows, forcing extra oxygen into the bloodstream to power the lifting of the great weight. That meant high fuel consumption too, he remembered. No wonder Erannath traveled alone, if he had no vehicle. This land couldn't support two of him inside a practical radius of operations.

"He's gorgeous," Fraina whispered to Ivar. "What did you call him?"

"Ythrian," the Firstling replied. "You mean you don't know?"

"I guess I have heard, vaguely, but I'm an ignorant wanderfoot, Rolf. Will you tell me later?"

Ha! Won't I?

Mikkal settled himself back in the shade where he had been. "Might I ask what brings you, stranger?"

"Circumstances," Erannath replied. His race tended to be curt. A large part of their own communication lay in nuances indicated by the play of marvelously controllable quills.

Mikkal laughed. "In other words, yes, I might ask, but no, I might not get an answer. Wouldn't you like to palaver a while anyhow? Yo, Fraina, Rolf, join the party."

They did. Erannath's gaze lingered on the Firstling. "I have not hitherto observed your breed fare thus," he said.

"I—wanted a change—" Ivar faltered.

"He hasn't told exactly why, and no need for you to, either," Mikkal declared. "But see here, Aeronaut, your remark implies you *have* been observing, and pretty extensively too. Unless you're given to reckless generalization, which I don't believe your kind is."

Expressions they could not read rippled across the feathers. "Yes," the Ythrian said after a moment, "I am interested in this planet. As an Avalonian, I am naturally familiar with humans, but of a rather special sort. Being on Aeneas, I am taking the opportunity to become acquainted, however superficially, with a few more."

"U-u-uh-huh." Mikkal lounged crosslegged, smoking, idly watching the sky, while he drawled. "Somehow I doubt they've heard of you in Nova Roma. The occupation authorities have planted their heaviest buttocks on space traffic, in and out. Want to show me your official permit to flit around? As skittery as the guiders of our Terran destinies are nowadays, would they give a visitor from our esteemed rival empire the freedom of a key near-the-border world? I'm only fantasizing, but it goes in the direction of you being stranded here. You came in during the revolt, let's suppose, when that was easy to do unbeknownst, and you're biding your time till conditions ease up enough for you to get home."

Ivar's fingers clenched on his gunstock. But Erannath sat imperturbable. "Fantasize as you wish," he said dryly, "if you grant me the same right." Again his eyes smote the Firstling.

"Well, our territory doesn't come near Nova Roma," Mikkal

continued. "We'd make you welcome, if you care to roll with us as you've probably done already in two or three other Trains. Your songs and stories should be uncommon entertaining. And . . . maybe when we reach the green and start giving shows, we can work you into an act."

Fraina gasped. Ivar smiled at her. "Yes," he whispered, "without that weed in him—unless he was in camp—Mikkal wouldn't have nerve to proposition those claws and dignity, would he?" Her hair tickled his face. She squeezed his hand.

"My thanks," Erannath said. "I will be honored to guest you, for a few days at least. Thereafter we can discuss further."

He went high above them, hovering, soaring, wheeling in splendor, while they rode back across the tilted land.

"What *is* he?" Fraina asked. Hoofbeats clopped beneath her voice. A breeze bore smoky odors of starkwood. They recalled the smell of the Ythrian, as if his forefathers once flew too near their sun.

"A sophont," Mikkal said redundantly. He proceeded: "More bright and tough than most. Maybe more than us. Could be we're stronger, we humans, simply because we outnumber them, and that simply because of having gotten the jump on them in space travel and, hm, needing less room per person to live in."

"A bird?"

"No," Ivar told her. "They're feathered, yes, warm-blooded, two sexes. However, you noticed he doesn't have a beak, and females give live birth. No lactation—no milk, I mean; the lips're for getting the blood out of prey."

"You bespoke an empire, Mikkal," she said, "and, ye-ih, I do remember mentions aforetime. Talk on, will you?"

"Let Rolf do that," the man suggested. "He's schooled. Besides, if he has to keep still much longer, he'll make an awful mess when he explodes."

Ivar's ears burned. True, he thought. But Fraina gave him such eager attention that he plunged happily forward.

"Ythri's planet rather like Aeneas, except for havin' cooler sun," he said. "It's about a hundred light-years from here, roughly in direction of Beta Centauri."

"That's the Angel's Eye," Mikkal interpolated.

Don't tinerans use our constellations? Ivar wondered. *Well, we don't use* Terra's; *our sky is different.* "After humans made contact, Ythrians rapidly acquired modern technology," he went on. "Altogether variant civilization, of course, if you can call it civilization, they never havin' had cities. Noneless, it lent itself to spacefaring same as Technic culture, and in time Ythrians began to trade and colonize, on smaller scale than humans. When League fell apart and Troubles followed, they suffered too. Men restored order at last by establishin' Terran Empire, Ythrians by their Domain. It isn't really an empire, Mikkal. Loose alliance of worlds.

"Still, it grew. So did Empire, Terra's, that is, till they met and clashed. Couple centuries ago, they fought. Ythri lost war and had to give up good deal of border territory. But it'd fought too stiffly for Imperium to think of annexin' entire Domain.

"Since, relations have been . . . variable, let's say. Some affrays, though never another real war; some treaties and joint undertakin's, though often skulduggery on both sides; plenty of trade, individuals and organizations visitin' back and forth. Terra's not happy about how Domain of Ythri is growin' in opposite direction from us, and in strength. But Merseia's kept Imperium too busy to do much in these parts—except stamp out freedom among its own subjects."

"Nothing like that to make a person objective about his government," Mikkal remarked aside.

"I see," Fraina said. "How clearly you explain. . . . Didn't I hear him tell he was, m-m, from Avalon?"

"Yes," Ivar replied. "Planet in Domain, colonized by humans and Ythrians together. Unique society. It'd be reasonable to send Avalonian to spy out Aeneas. He'd have more rapport with us, more insight, than ordinary Ythrians."

Her eyes widened. "He's a spy?"

"Intelligence agent, if you prefer. Not skulkin' around burglarizin' Navy bases or any such nonsense. Gatherin' what bits of information he can, to become part of their picture of Terran Empire. I really can't think what else he'd be. They must've landed him here while space-traffic control was broken down because of independence war. As Mikkal says, eventually he'll leave—I'd guess when Ythrians again have consulate in Nova Roma, that can arrange to smuggle him out."

"You don't care, Rolf?"

"Why should I? In fact—"

Ivar finished the thought in his head. *We got no Ythrian help in our struggle. I'm sure Hugh McCormac tried, and was refused. They wouldn't risk new war. But...if we could get clandestine aid—arms and equipment slipped to us, interstellar transport furnished, communications nets made available—we could build strength of freedom forces till—We failed because we weren't rightly prepared. McCormac raised standard almost on impulse. And he wasn't tryin' to split Empire, he wanted to rule it himself. What would Ythri gain by that? Whereas if our purpose was to break Sector Alpha Cruets loose, make it independent or even bring it under Ythri's easygoin' suzerainty—wouldn't that interest them? Perhaps be worth war, especially if we got Merseian help too*—He looked up at Erannath and dreamed of wings which stormed hitherward in the cause of liberty.

An exclamation drew him back to his body. They had topped a ridge. On the farther slope, mostly buried by a rockslide, were the remnants of great walls and of columns so slim and poised that it was as if they too were flying. Time had not dimmed their nacreous luster.

"Why...Builder relic," Ivar said. "Or do you call them Elders?"

"*La-Sarzen,*" Fraina told him, very low. "The High Ones." Upon her countenance and, yes, Mikkal's, lay awe.

"We're off our usual route," the man breathed. "I'd forgotten that this is where some of them lived."

He and his sister sprang from their saddles, knelt with uplifted arms, and chanted. Afterward they rose, crossed themselves, and spat: in this parched country, a deed of sacrifice. As they rode on, they gave the ruins a wide berth, and hailed them before dropping behind the next rise.

Erannath had not descended to watch. Given his vision, he need not. He cruised through slow circles like a sign in heaven.

After a kilometer, Ivar dared ask: "Is that...back yonder... part of your religion? I wouldn't want to be profane."

Mikkal nodded. "I suppose you could call it sacred. Whatever the High Ones are, they're as near godhood as makes no difference."

That doesn't follow, Ivar thought, keeping silence. *Why is it so nearly universal belief?*

"Some of their spirit must be left in what they made," Fraina said raptly. "We need its help. And, when they come back, they'll know we keep faith in them."

"Will they?" Ivar couldn't help the question.

"Yes," Mikkal said. In him, sober quiet was twice powerful. "Quite likely during our own lifetimes, Rolf. Haven't you heard the tale that's abroad? Far south, where the dead men dwell, a prophet has arisen to prepare the way—"

He shivered in the warmth. "I don't know if that's true, myself," he finished in a matter-of-fact tone. "But we can hope, can't we? C'mon, tingle up these lazy beasts and let's get back to the Train."

�֎ 9 �֎

The mail from Terra was in. Chunderban Desai settled back with a box of cigarettes, a samovar of tea, and resignation to the fact that he would eat lunch and dinner and a midnight snack off his desk. This did not mean he, his staff, or his equipment were inefficient. He would have no need to personally scan two-thirds of what was addressed to his office. But he did bear ultimate responsibility for a globe upon which dwelt 400 million human beings.

Lord Advisor Petroff of the Policy Board was proposing a shake-up of organizational structure throughout the occupied zone, and needed reports and opinions from every commissioner. Lord Advisor Chardon passed on certain complaints from Sector Governor Muratori, about a seeming lack of zeal in the reconstruction of the Virgilian System, and asked for explanations. Naval Intelligence wanted various operations started which would attempt to learn how active Merseian agents were throughout the Alpha Crucis region. BuEc wanted a fresh survey made of mineral resources in the barren planets of each system in the sector, and studies of their exploitability as a method of industrial recovery. BuSci wanted increased support for research on Dido, adding that that should help win over the Aeneans. BuPsy wanted Dido evacuated, fearing that its cloud cover and vast wildernesses made it potentially too useful to guerrillas. The Throne wanted immediate in-depth information on local results should His Majesty make a contemplated tour of the subjugated rebel worlds. . . .

Night filled the wall transparency, and a chill tiny Creusa hurtled above a darkened city, when a thing Desai himself had requested finally crossed the screen. He surged out of sleepiness with a gasp. *I'd better have that selector reprogrammed!* His fingers shook almost too badly for him to insert a fresh cigarette in his holder and inhale it to ignition. He never noticed how tongue, palate, throat, and lungs protested.

"—no planet named, nicknamed, or translated as Jean-Baptiste, assuredly not in any known language or dialect of the Empire, nor in any exterior space for which records are available. Saint John, Hagios Ioannes, and the continent of San Juan on Nuevo México were all named after a co-author of the basic Christian canon, a person distinct from the one who figures as active in events described therein and is termed in Fransai Jean-Baptiste, in Anglic John the Baptist...

"The origin of the individual self-denominated Aycharaych (v. note 3 on transcription of the voice print) has been identified, from measurement upon holographic material supplied (Ref. 2), with a probability deemed high albeit nonquantifiable due to paucity of data.

"When no good correlation was obtained with any species filed with the Imperial Xenological Register, application was made to Naval Intelligence. It was reported by this agency that as a result of a scan of special data banks, Aycharaych can be assumed to be from a planet subject to the Roidhun of Merseia. It was added that he should be considered an agent thereof, presumably dispatched on a mission inimical to the best interests of His Majesty.

"Unfortunately, very little is known about the planet in question. A full account is attached, but will be found scarcely more informative than the summary which follows.

"According to a few casual mentions made in the presence of Imperial personnel and duly reported by them, the planet is referred to as Chereion (v. note 3). It is recorded as having been called variously 'cold, creepy,' 'a mummy dwarf,' and 'a silent ancient,' albeit some favorable notice was taken of art and architecture. These remarks were made in conversation by Merseians (or, in one instance, a non-Merseian of the Roidhunate) by whom the planet had been visited briefly in the course of voyages directed elsewhere. From this it may perhaps be inferred that Chereion is terrestroid verging on subterrestroid, of low mean temperature, sufficiently small and/or old that a substantial loss of atmosphere and hydrosphere has been suffered. In short, it may be considered possibly not too dissimilar to Aeneas as the latter is described in the files. Nothing has been scanned which would make it possible for the sun to be located or spectrally classified. It must be emphasized that Chereion is obscure, seldom touched at, and never heard of by the average Merseian.

"Some indications were noted, which owing to lack of funds have not been pursued further by Intelligence, that Chereion may be more highly regarded than this by the top levels of the Roidhunate hierarchy, and that indeed the dearth of interest in it may have been deliberately instigated rather than straightforwardly caused by primitiveness, poverty, or other more usual factors. If so, presumably its entire populace has, effectively, been induced to cooperate, suggesting that some uniqueness may be found in their psychology.

"The Chereionites are not absolutely confined to their planet. Identification of subject Aycharaych as of this race was made from pictures taken with microcameras upon two different occasions, one a reception at the Terran Embassy on Merseia, one more recently during negotiations in re Jihannath. In either case, a large and mixed group being present, no more than brief queries were made, eliciting replies such as those listed above. But it should be pointed out that if a Chereionite was present at any affair of such importance (and presumably at others for which no data are on hand) then he must have been considered useful to the Roidhunate.

"As an additional fragment, the following last-minute and essentially anecdotal material is here inserted. Naval Intelligence, upon receipt of the request from this office, was moved to instigate inquiries among such of its own personnel as happened to be readily available. In response, this declaration, here paraphrased, was made by one Cmdr. Dominic Flandry:

"He had been on temporary assignment to Talwin, since he was originally concerned in events leading to the joint Terran-Merseian research effort upon that planet (v. note 27) and his special knowledge might conceivably help in gathering militarily useful data. While there, he cultivated the friendship of a young Merseian officer. The intimation is that he introduced the latter to various debaucheries; whatever the method was, he got him talking fairly freely. Having noticed a member of a species new to him in the Merseian group, Flandry asked what manner of sophont this might be. The officer, intoxicated at the time, gave the name of the planet, Chereion, then went on to mumble of a race of incredible antiquity, possessing powers his government keeps secret: a race which seemingly had once nurtured a high civilization, and which said officer suspected might now cherish ambitions wherein his own people are a mere means to an end. Flandry thinks the officer might well have said more; but abruptly the ranking Merseians present ended the occasion and left with all their personnel. Flandry would have pursued the matter further, but never saw his informant or the Chereionite again. He filed this story as part of his report, but Regional Data Processing did not evaluate it as more than a rumor, and thus did not forward it to the central banks.

"The foregoing is presented only in the interest of completeness. Sensationalism is to be discouraged. It is recommended that a maximum feasible effort be instigated for the apprehension of the being Aycharaych, while every due allowance is made for other programs which have rightfully been given a higher priority than the possible presence of a lone foreign operative. Should such effort be rewarded with success, the subject is to be detained while HQNI is notified...."

Desai stared into darkness. *But there is mention of Jean-Baptiste in the files on Llynathawr,* he thought. *Easy enough for an employee in Merseia's pay to insert false data... probably during the chaos of the civil war.... Uldwyr, you green devil, what have you or yours in mind for my planet?*

The Flone Valley is for the most part a gentler land than the edge of Ilion. Rolling on roads toward the great stream, Waybreak had no further need for the discipline of the desert. Exuberance kindled as spent energies returned.

On a mild night, the Train camped in a pasture belonging to a yeoman family with which it had made an agreement generations ago. There was no curfew; wood for a bonfire was plentiful; celebration lasted late. But early on, when Fraina had danced for them, she went to where Ivar sat and murmured, "Want to take a walk? I'll be back soon's I've swapped clothes"—before she skipped off to Jubilee.

His blood roared. It drowned the talk to which he had been listening while he watched a succession of performances. When he could hear again, the words felt dwindled and purposeless, like the hum of a midgeling swarm.

"Yes, I was briefly with two other nomad groups," Erannath was saying, "the Dark Stars north of Nova Roma, near the Julia River, and the Gurdy Men in the Fort Lunacy area. The differences in custom are interesting but, I judge, mere eddies in a single wind."

King Samlo, seated on his chair, the only one put out, tugged his beard. "You ought to visit the Magic Fathers, then, who I was apprenticed to," he said. "And the Glorious make women the heads of their wagons. But they're over in Tiberia, across the Antonine Seabed, so I don't know them myself."

"Perhaps I will go see," Erannath answered, "though I feel certain of finding the same basic pattern."

"Funny," said the yeoman. "You, xeno—no offense meant; I had some damn fine nonhuman shipmates durin' war of independence— you get around more on our planet than I ever have, or these professional travelers here."

He had come with his grown sons to join the fun. Minors and womenfolk stayed behind. Not only was the party sure to become licentious; brawls might explode. Fascinated by Erannath, he joined the king, Padro of Roadlord, the widow Mara of Tramper, and a few more in conversation on the fringes of the circle. They were older folk, their bodies dimmed; the feverish atmosphere touched them less.

What am I doin' here? Ivar wondered. Exultation: *Waitin' for Fraina, that's what.... Earlier, I thought I'd better not get too involved in things. Well, chaos take caution!*

The bonfire flared and rumbled at the center of the wagons. Whenever a stick went *crack,* sparks geysered out of yellow and red flames. The light flew across those who were seated on the ground, snatched eyes, teeth, earrings, bracelets, bits of gaudy cloth out of shadow, cast them back and brought forth instead a dice game, a boy and girl embraced, a playful wrestling match, a boy and girl already stealing off into the farther meadow. Around the blaze, couples had begun a stamping ring-dance, to the music of a lame guitarist, a hunchbacked drummer, and a blind man who sang in plangent Haisun. It smelled of smoke and humanity.

The flicker sheened off Erannath's plumage, turned his eyes to molten gold and his crest to a crown. In its skyey accent his speech did not sound pedantic: "Outsiders often do explore more widely than dwellers, Yeoman Vasiliev, and see more, too. People tend to take themselves for granted."

"I dunno," Samlo argued. "To you, don't the big differences shadow out the little ones that matter to us? You have wings, we don't; we have proper legs, you don't. Doesn't that make us seem pretty much alike to you? How can you say the Trains are all the same?"

"I did not say that, King," Erannath replied. "I said I have observed deep-going common factors. Perhaps you are blinkered by what you call the little differences that matter. Perhaps they matter more to you than they should."

Ivar laughed and tossed in: "Question is, whether we can't see forest for trees, or can't see trees for forest."

Then Fraina was back, and he sprang up. She had changed to a shimmerlyn gown, ragged from years but cut so as to be hardly less revealing than her dancer's costume. Upon her shoulder, alongside a blue-black cataract of hair, sat the luck of Jubilee, muffled in its mantle apart from the imp head.

"Coming?" she chirruped.

"N-n-n-need you ask?" Ivar gave the king a nord-style bow. "Will you excuse me, sir?"

Samlo nodded. A saturnine smile crossed his mouth.

As he straightened, Ivar grew aware of the intentness of Erannath. One did not have to be Ythrian to read hatred in erected quills and hunched stance. His gaze followed that of the golden orbs, and met the red triplet of the luck's. The animal crouched, bristled, and chittered.

"What's wrong, sweet?" Fraina reached to soothe her pet.

Ivar recalled how Erannath had declined the hospitality of any wagon and spent his whole time outdoors, even the bitterest nights, when he must slowly pump his wings while he slept to keep his metabolism high enough that he wouldn't freeze to death. In sudden realization, the Firstling asked him, "Don't you like lucks?"

"No," said the Ythrian.

After a moment: "I have encountered them elsewhere. In Planha we call them *liayalre*. Slinkers."

Fraina pouted. "Oh, foof! I took poor Tais along for a gulp of fresh air. C'mon, Rolf."

She tucked her arm beneath Ivar's. He forgot that he had never cared for lucks either.

Erannath stared after him till he was gone from sight.

Beyond the ring of vehicles, the meadow rolled wide, its dawn trava turf springy and sweet underfoot, silver-gray beneath heaven. Trees stood roundabout, intricacies of pine, massivenesses of hammerbranch, cupolas of delphi. Both moons tinged their boughs white; and of the shadows, those cast by Creusa stirred as the half-disc sped eastward. Stars crowded velvet blackness. The Milky Way was an icefall.

Music faded behind him and her, until they were alone with a tadmouse's trill. He was speechless, content to marvel at the fact that she existed.

She said at last, quietly, looking before her: "Rolf, there's got to be High Ones. This much joy can't just've happened."

"High Ones? Or God? Well—" *Non sequitur, my dear. To us this is beautiful because certain apes were adapted to same kind of weather, long ago on Terra. Though we may feel subtle enchantment in deserts, can we feel it as wholly as Erannath must?... But doesn't that mean that Creator made every kind of beauty? It's bleak, believin' in nothin' except accident.*

"Never mind philosophy," he said. Recklessly: "Waste of time I could spend by your side."

She slipped an arm around his waist. He felt it like fire. *I'm in love,* he knew through the thunders. *Never before like this. Tanya—*

She sighed. "Aye-ah. How much've we left?"

"Forever?"

"No. You can't stay in the Train. It's never happened."

"Why can't it?"

"Because you sitters—wait, Rolf, I'm sorry, you're too good for that word, you're a strider—you people who have rooted homes, you're—not weak—but you haven't got our kind of toughness."

Which centuries of deaths have bred.

"I'm afraid for you," Fraina whispered.

"What? Me?" His pride surged in a wave of anger that he knew, far off at the back of his mind, was foolish. "Hoy, listen, I survived Dreary crossin' as well as next man, didn't I? I'm bigger and stronger than anybody else; maybe not so wiry, not so quick, but by chaos, if we struck dryout, starveout, gritstorm, whatever, I'd stay alive!"

She leaned closer. "And you're smart, too, Rolf, full of book stories—what's more, full of skills we're always short on. Yet you'll have to go. Maybe because you're too much for us. What could we give you, for the rest of your life?"

You, his pulse replied. *And freedom to be myself.... Drop your damned duties, Ivor Frederiksen. You never asked to be born to them. Stop thinkin' how those lights overhead are political points, and let them again be stars.*

"I, I, I don't think I could ever get tired of traveling if you were along," he blurted. "And, uh, well, I can haul my load, maybe give Waybreak somethin' really valuable—"

"Until you got swittled, or knifed. Rolf, darling, you're innocent. You know in your bones that most people are honest and don't get violent without reason. It's not true. Not in the Trains, it isn't. How can you change your skeleton, Rolf?"

"Could you help me?"

"Oh, if I could!" The shifty moonlight caught a glimmer of tears.

Abruptly Fraina tossed her head and stated, "Well, if nothing else, I can shield you from the first and worst, Rolf."

"What do you mean?" By now used to mercurial changes of mood, he chiefly was conscious of her looks, touch, and fragrance. They were still walking. The luck on her shoulder, drawn into its mantle, had virtually seceded from visibility.

"You've a fair clutch of jingle along, haven't you?"

He nodded. Actually the money was in bills, Imperial credits as well as Aenean libras, most of it given him in a wad by Sergeant Astaff before he left Windhome. ("Withdrew my savin's, Firstlin'. No worry. You'll pay me back if you live, and if you don't live, what futterin' difference'll my account make?" How remote and unreal it seemed!) Tinerans had no particular concept of privacy. *(I've learned to accept that, haven't I? Privacy is in my brain. What matter if Dulcy casually goes through my pockets, if she and Mikkal and I casually dress and undress in their wagon, if they casually make love in bunk below mine?)* Thus it was general knowledge that Rolf Mariner was well-heeled. No one stole from a fellow in the Train. The guilt would have been impossible to hide, and meant exile. After pickpocket practice, the spoils were returned. He had declined invitations to gamble, that being considered a lawful way of picking a companion clean.

"We'll soon reach the river," Fraina said. "We'll move along it, from town to town, as far as our territory stretches. Carnival at every stop. Hectic—well, you've been to tineran pitches, you told me. The thing is, those times we're on the grab. It's us against—is 'against' the word?—*zans.* We don't wish harm on the sitters, but we're after everything we can hook. At a time like that, somebody might forget you're not an ordinary sitter. We even fall out with our kind, too often."

Why? passed across Ivar. *Granted this society hasn't same idea as mine of what constitutes property or contract. Still, if anything, shouldn't nomads be more alert than usual when among aliens, more united and coordinated? But no, I remember from Brotherband visits to Windhome, excitement always affected them too, till they'd as likely riot among each other as with Landfolk.*

He lost the question. They had halted near an argent-roofed delphi. Stars gleamed, moons glowed, and she held both his hands.

"Let me keep your moneta for you, Rolf," she offered. "I know how to stash it. Afterward—"

"There will be an afterward!"

"There's got to be," she wept, and came to him.

He let go all holds, save upon her. Soon they went into the moon-dappled grotto of the delphi. The luck stayed outside, waiting.

He who had been Jaan the Shoemaker, until Caruith returned after six million swings of the world around the sun, looked from the snag of a tower across the multitude which filled the marketplace. From around the Sea of Orcus, folk had swarmed hither for Radmas. More were on Mount Cronos this year than ever before in memory or chronicle. They knew the Deliverer was come and would preach unto them.

They made a blue-shadowy dimness beneath the wall whereon he stood: a face, a lancehead, a burnoose, a helmet, picked out of the dusk which still welled between surrounding houses and archways. Virgil had barely risen over the waters, and the Arena blocked off sight of it, so that a phantom mother-of-pearl was only just beginning to awaken in the great ruin. Some stars remained yet in the sky. Breath indrawn felt razor keen. Released, it ghosted. Endless underneath silence went the noise of the falls.

—Go, Caruith said.

Their body lifted both arms. Amplified, their voice spoke forth into the hush.

"People, I bring you stern tidings.

"You await rescue, first from the grip of the tyrant, next and foremost from the grip of mortality—of being merely, emptily human. You wait for transcendence.

"Look up, then, to yonder stars. Remember what they are, not numbers in a catalog, not balls of burning gas, but reality itself, even as you and I are real. We are not eternal, nor are they; but they are closer to eternity than we. The light of the farthest that we can see has crossed an eon to come to us. And the word it bears is that first it shone upon those have gone before.

"They shall return. I, in whom lives the mind of Caruith, pledge this, if we will make our world worthy to receive them.

"Yet that may not be done soon nor easily. The road before us is hard, steep, bestrewn with sharp shards. Blood will mark the footprints we leave, and at our backs will whiten the skulls of those who fell by the way. Like one who spoke upon Mother Terra, long after Caruith but long before Jaan, I bring you not peace but a sword."

✶ 10 ✶

Boseville was typical of the small towns along the Flone between Nova Roma and the Cimmerian Mountains. A cluster of neatly laid out, blocky but gaily colored buildings upon the right bank, it looked across two kilometers' width of brown stream to a ferry terminal, pastures, and timberlots. At its back, canals threaded westward through croplands. Unlike the gaunt but spacious country along the Ilian Shelf, this was narrow enough, and at the same time rich enough, that many of its farmers could dwell in the community. Besides agriculture, Boseville lived off service industries and minor manufacturing. Most of its trade with the outside world went through the Riverfolk. An inscribed monolith in the plaza commemorated its defenders during the Troubles. Nothing since had greatly disturbed it, including rebellion and an occupation force which it never saw.

Or was that true any longer? More and more, Ivar wondered.

He had accompanied Erannath into town while the tinerans readied their pitches. The chance of his being recognized was negligible, unless the Terrans had issued bulletins on him. He was sure they had not. To judge by what broadcasts he'd seen when King Samlo ordered the Train's single receiver brought forth and tuned in—a fair sample, even though the nomads were not much given to passive watching—the Wildfoss affair had been soft-pedaled almost to the point of suppression. Evidently

Commissioner Desai didn't wish to inspire imitations, nor make a hero figure out of the Firstling of Ilion.

Anyhow, whoever might identify him was most unlikely to call the nearest garrison.

Erannath wanted to explore this aspect of nord culture. It would be useful having a member of it for companion, albeit one from a different area. Since he was of scant help in preparing the shows, Ivar offered to come along. The Ythrian seemed worth cultivation, an interesting and, in his taciturn fashion, likable sort. Besides, Ivar discovered with surprise that, after the frenetic caravan, he was a bit homesick for his own people.

Or so he thought. Then, when he walked on pavement between walls, he began to feel stifled. How seldom these folk really laughed aloud! How drably they dressed! And where were the male swagger, the female ardor? He wondered how these sitters had gotten any wish to beget the children he saw. Why, they needed to pour their merriment out of a tankard.

Not that the beer wasn't good. He gulped it down. Erannath sipped.

They sat in a waterfront tavern, wood-paneled, rough-raftered, dark and smoky. Windows opened on a view of the dock. A ship, which had unloaded cargo here and taken on consignments for farther downstream, was girding to depart.

"Don't yonder crew want to stay for our carnival?" Ivar asked.

A burly, bearded man, among the several whom Erannath's exotic presence had attracted to this table, puffed his pipe before answering slowly: "No, I don't recall as how Riverfolk ever go to those things. Seems like they, m-m-m, shun tinerans. Maybe not bad idea."

"Why?" Ivar challenged. *Are they nonhuman, not to care for Fraina's dancin' or Mikkal's blade arts or—*

"Always trouble. I notice, son, you said, 'Our carnival.' Have care. It brings grief, tryin' to be what you're not born to be."

"I'll guide my private life, if you please."

The villager shrugged. "Sorry."

"If the nomads are a disturbing force," Erannath inquired, "why do you allow them in your territory?"

"They've always been passin' through," said the oldest man present. "Tradition gives rights. Includin' right to pick up part of their livin'—by entertainments, cheap merchandise, odd jobs, and, yes, teachin' prudence by fleecin' the foolish."

"Besides," added a young fellow, "they do bring color, excitement, touch of danger now and then. We might not live this quietly if Waybreak didn't overnight twice in year."

The jaws of the bearded man clamped hard on his pipestem before he growled, "We're soon apt to get oversupplied with danger, Jim."

Ivar stiffened. A tingle went through him. "What do you mean ... may I ask?"

A folk saying answered him: "Either much or little."

But another customer, a trifle drunk, spoke forth. "Rumors only. And yet, something astir up and down river, talk of one far south who's promised Elders will return and deliver us from Empire. Could be wishful thinkin', of course. But damn, it feels right somehow. Aeneas is special. I never paid lot of attention to Dido before; however, lately I've begun givin' more and more thought to everything our filosofs have learned there. I've gone out under Mornin' Star and tried to think myself toward Oneness, and you know, it's helped me. Should we let Impies crush us back into subjects, when we may be right at next stage of evolution?"

The bearded man frowned. "That's heathenish talk, Bob. Me, I'll hold my trust in God." To Ivar: "God's will be done. I never thought Empire was too bad, nor do I now. But it has gone morally rotten, and maybe we are God's chosen instruments to give it cleansin' shock." After a pause: "It's true, we'll need powerful outside help. Maybe He's preparin' that for us too." All their looks bent on Erannath. "I'm plain valley dweller and don't know anything," the speaker finished, "except that unrest is waxin', and hope of deliverance."

Hastily, the oldster changed the subject.

Night had toppled upon them when Firstling and Ythrian returned to camp. After they left town, stars gave winter-keen guidance to their feet. Otherwise the air was soft, moist, full of growth odors. Gravel scrunched beneath the tread of those bound the same way. Voices tended to break off when a talker noticed the nonhuman, but manners did not allow butting into a serious conversation. Ahead, lamps on poles glowed above wagons widespread among tents. The skirl of music loudened.

"What I seek to understand," Erannath said, "is this Aenean resentment of the Imperium. My race would resist such overlordship bitterly. But in human terms, it has on the whole been light, little more than a minor addition to taxes and the surrender of sovereignty over outside, not domestic, affairs. In exchange, you get protection, trade, abundant offplanet contacts. Correct?"

"Perhaps once," Ivar answered. The beer buzzed in his head. "But then they set that Snelund creature over us. And since, too many of us are dead in war, while Impies tell us to change ways of our forefathers."

"Was the late governorship really that oppressive, at least where Aeneas was concerned? Besides, can you not interpret the situation as that the Imperium made a mistake, which is being corrected? True, it cost lives and treasure to force the correction. But you people showed such deathpride that the authorities are shy of pushing you very hard. Simple cooperativeness would enable you to keep virtually all your institutions, or have them restored."

"How do you know?"

Erannath ignored the question. "I could comprehend anger at the start of the occupation," he said, "if afterward it damped out when the Imperial viceroy proved himself mild. Instead . . . my impression is that at first you Aeneans accepted your defeat with a measure of resignation—but since, your rebellious emotions have swelled; and lacking hopes of independence in reality, you project them into fantasy. *Why?*"

"I reckon we were stunned, and're startin' to recover. And could be those hopes aren't altogether wild." Ivar stared at the being who trotted along beside him so clumsily, almost painfully. Erannath's crest bobbed to the crutchlike swing of his wings; shadows along the ground dimmed luster of eyes and feathers. "What're you doin', anyway, tellin' me I should become meek Imperial subject? You're Ythrian—from free race of hunters, they claim—from rival power we once robbed of plenty real estate—What're you tryin' to preach at me?"

"Nothing. As I have explained before, I am a xenologist specializing in anthropology, here to gather data on your species. I travel unofficially, *hyai,* illegally, to avoid restrictions. More than this it would be unwise to say, even as you have not seen fit to detail your own circumstances. I ask questions in order to get responses which may help me map Aenean attitudes. Enough."

When an Ythrian finished on that word, he was terminating a discussion. Ivar thought: *Well, why shouldn't he pretend he's harmless? It'll help his case, get him merely deported, if Impies happen to catch him.... Yes, probably he is spyin', no more. But if I can convince him, make him tell them at home, how we really would fight year after year for our freedom, if they'd give us some aid—maybe they would!*

The blaze of it in him blent into the larger brilliance of being nearly back in camp, nearly back to Fraina.

And then—

They entered a crowd milling between faded rainbows of tent-cloth. Lamps overhead glared out the stars. Above the center pitch, a cylinder of colored panes rotated around the brightest light: red, yellow, green, blue, purple flickered feverish across the bodies and faces below. A hawker chanted of his wares, a barker of games of chance, a cook of the spiceballs whose frying filled every nostril around him. Upon a platform three girls danced, and though their performance was free and small-town nords were supposed to be close with a libra, coins glittered in arcs toward their leaping feet. Beneath, the blind and crippled musicians sawed out a melody which had begun to make visitors jig. No alcohol or other drugs were in sight; yet sober riverside men mingled with tinerans in noisy camaraderie, marveled like children at a strolling magician or juggler, whooped, waved, and jostled. Perched here and there upon wagons, the lucks of Waybreak watched.

It surged in Ivar: *My folk! My joy!*

And Fraina came by, scarcely clad, nestled against a middle-aged local whose own garb bespoke wealth. He looked dazed with desire.

Ivar stopped. Beside him, abruptly, Erannath stood on hands to free his wings.

"What goes?" Ivar cried through the racket. Like a blow to the belly, he knew. More often than not, whenever they could, nomad women did this thing.

But not Fraina! We're in love!

She rippled as she walked. Light sheened off blue-black hair, red skin, tilted wide eyes, teeth between half-parted lips. A musk of femaleness surfed outward from her.

"Let go my girl!" Ivar screamed.

He knocked a man over in his plunge. Others voiced anger as he thrust by. His knife came forth. Driven by strength and skill, that heavy blade could take off a human hand at the wrist, or go through a rib to the heart.

The villager saw. A large person, used to command, he held firm. Though unarmed, he crouched in a stance remembered from his military training days.

"Get away, clinkerbrain," Fraina ordered Ivar.

"No, you slut!" He struck her aside. She recovered too fast to fall. Whirling, he knew in bare time that he really shouldn't kill this yokel, that she'd enticed him and—Ivar's empty hand made a fist. He smote at the mouth. The riverdweller blocked the blow, a shock of flesh and bone, and bawled:

"Help! Peacemen!" That was the alarm word. Small towns kept no regular police; but volunteers drilled and patrolled together, and heeded each other's summons.

Fraina's fingernails raked blood from Ivar's cheek. "You starting a riot?" she shrilled. A Haisun call followed.

Rivermen tried to push close. Men of the Train tried to deflect them, disperse them. Oaths and shouts lifted. Scuffles broke loose.

Mikkal of Redtop slithered through the mob, bounded toward the fight. His belt was full of daggers. "*Il-krozny ya?*" he barked.

Fraina pointed at Ivar, who was backing her escort against a wagon. "*Vakhabo!*" And in loud Anglic: "Kill me that dog! He hit me—your sister!"

Mikkal's arm moved. A blade glittered past Ivar's ear, to thunk into a panel and shiver. "Stop where you're at," the tineran said. "Drop your slash. Or you're dead."

Ivar turned from an enemy who no longer mattered. Grief ripped through him. "But you're my friend," he pleaded.

The villager struck him on the neck, kicked him when he had tumbled. Fraina warbled glee, leaped to take the fellow's elbow, crooned of his prowess. Mikkal tossed knife after knife aloft, made a wheel of them, belled when he had the crowd's attention: "Peace! Peace! We don't want this stranger. We cast him out. You care to jail him? Fine, go ahead. Let's the rest of us get on with our fun."

Ivar sat up. He barely noticed the aches where he had been hit. Fraina, Waybreak were lost to him. He could no more understand why than he could have understood it if he had suddenly had a heart attack.

But a wanderer's aliveness remained. He saw booted legs close in, and knew the watch was about to haul him off. It jagged across his awareness that then the Imperials might well see a report on him.

His weapon lay on the ground. He snatched it and sprang erect. A war-whoop tore his throat. "Out of my way!" he yelled after, and started into the ring of men. If need be, he'd cut a road through.

Wings cannonaded, made gusts of air, eclipsed the lamps. Erannath was aloft.

Six meters of span roofed the throng in quills and racket. What light came through shone burnished on those feathers, those talons. Unarmed though he was, humans ducked away from scything claws, lurched from buffeting wingbones. "Hither!" Erannath whistled. "To me, Rolf Mariner! *Raiharo!*"

Ivar sprang through the lane opened for him, out past tents and demon-covered wagons, into night. The aquiline shape glided low above, black athwart the Milky Way. "Head south," hissed in darkness. "Keep near the riverbank." The Ythrian swung by, returned for a second pass. "I will fly elsewhere, in their view, draw off pursuit, soon shake it and join you." On the third swoop: "Later I will go to the ship which has left, and arrange passage for us. Fair winds follow you." He banked and was gone.

Ivar's body settled into a lope over the fields. The rest of him knew only: *Fraina. Waybreak. Forever gone? Then what's to live for?*

Nevertheless he fled.

✵ 11 ✵

After a boat, guided by Erannath, brought him aboard the *Jade Gate*, Ivar fell into a bunk and a twisting, nightmare-haunted sleep. He was almost glad when a gong-crash roused him a few hours later.

He was alone in a cabin meant for four, cramped but pleasant. Hardwood deck, white-painted overhead, bulkheads lacquered in red and black, were surgically clean. Light came dimly through a brass-framed window to pick out a dresser and washbowl. Foot-thuds and voices made a cheerful clamor beneath the toning of the bronze. He didn't know that rapid, musical language.

I suppose I ought to go see whatever this is, he thought, somewhere in the sorrow of what he had lost. It took his entire will to put clothes on and step out the door.

Crewfolk were bouncing everywhere around. A young man

noticed him, beamed, and said, "Ahoa to you, welcome passenger," in the singsong River dialect of Anglic.

"What's happenin'?" Ivar asked mechanically.

"We say good morning to the sun. Watch, but please to stand quiet where you are."

He obeyed. The pre-dawn chill lashed some alertness into him and he observed his surroundings with a faint growth of interest.

Heaven was still full of stars, but eastward turning wan. The shores, a kilometer from either side of the vessel, were low blue shadows, while the water gleamed as if burnished, except where mist went eddying. High overhead, the wings of a vulch at hover caught the first daylight. As gong and crew fell silent, an utter hush returned, not really broken by the faint pulse of engines.

The craft was more than 50 meters in length and 20 in the beam, her timber sides high even at the waist, then at the blunt bow raising sharply in two tiers, three at the rounded stern. Two sizable deckhouses bracketed the amidships section, their roofs fancifully curved at the eaves and carved at the ends. Fore and aft of them, kingposts supported cargo booms, as well as windmills to help charge the capacitors which powered the vessel. Between reared a mast which could be set with three square sails. Ivar glimpsed Erannath on the topmost yard. He must have spent the night there, for lack of the frame which would suit him better than a bunk.

An outsize red-and-gold flag drooped from an after staff. At the prow the gigantic image of a Fortune Guardian scowled at dangers ahead. In his left hand he bore a sword against them, in his right a lotus flower.

There posed an old man in robe and tasseled cap, beside him a woman similarly clad though bareheaded, near them a band who wielded gong, flutes, pipas, and drum. The crew, on their knees save for what small children were held by their mothers, occupied the decks beneath.

As light strengthened, the stillness seemed to deepen yet further, and frost on brightwork glittered like the stars.

Then Virgil stood out of the east. Radiance shivered across waters. The ancient raised his arms and cried a brief chant, the people responded, music rollicked, everybody cheered, the ship's business resumed.

Ivar stretched numbed hands toward the warmth that began to flow out of indigo air. Vapors steamed away and he saw the cultivated lands roll green, a flock of beasts, an early horseman or a roadborne vehicle, turned into toys by distance. Closer were the brood of *Jade Gate*. A stubby tug drew a freight-laden barge, two trawlers spread their nets, and in several kayaks, each accompanied by an osel, herders kept a pod of river pigs moving along.

For those not on watch, the first order of the day was evidently to get cleaned up. Some went below, some peeled off their clothes and dived overboard, to frisk about till they were ready to climb back on a Jacob's ladder. Merriment loudened. It was not like tineran glee. Such japes as he heard in Anglic were gentle rather than stinging, laughter was more a deep clucking than a shrill peal. Whoever passed near Ivar stopped to make a slight bow and bid him welcome aboard.

They're civilized without bein' rigid, strong without bein' cruel, happy without bein' foolish, shrewd without bein' crooked, respectful of learnin' and law, useful in their work, he knew dully; *but they are not wild red wanderers.*

Handsome enough, of course. They averaged a bit taller than tinerans, shorter than nords, the build stocky, skin tawny, hair deep black where age had not bleached it. Heads were round, faces broad and high of cheekbones, eyes brown and slightly oblique, lips full, noses tending to flatness though beaks did occur. Only old men let beards grow, and both sexes banged their hair across the brows and bobbed it off just under the ears. Alike too was working garb, blue tunics and bell-bottomed trousers. Already now, before the frost was off, many went barefoot; and the nudity of the swimmers showed a fondness for elaborate tattoos.

He knew more about them than he had about the nomads. It was still not much. This was his first time aboard a craft of theirs, aside from once when one which plied as far north as Nova Roma held open house. Otherwise his experience was confined to casual reading and a documentary program recorded almost a century ago.

Nevertheless the Kuang Shih had bonds to the ruling culture of Aeneas, in a way that the tinerans did not. They furnished the principal transportation for goods, and for humans who weren't in a hurry, along the entire lower Flone—as well as fish, flesh, and fiber taken from the river, and incidental handicrafts, exchanged for the products and energy recharges of industrial culture.

If they held themselves aloof when ashore, it was not due to hostility. They were amply courteous in business dealings, downright cordial to passengers. It was simply that their way of life satisfied them, and had little in common with that of rooted people. The most conservative Landfolk maintained less far-reaching and deep-going blood ties—every ship and its attendants an extended family, strictly exogamous and, without making a fuss about it, moral—not to speak of faith, tradition, law, custom, arts, skills, hopes, fears altogether different.

I dreamed Waybreak might take me in, and instead it cast me out. Jade Gate—is that her name?—will no doubt treat me kindly till we part, but I'd never imagine bein' taken into her.

No matter. O Fraina!

"Sir—"

The girl who shyly addressed him brought back the dancer, hurtfully, by her very unlikeness. Besides her race, she was younger, he guessed eight or nine, demurely garbed so that he couldn't be sure how much her slight figure had begun to fill out. (Not that he cared.) Her features were more delicate than usual, and she bowed lower to him.

"Your pardon, please, welcome passenger," she said in a thin voice. "Do you care for breakfast?"

She offered him a bowl of cereals, greens, and bits of meat cooked together, a cup of tea, a napkin, and eating utensils such as he was used to. He grew aware that crewfolk were in line at the galley entrance. A signal must have called them without his noticing through the darkness that muffled him. Most found places on deck to hunker and eat in convivial groups.

"Why, why, thank you," Ivar said. He wasn't hungry, but supposed he could get the food down. It smelled spicy.

"We have one dining saloon below, with table and benches, if you wish," the girl told him.

"No!" The idea of being needlessly enclosed, after desert heavens and then nights outdoors in valley summer with Fraina, sickened him.

"Pardon, pardon." She drew back a step. He realized he had yelled.

"I'm sorry," he said. "I'm in bad way. Didn't mean to sound angry. Right here will be fine." She smiled and set her burden down on the planks, near a bulwark against which he could rest. "Uh, my name is Iv—Rolf Mariner."

"This person is Jao, fourth daughter to Captain Riho Mea. She bade me to see to your comfort. Can I help you in any wise, Sir Mariner?" The child dipped her head above bridged fingertips.

"I ... well, I don't know." *Who can help me, ever again?*

"Perhaps if I stay near you one while, show you over our ship later? You may think of something then."

Her cleanliness reminded him of his grime and sour sweat-smell, unkempt hair and stubbly chin. "I, uh, I should have washed before breakfast."

"Eat, and I will lead you to the bath, and bring what else you need to your cabin. You are our only guest this trip," Her glance swept aloft and came aglow. "Ai, the beautiful flyer from the stars. How could I forget? Can you summon him while I fetch his food?"

"He eats only meat, you know. Or, no, I reckon you wouldn't. Anyhow, I'll bet he's already caught piece of wild game. He sees us, and he'll come down when he wants to."

"If you say it, sir. May I bring my bowl, or would you rather be undisturbed?"

"Whatever you want," Ivar grunted. "I'm afraid I'm poor company this mornin'."

"Perhaps you should sleep further? My mother the captain will not press you. But she said that sometime this day she must see you and your friend, alone."

Passengers had quarters to themselves if and when a vessel was operating below capacity in that regard. Crew did not. Children were raised communally from birth ... physically speaking. The ties between them and their parents were strong, far stronger than among tinerans, although their ultimate family was the ship as a whole. Married couples were assigned cubicles, sufficient for sleeping and a few personal possessions. Certain soundproofed cabins were available for study, meditation, or similar purposes. Aside from this, privacy of the body did not exist, save for chaplain and captain.

The latter had two chambers near the bridge. The larger was living room, dining room, office, and whatever else she deemed necessary.

Her husband greeted her visitors at the door, then politely excused himself. He was her third, Jao had remarked to Ivar. Born on the *Celestial Peace,* when quite a young girl Mea had been wedded by the usual prearrangement to a man of the *Red Bird Banner*. He drowned when a skiff capsized; the Flone had many treacheries. She used her inheritance in shrewd trading, garnering wealth until the second officer of the *Jade Gate* met her at a fleet festival and persuaded her to move in with him. He was a widower, considerably older than she; it was a marriage of convenience. But most were, among the Kuang Shih. Theirs functioned well for a number of years, efficiently combining their talents and credit accounts, incidentally producing Jao's youngest sister. At last an artery in his brain betrayed him and rather than linger useless he requested the Gentle Cup. Soon afterward, the captain died also, and the officers elected Riho Mea his successor. Lately she had invited Haleku Uan of the *Yellow Dragon* to marry her. He was about Ivar's age.

Jao must have read distaste on the Firstling's countenance, for she had said quietly: "They are happy together. He is merely one carpenter, nor can she raise him higher, nor can he inherit from her except in *lung*—pro-por-tion to children of hers that are his too; and she is past childbearing and he knew it."

He thought at the time that she was defending her mother, or even her stepfather. As days passed, he came to believe she had spoken unspectacular truth. The Riverfolk had their own concept of individuality.

To start with, what did riches mean? Those who were not content to draw their regular wage, but drove personal bargains with the Ti Shih, the Shorefolk, could obtain no more than minor luxuries for themselves; a ship had room for nothing else. Beyond that, they could simply make contributions to the floating community. That won rewards of prestige. But anybody could get the same by outstanding service or, to a lesser extent, unusual prowess or talent.

Prestige might bring promotion. However, authority gave small chance for self-aggrandizement either, in a society which followed the same peaceful round through century after century.

Why, then, did the people of the land think of Riverfolk as hustlers, honest but clever, courteous but ambitious? Ivar decided that these were the personality types who dealt with the people of the land. The rest kept pretty much to themselves. And yet, that latter majority had abundant ways to express itself.

These ideas came to him later. They did have their genesis the evening he first entered the cabin of Captain Riho.

Sunbeams struck level, amber-hued, through the starboard windows of the main room. They sheened off a crystal on a shelf, glowed off a scroll of trees and calligraphy above. The chamber was so austerely furnished as to feel spacious. In one corner, half-hidden by a carved screen, stood a desk and a minimum of data and communications equipment. In another stood a well-filled bookcase. Near the middle of the reed matting which covered the deck was a padded, ring-shaped bench, with a low table at the center and a couple of detachable back rests for the benefit of visiting Ti Shih.

The skipper came forward, and Ivar began changing his mind about her and her man. She was of medium height, plump yet extraordinarily light on her feet. Years had scarcely touched the snubnosed, dark-ivory face, apart from crinkles around the eyes and scattered white in the hair. Her mouth showed capacity for a huge grin. She worn the common blue tunic and trousers, zori on bare feet, fireburst tattoo on the arm which slid from its sleeve as she offered her hand. The palm was warm and callused.

"Ahoa, welcome passengers." Her voice verged on hoarseness. "Will you not honor me by taking seats and refreshment?" She bowed them toward the bench, and from the inner room fetched a trayful of tea, cakes, and slices of raw ichthyoid flesh. The ship lurched in a crosscurrent off a newly formed sandbar, and she came near dropping her load. She rapped out a phrase. Catching Erannath's alert look, she translated it for him. Ivar was a little shocked. He had thought soldiers knew how to curse.

She kicked off her sandals, placed herself crosslegged opposite her guests, and opened a box of cigars that stood on the table. "You want?" she offered. They both declined. "Mind if I do?" Ivar didn't—*What has creation got that's worth mindin'?*—and Erannath stayed mute though a ripple passed over his plumes. Captain Riho stuck a fat black cylinder between her teeth and got it ignited. Smoke smote the air.

"I hope you are comfortable?" she said. "Sir . . . Erannath . . . if you will give my husband the specs for your kind of bed—"

"Later, thank you," the flyer snapped. "Shall we get to the point?"

"Fine. Always I was taught, Ythrians do not waste words. Here is my first pleasure to meet your breed. If you will please to pardon seeming rudeness—you *are* aboard curious-wise. I would not pry but must know certain things, like where you are bound."

"We are not sure. How far do you go?"

"Clear to the Linn, this trip. Solstice comes near, our Season of Returnings."

"Fortunate for us, if I happen to have cash enough on my person to buy that long a passage for two." Erannath touched his pocketed apron.

I have none, Ivar thought. *Fraina swittled me out of everything, surely knowin' I'd have to leave Train. Only, did she have to provoke my leavin' so soon?* He paid no attention to the dickering.

"—well," Erannath finished. "We can come along to the end of the river if we choose. We may debark earlier."

Riho Mea frowned behind an acrid blue veil. "Why might that be?" she demanded. "You understand, sirs, I have one ship to worry about, and these are much too interesting times."

"Did I not explain fully enough, last night when I arrived on board? I am a scientist studying your planet. I happened to join a nomad group shortly after Rolf Mariner did—for reasons about which he has the right not to get specific. As often before, violence lofted at the carnival. It would have led either to his death at nomad hands, or his arrest by the Bosevilleans. I helped him escape."

"Yes, those were almost your exact words."

"I intended no offense in repeating them, Captain. Do humans not prefer verbal redundancy?"

"You miss my course, Sir Erannath," she said a touch coldly. "You have *not* explained enough. We could take you on in emergency, for maybe that did save lives. However, today is not one such hurry. Please to take refreshment, you both, as I will, to show good faith. I accuse you of nothing, but you are intelligent and realize I must be sure we are not harboring criminals. Matters are very skittly, what with the occupation."

She laid her cigar in an ashtray, crunched a cookie, slurped a mouthful of tea. Ivar bestirred himself to follow suit. Erannath laid claws on a strip of meat and ripped it with his fangs. "Good," said the woman. "Will you tell your tale, Sir Mariner?"

Ivar had spent most of the day alone, stretched on his bunk. He didn't care what became of him, and his mind wasn't working especially well. But from a sense of duty, or whatever, he had rehearsed his story like a dog mumbling a bone. It plodded forth:

"I'm not guilty of anything except disgust, Captain, and I don't think that's punishable, unless Impies have made it illegal since I left.

You may know, besides banning free speech, they razed McCormac Memorial in Nova Roma. My parents ... well, they don't condone Imperium, but they kept talkin' about compromise and how maybe we Aeneans were partly in wrong, till I couldn't stand it. I went off into wilderness to be by myself—common practice ashore, you probably know—and met tineran Train there. Why not join them for while? It'd be change for me, and I had skills they could use. Last night, as my friend told, senseless brawl happened. I think, now, it was helped along by tinerans I'd thought were my ... friends ... so they could keep money and valuable rif—article I'd left with them."

"As a matter of fact," Erannath said, "he is technically guilty of assault upon a Boseville man. He did no harm, though. He merely suffered it. I doubt that any complaint has been filed. These incidents are frequent at those affairs, and everyone knows it." He paused. "They do not know why this is. I do."

Startled from his apathy, Ivar regarded the Ythrian almost as sharply as Riho Mea did. He met their gazes in turn—theirs were the eyes which dropped—and let time go by before he said with no particular inflection: "Perhaps I should keep my discovery for the Intelligence service of the Domain. However, it is of marginal use to us, whereas Aeneans will find it a claw struck into their backs."

The captain chewed her cigar before she answered: "You mean you will tell me if I let you stay aboard." Erannath didn't bother to speak his response. "How do I know—" She caught herself. "Please to pardon this person. I wonder what evidence you have for whatever you will say."

"None," he admitted. "Once given the clue, you humans can confirm the statement."

"Say on."

"If I do, you will convey us, and ask no further questions?"

"I will judge you by your story."

Erannath studied her. At length he said: "Very well, for I hear your deathpride." He was still during a heartbeat. "The breath of tineran life is that creature they call the luck, keeping at least one in every wagon. We call it the slinker."

"Hoy," broke from Ivar, "how would you know—?"

"Ythrians have found the three-eyed beasts on a number of planets." Erannath did not keep the wish to kill out of his voice; and his feathers began to stand erect. "Not on our home. God did not lay that particular snare for us. But on several worlds like it, which naturally we investigated more thoroughly than your race normally does—the lesser terrestroid globes. Always slinkers are associated with fragments of an earlier civilization, such as Aeneas has. We suspect they were spread by that civilization, whether deliberately, accidentally, or through their own design. Some of us theorize that they caused its downfall."

"Wait a minute," Ivar protested. "Why have we humans never heard of them?"

"You have, on this world," Erannath replied. "Probably else-where too, but quite incidentally, notes buried in your data banks, because you are more interested in larger and moister planets. And for our part, we have had no special reason to tell you. We learned what slinkers are early in our starfaring, when first we had scant contact with Terrans, afterward hostile contact. We developed means to eradicate them. They long ago ceased to be a problem in the Domain, and no doubt few Ythrians, even, have heard of them nowadays."

Too much information, too big a universe, passed through Ivar.

"Besides," Erannath went on, "it seems humans are more sus-ceptible than Ythrians. Our two brain-types are rather differently organized, and the slinkers' resonate better with yours."

"Resonate?" Captain Riho scowled.

"The slinker nervous system is an extraordinarily well-developed telepathic transceiver," Erannath said. "Not of thoughts. We really don't know what level of reasoning ability the little abominations possess. Nor do we care, in the way that human scientists might. When we had established what they do, our overwhelming desire was merely to slay them."

"What do they do, then?" Ivar asked around a lump of nausea.

"They violate the innermost self. In effect, they receive emotions and feed these back; they act as amplifiers." It was terrifying to see Erannath where he crouched. His dry phrases ripped forth. "Perhaps those intelligences you call the Builders developed them as pets, pleasure sources. The Builders may have had cooler spirits than you or we do. Or perhaps they degenerated from the effects, and died.

"I said that the resonance with us Ythrians is weak. Nonethe-less we found explorers and colonists showing ugly behavior. It would start as bad dreams, go on to murderously short temper, to year-around ovulation, to—Enough. We tracked down the cause and destroyed it.

"You humans are more vulnerable, it appears. You are lucky that slinkers prefer the deserts. Otherwise all Aeneans might be addicted.

"Yes, addiction. They don't realize it themselves, they think they keep these pets merely because of custom, but the tinerans are a nation of addicts. Every emotion they begin to feel is fed back into them, amplified, radiated, reamplified, to the limit of what the organism can generate. Do you marvel that they act like constitutional psychopaths? That they touch no drugs in their caravans, but require drugs when away, and cannot survive being away very long?

"At that, they must have adapted; there must have been natural selection. Many can think craftily, like the female who reaved your holdings, Rolf Mariner. I wonder if her kind are not born dependent on the poison.

"You should thank her, though, that she got you cast out as early as she did!"

Ivar covered his face. "O God, no."

"I need clean sky and a beast to hunt," Erannath grated. "I will be back tomorrow."

He left. Ivar wept on Riho Mea's breast. She held him close, stroked his hair and murmured.

"You'll get well, poor dear, we'll make you well. The river flows, flows, flows.... Here is peace."

Finally she left him on her husband's bunk, exhausted of tears and ready to sleep. The light through the windows was gold-red. She changed into her robe and went onto the foredeck, to join chaplain and crew in wishing the sun goodnight.

☼ 12 ☼

South of Cold Landing the country began to grow steep and stony, and the peaks of the Cimmerian range hung ghostlike on its horizon. There the river would flow too swiftly for the herds. But first it broadened to fill a valley with what was practically a lake: the Green Bowl, where ships bound farther south left their animals in care of a few crewfolk, to fatten on water plants and molluscoids.

Approaching that place, Ivar paddled his kayak with an awkwardness which drew amiable laughter from his young companions. They darted spearfly-fast over the surface; or, leaping into the stream, they raced the long-bodied webfooted brown osels which served them for herd dogs, while he wallowed more clumsily than the fat, flippered, snouted chuho—water pigs—which were being herded.

He didn't mind. Nobody is good at everything, and he was improving at a respectable pace.

Wavelets blinked beneath violet heaven, chuckled, swirled, joined livingly with his muscles to drive the kayak onward. This was the reality which held him, not stiff crags and dusty-green brush on yonder hills. A coolness rose from it, to temper wind-less warmth of air. It smelled damp, rich. Ahead, *Jade Gate* was a gaudily painted castle; farther on moved a sister vessel; trawl-ers and barges already waited at Cold Landing. Closer at hand, the chuho browsed on wetcress. Now and then an osel heeded the command of a boy or girl and sped to turn back a straggler. Herding on the Flone was an ideal task, he thought. Exertion and alertness kept a person fully alive, while nevertheless letting him enter into that peace, beauty, majesty which was the river.

To be sure, he was a mere spectator, invited along because these youngsters liked him. That was all right.

Jao maneuvered her kayak near his. "Goes it well?" she asked. "You do fine, Rolf." She flushed, dropped her glance, and added timidly: "I think not I could do that fine in your wilderness. But sometime I would wish to try."

"Sometime... I'd like to take you," he answered.

On this duty in summer, one customarily went nude, so as to be ready at any time for a swim. Ivar was too fair-skinned for that, and wore a light blouse and trousers Erannath had had made for him. He turned his own eyes elsewhere. The girl was far too young for the thoughts she was old enough to arouse—besides being foreign to him—no, never mind that, what mattered was that she was sweet and trusting and—

Oh, damnation, I will not be ashamed of thinkin' she's female. Thinkin' is all it'll ever amount to. And that I do, that I can, mea-sures how far I've gone toward gainin' back my sanity.

The gaiety and the ceremoniousnesses aboard ship; the little towns where they stopped to load and unload, and the long green reaches between; the harsh wisdom of Erannath, serene wisdom of Iang Weii the chaplain, pragmatic wisdom of Riho Mea the captain, counseling him; the friendliness of her husband and other people his age; the, yes, the way this particular daughter of hers followed him everywhere around; always the river, mighty as time, days and nights, days and nights, feeling like a longer stretch than they had been, like a foretaste of eternity: these had healed him.

Fraina danced no more through his dreams. He could summon a memory for inspection, and understand how the reality had never come near being as gorgeous as it seemed, and pity the wanderers and vow to bring them aid when he became able.

When would that be? How? He was an outlaw. As he emerged from his hurt, he saw ever more clearly how passive he had been. Erannath had rescued him and provided him with this berth—why? What reason, other than pleasure, had he to go to the river's end? And if he did, what next?

He drew breath. *Time to start actin' again, instead of bein' acted on. First thing I need is allies.*

Jao's cry brought him back. She pointed to the nigh shore. Her paddle flew. He toiled after. Their companions saw, left one in charge of the herd, and converged on the same spot.

A floating object lay caught in reeds: a sealed wooden box, arch-lidded, about two meters in length. Upon its black enamel he identified golden symbols of Sun, Moons, and River.

"*Ai-ya, ai-ya, ai-ya,*" Jao chanted. Suddenly solemn, the rest chimed in. Though ignorant of the Kuang Shih's primary language, Ivar could recognize a hymn. He held himself aside.

The herders freed the box. Swimmers pushed it out into midstream. Osels under sharp command kept chuhos away. It drifted on south. They must have seen aboard *Jade Gate,* because the flag went to half-mast.

"What was that?" Ivar then ventured to ask.

Jao brushed the wet locks off her brow and answered, surprised, "Did you not know? That was one coffin."

"Huh? I—Wait, I beg your pardon, I do seem to remember—"

"All our dead go down the river, down the Yun Kow at last—the Linn—to the Tien Hu, what you call the Sea of Orcus. It is our duty to launch again any we find stranded." In awe: "I have heard about one seer who walks there now, who will call back the Old Shen from the stars. Will our dead then rise from the waters?"

Tatiana Thane had never supposed she could mind being by herself. She had always had a worldful of things to do, read, watch, listen to, think about.

Daytimes still weren't altogether bad. Her present work was inherently solitary: study, meditation, cut-and-try, bit by bit the construction of a semantic model of the language spoken around Mount Hamilcar on Dido, which would enable humans to converse with the natives on a more basic level than pidgin allowed. Her dialogues were with a computer, or occasionally by vid with the man under whom she had studied, who was retired to his estate in Heraclea and too old to care about politics.

Since she became a research fellow, students had treated her respectfully. Thus she took a while—when she missed Ivar so jaggedly, when she was so haunted by fear for him—to realize that this behavior had become an avoidance. Nor was she overtly snubbed at faculty rituals, meetings, dining commons, chance encounters in corridor or quad. These days, people didn't often talk animatedly. Thus likewise she took a while to realize that they never did with her any more, and, except for her parents, had let her drop from their social lives.

Slowly her spirit wore down.

The first real break in her isolation came about 1700 hours on a Marsday. She was thinking of going to bed, however poorly she would sleep. Outside was a darker night than ordinary, for a great dustcloud borne along the tropopause had veiled the stars. Lavinia was a blurred dim crescent above spires and domes. Wind piped. She sprawled in her largest chair and played with Frumious Bandersnatch. The tadmouse ran up and down her body, from shins to shoulders and back, trilling. The comfort was as minute as himself.

The knocker rapped. For a moment she thought she hadn't heard aright. Then her pulse stumbled, and she nearly threw her pet off in her haste to open the door. He clung to her sweater and whistled indignation.

A man stepped through, at once closing the door behind him. Though the outside air that came along was cold as well as ferric-harsh, no one would ordinarily have worn a nightmask. He doffed his and she saw the bony middle-aged features of Gabriel Stewart. They had last been together on Dido. His work was to know the Hamilcar region backwards and forwards, guide scientific parties and see to their well-being.

"Why...why...hello," she said helplessly.

"Draw your blinds," he ordered. "I'd as soon not be glimpsed from beneath."

She stared. Her backbone pringled. "Are you in trouble, Gabe?"

"Not officially—yet."

"I'd no idea you were on Aeneas. Why didn't you call?"

"Calls can be monitored. Now cover those windows, will you?"

She obeyed. Stewart removed his outer garments. "It's good to see you again," she ventured.

"You may not think that after I've spoken my piece." He unbent a little. "Though maybe you will. I recall you as bold lass, in your quiet way. And I don't suppose Firstlin' of Ilion made you his girl for nothin'."

"Do you have news of Ivar?" she cried.

"'Fraid not. I was hopin' you would. . . . Well, let's talk."

He refused wine but let her brew a pot of tea. Meanwhile he sat, puffed his pipe, exchanged accounts of everything that had happened since the revolution erupted. He had gone outsystem, in McCormac's hastily assembled Intelligence corps, and admitted ruefully that meanwhile the war was lost in his own bailiwick. As far as he could discover, upon being returned after the defeat, some Terran agent had not only managed to rescue the Admiral's wife from Snelund—a priceless bargaining counter, no doubt—but while on Dido had hijacked a patriot vessel whose computer held the latest codes. . . . "I got wonderin' about possibility of organizin' Didonians to help fight on, as guerrillas or even as Navy personnel. At last I hitched ride to Aeneas and looked up my friend—m-m, never mind his name; he's of University too, on a secondary campus. Through him, I soon got involved in resistance movement."

"There is one?"

He regarded her somberly. "You ask that, Ivar Frederiksen's bride to be?"

"I was never consulted." She put teapot and cups on a table between them, sank to the edge of a chair opposite his, and stared at the fingers wrestling in her lap. "He—It was crazy impulse, what he did. Wasn't it?"

"Maybe then. Not any longer. Of course, your dear Commissioner Desai would prefer you believe that."

Tatiana braced herself and met his look. "Granted," she said, "I've seen Desai several times. I've passed on his remarks to people I know—not endorsin' them, simply passin' them on. Is that why I'm ostracized? Surely University folk should agree we can't have too much data input."

"I've queried around about you," Stewart replied. "It's curious kind of tension. Outsider like me can maybe identify it better than those who're bein' racked. On one hand, you are Ivar Frederiksen's girl. It could be dangerous gettin' near you, because he may return any day. That makes cowardly types ride clear of you. Then certain others—Well, you do have *mana*. I can't think of better word for it. They sense you're big medicine, because of bein' his chosen, and it makes them vaguely uncomfortable. They aren't used to that sort of thing in their neat, scientifically ordered lives. So they find excuses to themselves for postponin' any resumption of former close relations with you.

"On other hand"—he trailed a slow streamer of smoke—"you are, to speak blunt, lettin' yourself be used by enemy. You may think you're relayin' Desai's words for whatever these're worth as information. But mere fact that you will receive him, will talk civilly with him, means you lack full commitment. And this gets you shunned by those who have it. Cut off, you don't know how many already do. Well, they *are* many. And number grows day by day."

He leaned forward. "When I'd figured how matters stand, I had to come see you, Tatiana. My guess is, Desai's half persuaded you to try wheedlin' Frederiksen into surrender, if and when you two get back in touch. Well, you mustn't. At very least, hold apart from Impies." Starkly: "Freedom movement's at point where we can start makin' examples of collaborators. I know you'd never be one, consciously. Don't let yon Desai bastard snare you."

"But," she stammered in her bewilderment, "but what do you mean to do? What can you hope for? And Ivar—he's nothin' but young man who got carried away—fugitive, completely powerless, if, if, if he's still alive at all—"

"He is," Stewart told her. "I don't know where or how, or what he's doin', but he is. Word runs too widely to have no truth behind it." His voice lifted. "You've heard also. You must have. Signs, tokens, precognitions. . . . Never mind his weaklin' father. Ivar is rightful leader of free Aeneas—when Builders return, which they will, which they will. And you are his bride who will bear his son that Builders will make more than human."

Belief stood incandescent in his eyes.

✵ 13 ✵

South of the Green Bowl, hills climbed ever faster. Yet for a while the stream continued to flow peaceful. Ivar wished his blood could do likewise.

Seeking tranquility, he climbed to the foredeck for a clear view across night. He stopped short when he spied others on hand than the lookout who added eyes to the radar.

Through a crowd of stars and a torrent of galaxy, Creusa sped past Lavinia. Light lay argent ashore, touching crests and crags, swallowed by shadows farther down. It shivered and sparked on the water, made ghostly the sails which had been set to use a fair wind. That air murmured cold through quietness and a rustle at the bows.

Fore and aft, separated by a few kilometers for safety, glowed the lights of three companion vessels. No few were bound this way, to celebrate the Season of Returnings.

Ivar saw the lookout on his knees under the figurehead, and a sheen off Erannath's plumage, and Riho Mea and Iang Weii in their robes. Captain and chaplain were completing a ritual, it seemed. Mute, now and then lifting hands or bowing heads, they had watched the moons draw near and again apart.

"Ah," Mea gusted. The crewman rose.

"I beg pardon," Erannath said. "Had I known a religious practice was going on, I would not have descended here. I stayed because that was perhaps less distracting than my takeoff would have been."

"No harm done," Mea assured him. "In fact, the sight of you coming down gave one extra glory."

"Besides," Iang said in his mild voice, "though this is something we always do at certain times, it is not strictly religious." He stroked his thin white beard. "Have we Kuang Shih religion, in the same sense as the Christians or Jews of the Ti Shih or the pagans of the tineran society? This is one matter of definition, not so? We preach nothing about gods. To most of us that whole subject is not important. Whether or not gods, or God, exist, is it not merely one scientific question—cosmological?"

"Then what do you hunt after?" the Ythrian asked.

"Allness," the chaplain replied. "Unity, harmony. Through rites and symbols. We know they are only rites and symbols. But they say to the opened mind what words cannot. The River is ongoing-ness, fate; the Sun is life; Moons and Stars are the transhuman."

"We contemplate these things," Riho Mea added. "We try to merge with them, with everything that is." Her glance fell on Ivar. "Ahoa, Sir Mariner," she called. "Come, join our party."

Iang, who could stay solemn longer than her, continued: "Our race, or yours, has less gift for the whole *chan*—understanding—than the many-minded people of the Morning Star. However, when the Old Shen return, mankind will gain the same immortal singleness, and have moreover the strengths we were forced to make in ourselves, in order to endure being alone in our skulls."

"You too?" Erannath snapped. "Is everybody on Aeneas waiting for these mentors and saviors?"

"More and more, we are," Mea said. "Up the Yun Kow drifts word—"

Ivar, who had approached, felt as if touched by lightnings. Her gaze had locked on him. He knew: *These are* not *just easy-goin', practiced sailors. I should've seen it earlier. That coffin—and fact they're bound on dangerous trip to honor both their ancestors and their descendants—and now this—no, they're as profoundly escha-tological as any Bible-and-blaster yeoman.*

"Word about liberation?" he exclaimed.

"Aye, though that's the bare beginning," she answered. Iang nodded, while the lookout laid hand on sheath knife.

Abruptly she said, "Would you like to talk about this... Rolf Mariner? I'm ready for one drink and cigar in my cabin anyway."

His pulses roared. "You also, good friend and wise man," he heard her propose to Iang.

"I bid you goodnight, then," Erannath said.

The chaplain bowed to him. "Forgive us our confidentiality."

"Maybe we should invite you along," Mea said. "Look here, you are not one plain scientist like you claim. You are one Ythrian secret agent, collecting information on the key human planet Aeneas, no?" When he stayed silent, she laughed. "Never mind. Point is, we and you have the same enemy, the Terran Empire. At least, Ythri shouldn't mind if the Empire loses territory."

"Afterward, though," Iang murmured, "I cannot help but wonder how well the carnivore soul may adapt to the enlightenment the Old Shen will bring."

Moonlight turned Erannath's feather to silver, his eyes to mercury.

"Do you look on your species as a chosen people?" he said, equally low. At once he must have regretted his impulse, for he went on: "Your intrigues are no concern of mine. Nor do I care if you decide I am something more than an observer. If you are opposed to the occupation authorities, presumably you won't betray me to them. I wish to go on a night hunt. May fortune blow your way."

His wings spread, from rail to rail. The wind of his rising gusted and boomed. For a while he gleamed high aloft, before vision lost him among the stars.

Mea led Iang and Ivar to her quarters. Her husband greeted them, and this time he stayed: a bright and resolute young man, the dream of freedom kindled within him.

When the door had been shut, the captain said: "Ahoa, Ivar Frederiksen, Firstling of Ilion."

"How did you know?" he whispered.

She grinned, and went for the cigar she had bespoken. "How obvious need it be? Surely that Ythrian has suspected. Why else should he care about one human waif? But to him, humans are so foreign—so alike-seeming—and besides, being a spy, he couldn't dare use data services—he must have been holding back, trying to confirm his guess. Me, I remembered some choked-off news accounts. I called up Nova Roma public files, asked for pictures and—O-ah, no fears. I am one merchant myself, I know how to disguise my real intents."

"You, you will . . . help me?" he faltered.

They drew close around him, the young man, the old man, the captain. "You will help us," Iang said. "You are the Firstling—our rightful leader that every Aenean can follow—to throw out those mind-stifling Terrans and make ready for the Advent that is promised—What can we do for you, lord?"

Chunderban Desai broke the connection and sat for a while staring before him. His wife, who had been out of the room, came back in and asked what was wrong.

"Peter Jowett is dead," he told her.

"Oh, no." The two families had become friendly in the isolation they shared.

"Murdered."

"What?" The gentleness in her face gave way to horror.

"The separatists," he sighed. "It has to be. No melodramatic message left. He was killed by a rifle bullet as he left his office. But who else hated him?"

She groped for the comfort of his hand. He returned the pressure. "A real underground?" she said. "I didn't know."

"Nor I, until now. Oh, I got reports from planted agents, from surveillance devices, all the usual means. Something was brewing, something being organized. Still, I didn't expect outright terrorism this soon, if ever."

"The futility is nearly the worst part. What chance have they?"

He rose from his chair. Side by side, they went to a window. It gave on the garden of the little house they rented in the suburbs: alien plants spiky beneath alien stars and moons, whose light fell on the frosted helmet of a marine guard.

"I don't know," he said. Despite the low gravity, his back slumped. "They must have some. It isn't the hopeless who rebel, it's those who think they see the end of their particular tunnels, and grow impatient."

"You have given them hope, dear."

"Well ... I came here thinking they'd accept their military defeat and work with me like sensible people, to get their planet reintegrated with the Empire. After all, except for the Snelund episode, Aeneas has benefited from the Imperium, on balance; and we're trying to set up precautions against another Snelund. Peter agreed. Therefore they killed him. Who's next?"

Her fingers tightened on his. "Poor Olga. The poor children. Should I call her tonight or, or what?"

He stayed in the orbit of his own thoughts. "Rumors of a deliverer—not merely a political liberator, but a savior—no, a whole race of saviors—that's what's driving the Aeneans," he said. "And not the dominant culture alone. The others too. In their different ways, they all wait for an apocalypse."

"Who is preaching it?"

He chuckled sadly. "If I knew that, I could order the party arrested. Or, better yet, try to suborn him. Or them. But my agents hear nothing except these vague rumors. Never forget how terribly few we are, and how marked, on an entire world.... We did notice what appeared to be a centering of the rumors on the Orcan area. We investigated. We drew blank, at least as far as finding any proof of illegal activities. The society there, and its beliefs, always have been founded on colossal prehuman ruins, and evidently has often brought forth millennialist prophets. Our people had more urgent things to do than straggle with the language and ethos of some poverty-stricken dwellers on a dead sea floor." His tone strengthened. "Though if I had the personnel for it, I would probe further indeed. This wouldn't be the first time that a voice from the desert drove nations mad."

The phone chimed again. He muttered a swear word before he returned to accept the call. It was on scramble code, which automatically heterodyned the audio output so that Desai's wife could not hear what came to him a couple of meters away. The screen was vacant, too.

She could see the blaze on his face; and she heard him shout after the conversation ended, as he surged from his chair: "Brahma's mercy, yes! We'll catch him and end this thing!"

✵ 14 ✵

Jade Gate had nearly reached the Linn when the Terrans came.

The Cimmerian Mountains form the southern marge of Ilion. The further south the Flone goes through them, until its final incredible plunge off the continental rim, the steeper and deeper is the gorge it has cut for itself. In winter it runs quiet between those walls, under a sheath of ice. But by midsummer, swollen with melt off the polar cap, it is a race, and they must have skillful pilots who would venture along that violence.

At the port rail of the main deck, Ivar and Jao watched. Water brawled, foamed, spouted off rocks, filled air with an ongoing cannonade and made the vessel rock and shudder. Here the stream had narrowed to a bare 300 meters between heaped boulders and talus. Behind, cliffs rose for a pair of kilometers. The rock was gloomy-hued and there was only a strip of sky to see, from which Virgil had already sunk. The brighter stars gleamed in its duskiness. Down under the full weight of shadow, it was cold. Spray dashed into faces and across garments. Forward, the canyon dimmed out in mist. Nevertheless he spied three ships in that direction, and four aft. More than these were rendezvous-bound.

As the deck pitched beneath her, the girl caught his arm. "What was that?" he shouted through the noise, and barely heard her reply:

"Swerve around one obstacle, I'm sure. Nothing here is ever twice the same."

"Have you had any wrecks?"

"Some few per century. Most lives are saved."

"God! You'll take such risk, year after year, for . . . ritual?"

"The danger is part of the ritual, Rolf. We are never so one with the world as when—Ai-ah!"

His gaze followed hers aloft, and his heart lurched. Downward came slanting the torpedo shape of a large flyer. Upon its armored flank shone the sunburst of Empire.

"Who is that?" she cried innocently.

"A marine troop. After me. Who else?" He didn't rasp it loud enough for her to hear. When he wrenched free and ran, she stared in hurt amazement.

He pounded up the ladder to the bridge, where he knew Mea stood by the pilot. She came out to meet him. Grimness bestrode her countenance. She had bitten her cigar across. "Let's get you below," she snapped, and shoved at him.

He stumbled before her, among crewfolk who boiled with excitement. The aircraft whined toward the lead end of the line. "*Chao yu li!*" Mea exclaimed. "We've that much luck, at least. They don't know which vessel is ours."

"They might know its name," he replied. "Whoever gave me away—"

"Aye. Here, this way. . . . Hold." Erannath had emerged from his cabin. "You!" She pointed at the next deckhouse. "Into that door!"

The Ythrian halted, lifted his talons. "Move!" the captain bawled. "Or I'll have you shot!"

For an instant his crest stood stiff. Then he obeyed. The three of them entered a narrow, throbbing corridor. Mea bowed to Erannath. "I am sorry, honored passenger," she said. Partly muffled by bulkheads, the air was less thunderous here. "Time lacked for requesting your help courteously. You are most good that you obliged regardless. Please to come."

She trotted on. Ivar and Erannath followed, the Ythrian rocking clumsily along on his wing-feet while he asked, "What has happened?"

"Impies," the young man groaned. "We had to get out of sight from above. If either of us got glimpsed, that'd've ended this game. Not that I see how it can go on much longer."

Erannath's eyes smoldered golden upon him. "What game do you speak of?"

"I'm fugitive from Terrans."

"And worth the captain's protection? A-a-a-ah..."

Mea stopped at an intercom unit, punched a number, spoke rapid-fire for a minute. When she turned back to her companions, she was the barest bit relaxed.

"I raised our radioman in time," she said. "Likely the enemy will call, asking which of us is *Jade Gate*. My man is alerting the others in our own language, which surely the Terrans don't understand. We Riverfolk stick together. Everybody will act stupid, claim they don't know, garble things as if they had one poor command of Anglic." Her grin flashed. "To act stupid is one skill of our people."

"Were I the Terran commander," Erannath said, "I would thereupon beam to each ship individually, requiring its name. And were I the captain of any, I would not court punishment by lying, in a cause which has not been explained to me."

Mea barked laughter. "Right. But I suggested *Portal of Virtue* and *Way to Fortune* both answer they are *Jade Gate,* as well as this one. The real names could reasonably translate to the same as ours. They can safely give the Terrans that stab."

She turned bleak again: "At best, though, we buy short time to smuggle you off, Ivar Frederiksen, and you, Erannath, spy from Ythri. I dare not give you any firearms. That would prove our role, should you get caught." The man felt the knife he had kept on his belt since he left Windhome. The nonhuman wasn't wearing his apron, thus had no weapons. The woman continued: "When the marines flit down to us, we'll admit you were here, but claim we had no idea you were wanted. True enough, for everybody except three of us; and we can behave plenty innocent. We'll say you must have seen the airboat and fled, we know not where."

Ivar thought of the starkness that walled them in and pleaded, "Where, for real?"

Mea led them to a companionway and downward. As she hastened, she said across her shoulder: "Some Orcans always climb the Shelf to trade with us after our ceremonies are done. You may meet them at the site, otherwise on their way to it. Or if not, you can probably reach the Tien Hu by yourselves, and get help. I feel sure they will help. Theirs is the seer they've told us of."

"Won't Impies think of that?" Ivar protested.

"No doubt. Still, I bet it's one impossible country to ransack."

Mea stopped at a point in another corridor, glanced about, and rapped, "Aye, you may be caught. But you *will* be caught if you stay aboard. You may drown crossing to shore, or break your neck off one cliff, or thousand other griefs. Well, are you our Firstling or not?"

She flung open a door and ushered them through. The room beyond was a storage space for kayaks, and also held a small crane for their launching. "Get in," she ordered Ivar. "You should be able to reach the bank. Just work at not capsizing and not hitting anything, and make what shoreward way you can whenever you find one stretch not too rough. Once afoot, send the boat off again. No sense leaving any clue to where you landed. Afterward, rocks and mist should hide you from overhead, if you go carefully. . . . Erannath, you fly across, right above the surface."

Half terrified and half carried beyond himself, Ivar settled into the frail craft, secured the cover around his waist, gripped the paddle. Riho Mea leaned toward him. He had never before seen tears in her eyes. "All luck sail with you, Firstling," she said unsteadily, "for all our hopes do." Her lips touched his.

She opened a hatch in the hull and stood to the controls of the crane. Its motor whirred, its arm descended to lay hold with clamps to rings fore and aft, it lifted Ivar outward and lowered him alongside.

The river boomed and brawled. The world was a cold wet grayness of spray blown backward from the falls. Phantom cliffs showed through. Ivar and Erannath rested among house-sized boulders.

Despite his shoes, the stones along the bank had been cruel to the human. He ached from bruises where he had tripped and slashes where sharp edges had caught him. Weariness filled every bone like a lead casting. The Ythrian, who could flutter above obstacles, was in better shape, though prolonged land travel was always hard on his race.

By some trick of echo in their shelter, talk was possible at less than the top of a voice. "No doubt a trail goes down the Shelf to the seabed," Erannath said. "We must presume the Terrans are not fools. When they don't find us aboard any ship, they will suppose us bound for Orcus, and call Nova Roma for a stat of the most detailed geodetic survey map available. They will then cruise above that trail. We must take a roundabout way."

"That'll likely be dangerous to me," Ivar said dully.

"I will help you as best I can," Erannath promised. Perhaps the set of his feathers added: *If God the Hunter hurls you to your death, cry defiance as you fall.*

"Why are you interested in me, anyhow?" Ivar demanded.

The Ythrian trilled what corresponded to a chuckle. "You and your fellows have taken for granted I'm a secret agent of the Domain. Let's say, first, that I wondered if you truly were plain Rolf Mariner, and accompanied you to try to find out. Second, I have no desire myself to be taken prisoner. Our interests in escape coincide."

"Do they, now? You need only fly elsewhere."

"But you are the Firstling of Ilion. Alone, you'd perish or be captured. Captain Riho doesn't understand how different this kind of country is from what you are used to. With my help, you have a fair chance."

Ivar was too worn and sore to exult. Yet underneath, a low fire awoke. *He is interested in my success! So interested he'll gamble his whole mission, everything he might have brought home, to see me through. Maybe we really can get help from Ythri, when we break Sector Alpha Crucis free.*

This moment was premature to voice such things aloud. Presently the two of them resumed their crawling journey.

For a short stretch, the river again broadened until a fleet could lie to, heavily anchored and with engineers standing by to supply power on a whistle's notice. The right bank widened also, in a few level hectares which had been cleared of detritus. There stood an altar flanked by stone guardians, eroded almost shapeless. There too lay traces of campfires; but no Orcans had yet arrived. Here the rush of current was lost under the world-shivering steady roar of the Linn, only seven kilometers distant. Its edge was never visible through the spray flung aloft.

Tonight the wind had shifted, driving the perpetual fog south till it hung as a moon-whitened curtain between vast black walls. The water glistened. Darkling upon it rested those vessels which had arrived. Somehow their riding lights and the colored lanterns strung throughout their rigging lacked cheeriness, when the Terran warcraft hung above on its negafield and watched. The air was cold; ice crackled in Ivar's clothes and Erannath's feathers.

Humans have better night vision than Ythrians. Ivar was the

first to see. "Hsssh!" He drew his companion back, while sickness caught his throat. Then Erannath identified those shimmers and shadows ahead. Three marines kept watch on the open ground.

No way existed to circle them unnoticed; the bank lay bare and moonlit to the bottom of an unscalable precipice. Ivar shrank behind a rock, thought wildly of swimming and knew that here he couldn't, of weeping and found that now he couldn't.

Unheard through the noise, Erannath lifted. Moon-glow tinged him. But sight was tricky for men who sat high in a hull. Otherwise they need not have placed sentries.

Ivar choked on a breath. He saw the great wings scythe back down. One man tumbled, a second, a third, in as many pulse-beats. Erannath landed among them where they sprawled and beckoned the Firstling.

Ivar ran. Strangely, what broke from him was, "Are they dead?"

"No. Stunned. I hold a Third Echelon in *hyai-lu*. I used its triple blow, both alatan bones and a...do you say rabbit punch?" Erannath was busy. He stripped the two-ways off wrists, grav units off torsos, rifles off shoulders, gave one of each to Ivar and tossed the rest in the Flone. When they awoke, the marines would be unable to radio, rise, or fire signals, and must wait till their regular relief descended.

If they awoke. The bodies looked ghastly limp to Ivar. He thrust that question aside, unsure why it should bother him when they were the enemy and when in joyous fact he and his ally had lucked out, had won a virtually certain means of getting to their goal.

They did not hazard immediate flight. On the further side of the meeting round the Orcan trail began. Though narrow, twisting, and vague, often told only by cairns, it was better going than the shoreline had been. Anything would be. Ivar limped and Erannath hobbled as if unchained.

When they entered the concealing mists, they dared rise. And that was like becoming a freed spirit. Ivar wondered if the transcendence of humanness which the prophet promised could feel this miraculous. The twin cylinders he wore drove him through roaring wet smoke till he burst forth and beheld the side of a continent.

It toppled enormously, more steep and barren than anywhere in the west, four kilometers of palisades, headlands, ravines, raw slopes of old landslides, down and down to the dead ocean floor. Those were murky heights beneath stars and moons; but over them cascaded the Linn. It fell almost half the distance in a single straight leap, unhidden by spume, agleam like a drawn sword. The querning of it toned through heaven.

Below sheened the Orcan Sea, surrounded by hills which cultivation mottled. Beyond, desert glimmered death-white.

Erannath swept near. "Quick!" he commanded. "To ground before the Terrans come and spot us."

Ivar nodded, took his bearings from the constellations, and aimed southwest, to where Mount Cronos raised its dim bulk. They might as well reduce the way they had left to go.

Air skirled frigid around him. His teeth clattered till he forced them together. This was not like the part of the Antonine Seabed under Windhome. There it was often warm of summer nights, and never too hot by day. But there it was tempered by plenteous green life.

Yonder so-called Sea of Orcus was no more than a huge lake, dense and bitter with salts leached into it. Mists and lesser streams off the Linn gave fresh water to the rim of its bowl. And that was all. Nothing ran far on southward. Winds bending up from the equator sucked every moisture into themselves and scattered it across immensities. That land lay bare because those same winds had long ago blown away the rich bottom soil which elsewhere was the heritage left Aeneas by its oceans.

Here was the sternest country where men dwelt upon this planet. Ivar knew it had shaped their tribe, their souls. He knew little more. No outsider did.

Aliens—He squinted at Erannath. The Ythrian descended as if upon prey, magnificent as the downward-rushing falls. *I thought for a moment you must've been one who betrayed me,* passed through Ivar. *Can't be, I reckon.*

Then: who did?

❈ 15 ❈

Dawnlight shivered upon the sea and cast sharp blue shadows across dust. From the Grand Tower, a trumpet greeted the sun. Its voice blew colder than the windless air.

Jaan left his mother's house and walked a street which twisted between shuttered gray blocks of houses, down to the wharf. What few people were abroad crossed arms and bowed to him, some in awe, some in wary respect. In the wall-enclosed narrowness dusk still prevailed, making their robes look ghostly.

The wharf was Ancient work, a sudden dazzling contrast to the drabness and poverty of the human town. Its table thrust irides- cent, hard and cool beneath the feet, out of the mountainside. Millions of years had broken a corner off it but not eroded the substance. What they had done was steal the waves which once lapped its lower edge; now brush-grown slopes fell steeply to the water a kilometer beneath.

The town covered the mountain for a similar distance upward, its featureless adobe cubicles finally huddling against the very flanks of the Arena which crowned the peak. That was also built by the Ancients, and even ruined stood in glory. It was of the same shining, enduring material as the wharf, elliptical in plan, the major axis almost a kilometer and the walls rearing more than 30 meters before their final upthrust in what had been seven towers and remained three. Those walls were not sheer; they fountained, in pillars, terraces, arches, galleries, setbacks, slim bridges, wing- like balconies, so that light and shadow played endlessly and the building was like one eternal cool fire.

Banners rose, gold and scarlet, to the tops of flagstaffs on the parapets. The Companions were changing their guard.

Jaan's gaze turned away, to the northerly horizon where the continent reared above the Sea of Orcus. With Virgil barely over them, the heights appeared black, save for the Linn. Its dim thunder reverberated through air and earth.

—I do not see them flying, he said.

—No, they are not, replied Caruith. For fear of pursuit, they landed near Alsa and induced a villager to convey them in his truck. Look, there it comes.

Jaan was unsure whether his own mind or the Ancient's told his head to swing about, his eyes to focus on the dirt road snaking uphill from the shoreline. Were the two beginning to become one already? It had been promised. To be a part, no, a characteristic, a memory, of Caruith...oh, wonder above wonders....

He saw the battered vehicle more by the dust it raised than anything else, for it was afar, would not reach the town for a while yet. It was not the only traffic at this early hour. Several groundcars moved along the highway that girdled the sea; a couple of tractors were at work in the hills behind, black dots upon brown and wan green, to coax a crop out of niggard soil; a boat slid across the thick waters, trawling for creatures which men could not eat but whose tissues concentrated minerals that men could use. And above the Arena there poised on its negafield an aircraft the Companions owned. Though unarmed by Imperial decree, it was on guard. These were uneasy times.

"Master."

Jaan turned at the voice and saw Robhar, youngest of his disciples. The boy, a fisherman's son, was nearly lost in his ragged robe. His breath steamed around shoulder-length black elflocks. He made his bow doubly deep. "Master," he asked, "can I serve you in aught?"

—He kept watch for hours till we emerged, and then did not venture to address us before we paused here, Caruith said. His devotion is superb.

—I do not believe the rest care less, Jaan replied out of his knowledge of humankind—which the mightiest nonhuman intellect could never totally sound. They are older, lack endurance to wait sleepless and freezing on the chance that we may want them; they have, moreover, their daily work, and most of them their wives and children.

—The time draws nigh when they must forsake those, and all others, to follow us.

—They know that. I am sure they accept it altogether. But then should they not savor the small joys of being human as much as they may, while still they may?

—You remain too human yourself, Jaan. You must become a lightning bolt.

Meanwhile the prophet said, "Yes, Robhar. This is a day of destiny." As the eyes before him flared: "Nonetheless we have practical measures to take, no time for rejoicing. We remain only men, chained to the world. Two are bound hither, a human and an Ythrian. They could be vital to the liberation. The Terrans are after them, and will surely soon arrive in force to seek them out. Before then, they must be well hidden; and as few townsfolk as may be must know about them, lest the tale be spilled.

"Hurry. Go to the livery stable of Brother Boras and ask him to lend us a statha with a pannier large enough to hide an Ythrian—about your size, though we will also need a blanket to cover his wing-ends that will stick forth. Do not tell Boras why

I desire this. He is loyal, but the tyrants have drugs and worse, should they come to suspect anyone knows something. Likewise, give no reasons to Brother Ezzara when you stop at his house to borrow a robe, sandals, and his red cloak with the hood. Order him to remain indoors until further word.

"Swiftly!"

Robhar clapped hands in sign of obedience and sped off, over the cobblestones and into the town.

Jaan waited. The truck would inevitably pass the wharf. Meanwhile, nobody was likely to have business here at this hour. Any who did chance by would see the prophet's lonely figure limned against space, and bow and not venture to linger.

—The driver comes sufficiently near for me to read his mind, whispered Caruith. I do not like what I see.

—What? asked Jaan, startled. Is he not true to us? Why else should he convey two outlaws?

—He is true, in the sense of wishing Aeneas free of the Empire and, indeed, Orcus free of Nova Roma. But he has not fully accepted our teaching, nor made an absolute commitment to our cause. For he is an impulsive and vacillating man. Ivar Frederiksen and Erannath of Avalon woke him up with a story about being scientists marooned by the failure of their aircraft, in need of transportation to Mount Cronos where they could get help. He knew the story must be false, but in his resentment of the Terrans agreed anyway. Now, more and more, he worries, he regrets his action. As soon as he is rid of them, he will drink to ease his fears, and the drink may well unlock his tongue.

—Is it not ample precaution that we transfer them out of his care? What else should we do? . . . No! Not murder!

—Many will die for the liberation. Would you hazard their sacrifice being in vain, for the sake of a single life today?

—Imprisonment, together with the Ythrian you warn me about—

—The disappearance of a person who has friends and neighbors is less easy to explain away than his death. Speak to Brother Velib. Recall that he was among the few Orcans who went off to serve with McCormac; he learned a good deal. It is not hard to create a believable "accident."

—No.

Jaan wrestled; but the mind which shared his brain was too powerful, too plausible. It is right that one man die for the people.

Were not Jaan and Caruith themselves prepared to do so? By the time the truck arrived, the prophet had actually calmed.

By then, too, Robhar had returned with the statha and the disguise. Everybody knew Ezzara by the red cloak he affected. Its hood would conceal a nord's head; long sleeves, and dirt rubbed well into sandaled feet, would conceal fair skin. Folk would observe nothing save the prophet, accompanied by two of his disciples, going up to the Arena and in through its gates, along with a beast whose burden might be, say, Ancient books that he had found in the catacombs.

The truck halted. Jaan accepted the salutation of the driver, while trying not to think of him as really real. The man opened the back door, and inside the body of the vehicle were the Ythrian and the Firstling of Ilion.

Jaan, who had never before seen an Ythrian in the flesh, found he was more taken by that arrogance of beauty (which must be destroyed, it mourned within him) than by the ordinary-looking blond youth who had so swiftly become a hinge of fate. He felt as if the blue eyes merely stared, while the golden ones searched.

They saw: a young man, more short and stocky than was common among Orcans, in an immaculate white robe, rope belt, sandals he had made himself. The countenance was broad, curve-nosed, full-lipped, pale-brown, handsome in its fashion; long hair and short beard were mahogany, clean and well-groomed. His own eyes were his most striking feature, wide-set, gray, and enormous. Around his brows went a circlet of metal with a faceted complexity above the face, the sole outward token that he was an Ancient returned to life after six million years.

He said, in his voice that was as usual slow and soft: "Welcome, Ivar Frederiksen, deliverer of your world."

Night laired everywhere around Desai's house. Neighbor lights felt star-distant; and there went no whisper of traffic. It was almost with relief that he blanked the windows.

"Please sit down, Prosser Thane," he said. "What refreshment may I offer you?"

"None," the tall young woman answered. After a moment she added, reluctantly and out of habit: "Thank you."

"Is it that you do not wish to eat the salt of an enemy?" His smile was wistful. "I shouldn't imagine tradition requires you refuse his tea."

"If you like, Commissioner." Tatiana seated herself, stiff-limbed in her plain coverall. Desai spoke to his wife, who fetched a tray with a steaming pot, two cups, and a plate of cookies. She set it down and excused herself. The door closed behind her.

To Desai, that felt like the room closing in on him. It was so comfortless, so ... impoverished, in spite of being physically adequate. His desk and communications board filled one corner, a reference shelf stood nearby, and otherwise the place was walls, faded carpet, furniture not designed for a man of his race or culture: apart from a picture or two, everything rented, none of the dear clutter which makes a home.

Our family moves too much, too often, too far, like a bobbin shuttling to reweave a fabric which tears because it is rotted. I was always taught on Ramanujan that we do best to travel light through life. But what does it do to the children, this flitting from place to place, though always into the same kind of Imperial-civil-servant enclave? He sighed. The thought was old in him.

"I appreciate your coming as I requested," he began. "I hope you, ah, took precautions."

"Yes, I did. I slipped into alley, reversed my cloak, and put on my nightmask."

"That's the reason I didn't visit you. It would be virtually impossible to conceal the fact. And surely the terrorists have you under a degree of surveillance."

Tatiana withheld expression. Desai plodded on: "I hate for you to take even this slight risk. The assassins of a dozen prominent citizens might well not stop at you, did they suspect you of, um, collaboration."

"Unless I'm on their side, and came here to learn whatever I can for them," Tatiana said in a metallic tone.

Desai ventured a smile. "That's the risk I take. Not very large, I assume." He lifted the teapot and raised his brows. She gave a faint nod. He poured for her and himself, lifted his cup and sipped. The heat comforted.

"How about gettin' to business?" she demanded.

"Indeed. I thought you would like to hear the latest news of Ivar Frederiksen."

That caught her! She said nothing, but she sat bolt upright and the brown gaze widened.

"This is confidential, of course. From a source I shan't describe,

I have learned that he joined a nomad band, later got into trouble with it, and took passage on a southbound ship of Riverfolk together with an Ythrian who may or may not have met him by chance but is almost certainly an Intelligence agent of the Domain. They were nearly at the outfall when I got word and sent a marine squad to bring him in. Thanks to confusion—obviously abetted by the sailors, though I don't plan to press charges—he and his companion escaped."

Red and white ran across her visage. She breathed quickly and shallowly, caught up her cup and gulped deep.

"You know I don't want him punished if it can be avoided," Desai said. "I want a chance to reason with him."

"I know that's what you claim," Tatiana snapped.

"If only people would understand," Desai pleaded. "Yes, the Imperium wronged you. But we are trying to make it good. And others would make tools of you, for prying apart what unity, and safety in unity, this civilization has left."

"What d'you mean? Ythrians? Merseians?" Her voice gibed.

Desai reached a decision. "Merseians. Oh, they are far off. But if they can again preoccupy us on this frontier—They failed last time, because McCormac's revolt caught them, too, by surprise. A more carefully engineered sequel would be different. Terra might even lose this entire sector, while simultaneously Merseia grabbed away at the opposite frontier. The result would be a truncated, shaken, weakened Empire, a strengthened Roidhunate flushed with success... and the Long Night brought that much closer."

He said into her unvoiced but unmistakable scorn: "You disbelieve? You consider Merseia a mere bogeyman? Please listen. A special agent of theirs is loose on Aeneas. No common spy or troublemaker. A creature of unique abilities; so important that, for the sake of his mission, a whole nonexistent planet was smuggled into the data files at Catawrayannis; so able—including fantastic telepathic feats—that all by himself he easily, almost teasingly escaped our precautions and disappeared into the wilds. Prosser Thane, Merseia is risking more than this one individual. It's giving away to us the fact that the Roidhunate includes such a species, putting us on our guard against more like him. No competent Intelligence service would allow that for anything less than the highest stakes.

"Do you see what a net your betrothed could get tangled in?"

Have I registered? Her face has gone utterly blank.

After a minute, she said: "I'll have to think on that, Commissioner. Your fears may be exaggerated. Let's stay with practicalities tonight. You were wonderin' about Ivar and this companion of his...who suggests Ythri may also be stickin' claws into our pot, right? Before I can suggest anything, you'd better tell me what else you know."

Desai armored himself in dryness. "Presumably they took refuge in the Orcan country," he said. "I've just had a report from a troop dispatched there to search for them. After several days of intensive effort, including depth quizzing of numerous people who might be suspected of knowledge, they have drawn blank. I can't leave them tied down, futile except for fueling hatred of us by their presence: not when sedition, sabotage, and violence are growing so fast across the whole planet. We need them to patrol the streets of, say, Nova Roma."

"Maybe Ivar didn't make for Orcus," Tatiana suggested.

"Maybe. But it would be logical, no?"

She uttered a third "Maybe," and then surprised him: "Did your men quiz that new prophet of theirs?"

"As a matter of fact, yes. No result. He gave off weird quasi-religious ideas that we already know a little about; they're anti-Imperial, but it seems better to let him vent pressure on behalf of his followers than to make a martyr of him. No, he revealed no knowledge of our Firstling. Nor did such as we could find among those persons who've constituted themselves an inner band of apostles."

It was clear that Tatiana stayed impersonal only by an effort. Her whole self must be churning about her sweetheart. "I'm astonished you got away with layin' hands on him or them. You could've touched off full-dress revolt, from all I've heard."

"I did issue instructions to handle cult leaders with micromanipulators. But after the search had gone on for a while, this... Jaan...voluntarily offered to undergo narco with his men, to end suspicion and, as he put it, leave the Terrans no further reason to remain. A shrewd move, if what he wanted was to get rid of them. After that big a concession from his side, they could scarcely do less than withdraw."

"Well," she challenged, "has it occurred to you that Ivar may *not* be in yon area?"

"Certainly. Although...the head technician of the quiz team reported Jaan showed an encephalogram not quite like any ever recorded before. As if his claim were true, that—what is it?—he is possessed by some kind of spirit. Oh, his body is normal-human. There's no reason to suppose the drug didn't suppress his capacity to lie, as it would for anyone else. But—"

"Mutation, I'd guess, would account for brain waves. They're odd and inbred folk, in environment our species never was evolved for."

"Probably. I'd have liked to borrow a Ryellian telepath from the governor's staff—considered it seriously, but decided that the Merseian agent, with the powers and knowledge he must have, would know how to guard against that, if he were involved. If I had a million skilled investigators, to study every aspect of this planet and its different peoples for a hundred intensive years—"

Desai abandoned his daydream. "We don't escape the possibility that Ivar and the Ythrian are in that region, unbeknownst to the prophet," he said. "A separate group could have smuggled them in. I understand Mount Cronos is riddled with tunnels and vaults, dug by the Elder race and never fully explored by men."

"But 'twould be hopeless quest goin' through them, right?" Tatiana replied.

"Yes. Especially when the hiding place could as well be far out in the desert." Desai paused. "This is why I asked you to come here, Prosser Thane. You know your fiancé. And surely you have more knowledge of the Orcans than our researchers can dig out of books, data banks, and superficial observation. Tell me, if you will, how likely would Ivar and they be to, m-m, get together?"

Tatiana fell silent. Desai loaded his cigarette holder and puffed and puffed. Finally she said, slowly:

"I don't think close cooperation's possible. Differences go too deep. And Ivar, at least, would have sense enough to realize it, and not try."

Desai refrained from comment, merely saying, "I wish you would describe that society for me."

"You must've read reports."

"Many. All from an outside, Terran viewpoint, including summaries my staff made of nord writings. They lack feel. You, however—your people and the Orcans have shared a world for centuries. If nothing else, I'm trying to grope toward an intuition of the relationship: not a bald socio-economic redaction, but a sense of the spirit, the tensions, the subtle and basic influences between cultures."

Tatiana sat for another time, gathering her thoughts. At last she said: "I really can't tell you much, Commissioner. Would you like capsule of history? You must know it already."

"I do not know what you consider important. Please."

"Well... these're by far our largest, best-preserved Builder relics, on Mount Cronos. But they were little studied, since Dido commanded most attention. Then Troubles came, raids, invasions, breakdown toward feudalism. Certain non-nords took refuge in Arena for lack of better shelter."

"Arena?" Desai wondered.

"Giant amphitheater on top of mountain, if amphitheater is what it was."

"Ah, that's not what 'arena' means.... No matter. I realize words change in local dialects. Do go on."

"They lived in that fortresslike structure, under strict discipline. When they went out to farm, fish, herd, armed men guarded them. Gradually these developed into military order, Companions of Arena, who were also magistrates, technical decision-makers—land bein' held in common—and finally became leaders in religious rites, religion naturally comin' to center on those mysterious remains.

"When order was restored, at first Companions resisted planetary government, and had to be beaten down. That made them more of priesthood, though they keep soldierly traditions. Since, they've given Nova Roma no particular trouble; but they hold aloof, and see their highest purpose as findin' out what Builders were, and are, and will be."

"Hm." Desai stroked his chin. "Are their people—these half million or so who inhabit the region—would you call them equally isolated from the rest of Aeneas?"

"Not quite. They trade, especially caravans across Antonine Seabed to its more fertile parts, bringin' minerals and bioproducts in exchange for food, manufactures, and whatnot. Number of their young men take service with nords for several years, to earn stake; they've high talent for water dowsin', which bears out what I said earlier about mutations among them. On whole, though, average continent dweller never sees an Orcan. And they do keep apart, forbid outside marriages on pain of exile, hold themselves to be special breed who will at last play special role related to Builders. Their history's full of prophets who had dreams about that. This Jaan's merely latest one."

Desai frowned. "Still, isn't his claim unique—that he is, at last, the incarnation, and the elder race will return in his lifetime—or whatever it is that he preaches?"

"I don't know." Tatiana drew breath. "One thing, however; and this's what you called me here for, right? In spite of callin' itself objective rather than supernatural, what Orcans have got behaves like religion. Well, Ivar's skeptic; in fact, he's committed unbeliever. I can't imagine him throwin' with gang of visionaries. They'd soon conflict too much."

Now Desai went quiet to ponder. *The point is well taken. That doesn't mean it's true.*

And yet what can I do but accept it . . . unless and until I hear from my spy, whatever has happened to him? (And that is something I may well never know.)

He shook himself. "So whether or not Ivar received help from an individual Orcan or two, you doubt he's contacted anyone significant, or will have any reason to linger in so forbidding an area. Am I correct, Prosser Thane?"

She nodded.

"Could you give me an idea as to where he might turn, how we might reach him?" Desai pursued.

She did not deign to answer.

"As you will," he said tiredly. "Bear in mind, he's in deadly danger as long as he is on the run: danger of getting shot by a patrol, for instance, or of committing a treasonable act which it would be impossible to pardon him for."

Tatiana bit her lip.

"I will not harass you about this," he promised. "But I beg you—you're a scientist, you should be used to entertaining radical new hypotheses and exploring their consequences—I beg you to consider the proposition that his real interests, and those of Aeneas, may lie with the Empire."

"I'd better go pretty soon," she said.

Later, to Gabriel Stewart, she exulted:

"He's got to be among Orcans. Nothin' else makes sense. He our rightful temporal leader, Jaan our mental one. Word'll go like fire in dry trava under a zoosny wind."

"But if prophet didn't know where he was—" fretted the scout.

Tatiana rapped forth a laugh. "Prophet did know! Do you

imagine Builder mind couldn't control human body reactions to miserable dose of narcotic? Why, simple schizophrenia can cause that."

He considered her. "You believe those rumors, girl? Rumors they are, you understand, nothin' more. Our outfit has no liaison with Arena."

"We'd better develop one.... Well, I admit we've no proof Builders are almost ready to return. But it makes sense." She gestured as if at the stars which her blinded window concealed. "Cosmenosis—What'd be truly fantastic is no purpose, no evolution, in all of that yonder." Raptly: "Desai spoke about Merseian agent operatin' on Aeneas. Not Merseian by race, though. Somebody strange enough to maybe, just maybe, be forerunner for Builders."

"Huh?" he exclaimed.

"I'd rather not say more at this point, Gabe. However, Desai also spoke about adoptin' workin' hypothesis. Until further notice, I think this ought to be ours, that there is at least *somethin'* to those stories. We've got to dig deeper, collect hard information. At worst, we'll find we're on our own. At best, who knows?"

"If nothin' else, it'd make good propaganda," he remarked cynically. He had not been back on Aeneas sufficiently long to absorb its atmosphere of expectation. "Uh, how do we keep enemy from reasonin'. and investigatin' along same lines?"

"We've no guaranteed way," Tatiana said. "I've been thinkin', though, and—Look, suppose I call Desai tomorrow or next day, claim I've had change of heart, try wheedlin' more out of him concernin' yon agent. But mainly what I'll do is suggest he check on highlanders of Chalce. They're tough, independent-minded clansmen, you probably recall. It's quite plausible they'd rally 'round Ivar if he went to them, and that he'd do so on his own initiative. Well, it's big and rugged country, take many men and lots of time to search over. Meanwhile—"

✵ 16 ✵

The room within the mountain was spacious, and its lining of Ancient material added an illusion of dreamlike depths beyond. Men had installed heated carpeting, fluoropanels, furniture, and other basic necessities, including books and an eidophone to while away the time. Nevertheless, as hours stretched into days he did not see, Ivar grew half wild. Erannath surely suffered worse; from a human viewpoint, all Ythrians are born with a degree of claustrophobia. But he kept self-control grimly in his talons. Conversation helped them both. Erannath even reminisced: "—wing-free. As a youth I wandered the whole of Avalon...hai-ha, storm-dawns over seas and snowpeaks! Hunting a spathodont with spears! Wind across the plains, that smelled of sun and eternity!... Later I trained to become a tramp spacehand. You do not know what that is? An Ythrian institution. Such a crewman may leave his ship whenever he wishes to stay for a while on some planet, provided a replacement is available; and one usually is." His gaze yearned beyond the shimmering walls. "Khrrr, this is a universe of wonders. Treasure it, Ivar. What is outside our heads is so much more than what can nest inside them."

"Are you still spaceman?" the human asked.

"No. I returned at length to Avalon with Hlirr, whom I had met and wedded on a world where rings flashed rainbow over oceans the color of old silver. That also is good, to ward a home and raise a brood. But they are grown now, and I, in search of a last long-faring before God stoops on me, am here"—he gave a harsh equivalent of a chuckle—"in this cave."

"You're spyin' for Domain, aren't you?"

"I have explained, I am a xenologist, specializing in anthropology. That was the subject I taught throughout the settled years on Avalon, and in which I am presently doing field work."

"Your bein' scientist doesn't forbid your bein' spy. Look, I don't hold it against you. Terran Empire is my enemy same as yours, if not more. We're natural allies. Won't you carry that word back to Ythri for me?"

Ripplings went over Erannath's plumage. "Is every opponent of the Empire your automatic friend? What of Merseia?"

"I've heard propaganda against Merseians till next claim about their bein' racist and territorially aggressive will throw me into anaphylactic shock. Has Terra *never* provoked, yes, menaced them? Besides, they're far off: Terra's problem, not ours. Why should Aeneas supply young men to pull Emperor's fat out of fire? What's he ever done for us? And, God, what hasn't he done to us?"

Erannath inquired slowly, "Do you indeed hope to lead a second, successful revolution?"

"I don't know about leadin'," Ivar said, hot-faced. "I hope to help."

"For what end?"

"Freedom."

"What is freedom? To do as you, an individual, choose? Then how can you be certain that a fragment of the Empire will not make still greater demands on you? I should think it would have to."

"Well, uh, well, I'd be willin' to serve, as long as it was my own people."

"How willing are your people themselves to be served—as individuals—in your fashion? You see no narrowing of your freedom in whatever the requirements may be for a politically independent Alpha Crucis region, any more than you see a narrowing of it in laws against murder or robbery. These imperatives accord with your desires. But others may feel otherwise. What is freedom, except having one's particular cage reach further than one cares to fly?"

Ivar scowled into the yellow eyes. "You talk strange, for Ythrian. For Avalonian, especially. Your planet sure resisted bein' swallowed up by Empire."

"That would have wrought a fundamental change in our lives: for example, by allowing unrestricted immigration, till we were first crowded and then outvoted. You, however—In what basic way might an Alpha Crucian Republic, or an Alpha Crucian province of the Domain, differ from Sector Alpha Crucis of the Empire? You get but one brief flight through reality, Ivar Frederiksen. Would you truly rather pass among ideologies than among stars?"

"Uh, I'm afraid you don't understand. Your race doesn't have our idea of government."

"It's irrelevant to us. My fellow Avalonians who are of human stock have come to think likewise. I must wonder why you are so intense, to the point of making it a deathpride matter, about the precise structure of a political organization. Why do you not, instead, concentrate your efforts toward arrangements whereby it will generally leave you and yours alone?"

"Well, if our motivation here is what puzzles you, then tell them on Ythri—" Ivar drew breath.

Time wore away; and all at once, it was not a single man who came in a plain robe, bringing food and removing discards: it was a figure in uniform that trod through the door and announced, "The High Commander!"

Ivar scrambled to his feet. The feather-crest stood stiff upon Erannath's head. For this they had abided.

A squad entered, forming a double line at taut attention. They were typical male Orcans: tall and lean, brown of skin, black and bushy of hair and closely cropped beard, their faces mostly oval and somewhat flat, their nostrils flared and lips full. But these were drilled and dressed like soldiers. They wore steel helmets which swept down over the neck and bore self-darkening vitryl visors now shoved up out of the way; blue tunics with insignia of rank and, upon the breast of each, an infinity sign; gray trousers tucked into soft boots. Besides knives and knuckledusters at their belts they carried, in defiance of Imperial decree, blasters and rifles which must have been kept hidden from confiscation.

Yakow Harolsson, High Commander of the Companions of the Arena, followed. He was clad the same as his men, except for adding a purple cloak. Though his beard was white and his features scored, the spare form remained erect. Ivar snapped him a salute.

Yakow returned it and in the nasal Anglic of the region said: "Be greeted, Firstling of Ilion."

"Have . . . Terrans gone . . . sir?" Ivar asked. His pulse banged, giddiness passed through him, the cool underground air felt thick in his throat.

"Yes. You may come forth." Yakow frowned. "In disguise, naturally, garb, hair and skin dyes, instruction about behavior. We dare not assume the enemy has left no spies or, what is likelier, hidden surveillance devices throughout the town—perhaps in the very Arena." From beneath discipline there blazed: "Yet forth shall you come, to prepare for the Deliverance."

Erannath stirred. "I could ill pass as an Orcan," he said dryly.

Yakow's gaze grew troubled as it sought him. "No. We have provided for you, after taking counsel."

A vague fear made Ivar exclaim, "Remember, sir, he's liaison with Ythri, which may become our ally."

"Indeed," Yakow said without tone. "We could simply keep you here, Sir Erannath, but from what I know of your race, you would find that unendurable. So we have prepared a safe place elsewhere. Be patient for a few more hours. After dark you will be led away."

To peak afar in wilderness, Ivar guessed, happy again, *where he can roam skies, hunt, think his thoughts, till we're ready for him to rejoin us—or we rejoin him—and afterward send him home.*

On impulse he seized the Ythrian's right hand. Talons closed sharp but gentle around his fingers. "Thanks for everything, Eran-nath," Ivar said. "I'll miss you ... till we meet once more."

"That will be as God courses," answered his friend.

The Arena took its name from the space it enclosed. Through a window in the Commander's lofty sanctum, Ivar looked across tier after tier, sweeping in an austere but subtly eye-compelling pattern of grand ellipses, down toward the central pavement. Those levels were broad enough to be terraces rather than seats, and the walls between them held arched openings which led to the halls and chambers of the interior. Nevertheless, the sugges-tion of an antique theater was strong.

A band of Companions was drilling; for though it had seldom fought in the last few centuries, the order remained military in character, and was police as well as quasi-priesthood. Distance and size dwindled the men to insects. Their calls and footfalls were lost in hot stillness, as were any noises from town; only the Linn resounded, endlessly grinding. Most life seemed to be in the building itself, its changeful iridescences and the energy of its curves.

"Why did Elders make it like this?" Ivar wondered aloud.

A scientific base, combining residences and workrooms? But the ramps which connected floors twisted so curiously; the floors themselves had their abrupt rises and drops, for no discernible reason; the vaulted corridors passed among apartments no two of which were alike. And what had gone on in the crater middle? Mere gardening, to provide desert-weary eyes with a park? (But these parts were fertile, six million years ago.) Experiments? Games? Rites? Something for which man, and every race known to man, had no concept?

"Jaan says the chief purpose was to provide a gathering place, where minds might conjoin and thus achieve transcendence," Yakow answered. He turned to his escort. "Dismissed," he snapped. They saluted and left, closing behind them the human-installed door.

It had had to be specially shaped, to fit the portal of this suite. The outer office where the two men stood was like the inside of a multi-faceted jewel; colors did not sheen softly, as they did across the exterior of the Arena, but glanced and glinted, fire-fierce, wher-ever a sunbeam struck. Against such a backdrop, the few articles of furniture and equipment belonging to the present occupancy seemed twice austere: chairs fashioned of gnarly starkwood, a similar table, a row of shelves holding books and a comset, a carpet woven from the mineral-harsh plants that grew in Orcan shallows.

"Be seated, if you will," Yakow said, and folded his lankness down.

Won't he offer me anyhow a cup of tea? flickered in Ivar. Then, recollection from reading: *No, in this country, food or drink shared creates bonds of mutual obligation. Reckon he doesn't feel quite ready for that with me.*

Do I with him? Ivar took a seat confronting the stern old face.

Disconcertingly, Yakow waited for him to start conversation. After a hollow moment, Ivar attempted: "Uh, that Jaan you speak of, sir. Your prophet, right? I'd not demean your faith, please believe me. But may I ask some questions?"

Yakow nodded; the white beard brushed the infinity sign on his breast. "Whatever you wish, Firstling. Truth can only be clarified by questionings." He paused. "Besides—let us be frank from our start—in many minds it is not yet certitude that Jaan has indeed been possessed by Caruith the Ancient. The Companions of the Arena have taken no official position on the mystery."

Ivar started. "But I thought—I mean, religion—"

Yakow lifted a hand. "Pray hearken, Firstling. We serve no religion here."

"What? Sir, you believe, you've believed for, for hundreds of years, in Elders!"

"As we believe in Virgil or the moons." A ghost-smile flickered. "After all, we see them daily. Likewise do we see the Ancient relics."

Yakow grew earnest. "Of your patience, Firstling, let me explain a little. 'Religion' means faith in the supernatural, does it not? Most Orcans, like most Aeneans everywhere, do have that kind of faith. They maintain a God exists, and observe different ceremonies and injunctions on that account. If they have any sophistication, however, they admit their belief is nonscientific. It is not subject to empirical confirmation or disconfirmation. Miracles may have happened through divine intervention; but a miracle, by definition, involves a suspension of natural law, hence cannot be experimen- tally repeated. Aye, its historical truth or falsity can be indirectly investigated. But the confirmation of an event proves nothing, since it *could* be explained away scientifically. For example, if we could show that there was in fact a Jesus Christ who did in fact rise from his tomb, he may have been in a coma, not dead.

Likewise, disconfirmation proves nothing. For example, if it turns out that a given saint never lived, that merely shows people were naive, not that the basic creed is wrong."

Ivar stared. *This talk—and before we've even touched on any practicalities—from hierophant of impoverished isolated desert dwellers?*

He collected his wits. *Well, nobody with access to electronic communications is truly isolated. And I wouldn't be surprised if Yakow studied at University. I've met a few Orcans there myself.*

Just because person lives apart, in special style, it doesn't mean he's ignorant or stupid.... M-m, do Terrans think this about us? The question aroused a mind-sharpening resentment.

"I repeat," Yakow was saying, "in my sense of the word, we have no shared religion here. We do have a doctrine.

"It is a fact, verifiable by standard stratigraphic and radioisotopic dating methods, a fact that a mighty civilization kept an outpost on Aeneas, six thousand thousand years ago. It is a reasonable inference that those beings did not perish, but rather went elsewhere, putting childish things away as they reached a new stage of evolution. And it may conceivably be wishful thinking, but it does seem more likely than otherwise, that the higher sentiences of the cosmos take a benign interest in the lower, and seek to aid them upward.

"This hope, if you wish to call it no more than that, is what has sustained us."

The words were in themselves dispassionate; and though the voice strengthened, the tone was basically calm. Yet Ivar looked into the countenance and decided to refrain from responding:

What proof have we of any further evolution? We've met many different races by now, and some are wildly different, not just in their bodies but in their ways of thinkin' and their capabilities. Still, we've found none we could call godlike. And why should intelligence progress indefinitely? Nothin' else in nature does. Beyond that point where technology becomes integral to species survival, what selection pressure is there to increase brains? If anything, we sophonts already have more than's good for us.

He realized: *That's orthodox modern attitude, of course. Maybe reflectin' sour grapes, or weariness of decadent society. No use denyin', what we've explored is one atom off outer skin of one dustmote galaxy....*

Aloud, he breathed, "Now Jaan claims Elders are about to return? And mind of theirs is already inside him?"

"Crudely put," Yakow said. "You must talk to him yourself, at length." He paused. "I told you, the Companions do not thus far officially accept his claims. Nor do we reject them. We do acknowledge that, overnight, somehow a humble shoemaker gained certain powers, certain knowledge. 'Remarkable' is an altogether worthless word for whatever has happened."

"Who is he?" Ivar dared ask. "I've heard nothin' more than rumors, hints, guesses."

Yakow spoke now as a pragmatic leader. "When he first arose from obscurity, and ever more people began accepting his preachments: we officers of the Arena saw what explosive potential was here, and sought to hold the story quiet until we could at least evaluate it and its consequences. Jaan himself has been most cooperative with us. We could not altogether prevent word from spreading beyond our land. But thus far, the outside planet knows only vaguely of a new cult in this poor corner."

It may not know *any more than that,* Ivar thought; *however, it's sure ready to* believe *more. Could be I've got news for you, Commander.* "Who is he, really?"

"The scion of a common family, though once well-to-do as prosperity goes in Orcus. His father, Gileb, was a trader who owned several land vehicles and claimed descent from the founder of the Companions. His mother, Nomi, has a genealogy still more venerable, back to the first humans on Aeneas."

"What happened?"

"You may recall, some sixteen years ago this region suffered a period of turmoil. A prolonged sandstorm brought crop failure and the loss of caravans; then quarreling over what was left caused old family feuds to erupt anew. They shook the very Companions. For a time we were ineffective."

Ivar nodded. He had been searching his memory for news stories, and come upon accounts of how this man had won to rule over the order, restored its discipline and morale, and gone on to rescue his entire society from chaos. But that had been the work of years.

"His possessions looted by enemies who sought his blood, Gileb fled with his wife and their infant son," Yakow went on in a level tone. "They trekked across the Antonine, barely surviving, to a small nord settlement in the fertile part of it. There they found poverty-stricken refuge.

"When Gileb died, Nomi returned home with her by then half-dozen children, to this by then pacified country. Jaan had learned the shoemaker's trade, and his mother was—is—a skillful weaver. Between them, they supported the family. There was never enough left over for Jaan to consider marrying.

"Finally he had his revelation . . . made his discovery . . . whatever it was."

"Can you tell me?" Ivar asked low.

The gaze upon him hardened. "That can be talked of later," said Yakow. "For now, methinks best we consider what part you might play, Firstling, in the liberation of Aeneas from the Empire—maybe of mankind from humanness."

✲ 17 ✲

In headcloth, robe, and sandals, skin stained brown and hair black, Ivar would pass a casual glance. His features, build, and blue eyes were not typical; but though the Orcans had long been endogamous, not every gene of their originally mixed heritage was gone, and occasional throwbacks appeared; to a degree, the prophet himself was one. More serious anomalies included his dialect of Anglic, his ignorance of the native language, his imperfect imitation of manners, gait, a thousand subtleties.

Yet surely no Terran, boredly watching the playback from a spy device, would notice those differences. Many Orcans would likewise fail to do so, or would shrug off what they did see. After all, there were local and individual variations within the region; besides, this young man might well be back from several years' service among nords who had influenced him.

Those who looked closely and carefully were the least likely to mention a word of what they saw. For the stranger walked in company with the shoemaker.

It had happened erenow. Someone would hear Jaan preach, and afterward request a private audience. Customarily, the two of them went off alone upon the mountain.

Several jealous pairs of eyes followed Jaan and Ivar out of town. They spoke little until they were well away from people, into a great and aloof landscape.

Behind and above, rocks, bushes, stretches of bare gray dirt reached sharply blue-shadowed, up toward habitation and the crowning Arena. Overhead, the sky was empty save for the sun and one hovering vulch. Downward, land tumbled to the sullen flatness of the sea. Around were hills which bore thin green and scattered houses. Traffic trudged on dust-smoking roads. Ilion reared dark, the Linn blinding white, to north and northeast; elsewhere the horizon was rolling nakedness. A warm and pungent wind stroked faces, fluttered garments, mumbled above the mill-noise of the falls.

Jaan's staff swung and thumped in time with his feet as he picked a way steadily along a browser trail. Ivar used no aid but moved like a hunter. That was automatic; his entire consciousness was bent toward the slow words:

"We can talk now, Firstling. Ask or declare what you will. You cannot frighten or anger me, you who have come as a living destiny."

"I'm no messenger of salvation," Ivar said low. "I'm just very fallible human bein', who doesn't even believe in God."

Jaan smiled. "No matter. I don't myself, in conventional terms. We use 'destiny' in a most special sense. For the moment, let's put it that you were guided here, or aided to come here, in subtle ways"—his extraordinary eyes locked onto the other and he spoke gravely—"because you have the potential of becoming a savior."

"No, I, not me."

Again Jaan relaxed, clapped him on the shoulder, and said, "I don't mean that mystically. Think back to your discussions with High Commander Yakow. What Aeneas needs is twofold, a uniting faith and a uniting secular leader. The Firstman of Ilion, for so you will become in time, has the most legitimate claim, most widely accepted, to speak for this planet. Furthermore, memory of Hugh McCormac will cause the entire sector to rally around him, once he raises the liberation banner afresh.

"What Caruith proclaims will fire many people. But it is too tremendous, too new, for them to live with day-to-day. They must have a . . . a political structure they understand and accept, to guide them through the upheaval. You are the nucleus of that, Ivar Frederiksen."

"I, I don't know—I'm no kind of general or politician, in fact I failed miserably before, and—"

"You will have skilled guidance. But never think we want you for a figurehead. Remember, the struggle will take years. As you grow in experience and wisdom, you will find yourself taking the real lead."

Ivar squinted through desert dazzlement at a far-off dust devil, and said with care:

"I hardly know anything so far...Jaan...except what Yakow and couple of his senior officers have told me. They kept insistin' that to explain—religious?—no, transcendental—to explain tran-scendental aspect of this, only you would do."

"Your present picture is confused and incomplete, then," Jaan said.

Ivar nodded. "What I've learned—Let me try and summarize, may I? Correct me where I'm wrong.

"All Aeneas is primed to explode again. Touchoff spark would be hope, any hope. Given some initial success, more and more peoples elsewhere in Sector Alpha Crucis would join in. But how're we to start? We're broken, disarmed, occupied.

"Well, you preach that superhuman help is at hand. My part would be to furnish political continuity. Aeneans, especially nords, who couldn't go along with return of Elders, might well support Firstman of Ilion in throwin' off Terran yoke. And even true believers would welcome that kind of reinforcement, that human touch: especially since we men must do most of work, and most of dyin', ourselves."

Jaan nodded. "Aye," he said. "Deliverance which is not earned is of little worth in establishing freedom that will endure, of no worth in raising us toward the next level of evolution. The Ancients will *help* us. As we will afterward help them, in their millennial battle....I repeat, we must not expect an instant revolution. To prepare will take years, and after that will follow years more of cruel strife. For a long time to come, your chief part will be simply to stay alive and at large, to be a symbol that keeps the hope of eventual liberation alight."

Ivar nerved himself to ask, "And you, meanwhile, do what?"

"I bear the witness," Jaan said; his tone was nearer humble than proud. "I plant the seeds of faith. As Caruith, I can give you, the Companions, the freedom leaders everywhere, some practical help: for instance, by reading minds under favorable circumstances. But in the ultimate, I am the embodiment of that past which is also the future.

"Surely at last I too must go hide in the wilds from the Terrans, after they realize my significance. Or perhaps they will kill me.

No matter. That only destroys this body. And in so doing, it creates the martyr, it fulfills the cycle. For Caruith shall rise again."

The wind seemed to blow cold along Ivar's bones. "Who is Caruith? What is he?"

"The mind of an Ancient," Jaan said serenely.

"Nobody was clear about it, talkin' to me—"

"They felt best I explain to you myself. For one thing, you are not a semi-literate artisan or herdsman. You are well educated; you reject supernaturalism; to you, Caruith must use a different language from my preachings to common Orcans."

Ivar walked on, waiting. A jackrat scuttered from the bleached skull of a statha.

Jaan looked before him. He spoke in a monotone that, somehow, sang.

"I will begin with my return hither, after the exile years. I was merely a shoemaker, a trade I had learned in what spare time I found between the odd jobs which helped keep us alive. Yet I had also the public data screens, to read, watch, study, learn somewhat of this universe; and at night I would often go forth under the stars to think.

"Now we came back to Mount Cronos. I dreamed of enlisting in the Companions, but that could not be; their training must begin at a far earlier age than mine. However, a sergeant among them, counselor and magistrate to our district, took an interest in me. He helped me carry on my studies. And at last he arranged for me to assist, part time and for a small wage, in archeological work.

"You realize that that is the driving force behind the Companions today. They began as a military band, and continue as civil authorities. Nova Roma could easily reorganize that for us, did we wish. But generations of prophets have convinced us the Ancients cannot be dead, must still dwell lordly in the cosmos. Then what better work is there than to seek what traces and clues are left among us? And who shall better carry it out than the Companions?"

Ivar nodded. This was a major reason why the University had stopped excavation in these parts: to avoid creating resentment among the inhabitants and their leaders. The paucity of reported results, ever since, was assumed to be due to lack of notable finds. Suddenly Ivar wondered how much had been kept secret.

The hypnotic voice went on: "That work made me feel, in my depths, how vastly space-time overarches us and yet how we altogether belong in it. I likewise brooded upon the idea, an idea I first heard while in exile, that the Didonians have a quality of mind, of being, which is as far beyond ours as ours is beyond blind instinct. Could the Ancients have it too—not in the primitive dim unities of our Neighbors, but in perfection? Might *we* someday have it?

"So I wondered, and took ever more to wandering by myself, aye, into the tunnels beneath the mountain when no one else was there. And my heart would cry out for an answer that never came.

"Until—

"It was a night near midwinter. The revolution had not begun, but even here we knew how the oppression waxed, and the people seethed, and chaos grew. Even we were in scant supply of certain things, because offworld trade was becoming irregular, as taxation and confiscation caused merchantmen to move from this sector, and the spaceport personnel themselves grew demoralized till there was no proper traffic control. Yes, a few times out-and-out pirates from the barbarian stars slipped past a fragmented guard to raid and run. The woe of Aeneas was heavy on me.

"I looked at the blaze of the Crux twins, and at the darkness which cleaves the Milky Way where the nebulae hide from us the core of our galaxy: and walking along the mountainside, I asked if, in all that majesty, our lives alone could be senseless accidents, our pain and death for nothing.

"It was cruelly cold, though. I entered the mouth of a newly dug-out Ancient corridor, for shelter; or did something call me? I had a flashbeam, and almost like a sleepwalker found myself bound deeper and deeper down those halls.

"You must understand, the wonderful work itself had not collapsed, save at the entrance, after millions of years of earthquake and landslide. Once we dug past that, we found a labyrinth akin to others. With our scanty manpower and equipment, we might take a lifetime to map the entire complex.

"Drawn by I knew not what, I went where men had not yet been. With a piece of chalkstone picked from the rubble, I marked my path; but that was well-nigh the last glimmer of ordinary human sense in me, as I drew kilometer by kilometer near to my finality.

"I found it in a room where light shone cool from a tall thing off whose simplicity my eyes glided; I could only see that it must be an artifact, and think that most of it must be not matter but energy. Before it lay this which I now wear on my head. I donned it and—

"—there are no words, no thoughts for what came—

"After three nights and days I ascended; and in me dwelt Caruith the Ancient."

✣ 18 ✣

A bony sketch of a man, Colonel Mattu Luuksson had returned Chunderban Desai's greetings with a salute, declined refreshment, and sat on the edge of his lounger as if he didn't want to submit his uniform to its self-adjusting embrace. Nevertheless the Companion of the Arena spoke courteously enough to the High Commissioner of Imperial Terra.

"—decision was reached yesterday. I appreciate your receiving me upon such short notice, busy as you must be."

"I would be remiss in my duty, did I not make welcome the representative of an entire nation," Desai answered. He passed smoke through his lungs before he added, "It does seem like, um, rather quick action, in a matter of this importance."

"The order to which I have the honor to belong does not condone hesitancy," Mattu declared. "Besides, you understand, sir, my mission is exploratory. Neither you nor we will care to make a commitment before we know the situation and each other more fully."

Desai noticed he was tapping his cigarette holder on the edge of the ashtaker, and made himself stop. "We could have discussed this by vid," he pointed out with a mildness he didn't quite feel.

"No, sir, not very well. More is involved than words. An electronic image of you and your office and any number of your subordinates would tell us nothing about the total environment."

"I see. Is that why you brought those several men along?"

"Yes. They will spend a few days wandering around the city, gathering experiences and impressions to report to our council, to help us estimate the desirability of more visits."

Desai arched his brows. "Do you fear they may be corrupted?" The thought of fleshpots in Nova Roma struck him as weirdly funny; he choked back a laugh.

Mattu frowned—in anger or in concentration? *How can I read so foreign a face?* "I had best try to explain from the foundations, Commissioner," he said, choosing each word. "Apparently you have the impression that I am here to protest the recent ransacking of our community, and to work out mutually satisfactory guarantees against similar incidents in future. That is only a minor part of it.

"Your office appears to feel the Orcan country is full of rebellious spirits, in spite of the fact that almost no Orcans joined McCormac's forces. The suspicion is not unnatural. We dwell apart; our entire ethos is different from yours."

From Terra's sensate pragmatism, you mean, Desai thought. *Or its decadence, do you imply?* "As a keeper of law and order yourself," he said, "I trust you sympathize with the occasional necessity of investigating every possibility, however remote."

A Terran, in a position similar to Mattu's, would generally have grinned. The colonel stayed humorless: "More contact should reduce distrust. But this would be insufficient reason to change long-standing customs and policies.

"The truth is, the Companions of the Arena and the society they serve are not as rigid, not as xenophobic, as popular belief elsewhere has it. Our isolation was never absolute; consider our trading caravans, or those young men who spend years outside, in work or in study. It is really only circumstance which has kept us on the fringe—and, no doubt, a certain amount of human inertia.

"Well, the times are mutating. If we Orcans are not to become worse off, we must adapt. In the course of adaptation, we can better our lot. Although we are not obsessed with material wealth, and indeed think it disastrous to acquire too much, yet we do not value poverty, Commissioner; nor are we afraid of new ideas. Rather, we feel our own ideas have strength to survive, and actually spread among people who may welcome them."

Desai's cigarette was used up. He threw away the ill-smelling stub and inserted a fresh one. Anticipating, his palate winced. "You are interested in enlarged trade relationships, then," he said.

"Yes," Mattu replied. "We have more to offer than is commonly realized. I think not just of natural resources, but of hands and brains, if more of our youth can get adequate modern educations."

"And, hm-m-m, tourism in your area?"

"Yes," Mattu snapped. Obviously the thought was distasteful to him as an individual. "To develop all this will take time, which we have, and capital, which we have not. The nords were never interested... albeit I confess the Companions never made any proposal to them. We have now conceived the hope that the Imperium may wish to help."

"Subsidies?"

"They need not be great, nor continue long. In return, the Imperium gains not simply our friendship, but our influence, as Orcans travel further and oftener across Aeneas. You face a nord power structure which, on the whole, opposes you, and which you are unlikely to win over. Might not Orcan influence help transform it?"

"Perhaps. In what direction, though?"

"Scarcely predictable at this stage, is it? For that matter, we could still decide isolation is best. I repeat, my mission is no more than a preliminary exploration—for both our sides, Commissioner." Chunderban Desai, who had the legions of the Empire at his beck, looked into the eyes of the stranger; and it was Chunderban Desai who felt a tinge of fear.

The young lieutenant from Mount Cronos had openly called Tatiana Thane to ask if he might visit her "in order to make the acquaintance of the person who best knows Ivar Frederiksen. Pray understand, respected lady, we do not lack esteem for him. However, indirectly he has been the cause of considerable trouble for us. It has occurred to me that you may advise us how we can convince the authorities we are not in league with him."

"I doubt it," she answered, half amused at his awkward earnestness. The other half of her twisted in re-aroused pain, and wanted to deny his request. But that would be cowardice.

When he entered her apartment, stiff in his uniform, he offered her a token of appreciation, a hand-carved pendant from his country. To study the design, she must hold it in her palm close to her face; and she read the engraved question, *Are we spied on?*

Her heart sprang. After an instant, she shook her head, and knew the gesture was too violent. No matter. Stewart sent a technician around from time to time, who verified that the Terrans had planted no bugs. Probably the underground itself had done so.... The lieutenant extracted an envelope from his tunic and bowed as he handed it to her.

"Read at your leisure," he said, "but my orders are to watch you destroy this afterward."

He seated himself. His look never left her. She, in her own chair, soon stopped noticing. After the third time through Ivar's letter, she mechanically heeded Frumious Bandersnatch's plaintive demand for attention.

Following endearments which were nobody else's business, and a brief account of his travels:

"—prophet, though he denies literal divine inspiration. I wonder what difference? His story is latter-day Apocalypse.

"I don't know whether I can believe it. His quiet certainty carries conviction; but I don't claim any profound knowledge of people. I could be fooled. What is undeniable is that under proper conditions he can read my mind, better than any human telepath I ever heard of, better than top-gifted humans are supposed to be able to. Or nonhumans, even? I was always taught telepathy is not universal language; it's not enough to sense your subject's radiations, you have to learn what each pattern means to *him;* and of course patterns vary from individual to individual, still more from culture to culture, tremendously from species to species. And to this day, phenomenon's not too well understood. I'd better just give you Jaan's own story, though my few words won't have anything of overwhelming *impression* he makes.

"He says, after finding this Elder artifact I mentioned, he put 'crown' on his head. I suppose that would be natural thing to do. It's adjustable, and ornamental, and maybe he's right, maybe command was being broadcast. Anyhow, something indescribable happened, heaven and hell together, at first mostly hell because of fear and strangeness and uprooting of his whole mind, later mostly heaven—and now, Jaan says, neither word is any good, there are no words for what he experiences, what he is.

"In scientific terms, if they aren't pseudoscientific (where do you draw line, when dealing with unknown?), what he says happened is this. Long ago, Elders, or Ancients as they call them here, had base on Aeneas, same as on many similar planets. It was no mere research base. They were serving huge purpose I'll come to later. Suggestion is right that they actually caused Didonians to evolve, as one experiment among many, all aimed at creating more intelligence, more consciousness, throughout cosmos.

"At last they withdrew, but left one behind whom Jaan gives name of Caruith, though he says spoken name is purely for benefit of our limited selves. It wasn't original Caruith who stayed;

and original wasn't individual like you or me anyway, but part—aspect?—attribute?—of glorious totality which Didonians only hint at. What Caruith did was let heeshself be scanned, neurone by neurone, so entire personality pattern could be recorded in some incredible fashion.

"Sorry, darling, I just decided pronoun like 'heesh' is okay for Neighbors but too undignified for Ancients. I'll say 'he' because I'm more used to that; could just as well, or just as badly, be 'she,' of course.

"When Jaan put on circlet, apparatus was activated, and stored pattern was imposed on his nervous system.

"You can guess difficulties. What shabby little word, 'difficulties!' Jaan has human brain, human body; and in fact, Elders thought mainly in terms of Didonian finding their treasure. Jaan can't do anything his own organism hasn't got potential for. Original Caruith could maybe solve a thousand simultaneous differential equations in his 'head,' in split second, if he wanted to; but Caruith using Jaan's primitive brain can't. You get idea?

"Noneless, Elders had realized Didonians might not be first in that room. They'd built flexibility into system. Furthermore, all organisms have potentials that aren't ordinarily used. Let me give you clumsy example. You play chess, paint pictures, hand-pilot aircraft, and analyze languages. I know. But suppose you'd been born into world where nobody had invented chess, paint, aircraft, or semantic analysis. You see? Or think how sheer physical and mental training can bring out capabilities in almost anybody.

"So after three days of simply getting adjusted, to point where he could think and act at all, Jaan came back topside. Since then, he's been integrating more and more with this great mind that shares his brain. He says at last they'll become *one*, more Caruith than Jaan, and he rejoices at prospect.

"Well, what does he preach? What do Elders want? Why did they do what they have done?

"Again, it's impossible to put in few words. I'm going to try, but I know I will fail. Maybe your imagination can fill in gaps. You've certainly got good mind, sweetheart.

"Ancients, Elders, Builders, High Ones, Old Shen, whatever we call them—and Jaan won't give them separate name, he says that would be worse misleading than 'Caruith' already is—evolved billions of years ago, near galactic center where stars are older and closer together. We're way out on thin fringe of spiral arm, you remember. At that time, there had not been many generations of stars, elements heavier than helium were rare, planets with possibility of life were few. Elders went into space and found it lonelier than we can dream, we who have more inhabited worlds around than anybody has counted. They turned inward, they deliberately forced themselves to keep on evolving mind, lifetime after lifetime, because they had no one else to talk to—How I wish I could send you record of Jaan explaining!

"Something happened. He says he isn't yet quite able to understand what. Split in race, in course of millions of years; not ideological difference as we think of ideology, but two different ways of perceiving, of evaluating reality, two different purposes to impose on universe. We dare not say one branch is good, one evil; we can only say they are irreconcilable. Call them Yang and Yin, but don't try to say which is which.

"In crudest possible language, *our* Elders see goal of life as consciousness, transcendence of everything material, unification of mind not only in this galaxy but throughout cosmos, so its final collapse won't be end but will be beginning. While Others seek—mystic oneness with energy—supreme experience of Acceptance—No, I don't suppose you can fairly call them death-oriented.

"Jaan likes old Terran quotation I know, as describing Elders: 'To strive, to seek, to find, and not to yield.' (Do you know it?) And for Others, what? Not 'Kismet,' really; that at least implies doing God's will, and Others deny God altogether. Nor 'nihilism,' which I reckon implies desire for chaos, maybe as necessary for rebirth. What Others stand for is so alien that—Oh, I'll write, knowing I'm wrong, that they believe rise, fall, and infinite extinction are our sole realities, and sole fulfillment that life can ultimately have is harmony with this curve.

"In contrast, Jaan says life, if it follows Elder star, will at last *create* God, *become* God.

"To that end, Elders have been watching new races arise on new planets, and helping them, guiding them, sometimes even bringing them into being like Didonians. They can't watch always over everything; they haven't over us. For Others have been at work too, and must be opposed.

"It's not war as we understand war; not on that level. On our level, it is.

"Analogy again. You may be trying to arrive at some vital decision that will determine your entire future. You may be reasoning, you may be wrestling with your emotions, but it's all in your mind; nobody else need see a thing.

"Only it's *not* all in your mind. Unhealthy body means unhealthy thinking. Therefore, down on cellular level, your white blood corpuscles and antigens are waging relentless, violent war on invaders. And its outcome will have much to do with what happens in your head—maybe everything. Do you see?

"It's like that. What intelligent life (I mean sophonts as we know them; Elders and Others are trans-intelligent) does is crucial. And one tiny bit of one galaxy, like ours, can be turning point. Effects multiply, you see. Just as it took few starfaring races to start many more on same course, irreversible change, so it could take few new races who go over to wholly new way of evolution for rest to do likewise eventually.

"Will that level be of Elders or of Others? Will we break old walls and reach, however painfully, for what is infinite, or will we find most harmonious, beautiful, noble way to move toward experience of oblivion?

"You see what I was getting at, that words like 'positive' and 'negative,' 'active' and 'passive,' 'evolutionism' and 'nihilism,' 'good' and 'evil' don't mean anything in this context? Beings unimaginably far beyond us have two opposing ways of comprehending reality. Which are we to choose?

"We have no escape from choosing. We can accept authority, limitations, instructions; we can compromise; we can live out our personal lives safely; and it's victory for Others throughout space we know, because right now *Homo sapiens* does happen to be leading species in these parts. Or we can take our risks, strike for our freedom, and if we win it, look for Elders to return and raise us, like children of theirs, toward being more than what we have ever been before.

"That's what Jaan says. Tanya, darling, I just don't know—"

She lifted eyes from the page. It flamed in her: *I do. Already.*

Nomi dwelt with her children in a two-room adobe at the bottom end of Grizzle Alley. Poverty flapped and racketed everywhere around them. It did not stink, for even the poorest Orcans were of cleanly habits and, while there was scant water to spare for washing, the air quickly parched out any malodors. Nor were there beggars; the Companions took in the desperately needy, and assigned them what work they were capable of doing. But ragged shapes crowded this quarter with turmoil: milling and yelling children, women overburdened with jugs and baskets, men plying their trades, day laborer, muledriver, carter, scavenger, artisan, butcher, tanner, priest, minstrel, vendor chanting or chaffering about his pitiful wares. Among battered brown walls, on tangled lanes of rutted iron-hard earth, Ivar felt more isolated than if he had been alone in the Dreary.

The mother of the prophet put him almost at ease. They had met briefly. Today he asked for Jaan, and heard the latter was absent, and was invited to come in and wait over a cup of tea. He felt a trifle guilty, for he had in fact made sure beforehand that Jaan was out, walking and earnestly talking with his disciples, less teaching them than using them for a sounding board while he groped his own way toward comprehension and integration of his double personality.

But I must learn more myself, before I make that terrible commitment he wants. And who can better give me some sense of what he really is, than this woman?

She was alone, the youngsters being at work or in school. The inside of the hut was therefore quiet, once its door had closed off street noise. Sunlight slanted dusty through the glass of narrow windows; few Orcans could afford vitryl. The room was cool, shadowy, crowded but, in its neatness, not cluttered. Nomi's loom filled one corner, a half-finished piece of cloth revealing a subtle pattern of subdued hues. Across from it was a set of primitive kitchen facilities. Shut-beds for her and her oldest son took most of the remaining space. In the middle of the room was a plank table surrounded by benches, whereat she seated her guest. Food on high shelves or hung from the rafters—a little preserved meat, more dried vegetables and hardtack—made the air fragrant. At the rear an open doorway showed a second room, occupied mostly by bunks.

Nomi moved soft-footed across the clay floor, poured from the pot she had made ready, and sat down opposite Ivar in a rustle of skirts. She had been beautiful when young, and was still handsome in a haggard fashion. If anything, her gauntness enhanced a pair of wonderful gray eyes, such as Jaan had in heritage from her. The coarse blue garb, the hood which this patriarchal society laid over the heads of widows, on her were not demeaning; she had too much inner pride to need vanity.

They had made small talk while she prepared the bitter Orcan tea. She knew who he was. Jaan said he kept no secrets from her, because she could keep any he asked from the world. Now Ivar apologized: "I didn't mean to interrupt your work, my lady."

She smiled. "A welcome interruption, Firstling."

"But, uh, you depend on it for your livin'. If you'd rather go on with it—"

She chuckled. "Pray take not away from me this excuse for idleness."

"Oh. I see." He hated to pry, it went against his entire training, and he knew he would not be good at it. But he had to start frank discussion somehow. "It's only, well, it seemed to me you aren't exactly rich. I mean, Jaan hasn't been makin' shoes since—what happened to him."

"No. He has won a higher purpose." She seemed amused by the inadequacy of the phrase.

"Uh, he never asks for contributions, I'm told. Doesn't that make things hard for you?"

She shook her head. "His next two brothers have reached an age where they can work part time. It could be whole time, save that I will not have it; they must get what learning they can. And... Jaan's followers help us. Few of them can afford any large donation, but a bit of food, a task done for us without charge, such gifts mount up."

Her lightness had vanished. She frowned at her cup and went on with some difficulty: "It was not quite simple for me to accept at first. Ever had we made our own way, as did Gileb's parents and mine ere we were wedded. But what Jaan does is so vital that—Ay-ah, acceptance is a tiny sacrifice."

"You do believe in Caruith, then?"

She lifted her gaze to his, and his dropped as she answered, "Shall I not believe my own good son and my husband's?"

"Oh, yes, certainly, my lady," he floundered. "I beg your pardon if I seemed to—Look, I am outsider here, I've only known him few days and—Do you see? You have knowledge of him to guide you in decidin' he's not, well, victim of delusion. I don't have that knowledge, not yet, anyway."

Nomi relented, reached across the table and patted his hand. "Indeed, Firstling. You do right to ask. I am gladdened that in you he has found the worthy comrade he needs."

Has he?

Perhaps she read the struggle on his face, for she continued, low-voiced and looking beyond him:

"Why should I wonder that you wonder? I did likewise. When he vanished for three dreadful days, and came home utterly changed—Yes, I thought a blood vessel must have burst in his brain, and wept for my kind, hard-working first-born boy, who had gotten so little from life.

"Afterward I came to understand how he had been singled out as no man ever was before in all of space and time. But that wasn't a joy, Firstling, as we humans know joy. His glory is as great and as cruel as the sun. Most likely he shall have to die. Only the other night, I dreamed he was Shoemaker Jaan again, married to a girl I used to think about for him, and they had laid their first baby in my arms. I woke laughing...." Her fingers closed hard on the cup. "That cannot be, of course."

Ivar never knew if he would have been able to probe further. An interruption saved him: Robhar, the youngest disciple, knocking at the door.

"I thought you might be here, sir," the boy said breathlessly. Though the master had identified the newcomer only by a false name, his importance was obvious. "Caruith will come as soon as he can." He thrust forward an envelope. "For you."

"Huh?" Ivar stared.

"The mission to Nova Roma is back, sir," Robhar said, nigh bursting with excitement. "It brought a letter for you. The messenger gave it to Caruith, but he told me to bring it straight to you."

To Heraz Hyronsson stood on the outside. Ivar ripped the envelope open. At the end of several pages came the bold signature *Tanya*. His own account to her had warned her how to address a reply.

"Excuse me," he mumbled, and sat down to gulp it.

Afterward he was very still for a while, his features locked. Then he made an excuse for leaving, promised to get in touch with Jaan soon, and hurried off. He had some tough thinking to do.

☆ **19** ☆

None but a few high-ranking officers among the Companions had
been told who Ivar was. They addressed him as Heraz when in
earshot of others. He showed himself as seldom as feasible, dining
with Yakow in the Commander's suite, sleeping in a room nearby
which had been lent him, using rear halls, ramps, and doorways
for his excursions. In that vast structure, more than half of it
unpopulated, he was never conspicuous. The corps knew their
chief was keeping someone special, but were too disciplined to
gossip about it.

Thus he and Yakow went almost unseen to the chamber used
as a garage. Jaan was already present, in response to word from
a runner. A guard saluted as the three men entered an aircar;
and no doubt much went on in his head, but he would remain
close-mouthed. The main door glided aside. Yakow's old hands
walked skillfully across the console. The car lifted, purred forth
into the central enclosure, rose a vertical kilometer, and started
leisurely southward.

A wind had sprung up as day rolled toward evening. It whined
around the hull, which shivered. The Sea of Orcus bore whitecaps
on its steel-colored surface and flung waves against its shores;
where spray struck and evaporated, salt was promptly hoar. The
continental shelf glowed reddish from long rays filtered through
a dust-veil which obscured the further desert; the top of that
storm broke off in thin clouds and streamed yellow across blue-
black heaven.

Yakow put controls on automatic, swiveled his seat around,
and regarded the pair who sat aft of him. "Very well, we have
the meeting place you wanted, Firstling," he said. "Now will you
tell us why?"

Ivar felt as if knives and needles searched him. He flicked his
glance toward Jaan's mild countenance, remembered what lay
beneath it, and recoiled to stare out the canopy at the waters
which they were crossing. *I'm supposed to cope with these two?*
he thought despairingly.

Well, there's nobody else for job. Nobody in whole wide universe.
Against his loneliness, he hugged to him the thought that they
might prove to be in truth his comrades in the cause of liberation.

"I, I'm scared of possible spies, bugs," he said.

"Not in my part of the Arena," Yakow snapped. "You know how often and thoroughly we check."

"But Terrans have resources of, of entire Empire to draw on. They could have stuff we don't suspect. Like telepathy." Ivar forced himself to turn back to Jaan. "You scan minds."

"Within limits," the prophet cautioned. "I have explained."

Yes. He took me down into mountain's heart and showed me machine—device—whatever it is that he says held record of Caruith. He wouldn't let me touch anything, though I couldn't really blame him, and inside I was just as glad for excuse not to. And there he sensed my thoughts. I tested him every way 1 could imagine, and he told me exactly what I was thinkin', as well as some things I hadn't quite known I was thinkin'. Yes.

He probably wouldn't've needed telepathy to see my sense of privacy outraged. He smiled and told me—

"*Fear not. I have only my human nervous system, and it isn't among the half-talented ones which occur rarely in our species. By myself, I cannot resonate any better than you, Firstling.*" *Bleakly:* "*This is terrible for Caruith, like being deaf or blind; but he endures, that awareness may be helped to fill reality. And down here—*" *Glory:* "*Here his former vessel acts to amplify, to recode, like a living brain center. Within its range of operation, Caruith-Jaan is part of what he rightfully should be: of what he will be again, when his people return and make for us that body we will have deserved.*"

I can believe anyway some fraction of what he claimed. Artificial amplification and relayin' of telepathy are beyond Terran science; but I've read of experiments with it, in past eras when Terran science was more progressive than now. Such technology is not too far beyond our present capabilities: almost matter of engineerin' development rather than pure research.

Surely it's negligible advance over what we know, compared to recordin' of entire personality, and reimposition of pattern on member of utterly foreign species....

"Well," Ivar said, "if you, usin' artifact not really intended for your kind of organism, if you con minds within radius of hundred meters or so—then naturally endowed bein's ought to do better."

"There are no nonhumans in Orcan territory," Yakow said.

"Except Erannath," Ivar retorted.

Did the white-bearded features stiffen? Did Jaan wince? "Ah,

yes," the Commander agreed. "A temporary exception. No xenosophonts are in Arena or town."

"Could be human mutants, maybe genetic-tailored, who've infiltrated." Ivar shrugged. "Or maybe no telepathy at all; maybe some
gadget your detectors won't register. I repeat, you probably don't
appreciate as well as I do what variety must exist on thousands
of Imperial planets. Nobody can keep track. Imperium could well
import surprise for us from far side of Empire." He sighed. "Or,
okay, call me paranoid. Call this trip unnecessary. You're probably
right. Fact is, however, I've got to decide what to do—question
involvin' not simply me, but my whole society—and I feel happier
discussin' it away from any imaginable surveillance."

Such as may lair inside Mount Cronos.

*If it does, I don't think it's happened to tap my thoughts these
past several hours. Else my sudden suspicions that came from
Tanya's letter could've gotten me arrested.*

Jaan inquired shrewdly, "Has the return of our Nova Roma
mission triggered you?"

Ivar nodded with needless force.

"The message you received from your betrothed—"

"I destroyed it," Ivar admitted, for the fact could not be evaded
were he asked to show the contents. "Because of personal elements." They weren't startled; most nords would have done the
same. "However, you can guess what's true, that she discussed her
connection with freedom movement. My letter to her and talks
with your emissary had convinced her our interests and yours
are identical in throwin' off Imperial yoke."

"And now you wish more details," Yakow said.

Ivar nodded again. "Sir, wouldn't you? Especially since it looks
as if Commissioner Desai will go along with your plan. That'll
mean Terrans comin' here, to discuss and implement economic
growth of this region. What does that imply for our liberation?"

"I thought I had explained," said Jaan patiently. "The plan is
Caruith's. Therefore it is long-range, as it must be; for what hope
lies in mere weapons? Let us rise in force before the time is ready,
and the Empire will crush us like a thumb crushing a sand-mite."

Caruith's plan— The aircar had passed across the sea and the
agricultural lands which fringed its southern shore, to go out over
the true desert. This country made the Dreary of Ironland seem
lush. Worn pinnacles lifted above ashen dunes; dust scuddled and

whirled; Ivar glimpsed fossil bones of an ocean monster, briefly exposed for wind to scour away, the single token of life. Low in the west, Virgil glowered through a haze that whistled.

"Idea seems...chancy, over-subtle....Can any nonhuman fathom our character that well?" he fretted.

"Remember, in me he is half human," Jaan replied; "and he has a multimillion-year history to draw on. Men are no more unique than any other sophonts. Caruith espies likenesses among races to which we are blind."

"I too grow impatient," Yakow sighed. "I yearn to see us free, but can hardly live long enough. Yet Caruith is right. We must prepare all Aeneans, so when the day comes, all will rise together."

"The trade expansion is a means to that end," Jaan assured. "It should cause Orcans to travel across the planet, meeting each sort of other Aenean, leavening with faith and fire. Oh, our agents will not be told to preach; they will not know anything except that they have practical bargains to drive and arrangements to make. But they will inevitably fall into conversations, and this will arouse interest, and nords or Riverfolk or tinerans or whoever will invite friends to come hear what the outlander has to say."

"I've heard that several times," Ivar replied, "and I still have trouble understandin'. Look, sirs. You don't expect mass conversion to Orcan beliefs, do you? I tell you, that's impossible. Our different cultures are too strong in their particular reverences—traditional religions, paganism, Cosmenosis, ancestor service, whatever it may be."

"Of course," Jaan said softly. "But can you not appreciate, Firstling, their very conviction is what counts? Orcans will by precept and example make every Aenean redouble his special fervor. And nothing in my message contradicts any basic tenet of yonder faiths. Rather, the return of the Ancients fulfills all hopes, no matter what form they have taken."

"I know, I know. Sorry, I keep on bein' skeptical. But never mind. I don't suppose it can do any harm; and as you say, it might well help keep spirit of resistance alive. What about me, though? What am I supposed to be doin' meanwhile?"

"At a time not far in the future," Yakow said, "you will raise the banner of independence. We need to make preparations first; mustn't risk you being seized at once by the enemy. Most likely, you'll have to spend years offplanet, waging guerrilla warfare on Dido, for example, or visiting foreign courts to negotiate for their support."

Ivar collected his nerve and interrupted: "Like Ythri?"

"Well . . . yes." Yakow dismissed his own infinitesimal hesitation. "Yes, we might get help from the Domain, not while yours is a small group of outlaws, but later, when our cause comes to look more promising." He leaned forward. "To begin with, frankly, your role will be a gadfly's. You will distract the Empire from noticing too much the effects of Orcans traveling across Aeneas. You cannot hope to accomplish more, not for the first several years."

"I don't know," Ivar said with what stubbornness he could rally. "We might get clandestine help from Ythri sooner, maybe quite soon. Some hints Erannath let drop—" He straightened in his seat. "Why not go talk to him right away?"

Jaan looked aside. Yakow said, "I fear that isn't practical at the moment, Firstling."

"How come? Where is he?"

Yakow clamped down sternness. "You yourself worry about what the enemy may eavesdrop on. What you don't know, you cannot let slip. I must request your patience in this matter."

It shuddered in Ivar as if the wind outside blew between his ribs. He wondered how well he faked surrender and relaxation. "Okay."

"We had better start back," Yakow said. "Night draws nigh."

He turned himself around and then the aircraft. A dusk was already in the cabin, for the storm had thickened. Ivar welcomed the concealment of his face. And did outside noise drown the thud-thud-thud of his pulse? He said most slowly, "You know, Jaan, one thing I've never heard bespoken. What does Caruith's race look like?"

"It doesn't matter," was the reply. "They are more mind than body. Indeed, their oneness includes numerous different species. Think of Dido. In the end, all races will belong."

"Uh-huh. However, I can't help bein' curious. Let's put it this way. What did the body look like that actually lay down under scanner?"

"Why . . . well—"

"Come on. Maybe your Orcans are so little used to pictures that they don't insist on description. I assure you, companyo, other Aeneans are different. They'll ask. Why not tell me?"

"*Kah,* hm, *kah—*" Jaan yielded. He seemed a touch confused, as if the consciousness superimposed on his didn't work well at a large distance from the reinforcing radiations of the underground vessel. "Yes. He...male, aye, in a bisexual warm-blooded species... not mammalian; descended from ornithoids...human-seeming in many ways, but beautiful, far more refined and sculptured than us. Thin features set at sharp angles; hairless golden skin; blue feather-crest; great russet eyes; a speaking voice like music—No." Jaan broke off. "I will not say further. It has no significance."

You've said plenty, tolled in Ivar.

Talk was sparse for the rest of the journey. As the car moved downward toward an Arena that had become a bulk of blackness studded with a few lights, the Firstling spoke. "Please, I want to go off by myself and think. I'm used to space and solitude when I make important decisions. How about lendin' me this flitter? I'll fly to calm area, settle down, watch moons and stars—return before mornin' and let you know how things appear to me. May I?"

He had well composed and mentally rehearsed his speech. Yakow raised no objection; Jaan gave his shoulder a sympathetic squeeze. "Surely," said the prophet. "Courage and wisdom abide with you, dear friend."

When he had let the others out, Ivar lifted fast, and cut a thunderclap through the air in his haste to be gone. The dread of pursuit bayed at his heels.

Harsh through him went: *They aren't infallible. I took them by surprise. Jaan should've been prepared with any description but true one—one that matches what Tanya relayed to me from Commissioner Desai, about Merseian agent loose on Aeneas.*

Stiffening wind after sunset filled the air around the lower mountainside with fine sand. Lavinia showed a dim half-disc overhead, but cast no real light; and there were no stars. Nor did villages and farmsteads scattered across the hills reveal themselves. Vision ended within meters.

Landing on instruments, Ivar wondered if this was lucky for him. He could descend unseen, where otherwise he would have had to park behind some ridge or grove kilometers away and slink forward afoot. Indeed, he had scant choice. Walking any distance through a desert storm, without special guidance equipment he didn't have along, posed too much danger of losing his way. But coming so near town and Arena, he risked registering on the detectors of a guard post, and somebody dispatching a squad to investigate.

Well, the worst hazard lay in a meek return to his quarters. He found with a certain joy that fear had left him, as had the hunger and thirst of supperlessness, washed away by the excitement now coursing through him. He donned the overgarment everyone took with him on every trip, slid back the door, and jumped to the ground.

The gale hooted and droned. It sheathed him in chill and a scent of iron. Grit stung. He secured his nightmask and groped forward.

For a minute he worried about going astray in spite of planning. Then he stubbed his toe on a rock which had fallen off a heap, spoil from the new excavation. The entrance was dead ahead uphill, to that tunnel down which Jaan had taken him.

He didn't turn on the flashbeam he had borrowed from the car's equipment, till he stood at the mouth. Thereafter he gripped it hard, as his free hand sought for a latch.

Protection from weather, the manmade door needed no lock against a folk whose piety was founded on relics. When he had closed it behind him, Ivar stood in abrupt silence, motionless cold, a dark whose thickness was broken only by the wan ray from the flash. His breath sounded too loud in his ears. Fingers sought comfort from the heavy sheath knife he had borne from Windhome; but it was his solitary weapon. To carry anything more, earlier, would have provoked instant suspicion.

What will I find?

Probably nothin'. I can take closer look at Caruith machine, but I haven't tools to open it and analyze. As for what might be elsewhere . . . these corridors twist on and on, in dozen different sets.

Noneless, newest discovery, plausibly barred to public while exploration proceeds, is most logical place to hide—whatever is to be hidden. And—his gaze went to the dust of megayears, tumbled and tracked like the dust of Luna when man first fared into space—*I could find traces which'll lead me further, if any have gone before me.*

He began to walk. His footfalls clopped hollowly back off the ageless vaulting.

Why am I doin' this? Because Merseians may have part in events?

Is it bad if they do? Tanya feels happy about what she's heard. She thinks Roidhunate might really come to our aid, and hopes I can somehow contact that agent.

But Ythri might help too. In which case, why won't Orcan chiefs let me see Erannath? Their excuse rings thin.

And if Ancients are workin' through Merseians, as is imaginable, why have they deceived Jaan? Shouldn't he know?

(Does he? It wouldn't be information to broadcast. Terran Imperium may well dismiss Jaan's claims as simply another piece of cultism, which it'd cause more trouble to suppress than it's worth . . . but never if Imperium suspected Merseia was behind it! So maybe he is withholdin' full story. Except that doesn't feel right. He's too sincere, too rapt, and, yes, too bewildered, to play double game. Isn't he?)

I've got to discover truth, or lose what right I ever had to lead my people.

Ivar marched on into blindness.

✧ 20 ✧

A kilometer deep within the mountain, he paused outside the chamber of Jaan's apotheosis. His flashbeam barely skimmed the metal enigma before seeking back to the tunnel floor.

Here enough visits had gone on of late years that the dust was scuffed confusion. Ivar proceeded down the passage. The thing in the room cast him a last reflection and was lost to sight. He had but the one bobbing blob of luminance to hollow out a place for himself in the dark. Now that he advanced slowly, carefully, the silence was well-nigh total. *Bad-a-bad,* went his heart, *bad-a-bad, bad-a-bad.*

After several meters, the blurriness ended. He would not have wondered to see individual footprints. Besides Jaan, officers of the Companions whom the prophet brought hither had surely ventured somewhat further. What halted him was sudden orderliness. The floor had been swept smooth.

He stood for minutes while his thoughts grew fangs. When he continued, the knife was in his right fist.

Presently the tunnel branched three ways. That was a logical point for people to stop. Penetrating the maze beyond was a task for properly equipped scientists; and no scientists would be allowed here for a long while to come. Ivar saw that the broom, or whatever it was, had gone down all the mouths. *Quite reasonable,* trickled through him. *Visitors wouldn't likely notice sweepin' had been done, unless they came to place where change in dust layers was obvious. Or unless they half expected it, like me . . . expected strange traces would have to be wiped out. . . .*

He went into each of the forks, and found that the handiwork ended after a short distance in two of them. What reached onward was simply the downdrift of geological ages. The third had been swept for some ways farther, though not since the next-to-last set of prints had been made. Two sets of those were human, one Ythrian; only the humans had returned. Superimposed were other marks, which were therefore more recent.

They were the tracks of a being who walked on birdlike claws.

Again Ivar stood. Cold gnawed him.

Should I turn right around and run?

Where could I run to?

And Erannath—That decided him. What other friend remained to the free Aeneans? If the Ythrian was alive.

He stalked on. A pair of doorways gaped along his path. He flashed light into them, but saw just empty chambers of curious shape.

Then the floor slanted sharply downward, and he rounded a curve, and from an arch ahead of him in the right wall there came a wan yellow glow.

He gave himself no chance to grow daunted, snapped off his beam and glided to the spot. Poised for a leap, he peered around the edge.

Another cell, this one hexagonal and high-domed, reached seven meters into the rock. Shadows hung in it as heavy, chill, and stagnant as the air. They were cast by a ponderous steel table to which were welded a lightglobe, a portable sanitary facility, and a meter-length chain. Free on its top stood a plastic tumbler and water pitcher, free on the floor lay a mattress, the single relief from iridescent hardness.

"Erannath!" Ivar cried.

The Ythrian hunched on the pad. His feathers were dull and draggled, his head gone skull-gaunt. The chain ended in a manacle that circled his left wrist.

Ivar entered. The Ythrian struggled out of dreams and knew him. The crest erected, the yellow eyes came ablaze. "*Hyaa-aa,*" he breathed.

Ivar knelt to embrace him. "What've they done?" the man cried. "Why? My God, those bastards—"

Erannath shook himself. His voice came hoarse, but strength rang in it. "No time for sentiment. What brought you here? Were you followed?"

"I g-g-got suspicious." Ivar hunkered back on his heels, hugged his knees, mastered his shock. The prisoner was all too aware of urgency; that stood forth from every quivering plume. And who could better know what dangers dwelt in this tomb? Never before had Ivar's mind run swifter.

"No," he said, "I don't think they suspect me in turn. I made excuse to flit off alone, came back and landed under cover of dust storm, found nobody around when I entered. What got me wonderin' was letter today from my girl. She'd learned of Merseian secret agent at large on Aeneas, telepath of some powerful kind. His description answers to Jaan's of Caruith. Right away, I thought maybe cruel trick was bein' played. Jaan should've had less respect for my feelin's and examined—I didn't show anybody letter, and kept well away from Arena as much as possible, before returnin' to look for myself."

"You did well." Erannath stroked talons across Ivar's head; and the man knew it for an accolade. "Beware. Aycharaych is near. We must hope he sleeps, and will sleep till you have gone."

"Till *we* have."

Erannath chuckled. His chain clinked. He did not bother to ask, How do you propose to cut this?

"I'll go fetch tools," Ivar said.

"No. Too chancy. You must escape with the word. At that, if you do get clear, I probably will be released unharmed. Aycharaych is not vindictive. I believe him when he says he sorrows at having to torture me."

Torture? No marks. . . . Of course. Keep sky king chained, buried alive, day after night away from sun, stars, wind. It'd be less cruel to stretch him over slow fire. Ivar gagged on rage.

Erannath saw, and warned: "You cannot afford indignation either. Listen. Aycharaych has talked freely to me. I think he must be lonely, shut away down here with nothing but his machinations and the occasional string he pulls on his puppet prophet. Or is his reason that, in talking, he brings associations into my consciousness, and thus reads more of what I know? This is why I have been kept alive. He wants to drain me of data."

"What is he?" Ivar whispered.

"A native of a planet he calls Chereion, somewhere in the Merseian Roidhunate. Its civilization is old, old—formerly wide-faring and mighty—yes, he says the Chereionites were the Build-ers, the Ancients. He will not tell me what made them withdraw. He confesses that now they are few, and what power they wield comes wholly from their brains."

"They're not, uh, uh, super-Didonians, though . . . galaxy-unifyin' intellects . . . as Jaan believes?"

"No. Nor do they wage a philosophical conflict among them-selves over the ultimate destiny of creation. Those stories merely fit Aycharaych's purpose." Erannath hunched on the claws of his wings. His head thrust forward against nacre and shadow. "Listen," he said. "We have no more than a sliver of time at best. Don't interrupt, unless I grow unclear. Listen. Remember."

The words blew harshly forth, like an autumn gale: "They pre-serve remnants of technology on Chereion which they have not shared with their masters the Merseians—if the Merseians are really their masters and not their tools. I wonder about that. Well, we must not stop to speculate. As one would await, the technology relates to the mind. For they are extraordinary telepaths, more gifted than the science we know has imagined is possible.

"There is some ultimate quality of the mind which goes deeper than language. At close range, Aycharaych can read the thoughts of *any* being—any speech, any species, he claims—without need-ing to know that being's symbolism. I suspect what he does is almost instantly to analyze the pattern, identify universals of logic and conation, go on from there to reconstruct the whole mental configuration—as if his nervous system included not only sensitiv-ity to the radiation of others, but an organic semantic computer fantastically beyond anything that Technic civilization has built.

"No matter! Their abilities naturally led Chereionite scientists to concentrate on psychology and neurology. It's been ossified for millions of years, that science, like their whole civilization: ossified, receding, dying. . . . Perhaps Aycharaych alone is trying to act on reality, trying to stop the extinction of his people. I don't know. I do know that he serves the Roidhunate as an Intelligence officer with a roving commission. This involves brewing trouble for the Terran Empire wherever he can.

"During the Snelund regime, he looked through Sector Alpha

Crucis. It wasn't hard, when misgovernment had already produced widespread laxity and confusion. The conflict over Jihannath was building toward a crisis, and Merseia needed difficulties on this frontier of Terra's.

"Aycharaych landed secretly on Aeneas and prowled. He found more than a planet growing rebellious. He found the potential of something that might break the Empire apart. For all the peoples here, in all their different ways, are profoundly religious. Give them a common faith, a missionary cause, and they can turn fanatic."

"No," Ivar couldn't help protesting.

"Aycharaych thinks so. He has spent a great deal of his time and energy on your world, however valuable his gift would make him elsewhere."

"But—one planet, a few millions, against the—"

"The cult would spread. He speaks of militant new religions in your past—Islam, is that the name of one?—religions which brought obscure tribes to world power, and shook older dominions to their roots, in a single generation.

"I *must* hurry. He found the likeliest place for the first spark was here, where the Ancients brood at the center of every awareness. In Jaan the dreamer, whose life and circumstances chanced to be a veritable human archetype, he found the likeliest tinder.

"He cannot by himself project a thought into a brain which is not born to receive it. But he has a machine which can. That is nothing fantastic; human, Ythrian, or Merseian engineers could develop the same device, had they enough incentive. We don't, because for us the utility would be marginal; electronic communications suit our kind of life better.

"Aycharaych, though—Telepathy of several kinds belongs to evolution on his planet. Do you remember the slinkers that the tinerans keep? I inquired, and he admitted they came originally from Chereion. No doubt their effect on men suggested his plan to him.

"He called Jaan down to where he laired in these labyrinths. He drugged him and . . . thought at him . . . in some way he knows, using that machine—until he had imprinted a set of false memories and an idiom to go with them. Then he released his victim."

"Artificial schizophrenia. Split personality. A man who was sane, made to hear 'Voices.'" Ivar shuddered.

Erannath was harder-souled; or had he simply lived with the fact longer, in his prison? He went on: "Aycharaych departed, having other mischief to wreak. What he had done on Aeneas might or might not bear fruit; if not, he had lost nothing except his time.

"He returned lately, and found success indeed. Jaan was winning converts throughout the Orcan country. Rumors of the new message were spreading across a whole globe of natural apostles, always eager for anything that might nourish faith, and now starved for a word of hope.

"Events must be guided with craft and patience, of course, or the movement would most likely come to naught, produce not a revolution followed by a crusade, but merely another sect. Aycharaych settled down to watch, to plot, ever oftener to plant in Jaan, through his thought projector, a revelation from Caruith—"

The Ythrian chopped off. He hissed. His free hand raked the air. Ivar whirled on his heel, sprang to stand crouched.

The figure in the doorway, limned against unending night, smiled. He was more than half humanlike, tall and slender in a gray robe; but his bare feet ended in claws. The skin glowed golden, the crest on the otherwise naked head rose blue, the eyes were warm bronze. His face was ax-thin, superbly molded. In one delicate hand he aimed a blaster.

"Greeting," he almost sang.

"You woke and sensed," grated from Erannath.

"No," said Aycharaych. "My dreams always listen. Afterward, however, yes, I waited out your conversation."

"Now what?" asked Ivar from the middle of nightmare.

"Why, that depends on you, Firstling," Aycharaych replied with unchanged gentleness. "May I in complete sincerity bid you welcome?"

"You—workin' for Merseia—"

The energy gun never wavered; yet the words flowed serene: "True. Do you object? Your desire is freedom. The Roidhunate's desire is that you should have it. This is the way."

"T-t-treachery, murder, torture, invadin' and twistin' men's bein's—"

"Existence always begets regrettable necessities. Be not overly proud, Firstling. You are prepared to launch a revolutionary war if you can, wherein millions would perish, millions more be mutilated, starved, hounded, brought to sorrow. Are you not? I do no more than help you. Is that horrible? What happiness has Jaan lost that has not already been repaid him a thousandfold?"

"How about Erannath?"

"Heed him not," croaked Ythrian to human. "Think why Merseia wants the Empire convulsed and shattered. Not for the liberty of Aeneans. No, to devour us piecemeal."

"One would expect Erannath to talk thus." Aycharaych's tone bore the least hint of mirth. "After all, he serves the Empire."

"What?" Ivar lurched where he stood. "Him? No!"

"Who else can logically have betrayed you, up on the river, once he felt certain of who you are?"

"He came along—"

"He had no means of preventing your escape, as it happened. Therefore his duty was to accompany you, in hopes of sending another message later, and meanwhile gather further information about native resistance movements. It was the same basic reason as caused him earlier to help you get away from the village, before he had more than a suspicion of your identity.

"I knew his purpose—I have not perpetually lurked underground, I have moved to and fro in the world—and gave Jaan orders, who passed them on to Yakow." Aycharaych sighed. "It was distasteful to all concerned. But my own duty has been to extract what I can from him."

"Erannath," Ivar begged, "it isn't true!"

The Ythrian lifted his head and said haughtily, "Truth you must find in yourself, Ivar Frederiksen. What do you mean to do: become another creature of Aycharaych's, or strike for the life of your people?"

"Have you a choice?" the Chereionite murmured. "I wish you no ill. Nevertheless, I too am at war and cannot stop to weigh out single lives. You will join us, fully and freely, or you will die."

How can I tell what I want? Through dread and anguish, Ivar felt the roan eyes upon him. Behind them must be focused that intellect, watching, searching, reading. *He'll know what I'm about to do before I know myself.* His knife clattered to the floor. *Why not yield? It may well be right—for Aeneas—no matter what Erannath says. And elsewise—*

Everything exploded. The Ythrian seized the knife. Balanced on one huge wing, he swept the other across Ivar, knocking the human back behind the shelter of it.

Aycharaych must not have been heeding what went on in the hunter's head. Now he shot. The beam flared and seared. Ivar saw blinding blueness, smelled ozone and scorched flesh. He bent away from death.

Erannath surged forward. Behind him remained his chained hand. He had hacked it off at the wrist.

A second blaster bolt tore him asunder. His uncrippled wing smote. Cast back against the wall, Aycharaych sank stunned. The gun fell from him.

Ivar pounced to grab the weapon. Erannath stirred. Blood pumped from among blackened plumes. An eye was gone. Breath whistled and rattled.

Ivar dropped on his knees, to cradle his friend. The eye that remained sought for him. "Thus God . . . tracks me down. . . . I would it had been under heaven," Erannath coughed. "*Eyan haa wharr, Hlirr talya—*" The light in the eye went out.

A movement caught Ivar's glance. He snatched after the gun. Aycharaych had recovered, was bound through the doorway.

For a heartbeat Ivar was about to yell, Stop, we're allies! That stayed his hand long enough for Aycharaych to vanish. Then Ivar knew what the Chereionite had seen: that no alliance could ever be.

I've got to get out, or Erannath—everybody—has gone for naught. Ivar leaped to his feet and ran. Blood left a track behind him.

He noticed with vague surprise that at some instant he had recovered his flash. Its beam scythed. *Can't grieve yet. Can't be afraid. Can't do anything but run and think.*

Is Aycharaych ahead of me? He's left prints in both directions. No, I'm sure he's not. He realizes I'll head back aboveground; and I, whose forebears came from heavier world than his, would overhaul him. So he's makin' for his lair. Does it have line to outside? Probably not. And even if it does, would he call? That'd give his whole game away. No, he'll have to follow after me, use his hell-machine to plant "intuition" in Jaan's mind—

The room of revelations appeared. Ivar halted and spent a minute playing flame across the thing within. He couldn't tell if he had disabled it or not, but he dared hope.

Onward. Out the door. Down the mountainside, through the sharp dust, athwart the wind which Erannath had died without feeling. To the aircar. Aloft.

The storm yelled and smote.

He burst above, into splendor. Below him rolled the blown dry clouds, full of silver and living shadow beneath Lavinia and hasty Creusa. Stars blazed uncountable. Ahead reared the heights of Ilion; down them glowed and thundered the Linn.

This world is ours. No stranger will shape its tomorrows.

An image in the radar-sweep screen made him look behind. Two other craft soared into view. Had Aycharaych raised pursuit? Decision crystallized in Ivar, unless it had been there throughout these past hours, or latent throughout his life. He activated the radio.

The Imperials monitored several communication bands. If he identified himself and called for a military escort, he could probably have one within minutes.

Tanya, he thought, *I'm comin' home.*

21

Chimes rang from the bell tower of the University. They played the olden peals, but somehow today they sounded at peace.

Or was Chunderban Desai wishfully deceiving himself? He wasn't sure, and wondered if he or any human ever could be.

Certainly the young man and woman who sat side by side and hand in hand looked upon him with wariness that might still mask hostility. Her pet, in her lap, seemed touched by the same air, for it perched quiet and kept its gaze on the visitor. The window behind them framed a spire in an indigo sky. It was open, and the breeze which carried the tones entered, cool, dry, pungent with growth odors.

"I apologize for intruding on you so soon after your reunion," Desai said. He had arrived three minutes ago. "I shan't stay long. You want to take up your private lives again. But I did think a few explanations and reassurances from me would help you."

"No big trouble, half hour in your company, after ten days locked away by myself," Ivar snapped.

"I am sorry about your detention, Firstling. It wasn't uncomfortable, was it? We did have to isolate you for a while. Doubtless you understand our need to be secure about you while your story was investigated. But we also had to provide for your own safety after your release. That took time. Without Prosser Thane's cooperation, it would have taken longer than it did."

"Safety—huh?" Ivar stared from him to Tatiana.

She closed fingers on the tadmouse's back, as if in search of solace. "Yes," she said, barely audibly.

"Terrorists of the self-styled freedom movement," Desai stated, his voice crisper than he felt. "They had already assassinated a number of Aeneans who supported the government. Your turning to us, your disclosure of a plot which might indeed have pried this sector loose from the Empire—you, the embodiment of their visions—could have brought them to murder again."

Ivar sat mute for a time. The bells died away. He didn't break the clasp he shared with Tatiana, but his part lost strength. At last he asked her, "What did you do?"

She gripped him harder. "I persuaded them. I never gave names...Commissioner Desai and his officers never asked me for any...but I talked to leaders, I was go-between, and—There'll be general amnesty."

"For past acts," the Imperial reminded. "We cannot allow more like them. I am hoping for help in their prevention." He paused. "If Aeneas is to know law again, tranquillity, restoration of what has been lost, you, Firstling, must take the lead."

"Because of what I am, or was?" Ivar said harshly.

Desai nodded. "More people will heed you, speaking of reconciliation, than anyone else. Especially after your story has been made public, or as much of it as is wise."

"Why not all?"

"Naval Intelligence will probably want to keep various details secret, if only to keep our opponents uncertain of what we do and do not know. And, m-m-m, several high-ranking officials would not appreciate the news getting loose, of how they were infiltrated, fooled, and led by the nose to an appalling brink."

"You, for instance?"

Desai smiled. "Between us, I have persons like Sector Governor Muratori in mind. I am scarcely important enough to become a sensation. Now they are not ungrateful in Llynathawr. I can expect quite a free hand in the Virgilian System henceforward. One policy I mean to implement is close consultation with representatives of every Aenean society, and the gradual phasing over of government to them."

"Hm. Includin' Orcans?"

"Yes. Commander Yakow was nearly shattered to learn the truth; and he is tough, and had no deep emotional commitment to the false creed—simply to the welfare of his people. He agrees the Imperium can best help them through their coming agony."

Ivar fell quiet anew. Tatiana regarded him. Tears glimmered on her lashes. She must well know that same kind of pain. Finally he asked, "Jaan?"

"The prophet himself?" Desai responded. "He knows no more than that for some reason you fled—defected, he no doubt thinks—and afterward an Imperial force came for another search of Mount Cronos, deeper-going than before, and the chiefs of the Companions have not opposed this. Perhaps you can advise me how to tell him the truth, before the general announcement is made."

Bleakness: "What about Aycharaych?"

"He has vanished, and his mind-engine. We're hunting for him, of course." Desai grimaced. "I'm afraid we will fail. One way or another, that wily scoundrel will get off the planet and home. But at least he did not destroy us here."

Ivar let go of his girl, as if for this time not she nor anything else could warm him. Beneath a tumbled lock of yellow hair, his gaze lay winter-blue. "Do you actually believe he could have?"

"The millennialism he was engineering, yes, it might have, I think," Desai answered, equally low. "We can't be certain. Very likely Aycharaych knows us better than we can know ourselves. But . . . it has happened, over and over, through man's troubled existence: the Holy War, which cannot be stopped and which carries away kingdoms and empires, though the first soldiers of it be few and poor.

"Their numbers grow, you see. Entire populations join them. Man has never really wanted a comfortable God, a reasonable or kindly one; he has wanted a faith, a cause, which promises everything but mainly which requires everything.

"Like moths to the candle flame—

"More and more in my stewardship of Aeneas, I have come to see that here is a world of many different peoples, but all of them believers, all strong and able, all sharing some tradition about mighty forerunners and all unready to admit that those forerunners may have been as tragically limited, ultimately as doomed, as we.

"Aeneas was in the forefront of struggle for a political end. When defeat came, that turned the dwellers and their energies back toward transcendental things. And then Aycharaych invented for them a transcendence which the most devout religionist and the most hardened scientist could alike accept.

"I do not think the tide of Holy War could have been stopped this side of Regulus. The end of it would have been humanity and humanity's friends ripped into two realms. No, more than two, for there *are* contradictions in the faith, which I think must have been deliberately put there. For instance, is God the Creator or the Created?—Yes, heresies, persecutions, rebellions . . . states lamed, chaotic, hating each other worse than any outsider—"

Desai drew breath before finishing: "—such as Merseia. Which would be precisely what Merseia needs, first to play us off against ourselves, afterward to overrun and subject us."

Ivar clenched fists on knees. "Truly?" he demanded.

"Truly," Desai said. "Oh, I know how useful the Merseian threat has often been to politicians, industrialists, military lords, and bureaucrats of the Empire. That does not mean the threat isn't real. I know how propaganda has smeared the Merseians, when they are in fact, according to their own lights and many of ours, a fairly decent folk. That does not mean their leaders won't risk the Long Night to grasp after supremacy.

"Firstling, if you want to be worthy of leading your own world, you must begin by dismissing the pleasant illusions. Don't take my word, either. Study. Inquire. Go see for yourself. Do your personal thinking. But always follow the truth, wherever it goes."

"Like that Ythrian?" Tatiana murmured.

"No, the entire Domain of Ythri," Desai told her. "Erannath was my agent, right. But he was also theirs. They sent him by prearrangement: because in his very foreignness, his conspicuousness and seeming detachment, he could learn what Terrans might not.

"Why should Ythri do this?" he challenged. "Had we not fought a war with them, and robbed them of some of their territory?"

"But that's far in the past, you see. The territory is long ago assimilated to us. Irredentism is idiocy. And Terra did not try to take over Ythri itself, or most of its colonies, in the peace settlement. Whatever the Empire's faults, and they are many, it recognizes certain limits to what it may wisely do.

"Merseia does not.

"Naturally, Erannath knew nothing about Aycharaych when he arrived here. But he did know Aeneas is a key planet in this sector, and expected Merseia to be at work somewhere underground. Because Terra and Ythri have an overwhelming common interest—peace, stability, containment of the insatiable aggressor—

and because the environment of your world suited him well, he came to give whatever help he could."

Desai cleared his throat. "I'm sorry," he said. "I didn't intend that long a speech. It surprised me too. I'm not an orator, just a glorified bureaucrat. But here's a matter on which billions of lives depend."

"Did you find his body?" Ivar asked without tone.

"Yes," Desai said. "His role is another thing we cannot make public: too revealing, too provocative. In fact, we shall have to play down Merseia's own part, for fear of shaking the uneasy peace.

"However, Erannath went home on an Imperial cruiser; and aboard was an honor guard."

"That's good," Ivar said after a while.

"Have you any plans for poor Jaan?" Tatiana asked.

"We will offer him psychiatric treatment, to rid him of the pseudo-personality," Desai promised. "I am told that's possible."

"Suppose he refuses."

"Then, troublesome though he may prove—because his movement won't die out quickly unless he himself denounces it—we will leave him alone. You may disbelieve this, but I don't approve of using people."

Desai's look returned to Ivar. "Likewise you, Firstling," he said. "You won't be coerced. Nobody will pressure you. Rather, I warn you that working with my administration, for the restoration of Aeneas within the Empire, will be hard and thankless. It will cost you friends, and years of your life that you might well spend more enjoyably, and pain when you must make the difficult decision or the inglorious compromise. I can only hope you will join us."

He rose. "I think that covers the situation for the time being," he said. "You have earned some privacy, you two. Please think this over, and feel free to call on me whenever you wish. Now, good day, Prosser Thane, Firstling Frederiksen." The High Commissioner of the Terran Empire bowed. "Thank you."

Slowly, Ivar and Tatiana rose. They towered above the little man, before they gave him their hands.

"Probably we will help," Ivar said. "Aeneas ought to outlive Empire."

Tatiana took the sting out of that: "Sir, I suspect we owe you more thanks than anybody will ever admit, least of all you."

As Desai closed the door behind him, he heard the tadmouse begin singing.

✸   ✸   ✸

Jaan walked forth alone before sunrise.

The streets were canyons of night where he often stumbled. But when he came out upon the wharf that the sea had lapped, heaven enclosed him.

Behind this wide, shimmering deck, the town was a huddle turned magical by moonlight. High above lifted the Arena, its dark strength frosted with radiance. Beneath his feet, the mountain fell gray-white and shadow-dappled to the dim shield of the waters. North and east stood Ilion, cloven by the Linn-gleam.

Mostly he knew sky. Stars thronged a darkness which seemed itself afire, till they melted together in the cataract of the Milky Way. Stateliest among them burned Alpha and Beta Crucis; yet he knew many more, the friends of his life's wanderings, and a part of him called on them to guide him. They only glittered and wheeled. Lavinia was down and Creusa hastening to set. Low above the barrens hung Dido, the morning star.

Save for the distant falls it was altogether still here, and mortally cold. Outward breath smoked like wraiths, inward breath hurt.

—Behold what is real and forever, said Caruith.

—Let me be, Jaan said. You are a phantom. You are a lie.

—You do not believe that. We do not.

—Then why is your chamber now empty, and I alone in my skull?

—The Others have won—not even a battle, if we remain steadfast; a skirmish in the striving of life to become God. You are not alone.

—What should we do?

—Deny their perjuries. Proclaim the truth.

—But you are not there! broke from Jaan. You are a branded part of my own brain, hissing at me; and I can be healed of you.

—Oh, yes, Caruith said in terrible scorn. They can wipe the traces of me away; they can also geld you if you want. Go, become domesticated, return to making shoes. Those stars will shine on.

—Our cause in this generation, on this globe, is broken, Jaan pleaded. We both know that. What can we do but go wretched, mocked, reviled, to ruin the dreams of a last faithful few?

—We can uphold the truth, and die for it.

—Truth? What proves you are real, Caruith?

—The emptiness I would leave behind me, Jaan.

And that, he thought, would indeed be there within him,

echoing "Meaningless, meaningless, meaningless" until his second death gave him silence.

—Keep me, Caruith urged, and we will die only once, and it will be in the service of yonder suns.

Jaan clung to his staff. *Help me.* No one answered save Caruith.

The sky whitened to eastward and Virgil came, the sudden Aenean dawn. Everywhere light awoke. Whistles went through the air, a sound of wings, a fragrance of plants which somehow kept roots in the desert. Banners rose above the Arena and trumpets rang, whatever had lately been told.

Jaan knew: *Life is its own service. And I may have enough of it in me to fill me. I will go seek the help of men.*

He had never before known how steep the upward path was. ✳

But I pray you by the lifting skies,
And the young wind over the grass,
That you take your eyes from off my eyes,
And let my spirit pass.
—Kipling

TIGER BY THE TAIL

When Captain Dominic Flandry opened his eyes, he saw metal. At the same time came awareness of a thrum and quiver, almost subliminally faint but not to be mistaken for anything else in the universe. He was aboard a spacecraft running on hyperdrive.

He sat up fast. Pain stabbed him through the temples. What the blue-flaming hell? He'd gone to sleep in one of the stews of Catawrayannis, with no intention of departure from that city for weeks or months to come—or, wait, had he passed out? Memory failed. Yet he hadn't drunk much.

Realization chilled him. He was not in a ship meant for humans. The crew must be pretty manlike, to judge from the size and design of articles. He could breathe the air, though it was chilly, bore peculiar odors, and seemed a bit denser than Terran standard. The interior grav-field, while not handicapping to him, was perceptibly stronger too, laying several extra kilos on his body. Bunks, one of which he occupied, were made up with sheets of vegetable fiber and blankets woven of long bluish-gray hair. A chest which could, he supposed, double as a seat, was wooden, carved and inlaid in a style new to him; and planetary art forms were a hobby of his.

He buried face in hands and struggled to think. The headache and a vile taste in his mouth were not from liquor—at least, not from the well-chosen stuff he had been drinking in reasonable moderation. And it made no sense that he'd dropped off so early; the girl had been attractive and bouncy. Therefore—

Drugged. Oh, no! Don't tell me I've been as stupid as a hero of a holoplay. That idea is not to be borne.

Well, who would have awaited such a trick? Certainly his opposition had no reason to...had they? Flandry had just been out developing a further part of that structure of demimonde acquaintances and information which would eventually, by tortuous routes, bring him to those whom he sought. He had been enjoying his work as conspicuously as possible, so that no one might suspect that it *was* work. Then somehow—

He lurched to his feet and hunted blearily for his clothes. They were missing; he was naked. Damn, he'd paid three hundred credits for that outfit. He stamped across to a metal door. It wasn't automatic. In his state, he needed half a minute to figure out how the sliding latch, cast in the form of a monster's head, was operated. He flung the door open and stared down the projection cone of a blaster.

The weapon was not of any make he recognized. However, there was no doubt as to its nature. Flandry sighed, attempted to relax, and considered the guard who held it.

The being was remarkably humanoid. Certain differences of detail could quite likely be found beneath the clothes, and more basic ones beneath the skin. Among countless worlds, evolutionary coincidences are bound to happen now and then, but never evolutionary identities. Yet to the eye, crew member and captive resembled each other more than either resembled, say, a woman. *Or an alien female?* Flandry wondered. *I'll bet this is a male, and equipped pretty much like me, too.*

The stranger could almost have passed for a tall, heavily built human. Variations in bodily proportions were slight, within the normal range. To be sure, Terra had never brought forth a race with his combination of features. The skin was very white, the hair and beard tawny, but the nose rather flat, lips full, eyes oblique and violet-colored. The ears were quite foreign, pointed, motile, cowrie-convoluted. Heavy brow ridges sprouted a pair of small, jet-black horns—scarcely for combat; they might perhaps have some sensory or sexual function. On the whole, the esthetic effect was pleasing, exotic enough to excite but familiar enough to attract.

The trouble was, Flandry was not feeling pleasable. He scowled at the garb which confronted him. It consisted of a gaudily patterned kilt and tunic, cuirass and helmet of a reddish alloy, leather buskins, a murderous-looking dirk, and two shriveled right hands, hung at the belt, which had probably belonged to foes. *Barbarian!* Flandry knew.

The guard gestured him back, unslung a horn from his shoulder, and blew a howling blast. That was pure flamboyancy; anyone who could build or buy spaceships would have intercoms installed. Old customs often lingered, though, especially when a people acquired modern technology overnight.

Which too many have done, Flandry reflected with grimness. *One would have been too many, and as is—No surprise that I never heard about this folk; it is their existence that is the nasty surprise.*

No individual could remember all the scores of thousands of sophont species over which the Terran Empire claimed hegemony—not to speak of those in the domains of other starfaring civilizations, Ythrian and Merseian and the rest. The majority were obscure, primitive by the standards of space travelers, seldom if ever visited, their allegiance nominal. This meant that strange things could develop among them over centuries, unbeknownst to worlds beyond. And known space itself was the tiniest splinter off the outer part of a spiral arm of a galaxy whose suns numbered above a hundred billion.

Outside the Empire, knowledge faded swiftly away. Yet there had been sporadic contact with dwellers in the wilderness. Merchant adventurers had searched widely about in olden days, and not always been scrupulous about what they sold. In this way and that, individual natives had wangled passage to advanced planets, and sometimes brought back information of a revolutionizing sort. Often this got passed on to other societies.

And so, here and there, cultures arose that possessed things like starships and nuclear weapons, and played ancient games with these new toys. Barbarian raiders had fearfully harried about during the Troubles. In the long run, the practice of hiring rival barbarians as mercenaries against them only worsened matters. After the Empire brought the Pax, it soon established lethal discouragements of raids and attempts at conquest within its sphere. The marches lay long quiet. But now the Empire was in a bad way, it relied ever more on nonhuman hireling fighters, its grip upon the border stars was slipping...word got around, and latter-day buccaneers began to venture forth....

Barbarians could be bought off, or played off against each other, or cowed by an occasional punitive expedition—most of the time. But if ever somebody among them formed a powerful coalition, and saw an opportunity—*vae victis!* Even if the Imperialists broke him, the harm he did first would be catastrophic. *Vae victoris!*

Flandry halted his brooding. Footfalls rang in the corridor. A minute later, a party of his captors entered the cabin, seven warriors and a chieftain.

The leader overtopped the prisoner, who was of above average height for a Terran, by a head. His eyes were pale blue, beneath a golden coronet which represented three intertwined serpentine forms. Though it would be folly to try interpreting facial expressions on such short acquaintance, this one sent a line from the remote past across Flandry's mind: "—sneer of cold command." He wore a robe of iridescent shimmerlyn, bought or looted from an Imperial world, trimmed with strips of scaly leather. A belt upheld a blaster and a slim sword. The latter might not be entirely an archaic symbol; to judge from wear on hilt and guard, it had seen use.

His gaze went up and down the nude frame before him. Flandry gave back as bland a stare as possible. At length the newcomer spoke. His Anglic was heavily accented and his voice, which was deep, had subtle overtones hinting at a not quite human conformation of teeth, palate, tongue, and throat. Nevertheless he required no vocalizer to make the sounds understandable: "You seem to be in better condition than I awaited. You are not soft, but hard."

The man shrugged. "One tries to keep in shape. It maintains capacity for drinking and lovemaking."

The alien scowled. "Have a care. Show respect. You are a prisoner, Captain Dominic Flandry."

They went through my pockets, naturally. "May I ask a respectful question? Was that girl last night paid to slip a little something extra into my drink?"

"Indeed. The Scothani are not the brainless brutes of your folklore. Few of the so-called barbarians have ever been, in fact." A stern smile. "It can be useful having your folk believe we are."

"Scothani? I don't think I've had the pleasure—"

"Hardly. We are not altogether unknown to the Imperium, but hitherto we have avoided direct contact. However, we are they from whom the Alarri fled."

Flandry harked back. He had been a boy then, but he well remembered news accounts of the fleets that swept across the marches with nuclear fire and energy sword. The Battle of Mirzan had been touch and go for a while, till a Navy task force smashed the gathered enemy strength. Yet it turned out that the Alarri were the victims of still another tribe, who had overrun their planet and laid it under tribute. Such an incident would scarcely have come to the notice of an indifferent Imperium, had not one nation of the conquered refused to surrender but, instead, boarded hordes into spacecraft and set forth in hopes of winning a new home. (They expected the Empire would buy peace from them, payment to be assistance in finding a planet they could colonize, preferably outside its borders. Terrestroid real estate is a galactic rarity. Instead, the remnants of them scattered back into the stellar wilderness. Maybe a few still survived.)

"You must have a small empire of your own by now," Flandry said.

"Aye, though not small. The gods who forged our destiny saw to it that our ancestors did not learn the secrets of power from humans, who might afterward have paid heed to us and tried to stop our growth. It was others who came to our world and started the great change."

Flandry nodded his weary head. The historical pattern was time-worn; Terra herself had been through it, over and over, long before her children departed for the stars. By way of exploration, trade, missionary effort, or whatever, a culture met another which was technologically behind it. If the latter had sufficient strength to survive the encounter, it gained knowledge of the foreigner's tricks and tactics while losing awe of him. Perhaps in the end it overcame him.

The gap between, say, a preindustrial Iron Age and an assembly of modern machines was enormous. It was not uncrossable. Basic equipment could be acquired, in exchange for natural resources or the like. Educations could be gotten. Once a class of engineers and applied scientists was in existence, progress could be made at home; if everything worked out right, it would accelerate like a landslide. After all, when you knew more or less how to build something, and had an entire, largely unplundered planet to draw on, your industrial base would soon suffice for most purposes. Presently you would have an entire planetary system to draw on.

It wasn't necessary to educate whole populations. Automated machinery did the bulk of the work. Peasants with hoes and sickles might well toil in sight of a spacefield for generations after it had come into being. In fact, the ruling class might consider extensive schooling undesirable, particularly among nationalities which its own had conquered.

New instrumentalities—old, fierce ways—

The Scothani, though, must have truly exploded forth on their interstellar career. Else Terra would not remain ignorant of them. That was suggestive of deliberate purpose with a long perspective. A prickling went along Flandry's skin. "Who were those beings that aided you?" he asked slowly. *The Merseians? They'd dearly love to see us in trouble: the worse, the dearer.*

The chieftain lifted a hand. "You are overly forward," he growled. "Have you forgotten you are alone among us, in a ship already light-years from Llynathawr and bound for Scotha itself? If you would have mercy, conduct yourself as behooves you."

Flandry assumed a humble stance. "Dare I ask why you took me, my lord?"

"You are a ranking officer of the Imperial Intelligence service. As such, you may have hostage value; but primarily we want information."

"From me? I—"

"I know." The reply was clearly disgusted. "You're typical of your kind. I've studied the Empire long enough to recognize you; I've traveled there myself, incognito, and met persons aplenty. You are another worthless younger son, given a well-paid sinecure so you can wear a bedizened uniform and play at being a fighting man."

Flandry decided to register a bit of indignation. "Sir, that isn't fair." In haste: "Not to contradict you, of course."

The barbarian laughed. It was a very human-sounding laugh, save that its heartiness was seldom heard on Terra any more. "I know you," he said. "Did you imagine I had you snatched at random, without learning something first? Your mission was to find who the ultimate leaders were of a conspiracy against the throne which had lately been uncovered. How am I aware of this? Why, you registered under your proper name at the most luxurious hotel in Catawrayannis. On a seemingly unlimited expense account, you strutted about dropping hints about your business, hints which would have been childishly dark were they not transparent.

Your actual activities amounted to drinking, gambling, wenching every night and sleeping the whole day." Humor gleamed cold in the blue eyes. "Was it perhaps your intention that the Empire's enemies should be rendered helpless by mirth at the spectacle?"

Flandry cringed. "Then why was I worth kidnapping, lord?" he mumbled.

"You are bound to have some information, some of it useful. For example, details about the organization and undertakings of your corps; most of Terran Naval Intelligence is very good at secrecy. Then there are services you can perform, documents you can translate, potential allies within the Empire you can identify, perhaps liaisons you can make. Eventually you may earn your freedom, aye, and rich reward." A fist lifted. "In case you contemplate any holding back, any treachery, be sure that my torturers know their trade."

"You needn't get melodramatic," Flandry said sullenly.

The fist shot out. Flandry went to the deck with his headache gone shriekingly keen. Blood dripped from his face as he crawled to hands and knees. Above him, the voice boomed: "Little man, the first thing you will learn is how a slave addresses the crown prince of Scothania."

The Terran lurched up. The barbarian knocked him down again. Behind, hands rested on gun butts. "Does this help teach you?" inquired his owner.

Well, I dare hope he isn't a sadist, that he's merely a member of a society which values roughness and toughness. "Yes, my lord prince. Thank you."

After all, a slave in the Empire is subject to worse.

"You will be instructed what to do," said the Scothan, turned on his heel, and strode out. His guards followed, except for the sentry. The latter whipped forth his dirk and held it straight up, an obvious gesture of salute.

A couple of underlings returned his clothes to Flandry, minus the gold braid. He sighed over the soiled, ripped garments in which he had cut such a gallant figure. Conducted to a head, he cleaned himself as best he could. Its layout was not too puzzling; besides being so humanoid, his captors derived their technology ultimately from his, whether or not that had been by way of Merseia.

The blows hadn't damaged his face beyond healing. It looked back from the mirror, fair-complexioned, high in the cheekbones, straight in the nose, delicately formed lips but strong chin, sleek brown hair and a neat mustache. Sometimes he thought it was too handsome, but he'd been young when he ordered a biosculptor to reshape it for him. Maybe when he got out of this mess he should have his countenance made over to a more rugged form suitable for a man in his thirties.

The slightly dolichocephalic bone structure was his own, however, as were the eyes: large and bright, with a bare hint of slanting, their irises of that curious gray which can variously seem almost blue or green or gold. The body was natural too, and he deserved full credit for its trimness. He hated exercises, but went through a dutiful daily routine which maintained strength, coordination, and reflexes. Besides, a man in condition stood out among the flabby nobles of Terra; he'd found his figure no end of help in making his home leaves pleasant.

His cheeks were still smooth. Maybe he could promote a razor before his last dose of antibeard wore off. At the minimum, he'd need scissors if he wasn't to get all scraggly.

Well, can't stand here admiring yourself forever, old chap. Flandry did the best he could with his clothes, tilted his officer's cap at a properly rakish angle, and walked out to meet his new shipmates.

They were not such bad fellows, he soon learned. Big, lusty, gusty warriors, out for adventure and wealth and fame, they were nevertheless well disciplined, with courtesy for each other and a rough kindliness for him. They were brave, honest, loyal, capable of sentiment and even the appreciation of certain beauties in art or nature. However, they were much given to deadly rages, and scarcely an atom's worth to compassion; they might not be inherently stupid, but their interests were limited; and it would have been pleasanter if they washed more frequently.

Much of this came to Flandry just as impressions at first, though experience tended to confirm it. Few aboard the ship spoke any language he did. A couple of officers who had some Anglic—less than the prince's—told him various things, in exchange for a little satisfaction of their own curiosity. He bunked with common crew in the place where he had been confined and took his food in a mess where one stood to eat out of trenchers, sans utensils other than issue knives. Flandry, allowed none, must rely on his teeth to cut the meat and shred the vegetables. The rations had strange flavors and the cooking was uninspired, but he found everything edible and a few items tasty. Someone had thoughtfully acquired a large stock of dietary-supplement capsules for him, to supply vitamins that didn't occur on Scotha.

He was allowed to wander around pretty freely, for there was nothing he could harm and he was never out of sight. Though big, the ship was crowded, for she had been on a scouting and plundering cruise.

She was one of a dozen Cerdic had taken forth. (That was not quite the prince's name, but near enough to catch Flandry's fancy; he was a bit of a history buff.) The additional purpose was presumably to train crews. They'd descended on several worlds, not all habitable to oxygen-breathing water drinkers, and improved their warlike skills, afterward taking whatever loot they wanted. Flandry got the impression that a couple of those planets were under Terran suzerainty; but if so, the connection was tenuous, and no sentient beings had been left alive to bear witness. Cerdic was too shrewd to provoke the Empire . . . yet.

He had agents on Llynathawr, which world was the listening post for this whole Imperial sector. They were hirelings from various starfaring races, probably humans among them; they could well include a few Scothans, claiming to be of a subject people who lived in a distant part of the realm.

While his flotilla orbited beyond detection, a speedster had entered the system and made secret landing. That wasn't hard, when border forces were undermanned and underequipped. The spies aboard contacted the spies in place, and brought back the latest news to their master. Learning that a special agent from Terra was in Catawrayannis, on an assignment of apparent importance—no matter what a fop and fool he was—Cerdic had ordered Flandry picked up. It would be no giveaway, for a carouser in the wild part of town could readily come to grief and never be seen again.

Now they were homeward bound, triumphant. It was clear that this had been no ordinary barbarian pirating, that Cerdic and his father Penda (another word-play by Flandry) were no ordinary barbarian chiefs, and that Scothania was no ordinary barbarian nation. Could the Long Night really be drawing nigh—in Flandry's own sacrosanct lifetime?

He shoved the thought aside. Time was lacking for worry. Let him also dismiss fret about the job from which he had been snatched. It would go to the staff, who could doubtless handle it, albeit not with the Flandry style. He had suddenly acquired a new task, whereof the first part was plain, old-fashioned survival.

After a time he was conducted to Cerdic's cabin. The place had a number of ethnic touches, such as a huge pair of tusks displayed on a bulkhead between shields and swords, animal skins on the deck, and a grotesque idol in one corner. Flandry wondered if they were there merely because they were expected. Other furniture included a desk with infotrieve and computer terminal, bookrolls and a reader for them, a holoscreen, and, yes, a number of codex volumes bearing Anglic titles. The prince occupied an Imperial-made lounger, too. Jewelry glittered across his massive breast.

"Attention!" he barked. Flandry snapped a salute and stood braced. "At ease," Cerdic said with a measure of affability. "Have you somewhat accustomed yourself to us?"

"Yes, sir," Flandry replied. He'd better.

"Your first task will be to learn Frithian, the principal language of Scotha," Cerdic directed. "As yet, few of our people speak Anglic, and many nobles and officers will want to talk to you."

"Yes, sir." It was what he would most have desired, short of his release in the course of total disaster for Scotha.

"Also, you will organize your knowledge in coherent fashion. Writing materials and a recorder will be available to you. Beware of falsification. I have traveled and lived in the Empire, remember. I will have a sense for errors and omissions. If ever I begin to doubt you, you will be subjected to hypnoprobing."

Flandry felt an inward shiver. The instrument was bad enough when lightly employed by skilled men. In the hands of aliens, who had no proper understanding of the human psyche and would, moreover, dig deep, he'd soon have no mind left.

"I'll cooperate, sir," he promised. "Please, though, you do realize I can't produce an encyclopedia. I can't so much as think of everything I might know that would be helpful to you. I'll have to be questioned now and then, to guide my thoughts."

Cerdic gave the curious circular nod of his kind. "Understood. Different sorts of cooperation may be required of you as we learn more. If you satisfy, you shall be rewarded. In the end, working with subjugated humans on our account, you could gain considerable power."

"Sir," began Flandry in a tone of weak self-righteousness, "I could not become a—"

"Oh, aye, you could," Cerdic interrupted. "You will...become as thorough a traitor as your capabilities allow. I told you before, I have been in the Empire, on Terra's very self; and I have studied deeply, aided by data retrieval systems, the works of your own sociologists, and of nonhumans who have an outside view of your ways. I *know* the Empire—its self-seeking politicians and self-indulgent masses, corruption, intrigue, morality and sense of duty rotten to the heart, decline of art into craft and science into dogma, strength sapped by a despair too pervasive for you to realize what it is—aye, aye. You were a great race once, you humans; you were among the first who aspired to the stars. But that was long ago."

The accusation was oversimplified, probably disingenuous. Yet enough truth was in it to touch a nerve. Cerdic's voice rose: "The time has waxed ready for the young peoples, in their strength and courage and hopefulness, to set themselves free, burn away the decayed mass of the Empire and give the universe something that can grow!"

Only, thought Flandry, *first comes the Long Night. It begins with a pyrotechnic sunset across thousands of worlds, which billions of sentient beings will not see because they will be part of the flames. It deepens with famine, plague, more war, more destruction of what the centuries have built, until at last the wild folk howl in our temples—save where a myriad petty tyrants hold dreary court among the shards. To say nothing of an end to good music and high cuisine, taste in clothes and taste in women and conversation as a fine art.*

"My lord," he ventured, "one piece of information I must give you is that the Empire does remain, well, formidable. For instance, it holds the Merseians at bay and—pardon me, sir—they must be more powerful than the Scothani."

"True," Cerdic agreed. "We are not *vilimenn*—what is an Anglic word? We are not maniacs. We cherish no dream of overthrowing the Terrans in a single campaign, no, nor in our own lifetimes. But we can reave a good deal from them that they will be unable to regain. We can press inward, step by step, exploiting their weaknesses, finding allies not simply among their enemies, but among their subjects. Above all, their vices will work against them, for us and our cause."

He leaned forward. "Yes, that is what will decide the final outcome," he said. "We have that which you have lost. Honesty. The Scothani are a race of honest warriors."

"No doubt, sir," Flandry admitted.

"Oh, we have our evil persons, but they are few and the custom of private challenges keeps them few. Besides, their evil is clean and open compared to yours, it is mere lawlessness or rapacity or the like. The vast bulk of the Scothani abide by our code. It would never occur to a true male of us to break an oath or desert a comrade or play false to his lord or lie on his word of honor. As for our females, they don't run loose, making eyes at every male they come across. No, they're kept properly at home until marriage, and then they know their place as mothers and houseguiders. Our youth are raised to respect the gods and the king, to fight, and to speak truth. Death is a little thing, Flandry; it comes to everyone at his hour; but honor lives forever.

"That is why we will win."

Battleships help, thought the human. And then, looking into ice-bright eyes: *He's a fanatic. But smart. That kind is apt to harm the universe most.*

Aloud, he said, "Forgive me, sir. I'm trying to understand. Isn't any stratagem a matter of lies? Your own disguised travels through the Empire—"

"One does not charge blindly against necessity," the prince responded. "Nor is one bound in any way as to what may be done with aliens. They are not of the Blood."

The good old race superiority complex, too. Oh, well.

"I tell you this," said Cerdic, "because a wisp of conscience may be left in you, making you uneasy about serving us. Think on what you have been told, see where justice dwells, and enter gladly into its house, which today stands upon Scotha. You may yet accomplish some good in a hitherto wasted life.... Now, report to *Kraz*—Lieutenant Eril and commence your tasks."

"Yes, sir." Flandry smeared the unction thick. "Thank you for your patience, my lord."

"Go," snapped Cerdic.

Flandry went.

✡ ✡ ✡

At a reasonable cruising pseudospeed, the flotilla was three weeks en route to Scotha. It took Flandry about two of them to acquire an adequate command of the language. Pedagogical electronics and pharmacopoeia were unavailable, but he had a knack, which he had developed through years of study and practice; and he could work very hard when he chose.

He described, haltingly, how slow his progress was despite his best efforts. Often he complained that he hadn't followed what was said to him. A person picked up quite a bit of odd information when talkers supposed he didn't understand them. There was little of prime military significance, of course, but there was much interesting detail about organization, equipment, operations, and like—as well as general background, attitudes, beliefs, pieces of biography.... It all went into the neat files in Flandry's skull, to be correlated with whatever else he learned by different means.

The Scothan crew were amicable toward him, eager to hear about his fabulous civilization and to brag about their own wonderful past and future exploits. He swapped songs and dirty jokes, joined rough-and-tumble sports and did well enough to earn some respect, even received a few confidences from those who had troubles.

They were addicted to gambling. Flandry learned their games, taught them a few of his, and before journey's end had won several suits of good clothes for alteration, plus a well-stuffed purse. He almost, not quite, hated to take his winnings. These overgrown schoolboys had no idea what tricks were possible with cards and dice.

Day by day, he filled out the portrait of their home. The Frithian kings had brought the nations of Scotha under themselves a century ago, and gone onward to the stars. Certain tales suggested their tutors had indeed been Merseians; however, no such beings had been seen for a long time. The monarchy was powerful, if not absolute; it was expected to pay attention to the will of the great nobles, who had a sort of parliament; they in turn must respect the basic rights of free commoners, though these were liable to various types of service as well as taxes. Slaves had no rights, and subject peoples only what happened to be conceded them. On the whole, the Scothan king seemed rather stronger than the Terran Emperor. The latter was theoretically well-nigh omnipotent, but in practice was hedged in by the sheer impossibility of governing his realm in anything like detail.

The Scothan domain was less unmanageable. It had conquered some hundred planetary systems outright, but for the most was content to exact tribute from these, in the form of raw materials, manufactured goods, or specialized labor. It dominated everything else within that space. It had made client states of several chosen societies, helping them start their own industrial revolutions and their own enforced unifications of their species. Under Penda, the coalition had grown sufficiently confident to plan war on the Empire.

The objective was not simple plunder, albeit wealth did beckon. Goods could be produced at home without the risks of battle. Nor was it merely territorial aggrandizement. That could be more safely carried on by discovering new worlds off in the wilderness, whose inhabitants weren't able to fight back. Nevertheless, honest toil could never in hundreds of years yield what a victory would bring in overnight. And planets that Scothan or human could colonize were spread thinly indeed among the suns; long searches were necessary to find them, and then generations of struggle and sacrifice were usually needed to make them altogether fit. Terra had already made the investment.

Below and beyond these practical calculations were what Flandry saw as irrationalities and recognized as the true driving forces. Scotha—Scothan society, in the form it had taken—*needed* war and conquest. The great required outlets for ambition, that their names might match or outshine the forefathers'. Lesser folk wanted a chance to better their lot, a chance that the aristocratic, anti-commercial order at home could not offer them without undermining itself. Glory was a fetish, and scant glory remained to be won in the barbarian regions. Sheer adventurousness clamored, and that darker longing for submergence of self which humankind had also known, too often, too well. The needs, the drives came together and took the shape of crusading fervor, a sense of holy racial destiny.

Yet as Cerdic maintained, the lords of Scothania were not demented. From Flandry's viewpoint they were more than a little mad, but they were realistic about it. Their strength was considerable, their planners able. They would wait for the next of the Empire's recurrent internal crises—and Flandry had been on Llynathawr because a new one of those seemed to be brewing.

No matter how much might was at Terra's beck, it was no use unless it could be brought to bear as needed. If the best of the Navy was tied down elsewhere, the armadas of fearless fanatics could rip through defenses manned by time-serving mercenaries under drone officers. The Merseians might not directly join Penda, but they would not be idle on his behalf. The Imperial magnates would be terrified at the prospect of having their comfortable lives interrupted by heavy demands; if a major war seemed likely, they would snatch at any face-saving offer to stop it. None but a few eccentrics would point out that the dismemberment of the Empire had commenced and the Long Night was ineluctably on its way.

As expected, Scotha was fully terrestroid—a trifle bigger than the prototype, a trifle further from its sun, its seas made turbulent by three small moons. Seen from orbit, it had the same white-marbled blue loveliness. Descending in a tender, Flandry wangled permission to examine the view with instruments. He found the continent across which the boat slanted to be equally attractive, unlike most of his poor raddled planet.

Modern industries, built from scratch, had not wasted and poisoned soil, polluted air and water, scarred land with mines and highways or buried it under hideous hectares of megalopolis. No doubt some ruination had taken place, but before it had proceeded far, that sort of business moved out to space where it belonged. Meanwhile, population burgeoned, but not to unmanageability. The Frithian kings had feared that their nation might be outnumbered and overwhelmed by subject peoples of the same species, and enacted measures simple, harsh, and effective to forestall this. (For example, children were taxed at an upwardly graduated rate. Frithians, and others who were more or less Frithianized, could generally afford to pay for three or four; most couples in less advanced areas could not, but must be content with two. Contraceptive help was freely available. Infants on whom tax was not paid were taken to be sold as slaves.) Before long, space colonization began to give general relief, at first in artificial environments, later on planets in different systems.

There were approximately three billion Scothani by now, two-thirds of them off the mother globe. That did not lessen the danger, given their allies and their monstrous array of automated weapons. Nearly all of them could be mobilized. In contrast, unreckonable swarms of Imperial civilians in the target sector would be first hindrance, later hostage . . . and eventually contributory to the conqueror.

Just the same, Flandry liked what scenery he observed. The landscape was green, in delicately different shades from his home. He saw broad forests, rich plains under cultivation or grazing, picturesque old villages, steep-walled castles. Rivers and snow-peaks gleamed afar. The skies were thronged with winged life. Now and then, a glimpse of sleek industrial buildings, proud new towers in a city, or traffic through heaven reminded him of what had lately been achieved.

Iuthagaar, the capital, hove in view. Once it had been no more than a stronghold atop a small mountain which rose from a rolling valley floor. Today it sprawled down the slopes and across kilometers below. However foreign the architecture—lavish use of metal, multi-staged roofs, high-lifting buildings often fluted, enormous colonnades, wildwood parks—Flandry found himself admiring. But on the peak above, sprawling, gray, craggy-turreted, emblazoned with a golden sun disc above the main portal and topped by a hundred banners, the ancient seat of the Frithian kings still dominated.

The tender landed at a royal spacefield. Flandry was led off to temporary quarters. Next day (the rotation period was about nineteen hours) he was summoned before Penda.

The hall was vast and dim-lit, hung with weapons and trophies of past wars, chill despite the fires that blazed and crackled on a row of hearths. The dragon throne of the king-emperor stood elevated at the north end. Wrapped in furs, Penda sat waiting. He had the stern manner and bleak gaze of his eldest son, and the record indicated he was intelligent in his fashion. It also indicated that he lacked Cerdic's range of interests and knowledge.

The prince occupied a lower seat on his father's right. The queen stood on the left, shivering a bit in the damp draft. Down either wall stretched a row of guardsmen, firelight shimmery on their helmets, breastplates, and halberds; for business purposes they carried blasters. Others in attendance included younger sons of the royal house, generals, councillors, visiting nobles. A few of the latter belonged to non-Scothan species and did not appear to be receiving excessive politeness. A band of musicians behind the throne twanged forth a melody. Servants scurried, fetching and carrying as they were curtly ordered.

His escorting officer named Flandry to the king. As he had been directed, the man first knelt, then, having risen, gave the salute of the Terran Navy: an effective gesture of submission. Thereafter he met Penda's eye. His position was anomalous, technically Cerdic's captured property, actually—what? And potentially?

"Let your welcome be what you earn," Penda rumbled. He proceeded to ask several fairly shrewd questions. Among them were inquiries as to what Flandry would do in various situations; immediate answers were required.

At the end, the king tugged his whitening beard and said slowly: "You are not an utter fool, you. Maybe you are not a fool at all. Were you pretending, or were you only misunderstood? We shall see. Be you turned over to General Nartheof himself, head of Intelligence, to make your report." (The Scothani did not believe in fencing their leaders off behind row after row of bureaucrats.) "You may also make suggestions, if you wish to have hope of regaining your liberty, but remember always that treachery will soon be identified and death will be the welcome end of its punishment."

"I will be honest, mighty lord," Flandry avowed.

"Is any Terran honest?" Cerdic growled.

"My lord," Flandry said with a cheerful smile, "as long as I am paid, I serve most faithfully. I am now in your pay—willy-nilly, yes, but with some prospect of doing better than I could have in my former service."

"Argh!" exclaimed Cerdic. "I'd begun to think better of you. This makes me a little sick."

"Lord, it was your wish."

"Aye. A yeoman must needs wield a muckfork."

Flandry turned to Penda. "Mighty lord," he said, "in earnest of my intentions, may I begin at once by making a respectful proposal to your august self?"

The king grinned like a wolf. "You may."

"Mighty lord, I am a new-arrived stranger among your folk, and have scant knowledge of them or their ways. But I have lived and traveled in an Empire which rules over thousands and thousands of widely different races, and has done so for centuries. Before then, Terra had had earlier centuries of dealings with them. Grant us, I pray you, that we have learned something from experience.

"We have found it is not wise to scorn our subjects. That

would gain us nothing but needless hatred. Instead, we show them whatever honor is appropriate. Meritorious individuals are even given Terran citizenship. Indeed, several entire worlds of nonhumans are included in Great Terra. Thus they have the same stake as we do in the Empire.

"Forgive me if, in my ignorance, I appear insolent. Yet my own life has given me a certain judgment about such matters. It appears to me that here are allies of yours, present on your mutual business, who are shown less than complete respect. Indeed, one or two look physically miserable." Flandry nodded toward a reptile-like being who huddled in bulky garb. "As simple a gesture as installing radiant heating would be appreciated, perhaps more than many Scothani realize. Appreciation would breed trust and cooperativeness in higher degree than erstwhile."

He bowed and finished: "Such is my humble counsel."

Penda stroked his horns. Cerdic fairly snarled: "This is the House of the Dynasty. We observe the ways of the forebears here above all places. Shall we become soft and luxury-loving as you, we who hunt vorgari on ski?"

Flandry's glance, flitting about the chamber, caught furtive dissatisfaction on many faces. Inside, he grinned. Austerity was not the private ideal of most of these virile barbarians.

The queen spoke timidly: "Lord of my being, the captive has wisdom. What harm in being warm? I—I seem always to be cold, myself."

Flandry gave her an appreciative look. He had ascertained that Scothanian and human females were extremely similar in outward anatomy. Queen Gunli was a stunblast, with dark rippling hair, big violet eyes, daintily sculptured features, and a figure that a thin, clinging gown scarcely hid. Frithian males demanded perfect chastity of their wives, yet liked to show them off—an assertion of their own masculinity and their ability to kill any intruder.

He had picked up a trifle about her background. She was young, Penda's third; her predecessors had died at early ages, perhaps of the same weariness and grief he thought he saw in her. She was not Frithian by birth, but from a southerly country which had been more civilized. Too slow to adopt the new technology, it had been forcibly incorporated in the world state; but on shipboard he had noticed that personnel who hailed from it appeared to consider themselves the cultural superiors of the

Frithians, and right about it. Greeks versus Romans....He also had a notion that Gunli held, locked away, considerable natural liveliness. Did she curse the fate that gave her noble blood and hence a political marriage?

For just an instant, his gaze and hers crossed.

"Be still," Cerdic told her.

Gunli's hand fell lightly on Penda's. The king frowned. "Speak not so to your queen and stepmother," he reproved the prince. "In truth, the Terran's idea bears thinking about."

Flandry bowed his most ironical bow. Cocking an eye at the lady, he caught a twinkle. She alone had read his gesture aright.

General Nartheof made an impressive show of blunt honesty; but a quick brain dwelt behind that hairy countenance. He leaned back from his desk, scratched under his leather tunic, and threw a quizzical stare at the man who sat opposite him.

"If matters are as you claim—" he began.

"They are," said Flandry.

"Belike. Your statements do go along with what we already know. They simply warn me that the Imperial Naval Intelligence Corps is better than mine at what it is allowed to do. Not altogether a surprise. Your breed did once conquer everything across four hundred light-years or more." Nartheof lifted a finger. "However, your service is hobbled by politics; and the fighting units it advises are staffed by venial cowards."

Flandry said nothing, but he remembered gallantly mounted actions in his own lifetime. The haughty Scothani seemed unable to comprehend that a state as absolutely decadent as they imagined the Empire was wouldn't have endured long enough to be their rival.

"And yet," Nartheof went on thoughtfully, "your point is well taken, that if the war is prolonged, Intelligence operations will become of the first importance. Even if our victory is quick, we can expect a covert struggle with the remnant of the Empire. And the organization of this corps is inferior. I have the courage to admit that."

"Besides," Flandry reminded, "there are the Merseians, with ambitions of their own. Well may they help you at first, but you can be sure that later they'll turn against you. And the Ythrians may grow alarmed and decide to take measures. You need information about both those domains, and more, before you go out on the galactic stage."

"Yes, yes. Beginning with reorganization. It's ridiculous to make noble birth such a heavy factor, or a factor at all, in deciding promotions."

"And when you do advance commoners, you assume those who've done best in the ranks will make the best officers. That doesn't necessarily follow. No doubt it did, back when reckless courage and handiness with a sword counted most in battle. But now, the concept is as obsolete as . . . as your time-wasting requirement that everyone in the services learn how to use an edged weapon."

"You don't understand that certain practices are to honor our forebears," Nartheof said huffily. "You've lost all sense of race." After a moment: "Nevertheless, you're right about the need to become more, uh, rationalized before we move."

"In ten or twenty years, you might be ready," the Terran opined.

"Impossible. If nothing else, too much eagerness. I will argue for some postponement, and I will start planning how to whip my corps into better shape. Most of the bright lads are mine; and I feel I can count you in there." The general slapped his desk. "As for my fellow services, I can but try. Gods, the dunderheads that command some!" Quickly: "If you repeat that, it will go ill with you. A high-born warrior does not brook disrespect from a slave. He cannot."

Flandry gave as good an imitation of the Scothanian nod as his cervical vertebrae allowed. "Understood, sir. Yet I can serve you best, and thereby serve myself, if we can speak freely between us. Who are these less than brilliant persons?"

"*Urh-hai*, Nornagast, for one, head of the Quartermaster Corps. I've argued my gullet raw, trying to show him he's too inflexibly set up—war is full of unforeseeables, and if a naval division had its supply lines cut it would have to retreat the whole way home, for it cannot live off the country among alien planets—He listens not. And he's cousin to the king, whose life he saved once when they were young. Penda cannot dismiss him without betraying honor."

Flandry stroked his mustache. "An accident could happen to Nornagast," he murmured.

Nartheof jerked erect in his chair. "What? Did I mishear? What did you say?"

"Nothing seriously meant, sir." Flandry smiled and spread his palms. "But just for the sake of discussion, suppose—well, suppose some excellent swordsman should pick a quarrel with Nornagast. I don't doubt he has enemies. If he should unfortunately be killed in the duel, you could get to the king immediately after and have the first voice in choosing Nornagast's successor. To be sure, you would have to know beforehand that a duel was coming. This would require an arrangement with the excellent swordsman, since he'd need a guarantee against the royal wrath—oh, for example, a place to bide his time till the situation changed—"

The general's dagger flashed free. "Silence!" he roared.

"Of course, sir, if you order it." Flandry stared meekly downward and lowered his voice. "I did but speculate aloud. It strikes me as both unfair and unwise that a dolt should have power and glory when others could much better serve Scothania."

"No more of your Terran vileness." However, the knife lowered.

"Forgive me, sir. As I've repeatedly been told, mine is a low, dishonest, treacherous race. Though we did conquer widely, once."

"A warrior might go far, if only—No!" Nartheof clashed blade back in sheath. "A warrior does not bury his hands in muck."

"Certainly not. Prince Cerdic observed that a pitchfork is the proper tool for that. It doesn't mind getting dirty. Nor does he who orders its use need to soil his mind by asking how that use will proceed—" Flandry's manner grew frightened. "I *beg* your pardon, sir. I forgot myself again. May I offer amends?"

Nartheof squinted at him. "Of what sort?"

"A useful item of information I chance to possess. As you doubtless have guessed, many Imperial arsenals and munitions dumps are guarded by nothing but secrecy. Modern warfare, with its high proportion of materiel to men, doesn't cause the Navy to have enough personnel for keeping live watch on everything. And there are plenty of obscure storage places, unfindable among so many suns. I know of one not too far from here."

The Scothan grew utterly intent. His breath quickened, puffing frost-clouds into the chilly room.

"An uninhabited, barren system in the marches," Flandry continued. "The second planet has a mountain range that decks a dragon's warren of storage facilities crammed with spacecraft, weapons, auxiliary equipment, supplies—sufficient to keep a flotilla in action for months. A few ships of yours could go there, take

what they chose, destroy the rest, and be gone without trace. The
next periodic inspection would find no clue as to the identity of
the perpetrators. Or, better yet, I could show you how to plant
clues indicating it was a Merseian operation."

Nartheof gaped. "Is this truth? How do you know?"

Flandry buffed his fingernails. "You recall what my mission
was to Llynathawr. Had I discovered the local admiral is in the
conspiracy, which is imaginable, I was to inform a certain junior
officer whose loyalty is assured, so he could take precautions."

Nartheof shook his head. "I knew the Empire was far gone," he
muttered, "but I never imagined this. I find it hard to believe."

"You can easily send a few scouts to verify my story."

"Yes." Excitement quivered through the hard voice. "I will. And
notify Cerdic—"

"Or simply dispatch the expedition yourself, explaining afterward
that you felt there was no time to lose. Otherwise, you know,
Cerdic is bound to take charge of the raid."

"He would not like such a trick on him," said Nartheof dubiously. "The glory to be won—and glory means power—"

"Indeed. Frankly, sir, I feel you deserve more of that than
you've gotten thus far. The prince could scarcely fault you for so
bold and important a coup." Flandry leaned forward. "You'd gain
more of the influence you need for advancing your ideas, in the
service of Scothania."

"Aye. Aye. And . . . Cerdic has grown overbearing. We'd gain, were
he taken down a little." Abruptly Nartheof chuckled, deep in his
chest. "Aye, by Vailtam's whiskers, I'll do it!"

Then bemusement came over him. He stared long at the man
before he murmured, "It'll be a stiff blow to the Empire. Directly or
indirectly, it will take many human lives. Why have you told me?"

Flandry shrugged. "I've decided my best interests lie with you,
sir." He put on a grave demeanor. "Though I'm afraid I'll make
enemies here before all is done. I'll need a strong friend."

"You have one," declared the barbarian. "You're much too useful
to be slaughtered. And—and—the gods curse you for your treachery, you soulless monster—but somehow, I cannot help liking you."

In a chamber more elegant and comfortable than the highest
standards allowed—warmth, richly hued and textured hangings,
incense and recorded music sweet upon the air—dice rattled across

a table and came to a halt. Prince Torric swore good-naturedly as he shoved a pile of coins toward Flandry. "You have the luck of the damned with you," he laughed.

For a slave, I'm not doing too badly, reflected the man. *In fact, I'm by way of becoming well-to-do, unless my master finds out and confiscates my hoard.* "Say rather that fortune favors the weak," he purred. "The strong don't need it, highness."

"Forget titles when we're by ourselves." The young male was drunk, his cheeks flushed. Greenish wine of Scotha lay puddled near his goblet. "Yes, to the deathrealm with titles. We're friends, Dominic, good friends, not so? We've swapped many a yarn, many a song and jest. And when you straightened out those money matters for me—They could've brought disgrace on my name, you know."

"It was nothing . . . Torric. I've a head for figures, and of course a Terran education helps." Flandry regarded the coins. "I feel guilty at taking even this much from you. You do need more wealth than is yours, to maintain your proper station."

"Well, plenty waits in the Empire. I'm promised a whole planetary system to rule over."

Flandry pretended surprise. "A single system? No more, for a son of King Penda? Why, I understand males of less rank expect far larger fiefs."

"Cerdic's doing." Torric gulped from his cup, set it down with a clang, and glowered at the night in a window. "He's persuaded Father . . . any prince but him, who had any real power, might be too tempted to grasp after more . . . for only *he* is to have any claim to the supreme overlordship."

"That isn't traditional, is it? I've heard that in olden times a new king was elected, from among the sons of the royal house, by the assembly of nobles."

As a matter of fact, that system had led to a number of civil wars. Finally it was decided that a successor should be chosen while his father still reigned. Primogeniture was usual but not legally required. Penda had practically forced the parliament to name Cerdic, with the obvious aim of establishing the precedent that the first son would always be the next king. That would be a long step toward absolute monarchy.

Torric wove his head about. He was no political sophisticate. "Thus 'twas. They wanted whoever was best."

"Is Cerdic, then?"

"He'll tell you so. Hour after hour."

"I gather you don't agree. These are dangerous times. Isn't it your duty to work for the welfare of Scothania? And who embodies that welfare more than the king?"

The prince blinked. He had forgotten, or he had never noticed, how much about himself he had let slip in the course of weeks. "Can you hear my thinking, Dominic? I wonder 'bout you—" He shook himself. "But no. I mustn't. I can't."

Flandry raised forefingers to brows. He had developed the gesture as his version of the Scothanian touching of the horns, to express surprise. "Helpless, Torric? I didn't await such words from you—you, royal warrior, descended from Saagur the Mighty, and on your mother's side from—" He let his voice trail off. The other had grown up knowing that his mother, Penda's second queen, had been higher born than the first.

"Now, now wait." Hands fumbled with goblet. "You've been such a practical devil till now. Gone crazy, ha?"

"No, I trust not. I am simply reminding you that Cerdic's power, like that of any chieftain, rests on his supporters. The grandest of those is his father, of course. But King Penda—I mean no disrespect—the great lord will not live many more years. Cerdic is not widely liked. Someone with a lawful claim to the throne, who had spent those years quietly preparing, gathering allegiances of his own and winning them away from Cerdic—"

For a moment, shock cleared the eyes that looked into his. "Would you make a brotherslayer of me?"

"Oh, absolutely not," Flandry said. He had studied how to sound reassuring in Scothan ears. "Only an event of a kind that Terran history is full of. And for the higher good of the Race. No, I daresay Cerdic could be honorably retired to govern a planetary system. Or you, being generous, might grant him two."

"But—your sneaking ways—I, I know nothing about 'em," Torric stammered. "Don't want to . . . I suppose you mean to dish—disaffect his faction, promise more'n he gives. . . . What's that word? Not Frithian; Ilrian." Queen Gunli was from Ilria. "*Laionas,* yes, *laionas.*" Bribery. "I couldn't do that. Don't even want to hear about it."

"You wouldn't need to," Flandry replied softly. "You could leave the details to your friends. What's a male for, if he never helps a friend?"

☼   ☼   ☼

Earl Morgaar, who held the conquered world Zanthudia in fief, was a noble of more influence than his title suggested. ("Earl" was a rough translation into Anglic.) He was also notoriously avaricious.

In a private place he maintained for his visits to Iuthagaar, he told Flandry: "Terran, your suggestion about farming out my tax-gathering has more than doubled my revenues ... until lately. Now the natives are seething. They murder my folk, they hide their goods, a number have taken up arms as guerrillas. What do they do about *that* in the Empire?"

"Surely, sir, you could crush them," the man replied.

"Aye, at vast effort and cost. And the dead pay no taxes. Ken you no better way, before my whole domain is in chaos?"

"Several, sir." Flandry sketched a few—puppet native committees, propaganda shifting the blame onto scapegoats, splashy displays of governmental concern for a select few underdogs.... He did not add that these methods work only when skillfully administered.

"It is well," said the earl at last. His gaze probed at the man's smiling face. "You've made yourself valuable to many a lord, have you not? Like Nartheof; he's waxing mighty since he took that Imperial arsenal. And others, myself among them." He rubbed his horns. "Yet it seems much of this gain is at the expense of rival Scothani, rather than the Empire. I still wonder about Nornagast's death."

"History shows that the prospect of enormous gain always stirs up internal strife, sir," Flandry answered. "Often a strong, virtuous warrior has had to seize dominance, so that he could reunite his people against their common enemy. Think how the early Terran Emperors ended the civil wars, once they had power."

"Um-m-m—yes. It was a maxim of the forebears that wealth corrupts. Have I not seen its truth in our own royal court?"

"Sir," Flandry said, "we being alone, and I being a decadent human, permit me to recall that Frithia has seen many changes of dynasty in the past."

"What?" Morgaar sat bolt upright. "Do you imply—No! My oath is to the king!"

"Of course, of course," the man said quickly. "I was just thinking that not everyone is as virtuous as you. You yourself spoke of those who are not. I fear that good King Penda is more trustful than is wise. Evil could well take him unawares. Enthroned, it would soon destroy that uprightness which is the fountainhead of Scothanian strength."

Morgaar leaned forward. His voice dropped. "Do you imply it could become necessary to forestall—"

"Well, for the good of Scothania—"

They were discussing details within an hour. Flandry suggested that Prince Kortan was probably approachable—but one should be leery of Prince Torric, who had ambitions of his own—

Winter solstice was the occasion of religious ceremonies followed by feasting and merriment. Town and castle blazed with light, shouted with music and drunken laughter. Warriors and nobles swirled their finest robes about them and boasted of the havoc they would wreak in the Empire. On the dark side, the number of alcoholic quarrels leading to bloodshed was unusually high this year among the upper classes.

There were dark corners in buildings, too. Flandry stood in an alcove before a window and looked over a dazzle of city lights to the mountains that reared on the horizon, white beneath a hurtling moon. Winter-frosty stars seemed so near that he could reach out and pluck them from the sky. Cold breathed from the glass pane. The sounds of revelry came to him as if across a chasm.

A light footfall sounded beneath them, Flandry turned and saw Gunli the queen. Her form was shadowed, but moonlight came in to bring forth her countenance in elfin wise. She might have been a lovely girl of Terra, save for the little horns and—well—

She looks human, almost, but she isn't. I've been able to play on these people because they're trying to play a game that my *race invented. They and we will never truly understand each other's inwardness.* Flandry's lips quirked. *They do share a quaint belief often found in our history, that the female of the species has no talent for politics. I've a notion Gunli could enlighten them about that, after she's enlightened herself. In that respect, as well as in the delectable flesh, she's human enough for all practical purposes.*

The cynicism faded before an indefinable sadness. Damn it, he liked Gunli. They two had shared speech, songs, memories, even mirth now and then, throughout the past months; she was honest and warm-hearted and—well, no matter.

"Why are you here alone, Dominic?" she asked. Her tone was quiet. Her eyes glimmered huge in the shifty moonlight.

"It would be imprudent for me to stay at the party," he answered wryly. "I'd cause too many fights. Half the company hate my guts, and don't care much for the rest of me."

She smiled. "And the other half can't do without you." She tossed her head, her equivalent of a shrug. The dark hair sheened. "*Urh-hai*, I've come in search of solitude myself. Those savages pluck too hard on my nerves. At home—" She came to stand beside him and stared outward. He saw a glitter of tears. Scothans also wept.

"Don't cry, Gunli," he murmured. "This is the night when the sun turns, remember. A new year offers new hope."

"I can't forget the old years," she said with sudden bitterness.

Understanding touched him. He asked, softer yet: "You had somebody else once, didn't you?"

"Aye. A young knight. But he was of low degree, so they married me off to Penda, who is old and harsh. Later Jomana was killed in a raid of Cerdic's." She turned her head to regard him. "Jomana isn't what hurts, Dominic. He was dear to me, but wounds heal if we survive them. I am thinking of the other young males, and their sweethearts, wives, daughters, mothers—"

"War is what they want."

"But not what the females want. Not to wait and wait and wait for the ships to come back, never knowing whether only his sword will return. Not to rock a baby and know that a few years hence he will be a corpse on the shores of some alien planet. Not to—" She broke off and straightened her slim shoulders. "Let me not whimper. Naught can I do about it."

"You are very brave as well as beautiful, Gunli," said Flandry. "Your kind has changed fate erenow." And he sang, low, a stave he had made in the Scothan bardic form:

> "*So I see you standing,*
> *sorrowful in darkness.*
> *But the moonlight's broken*
> *by your eyes, tear-shining—*
> *moonlight in the maiden's*
> *magic net of tresses.*
> *Gods gave many gifts, but,*
> *Gunli, yours was greatest.*"

All at once she was in his arms.

✧ ✧ ✧

Sviffash of Sithafar was in a glacial rage. He paced between the stone walls of the secret chamber, tail lashing his bowed legs, fanged jaws biting off each accented Frithian word.

"Like a craieex they treat me," he hissed. "I, primary one of a planet and an intelligent species, must bow to the dirty barbarian Penda. Our ships have the worst assignments in the fleet, our crews the last chances at loot. Scothani on our world swagger about among us as if we were subjugated primitives, not civilized allies. It is unendurable!"

Flandry preserved deferential silence. He had carefully nursed along the herpetoid's resentment ever since he identified it, on an occasion when Sviffash had come to Iuthagaar for conference. But he wanted the nonhuman to think everything was his own idea.

"By the Dark Lord, were it possible, I think I'd take us over to the Imperial side!" burst from the scaly countenance. "Do you say they treat their subjects decently?"

"Yes, as you can verify by sending a commission of inquiry that the Scothans need not know about. We've learned that race prejudice is counterproductive. Besides, if only because the sheer number of peoples requires it, by and large we leave them their autonomy, except in certain matters of defense, commerce, and the like where we must have uniformity. That's to everyone's benefit. Actually, being located well outside the border, I expect Sithafar would be offered alliance rather than client status." *If the Policy Board feels it's worthwhile offering them anything,* Flandry's mind added. *I trust they'll have the wit not to make that clear until afterward.*

"My subordinates would gladly follow," said Sviffash. "They would rather sack and occupy Scothanian than Terran worlds. But they fear Penda's revenge."

"Several other leaderships feel likewise. Once a revolt began and bid fair to succeed, still more would join in. It's a matter of getting them together. You could arrange that, my lord, after I've told you who they are."

Lidless black eyes glistened in a stare. "You've been busy, Terran, have you not? Like a spinner-legs weaving its web. Say on." Pause. "You realize, things must be so planned that, if you are caught at your work, I will be able to disown you, convincingly."

"Of course, my lord. I have a scheme prepared in detail for your scrutiny."

A tongue flickered forth and back again. "If we can—if we can—s-s-s, I myself will direct the first missile against Scotha!"

"No, my lord," Flandry said. "Scotha must be spared."

"Why?"

"Because you see, my lord, we'll have Scothan allies. They'll cooperate only on that condition. Some of the power-seeking nobles...and an Ilrian nationalist movement, desiring independence from Frithia...which, I may tell you, has the secret help of the queen herself...."

Flandry's stare was as bleak as his voice: "It will do you less than no good to kill me, Duke Asdagaar. Credit me with brains. I have made my preparations. If I die or disappear, the evidence goes straight to the king and, by broadcast, the people."

The Scothan's hands clenched white about the arms of his chair. Impotent fury chattered: "You devil! You slime-worm!"

Flandry wagged a finger. "Tut-tut. You are poorly advised to call names, my dear Asdagaar. A parricide, a betrayer, a breaker of oaths, a blasphemer—Be sure that I have proof. Some of it is in writing. More consists of the names of scattered witnesses and accomplices, each of whom knows a little of the entirety about you. A male without honor can await nothing but a nasty death."

"How did you learn?" Hopelessness crept into the duke's tone; he began to tremble.

"In various ways," Flandry said. "I've been in my business a fair number of years, after all. For instance, I cultivated the acquaintance of your slaves and servants. You high-born forget that the lower classes can see and hear and draw conclusions, and that they talk among themselves. The clues they gave me pointed me onward."

"Uh, uh, uh." The noise was as of strangling. "What do you want?"

"Help for certain others," Flandry replied. "You have powerful forces at your disposal. You are the head of your clan, which has always felt more loyal to itself than to the throne—"

Spring breezes blew soft through the garden and woke rustling in trees. A deep odor of green life was upon it. Somewhere in twilight, a creature not unlike a bird was singing. The ancient promise of summer to come stirred in the blood.

Flandry told himself he must relax before his nerves snapped across. Matters were out of his hands now, or nearly so; the machinery he had built was in motion. The counsel was of scant use.

He had grown thin and hollow-eyed. Likewise had Gunli, though on her it heightened the loveliness. More than ever, she made him think of the elves, in myths that she had never heard.

They had gone their separate ways to meet here in this place where few came. (It was an Ilrian garden, to ease her homesickness a little.) How often had they stolen such brief whiles together? The longer times they had been able to find must be used for scheming.

Gravel scrunched beneath their feet as they walked. The path was narrow; the hands they did not link brushed hedges that had begun to flower. Flandry tried to keep his speech dry, but heard it as weary: "The spaceship got off this morning. Aethagir should have no trouble reaching Ifri. He'll have more obstacles in his way after he arrives, but he's a clever lad. He'll get my letter to Admiral Walton." A tic wakened in his cheek. "The timing's too bloody close, though. If our task force hits too soon, or too late, well, the menace to the Empire will be ended, but at what a cost!"

"I've not seen your confidence flag before," Gunli said.

"It was necessary to put on a good show, my beautiful. But the fact is, I've never juggled an empire before." Flandry drew breath. "The next several weeks will be touch and go. You'd better leave Scotha. Make an excuse; explain you need a rest, which is clear to see. Take it on Alagan or Gamlu or wherever, a safely out-of-the-way planet." He smiled with a corner of his mouth. "What point in a victory where you died? The universe would become drab."

She looked away from him. Her hand felt cold in his. "I ought to die, I who've betrayed my husband, my king."

"No, you ought to live, you who've freed your country and saved lives in the millionfold."

"But the broken oath—" Quite quietly, she started to weep.

"An oath is just a means to an end: helping people get along with each other."

"An oath is an oath. Dominic, m-my choice was to stand by Penda—or by you—"

He comforted her as well as he could. And he reflected that seldom had he felt himself so thoroughgoing a skunk.

✿   ✿   ✿

The unaided eye could never really see a battle in space. Nothing but flashes among the stars betokened rays, warheads, incandescent vapor clouds, astronomically nearby. Farther off, across distances measured in planetary orbits, the deaths of ships were invisible.

Instruments sensed more fully, and computers integrated their data to give a running history of the combat. Admiral Thomas Walton, Imperial Terran Navy, laid down the latest printout and smiled in stark satisfaction.

"We're scrubbing them out of the sky," he said. "We've twice their strength. Besides, it's gotten pretty obvious by now that they were demoralized from the start. I don't know how else to account for their sloppiness."

"Is it known yet who they are?" wondered Chang, captain of the flagship.

"Not yet. We may salvage a piece of wreckage that'll identify them for sure, though I won't spend time searching for any. They're split into such a flinkin' lot of factions—" Walton rubbed his chin. "Judging from what data we have, their radiant of origin and similar clues, on the basis of Flandry's report I'd say it's the command of—what is that outlandish name?—Duke Markagrav. He's a royalist. However, it might be Kelry. He's in revolt against the king, though not about to join meekly with us."

Chang whistled. "Son of a bitch! The whole hegemony has just disintegrated, hasn't it? Everybody at the throat of everybody else, and hell take the hindmost. What's happened?"

Walton chuckled. "Dominic Flandry is what happened. We'll find out the details later, but his signature is on everything in sight." He leaned back and bridged his fingers. "We've a moment to chat till the next decision has to be made. I'm not free to tell you all I know about Flandry's career to date. However, since the Llynathawr business has been terminated, I can describe his *modus operandi* there. It's typical of him, insofar as anything ever is.

"I've mentioned to you that he was handling it when those barbarians kidnapped him. Needless to say, he'd done his home-work, and he set up an excellent undercover operation which did eventually track down the conspirators. They'd have been caught long before, though, if he'd stayed on hand. Know what he was doing? He showed up with, practically, a brass band; he put on a perfect act as a political appointee using the case as an excuse to go roistering, which made the plotters ease off on their precautions; meanwhile he worked his way toward them through the shadier characters he met.

"I've no words for how relieved I was when his report came in and I knew his disappearance hadn't meant he was dead. At the same time, I couldn't help feeling sorry for the Scothanians. They'd grabbed hold of Captain Flandry!"

Mobs howled and roiled in the streets of Iuthagaar. Here and there, houses burned. No government remained to control horror and anger.

The remnants of Penda's troops had abandoned the city and were in flight northward from the advancing Ilrian Liberation Army. They would be harried by Torric's irregulars, who in turn were the fragments of a force smashed by Earl Morgaar after Penda was slain by Asdagaar's assassins. Asdagaar himself had died when Nartheof's fleet broke his. The clansfolk had not fought well; it had lately become known to them what kind of male their chief was.

But Nartheof had met death too, at the hands of Nornagast's vengeful kin. His seizure of the throne and attempt at restoring order had mainly worsened the chaos. Now the royalists were scattered through space, driven off rebellious subject planets, hunted by their erstwhile allies, annihilated piecemeal by the oncoming Terran armada.

Desperately, the Scothanian lords fought among themselves and scrabbled to retrieve something from the ruin, each without thought for the rest. Some went down; some made hasty surrender to the Empire. Battle still flamed between the stars, but it was fast guttering out; the means of waging it had crumbled.

A few guards kept watch around the nearly deserted castle, waiting for the Terrans to proclaim, "Peace, ye underlings." They knew nothing else they could do but wait.

Flandry stood at a window in a high room and looked across the city. He felt no elation. Down there in the smoke, sentient beings lay dead. More would perish before the end of upheaval. The whole number would be merely in the hundreds, he guessed; the dead of the entire war were probably less than a million. Yet each of those heads had borne a cosmos within it.

To him came Gunli. Her fairness had gone bone-white, and she walked and spoke unsteadily. She had not expected Penda's murder.

She halted before him. Tapestries on the walls behind her depicted former triumphs. "Proud Scotha lies fallen, in wreck and misery," she said.

"Be happy for that," Flandry replied tonelessly.

A slim hand touched a horn. "What?"

He thought a lecture might calm her, for sure it was that she was overwrought to the edge of endurance. "Barbarian conquests never last," he said. "Barbarians have to become civilized first, before they are fit to rule a civilization.

"And Scothania had not gone through that stage. I knew almost from the beginning that it had gone straight from barbarism to decadence. Its much-vaunted honesty was its undoing. By self-righteously denying the possibility of dishonor in its own society, it left that society ignorant, uninoculated, helpless against the infection. I never believed the germ was not present. Scothans are much too humanlike. But they made the mistake of taking their hypocrisy at face value.

"Most of my work amounted just to pointing out to their key males the rewards of treachery. If they'd been truly honest, I'd have died at the first suggestion. Instead, they wanted to hear more. They found they didn't object to bribery, blackmail, betrayal, anything that seemed to be to their private advantages. Most Terrans would have seen deeper, would have wondered if the despised slave was talking to others along the same lines, would have recollected the old saying that two can play at the same game... and so can three, four, any number, till the game becomes unstable and somebody at last kicks the board over.

"Don't mourn for lost honor, Gunli. It never was there."

"It was in me, once." A strange light kindled in her eyes. "I have lost it, and though my people may become free, I am not fit to reign over them. Dominic, dishonor can only be wiped out with blood."

Unease tingled through him. "What do you mean?"

She snatched his blaster from the holster and skipped back out of reach before he could move. "Hold!" she shrilled. "Hold or I shoot!" Calmer: "You are cunning. But are you brave?"

He froze. "I think—" He paused to grope for words. Had she gone berserk? No, he believed not. But she wasn't entirely human, and she had in her the barbarian's iron code as well as the milder philosophy of her civilization. "I think I took a few risks, Gunli."

"Aye. But you never fought, fairly and openly, as a warrior should." The thinned countenance twisted in pain. Breath rasped in and out. "I act for you as well as him, Dominic. He must have his chance to avenge his father—my husband—and fallen Scotha—and you must have the chance to redeem your honor. The gods will know where justice lies."

Trial by combat, Flandry knew, *three hundred light-years and more from old Terra.*

Cerdic came through the door. He carried a sword in either hand, and laughed as he entered.

"I let him in, Dominic," Gunli cried through tears. "I had to—for Penda—but kill him, kill him!"

She ran to a window. In a convulsive movement, she threw the blaster out. The prince's ravaged visage showed surprise. She clung to the sill and sobbed, "I was afraid I might shoot you, Cerdic."

"Thanks!" he said savagely. "I may remember that when I deal with you, traitress. First—" again he cackled laughter—"I'll cut your paramour into many small pieces. For who, among the so-civilized Terrans, can wield a sword?"

Gunli staggered. "Oh, almighty gods, I never thought of that!"

She flung herself at Cerdic, nails and teeth and horns. "Get him, Dominic!" she screamed.

The prince swung a brawny arm around. She fell to the stone floor and lay half stunned.

"Now," Cerdic grinned, "choose your weapon."

Flandry came forward and took a slender shape at random. His thoughts were mostly of the queen. Poor darling, she'd suffered more than flesh was meant to bear. May time henceforward be kinder to her.

Cerdic crossed blades with him. The Scothan's expression had gone dreamy. "I mean to take a while about this," he murmured. "Before you die, Terran, you will no longer be a male."

Steel rang. Flandry parried a slash. He point raked the prince's brow. Cerdic bellowed and stormed forward. Flandry retreated. Scothan physical strength exceeded his. The sword could be knocked out of his grasp if he wasn't careful.

His foe hewed. He was wide open for the simplest stop thrust, but Flandry preferred not to slay him. Instead, he parried again, then followed with a riposte that tore across the breast. Cerdic sprang back. Flandry made a lunge, a feint, and a glide. He took his opponent in the right forearm. Blood welled. The injury wasn't disabling, but Cerdic was shaken. Flandry executed a beat that deflected the opposing blade. With the flat of his own, he smote across knuckles. The Scothan gasped in pain, and Flandry's next blow sent his weapon spinning in midair. He stood with his enemy's point at his throat.

Flandry laughed into his stupefaction and told him: "My friend, you didn't study our decadence as thoroughly as you should have. Archaism accompanies it. *Scientific* fencing is quite popular among us."

The prince braced himself. "Then kill me and be done," he said.

"There's been too much killing. Besides, I have uses for you." The Terran cast his sword from him and cocked his fists. "However, here's one thing I've been waiting with exemplary patience for an opportunity to do."

Despite Cerdic's powerful but clumsy defense, Flandry proceeded to beat the living hell out of him.

Wind boomed around the highest tower of the castle, chill and thrusting; but save for tatters of cloud, the sky was blue with late afternoon. Golden-plumed, a few winged creatures wheeled over the deck where Flandry and Gunli stood. They had drawn cloaks about them against the blast, but she rested a hand on the parapet, and his lay across it. Below them, roofs and walls fell away toward a city where Ilrian patrols now kept the peace. Beyond, hills, fields, and woods reached green to a horizon of snowpeaks.

"What you did, girl," he said, "was nothing more or less than help save Scotha. All Scotha. Think. What would have happened if you'd gone into the Empire? Supposing you won your victory— which was always doubtful, because Terra is still mighty—but supposing you did, what would have come next? Why, the humans or the Merseians would soon have had you at civil war over the spoils. You'd have made yourselves prey for a conqueror who'd have shown small mercy. As is, the conflict did less harm, by orders of magnitude, than even your success would have; and the victors aren't vindictive."

She bowed her head. "We deserve to be subjected," she whispered.

"Oh, but you won't be," he assured her. "What gain in that for Terra, as far away as you are? Some drastic changes will be necessary, of course, to make sure no fresh danger will breed hereabouts. But the Imperial commission that decides on them will depend heavily on *my* advice. I feel pretty sure Scotha will end as a confederation of nations under Ilrian dominance, with you the queen, and a Terran resident who keeps an eye on things but generally lets you alone." His lips brushed her cheek. "Begin thinking what you would like to see happen."

Her smile was still wan, but he saw that something of her spirit was on its way home. "I don't believe the Empire is in such a bad state," she said. "Not when it has people like you."

No, he thought, *it's worse off; but why hurt you again by explaining?*

She brought her left hand from beneath the cloak and took both his. "And what will you be doing?" she asked.

He met her gaze. Loneliness was sudden within him. How beautiful she stood there.

But what she meant could never endure. They were too foreign to each other. Best he depart soon, that the memories remain untarnished in them both. She would find someone else at last, and he—well—"I have my work," he said.

Far above them, the first of the descending Imperial ships glittered in heaven like a falling star. ✴

HONORABLE
ENEMIES

The door opened behind him and a voice murmured, "Good evening, Captain Flandry."

He spun about, with a reflexive grab for his stun pistol, and found himself looking at a blaster. Slowly, then, he let his empty hand fall and stood poised. His eyes searched beyond the weapon and the six talon-like fingers that held it, to the tall gaunt body and sardonic smile.

The face there was humanoid, if you overlooked countless details of shape and proportion—lean, hook-nosed, golden-skinned. There was no hair, but a feathery blue crest rose high and plumelets formed brows above the eyes. Those eyes were sheer beauty, big and luminous bronze in hue. The being wore a simple, knee-length white tunic and his clawed feet were bare. However, jewels indicating rank hung from his neck and a cloak like a gush of blood from his shoulders.

The whole Merseian group is occupied elsewhere, Flandry thought in dismay. *I've seen to that. Or supposed I had. What's gone wrong?*

He forced relaxation of a sort upon himself, and even an answering smile. The main question was how he might get out of here with a whole skin. Assessment . . . this wasn't actually a Merseian, though a member of that party. It was Aycharaych of Chereion, who had arrived only a few days ago, presumably on a mission that corresponded to Flandry's.

"Pardon the intrusion," the Terran said. "Purely professional, I assure you. No offense meant."

"And none taken," replied Aycharaych with equal urbanity. He spoke perfect Anglic, save for a touch of accent that added a kind of harsh music to it.

Nevertheless, he could easily blast the man down and later express regret that he had mistaken an ace Intelligence officer of the Terran Empire for a common burglar.

Flandry dared hope the Chereionite would not be so crass. Little was known of that race—this was the first one that the human had ever met—but they were said to have a very ancient civilization and very subtle ways. Flandry had heard stories about Aycharaych's specific operations....

"You are right, Captain, I intend you no harm," the being said. Flandry started. Had his mind been read, or what? "I will be content with chiding. This attempt to search our quarters was deplorably crude, quite unworthy of you. I trust you will give us a better game in future."

Flandry gauged distances and angles. A vase on a table stood close to hand. If he could sweep it across Aycharaych's wrist—

"I would not advise that, either," said the Chereionite. He stepped aside. "You may go now. Goodnight."

The Terran moved slowly toward the door. He couldn't let himself suffer this—dismissal. It was vital that he learn what the Merseians were brewing in the way of trouble for the Empire. Yes, a karate leap and kick—

Hampered by a greater gravity than his species had evolved under, Aycharaych should not have dodged fast enough. Yet somehow he did. He wasn't there when the boot arrived. Momentum carried Flandry on past. The blaster butt cracked against the base of his skull. He fell and lay for a minute while darkness roared through him.

"You do disappoint me, Captain," said the other, most softly. "A person of your reputation should be above theatrics. Now I must bid you goodnight."

Sickly, the human got to his feet and stumbled out into the hall. Aycharaych watched, still smiling.

Long passages brought him to the suite, as capacious as a small hotel, assigned the Terran delegation. Its common room was empty, like most of the rest. A feast was going on elsewhere. Flandry mixed himself a stiff drink at the bar and settled down.

A light step and a suggestive rustle of a long shimmerlyn skirt brought his glance around. Aline Chang-Lei, the Lady Marr of Syrtis, had entered. The sight of her lifted his spirits a trifle. She was tall and slender, raven-haired and oblique-eyed and delicate of feature; the blue gown seemed to make her ivory complexion luminous. She was also one of Sol's top field agents and his teammate here.

"What's the matter?" she asked at once.

"Why are you back?" he responded. "I thought you'd be at the party, helping distract people."

She shrugged. "No further point in that, at the present stage of it. An official function on Alfzar almost makes me long for a staid and stuffy one on Terra. I wanted a little quiet and an absence of drunks who've decided they're God's gift to womankind." Her gaze upon him sharpened. "You've failed, then. How?"

"I'd trade my air-conditioned room in hell for an answer to that." Flandry rubbed the ache at the back of his head. His wits had not yet fully recovered from the blow; he heard his voice plod through the obvious: "Look, we prevailed on the Sartaz to throw a brawl with everybody invited. We made doubly sure that every Merseian in the palace would be there. They'd trust to their robolocks to keep their place safe. They had absolutely no way of knowing we can nullify that sort of lock." The obtaining of the necessary information had been a minor triumph of his not long ago. "But what happened? No sooner was I in than Aycharaych appeared." He struggled to pronounce the name properly, but it came out sounding more Scottish than Chereionite; his vocal organs were not shaped like the other's, nor as versatile. "He was elaborately polite. Nevertheless he kept a blaster on me the whole while, anticipated my every move—would you imagine a scarecrow like him could avoid an attack and slug me? At last he sent me off wishing I had a tail to tuck between my legs."

"Oh, dear." Aline examined the bruise and stroked gentle fingers across it. Then her tone hardened: "He's bad news for certain, isn't he? What *do* we know about him? You've roved around more than most. Do you have anything to tell?"

"Nothing but what you've already heard. Apparently the Chereionites have a privileged position in the Roidhunate, not subjected like most non-Merseian races though not exactly citizens either. I've never heard of anyone who claims even to have seen their planet, or to know its location. Aycharaych appears to be quite active as a field agent—spy, saboteur, general troublemaker—but of course that's impossible to verify, precisely because he is so good at it. I'm afraid our mission is rather badly compromised, Aline."

Flandry got up and walked out onto a balcony. Both moons of Alfzar were aloft and near the full, pouring coppery light over gardens beneath that blended, kilometers away, with forest. The breeze was warm, laden with scents of flowers that had never bloomed under Sol. From afar in the vastness of the palace drifted sounds of music at the feast, on a scale and out of instruments that had never been heard on Terra.

Stars showed faint through the radiance. As he beheld them, Flandry felt daunted. Even the four million or so suns over which his Emperor claimed suzerainty were too many to know; most had never been visited more than perhaps once, if that. Too many mutually alien races; rival imperia, too, Merseia before all. . . .

Aline joined him and took his arm. "Are you letting a single failure discourage you?" she asked with careful good cheer. "Dominic Flandry, the single-handed conqueror of Scothania, brought down by that overgrown buzzard?"

"I just can't understand what happened, how he knew," the man mumbled. "The greenest cub in the Corps shouldn't have gotten caught as I was. How many of our best people has he accounted for? I'm convinced it was he who made McMurtrie disappear, three years back. Who else? Is our turn coming?"

"Oh, now!" She tried to laugh. "You know the devil himself is no better than the organization he belongs to, and Merseian Intelligence isn't that good. Were you drinking *sorgan* when you first heard about Aycharaych?"

"Drinking what?" he asked.

"Ah, I can tell you something you don't know," she said, still valiantly smiling. "Not that it's especially important. I simply happened to pick it up as a bit of gossip from one of our Alfzarian opposite numbers. It's a drug produced on a planet of this system—Cingetor? Yes. For Alfzarians it's medicinal, but in humans it has the odd property of depressing certain brain centers. The victim loses all critical sense. He believes, without question, anything you tell him."

"Hm." Flandry stroked his mustache. "Could be useful in our line of work."

"Not very. There are better ways of interrogating a prisoner, or for that matter producing a fanatic. The drug has an antidote which also confers permanent immunity. The Sartaz has forbidden its sale to his subjects who're of our species, but mainly just because it could help certain types of criminals."

"I should think our Corps would like to keep a little of it stashed away anyhow, against contingencies. And, m-m, to be sure, certain gentlemen would find it an aid to seduction."

"What are you thinking of?" she teased.

"Nothing. I don't need it," he answered smugly.

The diversion had somewhat brightened his mood. "Let me put some painkiller on this bump and escort you back to the party," he suggested. "I'll fend off the amorous drunks."

"But it's so beautiful here—" she sighed. "Ah, well, if you really want to go."

The Betelgeusean System is an appropriate setting for mysteries. It has no theoretical business possessing half a dozen planets, out of forty-seven, with life upon them. After all, being considerably more massive than Sol, it was only on the main sequence for a short time, as astronomical time goes. Now it is dying, a red giant that has consumed its innermost attendants. True, the total radiation is great enough that the zone where water can be liquid includes the orbits of those six worlds. However, this condition will not prevail sufficiently long for biologies to develop, let alone intelligences.

Yet when the first Terrestrial explorers arrived, they found flourishing ecologies and a civilization whose spacecraft plied from edge to edge of the system. The Betelgeuseans had only dim traditions about ancestors who fled some catastrophe elsewhere—in slower-than-light ships, no doubt—and seeded the barrenness they found with life that transformed it. (Properly gene-engineered microorganisms could generate an oxynitrogen atmosphere in mere decades of exponential multiplication; meanwhile automated operations could produce soil in chosen areas; eventually full-sized plants and animals could be grown from cells and released; after that, life would spread of itself, being a geological force of great potency.) Perhaps the effort exhausted the pioneers, or perhaps the resource base was insufficient to maintain a high technology in that early phase. Whatever the cause, reliable records on the Betelgeusean worlds only go back for some thousands of years.

Their sun will not keep those worlds warm very much longer, and its dying gasps may well make them uninhabitable even before they start to freeze—but the span available is measured in geological rather than historical terms. It is ample for an orderly move to new homes, now that the Betelgeuseans have learned such tricks as travel at hyperdrive pseudovelocities. Meanwhile they are in no hurry about it, for they command abundant resources, with all that that implies in the way of power.

In Flandry's day, their political position was also one he often wished his own people could occupy. They had not attempted to establish an empire on the scale of Terra or Merseia, but were content to maintain hegemony over such few neighbor stars as were needed for the protection of their home. Generations of wily Sartazes had found it profitable to play potential enemies off against each other; and the great states had, in turn, found it expedient to maintain Betelgeuse as a buffer *vis-a-vis* their rivals and the peripheral barbarians.

That stability was ending, though, as tension ratcheted upward between Terra and Merseia. Squarely between the two domains, its navy commanding the most direct route and in a position to strike at the heart of either, Betelgeuse would be an invaluable ally. If Merseia could get that help, it might well be the last preparation considered necessary for all-out war. If Terra could get it, Merseia would suddenly have to make concessions.

Emissaries swarmed to the red sun, together with spies, genteel blackmailers, purveyors of large bribes, and other such agents, whom their governments promptly disowned whenever they got caught. Official negotiations had reached the point where—Flandry claimed—clandestine activities were a major industry on the capital planet Alfzar. He and Aline had lately been dispatched to join in, he chosen primarily for his experience with nonhumans, she for her talents with her own species. Quite a few members of it had been settled here for generations, as citizens, and some of those held key positions. And then came Aycharaych.

For the most distinguished of his foreign guests, the Sartaz gave a hunting party. That monarch evidently enjoyed watching mortal enemies forced to exchange courtesies. Doubtless this occasion did please most of the Merseians; hunting was their favorite sport. The Terrans were less happy, but could scarcely refuse.

Flandry was especially disgruntled. Though he kept in physical trim as a matter of necessity, his own favorite play was conducted in a horizontal position. Worse, he had too much else to do.

The best-laid plans of him and his colleagues were going disastrously agley. Whether Imperial, Betelgeusean, or more exotic, agent after Terran agent had come to grief. Their undertakings failed due to watchfulness, their covers were blown, their own offices were ransacked and the data banks made to yield secrets, they themselves were apt to suffer arrest, or disappearance, or unexplained demise. None among them had found the source of betrayal. Flandry's guess was generally discounted. No single being could be as effective as he thought Aycharaych must be. It just wasn't possible that the opposition could have known about so many projects, caches, contacts, hiding places—or for that matter, Flandry thought, that his rival was *never* vulnerable to any of his assassination schemes—yet, damnation, it was happening.

And now a bloody hunt!

Alfzar rotates at almost the same rate as Terra. This meant that Flandry's servant roused him at an unsanctified hour. He had no absolute prejudice against sunrise; in fact, it was quite a pretty end to an evening. To get up then was a perversion of God's gifts. Dawn here was an alien thing, too. Mist tinged blood-red drifted in dankness through the open windows of his bedroom. It smelled like wet iron. Someone was blowing a horn somewhere, doubtless with intentions of spreading cheer; but to him, local music sounded like a cat in a washing machine. Engines growled. He closed his palms around the warmth of a coffee cup and shivered.

But somebody has to prop up civilization, at least through my own lifetime, he told himself. *Consider the alternative.*

Breakfast made the universe slightly more tolerable. He dressed with some pleasure, too, in skintight green iridon, golden-hued cloak with cowl and goggles, mirrorlike boots. At his waist he secured a needle gun and the slender sword which Alfzarian custom required be worn in the royal presence. The long walk downstairs and out to a palace gate, the longer walk thence to the marshalling field, brought him fully alive.

A picturesque medley of beings moved about the area, talking, gesturing, making ready. The Sartaz himself was on hand—also quite humanoid to see, short, stocky, hairless, blue-skinned, his eyes huge and yellow in the round, blunt-faced head. He was more plainly clad than the nobles, guards, and attendants of his race who surrounded him. The Terrans were more or less in a cluster of their own, a great deal less animated than the Betelgeuseans; several seemed downright miserable. The Merseians likewise kept somewhat aloof; they had reason to feel happy, but haughtiness prevented them from showing it in more than body language.

Flandry gave and received formal greetings all around. Terra and Merseia were at peace, were they not?—however many beings died and cities burned on the marches. He kept his gray gaze sleepy, but it missed little.

Not that there was anything new to see. The average Merseian exceeded him in height, standing a bulky two meters in spite of the forward-leaning posture. Also hairless, their skins were pale green and faintly scaly in appearance, though the massive countenances approximated the human except for an absence of ear-flaps. A low serration ran from the brow, down the spine, to the end of the long and heavy tail. Form-fitting black garb, trimmed in silver, covered most of the body.

The Merseians said nothing overtly rude, but neither did they hide their contempt. *I can understand that,* Flandry thought, as he often compulsively did. *Their civilization is young and strong, its energies turned outward, while ours is old, sated, decadent. All we want to do is maintain the status quo, because we're comfortable in it. Hence we're in the way of their dream of galactic overlordship. We are the first ones they have to smash.*

Or so they believe. And so we believe. Never mind what the unascertainable objective truth of the matter may be. Belief is what brings on the killing.

Shadowy through streaming red mist, a figure approached. In unreasonable shock, Flandry recognized Aycharaych, also garbed for the chase. The Chereionite halted before him, smiled amicably, and said, "Good morning, Captain."

"Oh . . . yes," the man got out. "Same to you, I suppose."

But wait, I'm losing my manners, my suavity, I'm letting him rattle me, and that in itself is a petty defeat. Better I give him my petty defiance.

"I'm a bit surprised," he added. "Wouldn't have thought you cared for hunting."

"Why, are we not both hunters by trade?" Aycharaych replied. "True, as a rule I find sophonts to be much the most interesting quarry. However, what I have heard of the game we seek today has made it seem sufficiently challenging. One wonders whether the ancestral pioneers here developed them specifically for sport."

"And then designed the rest of the local ecology to accommodate them?" Flandry laughed. "Well, projects have taken weirder courses than that."

The conversation became animated, ranging over the peculiarities and mysteries of many intelligent races. When the final horn blew its summons, Terran and Chereionite exchanged a wryly regretful glance. *Too bad. We were enjoying this. Too bad also that we're on opposite sides... isn't it?*

Hunters swung themselves into tiny one-person airjet craft and secured the harness. Each flyer had a needle-beam energy projector in the nose. That was minimal armament against a Borthudian dragon. Flandry reflected that the Sartaz wouldn't mind if an indignant beast did away with a guest or three.

The squadron lifted in a chorus of banshee wails and streaked northward for the mountains. Breaking through the mist, pilots saw Betelgeuse as an enormous, vaguely bounded disc in a purplish sky. Presently its warmth drank up the vapors below, and landscape lay revealed in all its unearthliness. The range appeared ahead, gaunt peaks, violet-shadowed canyons, snowfields tinged bloody by the sunlight. Despite himself, Flandry thrilled.

Voices came over the radio, in the court language and occasionally, courteously, in accented Anglic or Eriau. Scouts had spotted dragons here and there. Jet after jet peeled away from the squadron to go in pursuit. Before long, Flandry found his craft alone with one other.

Then two forms rose from the ground and started winging off. His pulse accelerated, his belly muscles tightened, he brought his flyer downward in a steep dive.

Like most predators, the dragons weren't looking for trouble. Annoyed by the racket overhead, they had set off in search of peace and quiet. However, they had never had reason to acquire an instinct of fear, either. Ten scaly meters of jaws, neck, body, and tail snaked through heaven, beneath enormous leathery wings. The beasts were less heavy than they appeared, and glided more than they actually flew. Just the same, a high-energy metabolism kept such a mass aloft. Yonder teeth could rend steel.

Flandry took aim. The creature he had chosen grew monstrously in his sights. A sunbeam made an eye glare scarlet as the dragon banked to face him in battle.

He squeezed his trigger. A thin blade of lightning smote forth, to burn through scales and the vital organs beneath. Yet the monster held to its collision course. Flandry rolled out of the way. Wings buffeted air, meters from him.

He had not allowed for the tail. A sudden impact shivered his teeth together. The jet reeled and went into a spin. The dragon followed.

Flandry fought his controls and tore the craft around, upward. He barrel-rolled and confronted open jaws. His beam seared in between the fangs. The dragon stumbled in midflight. Flandry pulled away and fired into a wing, ripping it.

Another blow shuddered through him. He twisted his head about in time to see the fuselage bitten open. The second beast had come to the aid of its crippled mate.

Wind poured in, searingly cold. The dragon struck again, and this time clung. Unmanageable, the aircraft plunged groundward. Mountains reeled across Flandry's vision. *What an ending!* passed through him. *Brought down and maybe eaten by my own quarry—*

He was free. The other jet had arrived, firing with surgical precision. *All gods bless that pilot, whoever he is!* Cleanly slain, the great creature toppled Lucifer-like. Its killer whipped around to dispose of the one Flandry had wounded.

The Terran got his vehicle on an even keel. He'd better inspect the damage, though, and give his nerves a chance to untwist, before proceeding back. The dragon that nearly got him had crashed on a slope beneath a ledge big enough for a vertical landing. As he approached, he raised a hand in salute. There lay another brave animal, done in as an act of politics. He grounded and sat for a minute quietly shuddering.

A whistle shrilled him back to alertness. The second aircraft was on its way down, presumably for the pilot to see how he fared; his radio was *hors de combat*. He opened the cockpit and climbed out to stand on harsh yellow turf, in a gelid breeze, that he might give proper thanks.

The vehicle set down. Its engine whined into silence, its canopy drew back, its rider got out.

Aycharaych.

Flandry's reaction was well-nigh instantaneous. Here he stood, unrecognizable as an individual at the distance between, in cloak and hood and goggles. Yonder was his enemy, unsuspecting, and there were no witnesses and any agonies of conscience could be postponed till a convenient time—

His hand was on the butt of his needle gun when he saw that Aycharaych's weapon was already drawn and aimed at him. He froze. The Chereionite approached him at an easy, steady pace, until he could hear the quiet word: "No."

He kept both his hands well away from his person. "Do you mean to do the honors yourself, then?" he asked.

"Not at all, unless you absolutely force me," Aycharaych said. "I do wish you to take out your gun, drop it, and step a few meters aside. Thereafter you are free to determine if your vehicle is airworthy. If not, I will be glad to summon assistance for you."

"You ... are very ... kind, sir."

"You are very useful, Captain. I perceive that you now understand why."

Aycharaych smoothly declined to discuss the matter further.

Afternoon light streamed through a window of Aline's room, the most private place she and Flandry could find in the palace. Its ruddiness somehow seemed only to bring out the pallor on her face. "Can't be," she whispered through lips drawn tight.

"Is," Flandry replied grimly. "The only possible answer. How he knows everything about us, everything we try and plan and— think. He can read our minds."

"But telepathy—you know its limitations—"

Flandry nodded. "Low rate of data conveyance at those frequencies, as well as high noise levels and rapid degradation of the signal. Not to speak of the coding problem. Different races have such different brain-activity patterns that a telepath has to learn a whole new 'language' for each. In fact, he has to do it for every single member of a basically non-telepathic species like ours; we don't grow up in a shared communication mode, the way we do with our mother tongues."

He began to pace, back and forth across the enclosing chamber. "But Chereion's a very old planet," he said. "Its people have the reputation among the more superstitious Merseians of being sorcerers. Somehow, they must be able to detect and interpret something mental that intelligent beings have in common universally, or almost universally. I've been wondering about—oh, a fantastic inborn ability to acquire information, store it, chase it up and down every branch of a logic tree till the meaning emerges—in hours, *minutes, seconds*?"

He beat fist against palm. "I am reasonably sure he can only read surface thoughts, those in the immediate awareness. Otherwise he'd have found out so much about us that the Merseians would be swaggering around on Terra by now. However, what he can do is bad enough!"

"No wonder he spared your life," Aline said drearily. "You've become the most valuable man on his side."

"And not a thing I can do about it," Flandry sighed. "I'm so helpless—we all are—that he doesn't care that we learn about him. Rather, he's no doubt made our knowledge a factor in his plans—our loss of morale at the news, for instance—

"I don't know what the range of his mind reading is. Probably just several meters: on the basis of what we know about the physical nature of the carrier waves for telepathy. But he sees me every day; and every time, he skims whatever I'm thinking of." The man's laugh jarred forth. "How do I go about *not* thinking of my work? By chanting mantras every waking moment? Better I should return home. Better we all should, perhaps, and give up on Betelgeuse."

Aline rose from her chair and came to stand before him as he halted at the window. "We'll have to get a research and development effort mounted on Terra," she said. "For some kind of helmet or whatever, that screens off transmission of thoughts."

"Of course. That doesn't help us today. Nor very much in the long run, really. Our people don't often encounter Chereionites, do they?"

She touched his arm. "Can't you avoid him while we're here?"

Flandry shrugged. "Yes, if I want to become a cipher—and you, and everybody with us. You know flinkin' well that we can't carry on a political intrigue purely by eidophone."

"What *can* we do?" Aline stood silent while Flandry took forth a cigarette and puffed it into lighting, then continued: "Whatever it is had better be fast. The Sartaz is growing cooler to Terra by the day. One can't blame him too much, considering what a series of blunders we've been making; and I hardly expect he'd believe us if we claimed that was due to Aycharaych."

Flandry blew a veil of smoke between his eyes and the alienness beyond the window through which he stared. "No doubt I shouldn't be bemoaning our situation, but spinning some elaborate counterplot," he said. "Except that I'll have to appear at this evening's banquet for the hunting party, and *he* will engage me in the most delightful conversation—"

Aline drew a quick breath. Her hand closed about his. He turned to regard her. "What is it?" he asked.

Her smile flashed for an instant, but the words came stark: "You don't really want to hear, do you?"

"Why—I suppose not," he replied, taken aback. "Though you're as vulnerable to him as anybody else."

"Yes, but I don't think I've been ransacked anywhere near as thoroughly." A tinge of bitterness: "We Terran women are expected to be subordinate, aren't we? In practice if not in theory. Even a ranking officer does best to keep a low profile, if female. You've been the obvious target, together with a few other key men. I've actually seen almost nothing of Aycharaych the whole while I've been here, and the chances are that when I did, I wasn't concentrating on anything too important."

She leaned close and went on in a tone gone low and urgent: "Keep him away from me, Dominic. Talk to him, engage his attention, give him no excuse to come near this part of the palace. He'll realize that that's your intention, naturally, but he won't be able just to brush you aside...if you're as clever as your reputation has it. I won't be at the banquet tonight, since I wasn't hunting, and—yes, I'll claim illness, ask to have a light supper brought me in this room—Come back afterward."

His gaze intensified upon her. "Whatever you're hatching in that lovely head," he murmured, "be quick about it. He'll get at you soon, you know, one way or another."

"You'd better leave now, Dominic," she said. "Leave me to my nefarious activities."

As he departed, her look followed him, and again she smiled.

Flandry returned from the banquet late. Wine glowed and buzzed in his blood. He hadn't exactly set out to get drunk, but he had wanted what relaxation he could seize...and found it not in the orgiastic amusements offered, but in discourse with Aycharaych. The talk had had nothing to do with the conflict between them; mostly it had been about ancient history, both Terran and Merseian, and utterly fascinating. He could almost forget that the great mind before him had no need of his speech.

Aline let him in when the scanner at her door identified him. She had muted the illumination; it flowed golden across hair, ivory sculpture of features, shimmerlyn robe. Impulsively, he kissed her, though he remembered to keep the gesture brief and light. "Good evening," he said. "How've things gone?"

"For me, mainly in thought," she answered low. "Very hard thought. Before we talk, how about a nightcap?" She gestured at a carafe and a pair of ornate goblets which had not been on her table earlier.

"No, thanks," he declined. "I've had entirely too many."

"Please," she said with a grave upward curving of lips. "For me. I need to ease off a little too."

"Well, when a lady puts it that way—" He accepted the vessel she handed him. They touched rims and drank.

The wine had a peculiar taste. If he had not taken on a considerable load already, he would have refused it after the first sip. But Aline said, "You do want it, I can see that," and he decided that he did, in spite of a sudden slight dizziness.

He sat down on the bed. She joined him. "Potent stuff, this," he muttered. "Where in the galaxy is it from?"

"Oh, no matter; it was the best the staff could promote for me on short notice, when I scarcely dared make a fuss." Aline laughed. "Good enough for government work."

"Or government idling," he said, and drank further.

"Yes, we do need to escape for a while, before we go crazy. We have tonight . . . tonight, if nothing else." As he drained his goblet and set it down, she leaned against him. "And we have love."

"What?" he asked, adolescently clumsy. The vertigo was leaving him, but he felt strange.

"No euphemism for a romp in bed, Dominic, darling," she breathed. "We love each other."

He forgot everything else as that joyous knowledge took hold of him.

Toward dawn she kissed him awake. He reached for the warmth and fragrance of her, but she sat up and told him: "No. Not yet, beloved."

A measure of sense arose, to make him sit also, leaned on a hand, and foresay, "You've news for me."

"Yes. I've wondered and wondered, and finally taken it on myself to—Well, it was supposed to be my secret, I the inconspicuous woman, till I notified our superiors here at practically the last minute. But your revelation about Aycharaych has changed everything."

He stiffened. She spoke on with a steadiness altogether unbefitting the word she gave:

"I was told before I left Terra that the Emperor and the Policy Board were considering this. Our dispatches have decided them, and I've received notice by diplomatic courier.

"A task force is in the vicinity, just outside detection range." That was no surprise in itself, though Flandry had not been informed. One tried to provide against contingencies. No doubt the Merseians had a small fleet of their own somewhere in this stellar neighborhood. "They've slipped the minor craft closer, in orbit around Betelgeuse. Those now have their orders—to get in fast, seize a beachhead, and deliver an ultimatum to the Sartaz."

"But that's impossible!" Flandry protested.

"No, it's risky, but it has a fair chance of working; and if we do nothing, Betelgeuse will go to the Merseians anyway, by default, correct? We have enough agents remaining in the defense forces here that a squadron, at least, can reach Alfzar from the outer system, undetected till too late. It'll land in the Gunazar Valley, up in the Borthudian highlands, already the night after tomorrow. Then every important place on the globe is hostage to its missiles, including especially this palace. The pill will be sweetened by such things as an offer of very substantial 'aid' if the Sartaz expels the Merseians. Admiral Fenross has been at work on the case for a long time. His best judgment is that the Sartaz will yield, furiously but still not willing to hazard all-out war."

"Will the Merseians meekly resign from the game?" Flandry wondered.

"We dare hope they will—if the coup is fast enough and complete enough to catch them off balance. It's obviously vital to keep the Betelgeuseans from suspecting anything beforehand, except for our agents among them. My job is to coordinate the actions—and inactions—of those beings, preparing for hour zero."

Flandry shook his head, as if that could dislodge bewilderment.

"Why are you telling me?" he almost groaned. "Aycharaych will pluck the news right out of my skull."

"Because I can't carry out my duty alone," she explained. "I have to deal with a dozen or more officers and—well, you do *not* need to know exactly who or where. Obviously, Aycharaych will alert the Merseians, and they'll initiate some kind of counteraction."

"Such as warning the Sartaz."

"Perhaps. Though I think not; not the first thing, anyhow. They would have no proof, only Aycharaych's word, and even if he puts on a demonstration of mind reading, what is that word worth? If they do try it, we need someone on the spot to deny everything—and, of course, send out a signal to the Navy that the invasion must be cancelled. A clever man could reap advantage out of the situation, use it to discredit the Merseians or . . . or something. . . . And we've no man more clever among us than you, or better at dealing with nonhumans." She stroked his hair, brushed lips across his, and added in a whisper: "Humans, too, as I've learned."

That roused a fresh terror in him. "They'll certainly be on your trail," he said. "If they caught you, they and their damned assassins—"

"That's another thing I need your help in, seeing to it that they don't," she responded with a gallantry that twisted the heart in him. "I'm going to take a sleeping pill now that'll knock me out for the next few hours. You make sure that Aycharaych is elsewhere when I wake, and for a while afterward. I can shake any other operative, and disappear."

He nodded. "If need be, I'll attack him physically. But he'll know that, so I daresay he'll go along with the conversation I'll start. If we got into close quarters, I could break that skinny neck of his."

And fall prey to Betelgeusean justice, neither of them added.

She kissed him hard. "Thank you, dearest, dearest," she breathed. "I'd love to make love again, but we don't dare, do we?"

"We'll try to reserve a lifetime for that, afterward," he vowed.

She took her sedative and soon was easily breathing. He looked at her for a long spell before he went in search of Aycharaych.

He found the Chereionite admiring curious blossoms in a far part of the garden, under dim red moonlight; for the sun was not yet up. The telepath's gaunt countenance bent into a smile. "Good morning, Captain," he greeted. "A little early for you, no? But then, we both have a busy time ahead of us."

He knew.

☼   ☼   ☼

In the following pair of days, Flandry worked as he had seldom worked before. Paradoxically, there was almost nothing for him to do; but he had to keep moving about, maintain communications throughout his web of underlings, stay certain that no disaster caught him unawares. Maybe, he thought, that incessant strain was what dulled his wits and clouded his judgment; or maybe it was fear for Aline. Whatever the cause, thinking had become an effort and the intuition that separated truths from falsehoods had deserted him. For this reason alone, it was as well that events were mostly going on without him, even without his knowledge—whatever those events were.

He considered breaching security and passing the news the woman had given him on to the Terran Embassy, the special delegation, or at least certain members of the Intelligence team. But what good would that do? He'd merely increase the risk of premature disclosure to the Betelgeuseans.

Evidently the Merseians had decided against informing the Sartaz at once. Aline's estimate had been right. Yet they were not going to sit still for the operation. Aycharaych and a few of them had left in a speedster on the afternoon of the first day, giving out that they had reports to deliver at home. Flandry felt sure the reports were, in fact, going to whatever naval force the Roidhunate maintained in the offing; and its commander would have more discretion to act than an admiral of the Empire normally did.

No doubt the Merseians could smuggle some kind of combat units down onto Alfzar. The question, the really interesting question was whether they could mount an adequate effort on such short notice. Flandry guessed that they might attempt it and then, if it failed, bring in their fleet "to aid the valiant Betelgeuseans." If the Sartaz had not already capitulated to the Terrans—or even if he had, maybe—this would certainly make him a stout ally of the Roidhun.

Terra might pull the whole thing off, of course; its task force would not be far behind the initial squadron, and the Merseian chief might decide against a full-dress naval engagement. Might, might, might! The unknowns were like spiderwebs enmeshing Flandry.

He looked up Gunazar Valley on an infotrieve. It was desolate, uninhabited, the home of winds and the lair of dragons, a good site for a secret descent; but the secret no longer existed.

Flandry had the impression that only a few members of the Merseian party here had been informed, and they in confidence.

They were the ones who now regarded him, when he encountered them, with hatred rather than contempt. There would have been no point, and some hazard, in telling a lot of juniors. They were as helpless as the man felt himself to be.

Aline was gone. Likewise was General Frank Bronson, the human-Betelgeusean military officer whom she had made her personal property soon after she arrived. Flandry wondered if she had converted him to an actual traitor, as Imperial agents had done to a number of personnel, or simply convinced him that the best interests of his state lay with Terra. Flandry also wondered what she was getting him to do in aid of the invasion—and how; but he shied away from that second matter in an unwonted sickness of jealousy.

The red giant crossed heaven; sank; was away; rose; crossed heaven; sank; was away—and when it rose anew, nothing had happened.

Flandry paced, chain-smoked, made a muttered litany out of every curse in any language that he had ever learned. Nothing had happened. Among the first lessons given him when he was a cadet had been: "No operation ever goes according to plan." There could easily have been some hitch, occasioning delay. But every added hour gave the Merseians more time to make ready, and to act.

On the third evening, one of his informants called him in his quarters to declare breathlessly that General Bronson was back and had requested an audience with the Sartaz—at once. Minutes later, his phone screen lit up with Aline's image. "I'm home, darling," she said. "Come on to my room."

She let him in and stood back, serious, her gaze searching him so intently that he did not at once seek to embrace her but halted and stared back. At last she said low, "You are very tired, aren't you? More than I expected. What's been going on?"

"Hardly a thing," he answered, "but I've felt rotten, and mainly I was worried about you—"

"I can do something about that," she told him with never a smile. "I must. We haven't much time. The Sartaz has agreed to let Bronson give a demonstration of 'a crucial matter' just two hours from now. We've got to set the show up, and we'll want your best advice on the psychology of it, and—But kiss me first."

He did. It lasted a while. She was the one who disengaged, went to the table, picked up a tumbler, and handed it to him. "Medicine for what ails you," she said. "Drink."

Obedient as a machine, he tossed off the dark-brown liquid. It caught at him, his head roared and spun, he lurched against the bed and fell down. "What the devil—" he gasped.

The foul sensations faded. Through him spread a kind of coolness, like a breeze of Terran springtime along his nerves and into his head. It was like the hand that Aline had laid on his brow, soothing, heartening, loving.

Clearing!

He sprang to his feet. Suddenly the preposterousness of it all loomed before him. Bumbling and weak-willed the Empire might be, and on that account scarcely likely to attempt any bold stroke; but its general staff was not incompetent, and whatever it did would be better planned than—

And he didn't love Aline. She was brave and beautiful, but he didn't love her. Yet three minutes ago, he *had*—

He looked into her eyes. Tears brimmed them as she nodded. "Yes," she whispered, "that's how it was. I'm sorry, my dear. You'll never know how sorry I am."

A telescreen formed one wall of a conference chamber. Before it curved rows of empty seats. The place was already well occupied, however, for Bronson had taken the precaution of ranking royal guards whom he could trust along the sides—impassive blue faces above gray tunics and steel corselets, on the shoulders of which rested firearms.

The general prowled the stage, glancing at his watch every several seconds. Perspiration glistened on his skin and he reeked of it. Flandry stood relaxed, attired in court dress; when action was imminent, he could wait with panther patience. Aline seemed altogether detached, lost somewhere amidst her own thoughts.

"If this doesn't work, you know, we'll be lucky if we're hanged," Bronson said.

"You need more confidence in yourself," answered Flandry tonelessly. "Though if the scheme fails, it won't matter much whether we hang or not."

He was prevaricating there; he was most fond of living, in spite of being haunted by the ghosts of certain dreams.

A trumpet sounded, brassy between pillars and vaulted ceiling. The humans saluted and stood to attention as the Sartaz and his principal councillors entered.

He raked suspicious yellow eyes across them. "I *hope* this business is as important as you claim," he said.

Flandry took the word; that was his element. "It is, your Majesty. It is a matter so immense that it should have been revealed to you weeks ago. Unfortunately, circumstances did not permit—as this eminent gathering will soon see—and your Majesty's loyal officer was forced to act on his own authority with what help we of Terra could give him. But if our work has gone well, the moment of revelation should also be that of salvation."

The monarch settled into a chair at the center, higher than the rest. His attenders then dared seat themselves. "What new evil have the empires wrought?" he demanded.

I don't blame him for wishing a plague on both our houses, Flandry thought, while he continued, "Your Majesty, Terra has never wished Betelgeuse anything but well. We are about to offer proof of that. If—"

An amplified voice boomed through the air: "Great Majesty, the ambassador from Merseia requests immediate audience. He maintains that it is a business whereon destiny will turn."

"No!" Bronson shouted.

The Sartaz sat motionless for half a minute before he said, "Yes. Admit his Excellency and let us hear him too."

The huge green form of Korvash the Farseeing entered in a swirl of rainbow-colored robes, a flare of gold and jewelry. Beside him was Aycharaych.

Flandry heard Bronson make a strangled noise and Aline draw a gasp. If that player got back into the game, at this precarious stage of things—Silence thickened while the newcomers went up the aisle to pay their respects.

Not thought, but instinct and impulse surged through Flandry. He sprang down off the stage. The court sword hissed from the sheath at his hip. "Stop those two!" he roared. "They would murder the Sartaz!"

Aycharaych's eyes widened. He opened his mouth to denounce what he saw in the Terran's mind—and sprang back in bare time to avoid a thrust at his body.

His own rapier whipped into his hand. In a whirr of steel, the spies met.

Korvash had drawn blade in sheer reflex. "Strike him down before he kills!" Aline cried. Guards swarmed forward.

The ambassador dropped his weapon. "This is ridiculous—" he began. A stun pistol chopped off his words. He collapsed and lay in a heap.

"That was perhaps unnecessary," the Sartaz said shrewdly. "Remove him to medical attention ... with due care."

Flandry and Aycharaych moved across his view, viciously busy. "Get them separated!" the officer of the guards called.

"No," the Sartaz countermanded. "Let them have it out."

Aline clenched her hands together. Bronson stood appalled. Slowly, at the royal signal, the troopers resumed formation.

Flandry had thought himself a champion fencer, but Aycharaych was his match. Though the Chereionite was hampered by gravity, no human could equal his speed and precision. The blade he wielded whistled in and out and around, feinted, thrust, parried, flicked blood from his opponent's arm and shoulder; and always he smiled.

His telepathy did him little good. Fencing is a matter of reflexes more than of conscious thought. Perhaps it gave him an extra edge, compensating for the handicap of weight.

The *Totentanz* went on. Flandry began to score in his turn. Red drops flowed down the golden visage. *I am going to wear you out, Aycharaych,* the man thought. *You'll tire before I do.* He retreated, and his enemy had no choice but to follow in hopes of a fatal opening.

Almost, he got one. Flandry's guard went awry, Aycharaych lunged, his point reached the Terran's upper arm. But then a karate kick knocked the sword spinning from his grasp, and steel was at his throat.

"Do not kill!" the Sartaz exclaimed. "We'll hear all of you out. Guards, disarm them."

"Dominic, Dominic," Aline crooned, between tears and laughter; yet she held her place on stage.

"Your Majesty," Flandry panted, "please, I beg you for your own sake, let me keep this prisoner till we've finished what we started. Time's ghastly short, and if he gets a chance, he'll spin matters out till too late. You'll soon understand."

His mind projected: *Aycharaych, if you part your lips, so help me, I'll run you through and worry about the consequences to me afterward.*

The Chereionite made the faintest of shrugs. Was there irony in it? He must have anticipated the ruler's decision:

"Very well. That would be . . . fitting."

Flandry poised more at ease. What he had said was probably not altogether a lie. No doubt the Merseians had returned with the idea of shortly springing their own surprise; they had learned— quite likely from Aycharaych, who'd tapped the mind of some aide or whoever—that Bronson and Aline were back too, realized that a Terran scheme must also be afoot, and decided it was best to act immediately, no matter how much they must improvise; meanwhile, a warning must be on its way to their troops—

"You'd better take over the demonstration," he called to Aline and Bronson. He dared not to let his attention wander for an instant from the one he confronted. At the edge of vision, he saw the general give the woman a bewildered look, and stand back as she trod forward.

"Your Majesty and nobles," she began, and self-possession welled back up within her, "we pray pardon for the haste and disorderli- ness of this proceeding, but feel sure you will soon realize that that was forced on us. Full explanation will be forthcoming from the Terran Imperium in due course, though you will surely also realize that it will take time to collect all the facts.

"Basically, our mission discovered that Merseia has decided to cease negotiating for an alliance which may never be granted. Instead, the Merseian plan is to compel it by arms. A small force, aided by traitors in your own ranks, has occupied the Gunazar Valley in the Borthudian range and is, at this very moment, pre- paring a bridgehead for invasion. With Alfzar under its weapons, the whole planetary system must yield—"

She let the uproar subside before she resumed coolly: "It was not feasible for us to pass this information on at once as we should and as we wished, for several reasons. First, it came piecemeal. Second, though it was gathered by agents we trusted, we had no documentation that would convince you. Third, Merseian agents were everywhere, and we even had reason to believe one of them could read your minds. If they had known their plot was being revealed, they—and the Merseian strength out in space—might well have chosen to act precipitately. As representatives of Terra, we did not feel we had a right to hazard exposing the Betelgeusean worlds to a major conflict.

"Instead, we contacted General Bronson. It is no secret that he is sympathetic to us, though he remains a loyal subject of the Sartaz. We estimated that his position in your defense hierarchy was not high enough to merit much enemy attention; yet he has authority to order the actions we suggested.

"This included mounting telescopic pickups around the valley. Permit me to tune them in."

She turned a switch. An image sprang onto the screen, crags and cliffs beneath the sullen moons, stirrings and metallic gleams in the shadows beneath. The view swept around, became close, became panoramic, brightened under optical amplification. It was a view of spacecraft at rest on the ground, of armor and artillery that they had disgorged now deployed about them, of uniformed Merseians at work.

The Sartaz gave a tigerish snarl. A courtier demanded, "Can you prove this is not a counterfeit?"

"You can prove it for yourself, sir," Aline replied. "Plenty of scraps will remain. Our strategy has been simple. Before they landed, engineers in General Bronson's command planted nuclear mines. They are radio controlled." With a sense of drama that Flandry could not have bettered, she lifted, from the stage where it had lain, a red box with a switch. "The signal can be relayed from this. Perhaps your Majesty would care to start things?"

"Give me that," said the Sartaz thickly. Aline sprang down from the stage and handed it to him, curtsying low. He flipped the switch.

Blue-white hell-flame lit the screen. It gave a vision of soil fountaining upward, landslides, a black cloud, and darkness.

"The latest explosion destroyed the last camera we had," Aline told the assembly. "Let me urge that your Majesty dispatch airborne scouts at once. They will find the proof I bespoke.

"Let me suggest further that you no longer regard Merseia as a friendly power. A detachment of the Terran Navy has been contacted and is on its way. Needless to say, it will not cross your outermost orbital radius without express permission. However, it will stand by, ready to help a Betelgeusean navy that we assume will be put on alert status.

"I believe that after Lord Korvash awakens and is permitted to send a message or two, there will be no further immediate danger from Merseia. As for the longer-range danger, that is something your Majesty must decide in your wisdom."

For the time being, deportation orders stood for every Merseian in the Betelgeusean System. What units of theirs lingered clandestinely, in hidden places on barren planets and moons and asteroids, would be of scant use—far less than their Terran counterparts.

It did not follow that Betelgeuse would conclude an alliance with the Empire. Though the Merseian ambassador had not been able, under the circumstances, to make any very effective protestations of innocence: still, the Sartaz and his advisors knew better than to believe in the disinterested benevolence of Terra. Negotiations would continue. They might or might not lead to agreement.

That was outside Flandry's concern. Let the diplomats worry about it. He—no, Aline, and he as a helper—had done the job of their own group, which was to keep the possibility open for their side and foreclose it for the opposition.

One does not dismiss an ambassador and his staff without a certain amount of courtesy. Korvash got time to close down his affairs here in orderly fashion. On the evening before he was due to leave, Flandry invited him and Aycharaych around for drinks. The hostess was Aline, and they had the common room for the Terran delegation for a site, with nobody else present. They could have had much more than that had they asked, but settled for the most expensive liquor available.

"Matters have been somewhat too hectic for me to offer the congratulations that are your due," said the Chereionite to the man after everybody had begun to relax.

"Thank you," Flandry replied. "I don't pretend to be sportsman enough that I wish you success next time around. However, it's an amusing game that the empires underwrite for us, no?"

Inwardly he thought, and knew that the other knew he thought: *You've not lost hands down, Aycharaych. You've gotten a great deal of information from me that your side will find useful in future. But the half-life of that kind of advantage isn't usually very long, and I'll gather more when you aren't around, and I am forewarned.*

He glanced at Aline. Her demeanor was more sober than it

had been when he and she impulsively planned this occasion. Was she thinking of missiles that would not strike and sentient beings that would not die—not yet—and of the fact that Aycharaych followed her thought?

Korvash stirred, where he squatted on a tripod of legs and tail in the manner of his people. "I've been overwhelmed with work myself," he growled. "Now will you tell me exactly what it was that you did, you Terrans?"

"Aline did it," Flandry said. "Want to tell them?"

She shook her head. "You tell them, if you wish," she murmured. "Please."

Flandry leaned back in his lounger, sipped from the snifter of brandy in his grasp, and was nothing loth to expound. "Well, then. When we realized you could read our minds, Aycharaych, things looked pretty hopeless. How can you possibly hide anything from that kind of telepath, let alone deceive him? Aline hit on the answer. First deceive yourself.

"There's an obscure drug in these parts called *sorgan*. It's forbidden to humans, but that needn't stop any competent Intelligence agent. It has the intriguing property of making its user believe whatever he's told. She fed me some without my knowledge and spun me that yarn about Terra's plan to occupy Alfzar. I accepted it as absolute truth; you read it out of me."

"I was puzzled," admitted the Chereionite. "It did not seem reasonable. However, it seemed plausible to you . . . and I am, after all, not human."

"Aline's main problem thereafter was to keep out of your range," Flandry said. "You helped there by haring off to get a warm reception prepared for the Terrans, as she'd guessed you would. If you could've stopped that invasion, then offered your act as earnest of your altruistic love for Betelgeuse—Well, tonight we'd've been the *personae non gratae* and you, perhaps, throwing a farewell party for us."

Korvash gusted a sigh, quite humanlike except for its volume. "Let me be honest," he said. "The decision to send for naval units, mobilize our Betelgeusean organization, act boldly, that was mine. Aycharaych counselled more caution, but I overruled him."

"Well, nobody's perfect," Flandry replied. "I have my own vices, though energy is not among them."

"This is no time for recriminations, of self or of others,"

Aycharaych said gently. "There will be more tomorrows. Tonight let us enjoy our truce."

The drinking lasted well on toward dawn. When finally the aliens left, Korvash offered many tipsy expressions of regard, and even of regret that the covert hostility must begin again.

Aycharaych showed no sign of changed mood. He took Aline's right hand in his bony fingers, and his eyes searched hers, even as—she remembered with an odd, half welcome sense of surrender—his mind was doing.

"Goodbye, my dear," he said, too softly for the rest to overhear. "As long as there are women like you, your race will endure."

She watched his tall form go down the corridor and her vision blurred a little. It was strange to think that her enemy knew what the man beside her did not. ✳

THE GAME OF GLORY

 I

A murdered man on a winter planet gave Flandry his first clue. Until then, he had only known that a monster fled Conjumar in a poisoned wreck of a spaceship, which might have gone twenty light-years before killing its pilot but could surely never have crossed the Spican marches to refuge.

And the trouble was—even for the Terran Empire, which contained an estimated four million stars—a sphere twenty light-years across held a devil's number of suns.

Flandry went through motions. He sent such few agents as could be spared from other jobs, for they were desperately under-manned in the frontier provinces, to make inquiries on the more likely planets within that range. Of course they drew blanks. Probability was stacked against them. Even if they actually visited whatever world the fugitive had landed on, he would be lying low for a while.

Flandry swore, recalled his men to more urgent tasks, and put the monster under filed-but-not-forgotten. Two years went by. He was sent to Betelgeuse and discovered how to lie to a telepath. He slipped into the Merseian Empire itself, wormed and black-mailed until he found a suitable planet (uninhabited, terrestroid, set aside as a hunting preserve of the aristocrats) and got home

303

again: whereafter the Terran Navy quietly built an advanced base
there and Flandry wondered if the same thing had happened on
his side of the fence. He went to Terra on leave, was invited to
the perpetual banquet of the Lyonid family, spent three epochal
months, and was never quite sure whether he seduced the wrong
man's wife or she him. At any rate, he fought a reluctant duel,
gave up hope of early promotion to rear admiral, and accepted
re-assignment to the Spican province.

Thus it was he found himself on Brae.

This world had been more or less independent until a few
months ago. Then military considerations forced the establishment of a new base in the region. It did not have to be Brae, but
Brae was asked, by a provincial governor who thought its people
would be delighted at the extra trade and protection. The Braean
High Temple, which had long watched its old culture and religion
sapped by Terran influence, declined. One does not decline an
Imperial invitation. It was repeated. And again it was refused. The
provincial governor insisted. Brae said it would go over his head
and appeal to the Emperor himself. The governor, who did not
want attention drawn to his precise mode of government, called
for local Navy help.

Wherefore Flandry walked through smashed ruins under a
red dwarf sun, with a few snowflakes falling like blood drops
out of great clotted clouds. He was directing the usual project in
cases like this—search, inquiry, more search, more interrogation,
until the irreconcilables had been found and exiled, the safely
collaboration-minded plugged into a governmental framework.
But when the blaster crashed, he whirled and ran toward the
noise as if to some obscure salvation.

"Sir!" cried the sergeant of his escort. "Sir, not there—snipers,
terrorists—*wait!*"

Flandry leaped the stump of a wall, zigzagged across a slushy
street, and crouched behind a wrecked flyer. His own handgun
was out, weaving around; his eyes flickered in habitual caution.
On a small plaza ahead of him stood a squad of Imperial marines.
They must have been on routine patrol when someone had fired
at them from one of the surrounding houses. They responded
with tiger precision. A tracer dart, flipped from a belt almost
the moment the shot came, followed the trail of ions to a certain
facade. A rover bomb leaped from its shoulder-borne rack, and

the entire front wall of the house went up in shards. Before the explosion ended, the squad attacked. Some of the debris struck their helmets as they charged.

Flandry drifted to the plaza. He saw now why the men's reaction was to obliterate: it was an invariable rule when a marine was bushwhacked dead.

He stooped over the victim. This was a young fellow, African-descended, with husky shoulders; but his skin had gone gray. He gripped his magnetic rifle in drilled reflex (or was it only a convulsive clutching at his mother's breast, as a dying man's mouth will try to suck again?) and stared through frog-like goggles on a turtle-like helmet. He was not, after all, dead yet. His blood bubbled from a stomach ripped open, losing itself in muddy snow. Under that dim sun, it looked black.

Flandry glanced up. His escort had surrounded him, though their faces turned wistfully toward the crump-crump of blasters and bomb guns. They were marines too.

"Get him to a hospital," said Flandry.

"No use, sir," answered the sergeant. "He'd be dead before we arrived. We've no revival equipment here yet, either, or stuff to keep him functional till they can grow another belly on him."

Flandry nodded and hunkered down by the boy. "Can I help you son?" he asked, as gently as might be.

The wide lips shinned back from shining teeth. "Ah, ah, ah," he gasped. "It's him in Uhunhu that knows." The eyes wallowed in their sockets. "Ai! 'List nay, they said. Nay let recruiters 'list you ... damned Empire ... even to gain warskill, don't 'list ... shall freedom come from slave-masters, asked he in Uhunhu. He and his 'ull teach what we must know, see you?" The boy's free hand closed wildly on Flandry's. "D'you understand?"

"Yes," said Flandry. "It's all right. Go to sleep."

"Ai, ai, look at her up there, grinning—" Despite himself, Flandry stared skyward. He was crouched by a fountain, which now held merely icicles. A slender column rose from the center, and on top of it the nude statue of a girl. She was not really human, she had legs too long, and a tail and pouch and sleek fur, but Flandry had not often seen such dancing loveliness trapped in metal; she was springtime and a first trembling kiss under windy poplars. The waning marine screamed.

"Leave me 'lone, leave me 'lone, you up there, leave me 'lone!

Stop grinning! I 'listed for to learn how to make Nyanza free, you hear up there, don't lap my blood so fast. It's nay my fault I made more slaves. I wanted to be free too! Get your teeth out of me, girl... mother, mother, don't eat me, mother—" Presently the boy died.

Captain Sir Dominic Flandry, Intelligence Corps, Imperial Terrestrial Navy, squatted beside him, under the fountain, while the marines blew down another house or two for good measure. A squadron of full-armored infantry did a belt-flit overhead, like jointed faceless dolls. A stringed instrument keened from a window across the square: Flandry did not know the Braean scale, the music might be dirge or defiance or ballad or coded signal.

He asked finally: "Anyone know where this chap was from?"

His escort looked blank. "A colonial, sir, judging from the accent," ventured one of the privates. "We sign on a lot, you know."

"Tell me more," snapped Flandry. He brooded a while longer. "There'll be records, of course."

His task had suddenly shifted. He would have to leave another man in charge here and check the dead boy's home himself, so great was the personnel shortage. Those delirious babblings could mean much or nothing. Most likely nothing, but civilization was spread hideously thin out here, where the stars faded toward barbarism, and the Empire of Merseia beyond, and the great unmapped Galactic night beyond that.

As yet he did not think of the monster, only that he was lonesome among his fellow conquerors and would be glad to get off on a one-man mission. At least a world bearing some Africans might be decently warm.

He shivered and got up and left the square. His escort trudged around him, their slung rifles pointed at a thin blue sky. Behind them the girl on the fountain smiled.

✺ ❚ ✺

The planet was five parsecs from Brae. It was the third of an otherwise uninteresting F5 dwarf, its official name was Nyanza, it had been colonized some 500 years back during the breakup of the Commonwealth. It had been made an Imperial client about a century ago, a few abortive revolts were crushed, now there was only a resident—which meant a trouble-free but unimportant and little visited world. The population was estimated at 10^7. That was all the microfiles had to say about Nyanza.

Flandry had checked them after identifying the murdered man, who turned out to be Thomas Umbolu, 19, free-born commoner of Jairnovaunt on Nyanza, no dependents, no personal oaths or obligations of fealty, religion "Christian variant," height 1.82 meters, weight 84 kilos, blood type O plus.... His service record was clean, though only one year old. A routine pre-induction hypno had shown no serious disaffection; but of course that hadn't meant a damn thing since the techniques of deep conditioning became general knowledge; it was just another bureaucratic ritual.

Flandry took a high-speed flitter and ran from Brae. Even so, the enforced idleness of the trip was long enough to remind him acutely that he had been celibate for weeks. He spent a good deal of the time in calisthenics. It bored him rigid, but a trim body had saved his life more than once and made it easy to get bed partners on softened worlds like Terra.

When the robopilot said they were going into approach, he spent some while dressing himself. An Intelligence officer had wide latitude as regards uniforms, and Flandry took more advantage of it than most. After due consideration, he clad his tall form in peacock-blue tunic, with white cross-belts and as much gold braid as regulations would stand; red sash and matched guns, needler and blaster; iridescent white trousers; soft black boots of authentic Terran beefleather. He hung a scarlet cloak from his shoulders and cocked a winged naval cap on his long sleek head. Surveying himself in the mirror, he saw a lean sunlamp-browned face, gray eyes, seal-brown hair and mustache, straight nose, high cheekbones: yes, he knew his last plasmecosmetic job had made his face too handsome, but somehow never got around to changing it again. He put a cigarette between his lips, adjusted its jaunty angle with care, inhaled it to light, and went to his pilot's seat. Not that he had anything to do with the actual piloting.

Nyanza shone before him, the clearest and most beautiful blue of his life, streaked with white cloud-belts and shuddering with great auroral streamers. He spotted two moons, a smallish one close in and a large one further out. He scowled. Where were the land masses? His robot made radio contact and the screen offered him a caucasoid face above a short-sleeved shirt.

"Captain Sir Dominic Flandry, Imperial Navy Intelligence,

requesting permission to land." Sometimes he wondered what he
would do if his polite formula ever met a rude no.

The visage gaped, "Oh...oh...already?"

"Hm?" said Flandry. He caught himself. "Ah, yes," he said wisely.

"But only today, sir!" babbled the face. "Why, we haven't
even thought about sending a courier out yet—it's been such a
nightmare—oh, thank God you're here, sir! You'll see for yourself,
at once, there isn't a Technician in the City—on Altla—on all
Nyanza, who doesn't set loyalty to his Majesty above life itself!"

"I'm sure his Majesty will be very much relieved," said Flandry.
"Now, if you please, how about a landing beam?" After a pause,
a few clicks, and the beginning downward rush of his ship: "Oh,
by the way, Bubbles. Where did you put your continents today?"

"Continents, sir?"

"You know. Large dirty places to stand on."

"Of course I know, sir!" The control man drew himself up.
"We're no parochials in the City. I've been to Spica myself."

"Would it be despicable if you had not?" mused Flandry. Most
of him was listening to the fellow's accent. The inexhaustible
variations on Anglic were a hobby of his.

"But as for the continents, sir, why, I thought you would know.
Nyanza has none. Altla is just a medium-sized island. Otherwise
there are only rocks and reefs, submerged at double high tide,
or even at Loa high."

"Oh, I knew," said Flandry reassuringly. "I just wanted to be sure
you knew." He turned off the receiver and sat thinking. Damn those
skimpy pilot's manuals! He'd have had to go to Spica for detailed
information. If only there were a faster-than-light equivalent of
radio. Instant communications unified planets; but the days and
weeks and months between stars let their systems drift culturally
apart—let hell brew for years, unnoticed till it boiled over—made
a slow growth of feudalism, within the Imperial structure itself,
inevitable. Of course, that would give civilization something to
fall back on when the Long Night finally came.

The spaceport was like ten thousand minor harbors: little more
than a grav-grid, a field, and some ancillary buildings, well out of
town. Beyond the hangars, to west and south, Flandry saw a green-
ness of carefully tended forest. Eastward rose the spires of a small
ancient city. Northward the ground sloped down in harsh grass and
boulders until it met a smothering white surf and an impossibly

blue ocean. The sky above was a little darker than Terra's—less
dust to scatter light—and cloudless; the sun was blindingly fierce,
bluish tinged. It was local summer: Altla lay at 35° N. latitude on
a Terra-sized planet with a 21° axial tilt. The air held an illusion
of being cooler than it was, for it blew briskly and smelled of salt
and the ultraviolet-rich sun gave it a thunderous tinge of ozone.

Still, Flandry wished he had not been quite such a dude. The
portmaster, another blond caucasoid, looked abominably comfortable in shorts, blouse, and kepi. Flandry took a morose satisfaction
in noting that the comfort was merely physical.

"Portmaster Heinz von Sonderburg, sir, at your service. Naturally, we waive quarantine on your behalf; no Imperial knight
would—Ah. Your luggage will be seen to, Captain ... Flandry?
Of course. Most honored. I have communicated with her Excellency and am happy to report she can offer you the usual official
hospitality. Otherwise we would have had to do our poor best
for you in the City—"

"Her Excellency?" asked Flandry when they were airborne.

"Is that not the proper usage?" Von Sonderburg made washing motions with his hands. "Oh, dear, I am so sorry. This is
such an isolated planet—the occasion so seldom arises—Believe
me, sir, we are uncouth only in manner. The City, at least, has
an enlightened forward-looking spirit of absolute loyalty to the
Imperium which—"

"It's just that I thought, in a case like this, where the only
Terrans on the planet are the resident and family, they'd have
appointed a man." Flandry looked down toward the city. It was
old, haphazardly raised out of native stone, with steep narrow
streets, teeming pedestrians, very few cars or flyers.

But the docks were big, sleekly modern and aswarm with
ships. He made out everything from plastic pirogues to giant
submarines. There was a majority of sailing craft, which implied
an unhurried esthetic-minded culture; but they were built along
radical hydrodynamic lines, which meant that the culture also
appreciated efficiency. A powered tug was leaving the bay with a
long tail of loaded barges, and air transport was extensively in use.

Elsewhere Flandry recognized a set of large sea-water processing units and their attached factories, where a thousand dissolved
substances were shaped into usefulness. A twin-hulled freighter
was unloading bales of ... sea weed? ... at the dock of an obvious

plastics plant. So, he thought, most of Nyanza fished, hunted, and ranched the planet-wide ocean; this one island took the raw materials and gave back metal, chemical fuel, synthetic timbers and resins and glassites and fibers, engines. He was familiar enough with pelagic technics—most overpopulated worlds turned back at last to Mother Ocean. But here they had begun as sailors, from the very first. It should make for an interesting society....

Von Sonderburg's voice jerked back his attention. "But of course, poor Freeman Bannerji was a man. I am merely referring to his, ah, his relict, poor Lady Varvara. She is an Ayres by birth, you know, the Ayres of Antarctica. She has borne her loss with the true fortitude of Imperial aristocratic blood, yes, we can be very proud to have been directed by the late husband of Lady Varvara Ayres Bannerji."

Flandry constructed his sentence to preserve the illusion: "Do you know the precise time he died?"

"Alas, no, sir. You can speak to the City constabulary, but I fear even they would have no exact information. Sometime last night, after he retired. You understand, sir, we have not your advanced police methods here. A harpoon gun—oh, what a way to meet one's final rest!" Von Sonderburg shuddered delicately.

"The weapon has not been found?" asked Flandry impassively.

"No, I do not believe so, sir. The killer took it with him, portable, you know. He must have crept up the wall with vacsoles, or used a flung grapnel to catch the windowsill and—His Excellency was a sound sleeper and his lady, ah, preferred separate quarters. Ah . . . you can take it for granted, sir, I am certain, that the murderer did not go through the house to reach Freeman Bannerji's retiring chamber. The servants are all of Technician birth, and no Technician would dream of—"

The resident's mansion hove into view. It was probably 75 years old, but its metal and tinted plastic remained a blatant, arrogant leap in formal gardens, amidst a shrill huddle of tenements. As the aircar set down, Flandry noticed that the City population was mostly caucasoid, not even very dark-skinned. They were crowded together in child-pullulating streets, blowsy women waved excited arms and shouted their hagglings, such of the men as did not work in industry kept grimy little shops. A pair of native constables in helmet and breastplate stood guard at the mansion gates. Those were tall Africans, who used stepped-down shockbeams with a sort of casual contempt to prevent loitering.

Lady Varvara was caucasoid herself, though the Chinese strain in the Ayres pedigree showed in dark hair and small-boned body. She posed, exquisite in a simple white mourning gown, beside a full-length stereo of her late husband. Hurri Chundra Bannerji had been a little brown middle-aged Terran with wistful eyes: doubtless the typical fussy, rule-bound, conscientious civil servant whose dreams of a knighthood die slowly over the decades. And now he was murdered.

Flandry bowed over Lady Varvara's frail hand. "Your Ladyship," he said, "accept my most heartfelt sympathy, and grant me forgiveness that I must intrude at a moment of such loss."

"I am glad you came," she whispered. "So very glad."

It had a shaken sincerity that almost upset Flandry's court manners. He backed off with another ritual bow. "You must not trouble yourself further, your Ladyship. Let me deal with the authorities."

"Authorities!" The word was a bitter explosion among her few thin pieces of Terran crystal. Otherwise the room was dominated by the conch-whorls of an art that had not seen Earth in centuries. "What authorities? Did you bring a regiment with you?"

"No." Flandry glanced around the long low-ceilinged room. A noiseless City-bred butler had just placed decanter and glasses by the trellis-wall which opened on the garden. When he left, there did not seem to be anyone else in earshot. Flandry took out his cigarets and raised his brows inquiringly at the woman. He saw she was younger than himself.

Her colorless lips bent into a smile. "Thank you," she said, so low he could almost not hear it.

"Eh? For what, your Ladyship? I'm afraid it's a frosty comfort to have me here."

"Oh, no," she said. She moved closer. Her reactions were not wholly natural: too calm and frank for a new-made widow, then suddenly and briefly too wild. A heavy dose of mysticine, he guessed. It was quite the thing for upper-class Imperials to erect chemical walls against grief or fear or—What do you do when the walls come down? he thought.

"Oh, no," repeated Lady Varvara. Her words flowed quick and high-pitched. "Perhaps you do not understand, Captain. You are the first Terran I have seen, besides my husband, for...how long? Something like three Nyanzan years, and that's about four Terran.

And then it was just a red-faced military legate making a routine check. Otherwise, who did we see? The City Warden and his officers paid a few courtesy calls every year. The sea chiefs had to visit us too when they happened to be on Altla...not for our sake, you understand, not to curry favor, only because it was beneath their dignity not to observe the formalities. Their dignity!" Her cheeks flamed. She stood close to him now, glaring upward; her fists drew the skin tight over bird-like knuckles. "As you would feel obliged to notice the existence of an unwelcome guest!"

"So the Empire is not popular here?" murmured Flandry.

"I don't know," she said pallidly, relaxing. "I don't know. All I know is—the only people we ever saw, with any regularity—our only friends, God help us, friends!—were the Lubbers."

"The what, my lady?"

"City people. Technicians. Pinkskins. Whatever you want to call them. Like that fat little von Sonderburg." She was shrill again. "Do you know what it's like, Captain, to associate with no one but an inferior class? It rubs off on you. Your soul gets greasy. Von Sonderburg now...always toadying up to Hurri Chundra... he would never light a cigar in my presence without asking me, in the most heavy way—exactly the same words, I have heard them a million times, till I could scream—'Does my lady object if I have a little smoke?'"

Varvara whirled from him. Her bare shoulders shuddered. "Does my lady object? Does my lady object? And then you come, Captain—your lungs still full of Earth air, I swear—you come and take out a cigaret case and raise your eyebrows. Like that. No more. A gesture we all used at Home, a ritual, an assumption that I have eyes to see what you're doing and intelligence to know what you want—Oh, be welcome, Captain Flandry, be welcome!" She gripped the trellis with both hands and stared out into the garden. "You're from Terra," she whispered. "I'll come to you tonight, any time, right now if you want, just to repay you for being a Terran."

Flandry tapped a cigaret on his thumbnail, put it to his lips at half mast, and drew deeply. He glanced at the sad brown eyes of Hurri Chundra Bannerji and said without words: *Sorry, old chap. I'm not a ghoul, and I'll do what I can to avoid this, but my job demands I be tactful. For the Empire and the Race!*

"I'm sorry to intrude when you're overwrought, your Ladyship," he said. "Of course, I'll arrange for your passage to provincial headquarters, and if you want to return Home from there—"

"After all these years," she mumbled, "who would I know?"

"Uh...may I suggest my lady, that you rest for a while—?"

An intercom chime saved both of them. Varvara said a shaky "Accept" and the connection closed. The butler's voice came: "Beg pardon, madame, but I have just received word of a distinguished native person who has arrived. Shall I ask postponement of the formal visit?"

"Oh...I don't know." Varvara's tone was dead. She did not look at Flandry. "Who is it?"

"Lady Tessa Hoorn, madame, Lightmistress of Little Skua in Jairnovaunt."

☼ ∎∎∎ ☼

When they reached the Zurian Current, the water, which had been a Homeric blue, turned deep purple, streaked with foam that flashed like crystallized snow. "This bends to north beyond Iron Shoals and carries on past the Reefs of Sorrow," remarked Tessa Hoorn. "Gains us a few knots speed. Though we've naught to hurry for, have we?"

Flandry blinked through dark contact lenses at the incredible horizon. Sunlight flimmered off the multitudinous laughter of small waves. "I suppose the color is due to plankton," he said.

"Plankton-like organisms," corrected Tessa. "We're nay on Earth, Captain. But aye, off this feed the oilfish, and off them the decapus, both of use to us." She pointed. "Yonder flags bear Dilolo stripes, quartered on Saleth green: the fishing boats of the Prince of Aquant."

Flandry's dazzled eyes could hardly even see the vessels, in that merciless illumination. Since the wind dropped, the Hoorn ship had been running on its auxiliary engine and now there was no shade from the great sails. An awning was spread amidships and some superbly muscled deckhands sprawled under it, clapping time to an eerie chant-pipe, like young gods carved in oiled ebony. The Terran would have given much for some of that shadow. But since Tessa Hoorn stood here in the bows, he must submit. It was an endurance contest, he recognized, with all the advantages on her side.

"Does your nation fish this current too?" he asked.

"A little," she nodded. "But mostly we in Jairnovaunt sail west and north, with harpoons for the kraken—ha, it's a pale life never to have speared fast to a beast with more of bulk than your own ship!—and smaller game. Then T'chaka Kruger farms a great patch of beanweed in the Lesser Sargasso. And in sooth I confess, not alone the commons but some captains born will scrape the low-tide reefs for shells or dive after sporyx. Then there are carpenters, weavers, engineers, medics, machinists, all trades that must be plied: and mummers and mimes, though most such sport is given by wandering boats of actors, masterless madcap folk who come by as fancy strikes 'em." She shrugged broad shoulders. "The Commander can list you all professions in his realm if you wish it, Imperial."

Flandry regarded her with more care than pleasure. He had not yet understood her attitude. Was it contempt, or merely hatred?

The sea people of Nyanza were almost entirely African by descent, which meant that perhaps three-fourths of their ancestors had been negroid, back when more or less "pure" stocks still existed. In a world of light, more actinic than anything on Earth, reflected off water, there had been a nearly absolute selection for dark coloring: not a Nyanzan outside the city on Altla was any whiter than the ace of spades. Otherwise genes swapped around pretty freely—kinky hair, broad noses, and full lips were the rule, but with plenty of exceptions. Tessa's hair formed a soft, tightly curled coif around her ears; her nostrils flared, in a wide arch-browed face, but the bridge was aquiline. Without her look of inbred haughtiness, it would have been a wholly beautiful face. The rest of her was even more stunning, almost as tall as Flandry, full-breasted, slim-waisted, and muscled like a Siamese cat. She wore merely a gold medallion of rank on her forehead, a belt with a knife, and the inevitable aqualung on her back... which left plenty on view to admire. But even in plumes and gown and rainbow cloak, she had been a walking shout as she entered the resident's mansion.

However, thought Dominic Flandry, that word "stunning" can be taken two ways. I am not about to make a pass at the Light-mistress of Little Skua.

He asked cautiously: "Where are the Technicians from?"

"Oh, those." A faint sneer flickered on her red mouth. "Well, see you, the firstcomers here settled on Altla, but then as more folk came in, space was lacking, so they began to range the sea. That proved so much better a life that erelong few cared to work on land. So sith the positions stood open, ai-hai!—it swarmed in with dirt-loving men and their shes. Most came from Deutschwelt, as it happened. When we had enough of yon ilk, and knew they'd breed, we closed the sluice, for they dare nay work as sailors, they get skin sicknesses, and Altla has little room."

"I should think they'd be powerful on the planet, what with the essential refineries and—"

"Nay, Captain. Altla and all thereon is owned in common by the true Nyanzan nations. The Technicians are but hirelings. Though in sooth, they've a sticky way with money and larger bank accounts than many a skipper. That's why we bar them from owning ships."

Flandry glanced down at himself. He had avoided the quasi-uniform of the despised class and had packed outfits of blouse, slacks, zori, and sash for himself; the winged cap sat on his head bearing the sunburst of Empire. But he could not evade the obvious fact, that his own culture was more Lubberly than pelagic. And an Imperial agent was often hated, but must not ever allow himself to be despised. Hence Flandry cocked a brow (Sardonic Expression 22-C, he thought) and drawled:

"I see. You're afraid that, being more intelligent, they'd end up owning every ship on the planet."

He could not see if she flushed, under the smooth black sweat-gleaming skin, but her lips drew back and one hand clapped to her knife. He thought that the sea bottom was no further away than a signal to her crew. Finally she exclaimed, "Is it the new fashion on Terra to insult a hostess? Well you know it's nay a matter of inborn brain, but of skill. The Lubbers are reared from birth to handle monies. But how many of 'em can handle a rigging—or even name the lines? Can you?"

Flandry's unfairness had been calculated. So was his refusal to meet her reply squarely. "Well," he said, "the Empire tries to respect local law and custom. Only the most uncivilized practices are not tolerated."

It stung her, she bridled. Most colonials were violently sensitive to their isolation from the Galactic mainstream. They did not see that their own societies were not backward on that account—were often healthier—and the answer to that lay buried somewhere in the depths of human unreasonableness. But the fact could be used.

Having angered her enough, Flandry finished coldly: "And, of course, the Empire cannot tolerate treasonable conspiracies."

Tessa Hoorn answered him in a strained voice, "Captain, there's nay conspiring here. Free-born folk are honest with foemen, too. It's you who put on slyness. For see you, I happened by Altla homebound from The Kraal, and visited yon mansion for courtesy's sake. When you asked passage to Jairnovaunt, I granted it, sith such is nay refused among ocean people. But well I knew you fared with me, liefer than fly the way in an hour or two, so you could draw me out and spy on me. And you've nay been frank as to your reasons for guesting my country." Her deep tones became a growl. "That's Lubber ways! You'll nay get far 'long your mission, speaking for a planet of Lubbers and Lubberlovers!"

She drew her knife, looked at it, and clashed it back into the sheath. Down on the quarterdeck, the crewmen stirred, a ripple of panther bodies. It grew so quiet that Flandry heard the steady snore of the bow through murmurous waves, and the lap-lap on the hull, and the creak of spars up in the sky.

He leaned back against a blistering bulwark and said with care: "I'm going to Jairnovaunt because a boy died holding my hand. I want to find his parents...." He offered her a cigaret, and helped himself when she shook her head. "But I'm not going just to extend my personal sympathies. Imperial expense accounts are not quite that elastic. For that matter, while we're being honest, I admit I'd hardly invite Bubbles or Flutters to my own house."

He blew smoke; it was almost invisible in the flooding light. "Maybe you wouldn't conspire behind anyone's back, m' lady. Come to think of it, who would conspire in front of anyone's face? But somebody on Nyanza is hatching a very nasty egg. That kid didn't sign up when the Imperial recruiter stopped by for glory or money: he enlisted to learn modern militechnics, with the idea of turning them against the Empire. And he died in trampled snow, sniped by a local patriot he was chasing. Who lured that young fellow out to die, Lightmistress? And who sneaked up a wall and harpooned a harmless little lonely bureaucrat in his sleep? Rather more to the point, who sent that murderer-by-stealth, and why? Really, this is a pretty slimy business all around. I should think you'd appreciate my efforts to clean it off your planet."

Tessa bit her lip. At last, not meeting his shielded gaze, she said, "I'm nay wise of any such plots, Captain. I won't speak 'loud 'gainst your Empire—my thoughts are my own, but it's true we've nay suffered much more than a resident and some taxes—"

"Which were doubtless higher when every nation maintained its own defenses," said Flandry. "Yes, we settle for a single man on worlds like this. We'd actually like to have more, because enough police could smell out trouble before it's grown too big, and could stop the grosser barbarities left over from independent days—"

Again she bristled. He said in a hurry: "No, please, for once that's not meant to irritate. By and large, Nyanza looks as if it's always been quite a humane place. If you don't use all the latest technological gimcrackery, it's because it's nonfunctional in this culture, not because you've forgotten what your ancestors knew. I'm just enough of a jackleg engineer to see that these weird-looking sails of yours are aerodynamic marvels; I'm certain that paraboloidal jib uses the Venturi effect with malice aforethought. Your language is grammatically archaic but semantically efficient. I can envision some of the bucolic poets at court going into raptures over your way of life. And getting seasick if they tried it, but that's another story.... Therefore," he finished soberly, "I'm afraid I'm a little more sympathetic to Hurri Chundra Bannerji, who fussed about and established extrasystemic employment contacts for your more ambitious young men and built breakwaters and ordered vaccines and was never admitted to your clubs, than I am sorry for you."

She looked over the side, into curling white and purple water, and said very low, "The Empire was nay asked here."

"Neither was anyone else. The Terran Empire established itself in this region first. The Merseian Empire would be a rather more demanding master—if only because it's still vigorous, expansive, virtuous, and generally uncorrupted, while Terra is the easygoing opposite." That brought her up sharply in astonishment, as he had expected. "Since the Empire must protect its frontiers, lest Terra herself be clobbered out of the sky, we're going to stay. It would not be advisable for some young Nyanzan firebrains to try harpooning space dreadnoughts. Anyone who provokes such gallant idiocy is an enemy of yours as well as mine."

Her eyes were moody upon his. After a long time she asked him, "Captain, have you ever swum undersea?"

"I've done a little skindiving for fun," he said, taken aback. He had spoken half honestly and half meretriciously, never quite sure which sentence was one or another, and thought he had touched the proper keys. But this surprised him.

"Nay more? And you stand all 'lone on a world that's aloof of you where it doesn't, perchance, scheme murder? Captain, I repent me what I said 'bout your folk being Lubbers."

The relief was like a wave of weakness. Flandry sucked in his cheeks around his cigaret and answered lightly: "They cannot do worse than shoot me, which would distress only my tailor and my vintner. Have you ever heard that the coward dies a thousand deaths, the hero dies but once?"

"Aye."

"Well, after the 857th death I got bored with it."

She laughed and he continued a line of banter, so habitual by now that most of him thought on other affairs. Not that he seriously expected the Lightmistress of Little Skua to become bodily accessible to him; he had gathered an impression of a chaste folk. But the several days' voyage to Jairnovaunt could be made very pleasant by a small shipboard flirtation, and he would learn a great deal more than if his fellow voyagers were hostile. For instance, whether the imported wine he had noticed in the galley was preferable to native seaberry gin. He had not been truthful in claiming indifference whether he lived or died: not while a supple young woman stood clad in sunlight, and blooded horses stamped on the ringing plains of Ilion, and smoke curled fragrant about coffee and cognac on Terra. But half the pleasure came from these things being staked against darkness.

✧ **IV** ✧

A tide was flowing when they reached Jairnovaunt, and all the rocks, and the housings upon them, were meters under the surface. The Hoorn ship steered a way between pennant-gay buoys to one of the anchored floating docks. There swarmed the sea people, snorting like porpoises among moored hulls or up like squirrels in tall masts. Fish were being unloaded and sails repaired and engines overhauled, somewhere a flute and a drum underlay a hundred deep voices chanting *Way-o* as bare feet stamped out a rigadoon. Flandry noticed how silence spread ripple-fashion from the sight of him. But he followed Tessa overboard as soon as her vessel was secured.

No Nyanzan was ever far from his aqualung. They seemed to have developed a more advanced model here than any Flandry had seen elsewhere: a transparent helmet and a small capacitance-battery device worn on the back, which electrolyzed oxygen directly from the water and added enough helium from a high-compression tank to dilute. By regulating the partial pressures of the gases, one could go quite deep.

This was only a short swim, as casual as a Terran's stroll across the bridgeway. Slanting through clear greenish coolth, Flandry saw that Jairnovaunt was large—sunken domes and towers gleamed farther than his vision reached. Work went on: a cargo submarine, with a score of human midges flitting about it, discharged kelpite bales into a warehouse tube. But there were also children darting among the eerie spires and grottos of a coraloid park, an old man scattered seeds for a school of brilliant-striped little fish, a boy and a girl swam hand in hand through voiceless wonder.

When he reached the long white hall of the Commander, Jairnovaunt's hereditary chief executive, Flandry was still so bemused by the waving, fronded formal gardens that he scarcely noticed how graceful the portico was. Even the airlock which admitted him blended into the overall pattern, a curiously disturbing one to the Terran mind, for it contrasted delicate traceries and brutal masses as if it were the ocean itself.

When the water had been pumped out, an airblast dried them, Flandry's shimmerite clothes as well as Tessa's sleek skin. They stepped into a hallway muraled with heroic abstractions. Beyond two guards bearing the ubiquitous harpoon rifles, and beyond an emergency bulkhead, the passage opened on a great circular chamber lined with malachite pillars under a clear dome. Some twoscore Nyanzans stood about. Their ages seemed to range upward from 20 or so; some wore only a 'lung, others a light-colored shirt and kilt; all bore dignity like a mantle. Quite a few were women, gowned and plumed if they were clothed at all, but otherwise as free and proud as their men.

Tessa stepped forward and saluted crisply. "The Lightmistress of Little Skua, returning from The Kraal as ordered, sir."

Commander Inyanduma III was a powerfully built, heavy-faced man with graying woolly hair: his medallion of rank was tattooed, a golden Pole Star bright on his brows. "Be welcome," he said, "and likewise your guest. He is now ours. I call his name holy."

The Terran flourished a bow. "An honor, sir. I am Captain Dominic Flandry, Imperial Navy. Lightmistress Hoorn was gracious enough to conduct me here."

He met the Commander's eyes steadily, but placed himself so he could watch Tessa on his edge of vision. Inyanduma tipped an almost imperceptible inquiring gesture toward her. She nodded, ever so faintly, and made a short-lived O with thumb and forefinger. *I'd already wormed out that she went to The Kraal on official business,* remembered Flandry, *but she wouldn't say what and only now will she even admit it succeeded. Too secret to mention on her ship's radiophone! As human beings, we enjoyed each other's company, traveling here. But as agents of our kings—?*

Inyanduma swept a sailor's muscular hand about the room. "You see our legislative leaders, Captain. When the Lightmistress 'phoned you were hither-bound, we supposed it was because of his Excellency's slaying, which had been broadcast 'round the globe. It's a grave matter, so I gathered our chiefs of council, from both the House of Men and the Congress of Women."

A rustling and murmuring went about the green columns, under the green sea. There was withdrawal in it, and a sullen waiting. These were not professional politicians as Terra knew the breed. These were the worthies of Jairnovaunt: aristocrats and shipowners, holding seats *ex officio,* and a proportion of ships' officers elected by the commons. Even the nobles were functional—Tessa Hoorn had inherited not the right but the duty to maintain lightships and communications about the reefs called Little Skua. They had all faced more storms and underwater teeth than they had debate.

Flandry said evenly: "My visit concerns worse than a murder, sir and gentles. A resident might be killed by any disgruntled individual, that's an occupational hazard. But I don't think one living soul hated Bannerji personally. And that's what's damnable!"

"Are you implying treason, sir?" rumbled Inyanduma.

"I am, sir. With more lines of evidence than one. Could anybody direct me to a family named Umbolu?"

It stirred and hissed among the councillors of Jairnovaunt. And then a young man trod forth—a huge young man with a lion's gait, cragged features and a scar on one cheek. "Aye," he said so it rang in the hall. "I hight Derek Umbolu, captain of the

kraken-chaser *Bloemfontein.* Tessa, why brought you a damned
Impy hither?"

"Belay!" rapped Inyanduma. "We'll show courtoisie here."

Tessa exclaimed to the giant: "Derek, Derek, he could have flown
to us in an hour! And we meditate nay rebellion—" Her voice
trailed off; she stepped back from his smoldering gaze, her own
eyes widening and a hand stealing to her mouth. The unspoken
question shivered, Do we?

"Let 'em keep 'way from us!" growled Derek Umbolu. "We'll
pay the tribute and hold to the bloody Pax if they'll leave us and
our old ways 'lone. But they don't!"

Flandry stepped into collective horror. "I'm not offended," he
said. "But neither do I make policy. Your complaints against the
local administration should be taken to the provincial governor—"

"Yon murdering quog!" spat Derek. "I've heard about Brae,
and more."

Since Flandry considered the description admirable (he assumed
a quog was not a nice animal) he said hastily: "I must warn you
against lèse majesté. And now let's get to my task. It's not very
pleasant for me either. Captain Umbolu, are you related to an
Imperial marine named Thomas?"

"Aye. I've a younger brother who 'listed for a five-year hitch."

Flandry's tones gentled. "I'm sorry. It didn't strike me you might
be so closely—Thomas Umbolu was killed in action on Brae."

Derek closed his eyes. One great hand clamped on the hilt
of his sheath knife till blood trickled from beneath the nails.
He looked again at the world and said thickly: "You came here
swifter than the official news, Captain."

"I saw him die," said Flandry. "He went like a brave man."

"You've nay crossed space just to tell a colonial that much."

"No," said Flandry. "I would like to speak alone with you
sometime soon. And with his other kin."

The broad black chest pumped air, the hard fingers curved
into claws. Derek Umbolu rasped forth: "You'll nay torment my
father with your devilments, nor throw shame on us with your
secrecy. Ask it out here, 'fore 'em all."

Flandry's shoulder muscles tightened, as if expecting a bullet.
He looked to the Commander. Inyanduma's starred face was like
obsidian. Flandry said: "I have reason to believe Thomas Umbolu
was implicated in a treasonable conspiracy. Of course, I could be

wrong, in which case I'll apologize. But I must first put a great many questions. I am certainly not going to perform before an audience. I'll see you later."

"You'll leave my father be or I'll kill you!"

"Belay!" cried Inyanduma. "I said he was a guest." More softly: "Go, Derek, and tell Old John what you must."

The giant saluted, wheeled, and stalked from the room. Flandry saw tears glimmer in Tessa's eyes. The Commander bowed ponderously at him. "Crave your pardon, sir. He's a stout heart... surely you'll find nay treason in his folk... but the news you bore was harsh."

Flandry made some reply. The gathering became decorous, the Lightmasters and Coastwatchers offered him polite conversation. He felt reasonably sure that few of them knew about any plottings: revolutions didn't start that way.

Eventually he found himself in a small but tastefully furnished bedroom. One wall was a planetary map. He studied it, looking for a place called Uhunhu. He found it near the Sheikhdom of Rossala, which lay north of here; if he read the symbols aright, it was a permanently submerged area.

A memory snapped into his consciousness. He swore for two unrepeating minutes before starting a chain of cigarets. If that was the answer—

✧ **V** ✧

The inner moon, though smaller, raised the largest tides, up to nine times a Terrestrial high; but it moved so fast, five orbits in two of Nyanza's 30-hour days, that the ebb was spectacularly rapid. Flandry heard a roar through his wall, switched on the transparency, and saw water tumbling white from dark rough rock. It was close to sunset, he had sat in his thoughts for hours. A glance at the electric ephemeris over his bunk told him that Loa, the outer satellite, would not dunk the hall till midnight. And that was a much weaker flow, without the whirlpool effects which were dangerous for a lower-case lubber like himself.

He stubbed out his cigaret and sighed. Might as well get the nasty part over with. Rising, he shucked all clothes but a pair of trunks and a 'lung; he put on the swimshoes given him and buckled his guns—they were safely waterproof—into their holsters.

A directory-map of the immediate region showed him where Captain John Umbolu lived. He recorded a message that business called him out and his host should not wait dinner: he felt sure Inyanduma would be more relieved than offended. Then he stepped through the airlock. It closed automatically after him.

Sunset blazed across violet waters. The white spume of the breakers was turned an incredible gold; tide pools on the naked black skerry were like molten copper. The sky was deep blue in the east, still pale overhead, shading to a clear cloudless green where the sun drowned. Through the surf's huge hollow crashing and grinding, Flandry heard bells from one of the many rose-red spires... or did a ship's bell ring among raking spars, or was it something he had heard in a dream once? Beneath all the noise, it was unutterably peaceful.

No one bothered with boats for such short distances. Flandry entered the water at a sheltered spot, unfolded the web feet in his shoes, and struck out between the scattered dome-and-towered reefs. Other heads bobbed in the little warm waves, but none paid him attention. He was glad of that. Steering a course by marked buoys, he found old Umbolu's house after a few energetic minutes.

It was on a long thin rock, surrounded by lesser stones on which a murderous fury exploded. The Terran paddled carefully around, in search of a safe approach. He found it, two natural breakwaters formed by gaunt rusty coraloid pinnacles, with a path that led upward through gardens now sodden heaps until it struck the little hemisphere. Twilight was closing in, slow and deeply blue; an evening planet came to white life in the west.

Flandry stepped onto the beach under the crags. It was dark there. He did not know what reflex of deadly years saved him. A man glided from behind one of the high spires and fired a harpoon. Flandry dropped on his stomach before he had seen more than a metallic glitter. The killing missile hissed where he had been.

"*If* you please!" He rolled over, yanking for his sleepy-needle gun. A night-black panther shape sprang toward him. His pistol was only half unlimbered when the hard body fell upon his. One chopping, wrist-numbing karate blow sent the weapon a-clatter from his grasp. He saw a bearded, hating face behind a knife.

Flandry blocked the stab with his left arm. The assassin pulled his blade back. Before it could return, Flandry's thumb went after the nearest eye. His opponent should have ignored that distraction for the few necessary moments of slicing time—but, instead, grabbed the Terran's wrist with his own free hand. Flandry's right hand was still weak, but he delivered a rabbit punch of sorts with it and took his left out of hock by jerking past his enemy's thumb. Laying both hands and a knee against the man's knife arm, he set about breaking same.

The fellow screeched, writhed, and wriggled free somehow. Both bounced to their feet. The dagger lay between them. The Nyanzan dove after it. Flandry put his foot on the blade. "Finders keepers," he said. He kicked the scrabbling man behind the ear and drew his blaster.

The Nyanzan did not stay kicked. Huddled at Flandry's knees, he threw a sudden shoulder block. The Terran went over on his backside. He glimpsed the lean form as it rose and leaped; it was in the water before he had fired.

After the thunder-crash had echoed to naught and no body had emerged, Flandry retrieved his needler. Slowly, his breathing and pulse eased. "That," he confessed aloud, "was as ludicrous a case of mutual ineptitude as the gods of slapstick ever engineered. We both deserve to be tickled to death by small green centipedes. Well...if you keep quiet about it, I will."

He squinted through the dusk at the assassin's knife. It was an ordinary rustproof blade, but the bone hilt carried an unfamiliar inlaid design. And had he ever before seen a Nyanzan with a respectable growth of beard?

He went on up the path and pressed the house bell. The airlock opened for him and he entered.

The place had a ship's neatness, and it was full of models, scrimshaw, stuffed fish, all the sailor souvenirs. But emptiness housed in it. One old man sat alone with his dead; there was no one else.

John Umbolu looked up through dim eyes and nodded. "Aye," he said, "I 'waited you, Captain. Be welcome and be seated."

Flandry lowered himself to a couch covered with the softscaled hide of some giant swimming thing John Umbolu had once hunted down. The leather was worn shabby. The old man limped to him with a decanter of imported rum. When they had both been helped, he sat himself in a massive armchair and their goblets clinked together. "Your honor and good health, sir," said John Umbolu.

Flandry looked into the wrinkled face and said quietly: "Your son Derek must have told you my news."

"I've had the tidings," nodded Umbolu. He took a pipe from its rack and began to fill it with slow careful motions. "You saw him die, sir?"

"He held my hand. His squad was ambushed on a combat mission on Brae. He...it was soon over."

"Drowning is the single decent death," whispered the Nyanzan. "My other children, all but Derek, had that much luck." He lit his pipe and blew smoke for a while. "I'm sorry Tom had to go yon way. But it is kind of you to come tell me of it."

"He'll be buried with full military honors," said Flandry awkwardly. If they don't have so many corpses they just bulldoze them under. "Or if you wish, instead of the battle-casualty bonus you can have his ashes returned here."

"Nay," said Umbolu. His white head wove back and forth. "What use is that? Let me have the money, to build a reef beacon in his name." He thought for a while longer, then said timidly: "Perchance I could call further on your kindness. Would you know if...you're 'ware, sir, soldiers on leave and the girls they meet...it's possible Tom left a child somewhere..."

"I'm sorry, I wouldn't know how to find out about that."

"Well, well, I expected nay more. Derek must be wed soon then, if the name's to live."

Flandry drew hard on a cigaret, taken from a waterproof case. He got out: "I have to tell you what your son said as he lay dying."

"Aye. Say forth, and fear me nay. Shall the fish blame the hook if it hurts him a little?"

Flandry related it. At the end, the old man's eyes closed, just as Derek's had done, and he let the empty glass slip from his fingers.

Finally: "I know naught of this. Will you believe that, Captain?"

"Yes, sir," Flandry answered.

"You fear Derek may be caught in the same net?"

"I hope not."

"I too. I'd nay have any son of mine in a scheme that works by midnight murder—whatever they may think of your Empire. Tom...Tom was young and didn't understand what was involved. Will you believe that too?" asked John Umbolu anxiously. Flandry nodded. The Nyanzan dropped his head and cupped his hands about the pipe bowl, as if for warmth. "But Derek...why, Derek's in the Council. Derek would have open eyes—Let it nay be so!"

Flandry left him with himself for a time, then: "Where might any young man...first have encountered the agents of such a conspiracy?"

"Who knows, sir? 'Fore his growth is gained, an Umbolu boy has shipped to all ports of the planet. Or there are always sailors from every nation on Nyanza, right here in Jairnovaunt."

Flandry held out the knife he had taken. "This belongs to a bearded man," he said. "Can you tell me anything about it?"

The faded eyes peered close. "Rossala work." It was an instant recognition, spoken in a lifeless voice. "And the Rossala men flaunt whiskers."

"As I came ashore here," said Flandry, "a bearded person with this knife tried to kill me. He got away, but—"

He stopped. The old sea captain had risen. Flandry looked up at an incandescent mask of fury, and suddenly he realized that John Umbolu was a very big man.

Gigantic fists clenched over the Terran's head. The voice roared like thunder, one majestic oath after the next, until rage at last found meaningful words. "Sneak assassins on my very ground! 'Gainst my guest! By the blazing bones of Almighty God, sir, you'll let me question every Rossalan in Jairnovaunt and flay yon one 'live!"

Flandry rose too. An upsurging eagerness tingled in him, a newborn plot. And at the same time—Warily, child, warily! You'll not get cooperation at this counter without some of the most weasel-like arguments and shameless emotional buttonpushing in hell's three-volume thesaurus.

Well, he thought, that's what I get paid for.

❈ VI ❈

Hours had gone when he left the house. He had eaten there, but sheer weariness dragged at him. He swam quite slowly back to the Commander's rock. When he stood on it, he rested for a while, looking over the sea.

Loa was up, Luna-sized, nearly full, but with several times the albedo of Earth's moon. High in a clear blackness, it drowned most of the alien constellations. The marker lights about every rock, color-coded for depth so that all Jairnovaunt was one great jewelbox, grew pallid in the moon-dazzle off the ocean.

Flandry took out a cigaret. It was enough to be alone with that light: at least, it helped. Imperial agents ought to have some kind of conscienceectomy performed. . . . He drew smoke into his lungs.

"Can you nay rest, Captain?"

The low woman-voice brought him bounding around. When he saw the moonlight gleam off Tessa Hoorn, he put back his gun, sheepishly.

"You seem a wee bit wakeful yourself," he answered. "Unless you are sleep-walking, or sleep-diving or whatever people do here. But no, surely I am the one asleep. Don't rouse me."

The moon turned her into darknesses and lithe witcheries, with great marching waters to swirl beneath her feet. She had been swimming—Loa glistened off a million cool drops, her only garment. He remembered how they had talked and laughed and traded songs and recollections and even hopes, under tall skies or moonlit sails. His heart stumbled, and glibness died.

"Aye. My net would nay hold fast to sleep this night." She stood before him, eyes lowered. It was the first time she had not met his gaze. In the streaming unreal light, he saw how a pulse fluttered in her throat. "So I wended from my bunk and—" The tones faded.

"Why did you come here again?" he asked.

"Oh . . . it was a place to steer for. Or perchance . . . Nay!" Her lips tried to smile, but were not quite steady. "Where were you this evening, sith we are so curious?"

"I spoke to Old John," he said, because so far truth would serve his purpose. "It wasn't easy."

"Aye. I wouldn't give your work to an enemy, Dominic. Why do you do it?"

He shrugged. "It's all I really know how to do."

"Nay!" she protested. "To aid a brute of a governor or a null of a resident—you're too much a man. You could come . . . here, even—Nay, the sun wouldn't allow it for long. . . ."

"It's not quite for nothing," he said. "The Empire is—" he grinned forlornly—"less perfect than myself. True. But what would replace it is a great deal worse."

"Are you so sure, Dominic?"

"No," he said in bitterness.

"You could dwell on a frontier world and do work you are sure is worth yourself. I . . . even I have thought, there is more in this universe than Nyanza . . . if such a planet had oceans, I could—"

Flandry said frantically: "Didn't you mention having a child, Tessa?"

"Aye, a Commander-child, but sith I'm unwed as yet the boy was adopted out." He looked his puzzlement and she explained, as glad as he to be impersonal: "The Commander must not wed, but lies with whom he will. It's a high honor, and if she be husbandless the woman gets a great dowry from him. The offspring of these unions are raised by the mothers' kin; when they are all old enough, the councillors elect the best-seeming son heir apparent."

Somewhere in his rocking brain, Flandry thought that the Terran Emperors could learn a good deal from Nyanza. He forced a chuckle and said: "Why, that makes you the perfect catch, Tessa—titled, rich, and the mother of a potential chieftain. How did you escape so far?"

"There was nay the right man," she whispered. "Inyanduma himself is so much a man, see you, for all his years. Only Derek Umbolu—how you unlock me, Terran!—and him too proud to wed 'bove his station." She caught her breath and blurted desperately: "But I'm nay more a maid, and I will nay wait until Full Entropy to be again a woman."

Flandry could have mumbled something and gotten the devil out of there. But he remembered through a brawling in his blood that he was an Imperial agent and that something had been done by this girl in southern waters which they kept secret from him.

He kissed her.

She responded shyly at first, and then with a hunger that tore at him. They sat for a long while under the moon, needing no words, until Flandry felt with dim surprise that the tide was licking his feet.

Tessa rose. "Come to my house," she said.

It was the moment when he must be a reptile-blooded scoundrel ... or perhaps a parfait gentil knight, he was desolately uncertain which. He remained seated, looking up at her, where she stood crowned with stars, and said:

"I'm sorry. It wouldn't do."

"Fear me naught," she said with a small catch of laughter, very close to a sob. "You can leave when you will. I'd nay have a man who wouldn't stay freely. But I'll do my best to keep you, Dominic, dearest."

He fumbled after another cigaret. "Do you think I'd like anything better?" he said. "But there's a monster loose on this planet,

I'm all but sure of it. I will not give you just a few hours with half my mind on my work. Afterward—" He left it unfinished.

She stood quiet for a time that stretched.

"It's for Nyanza too," he pleaded. "If this goes on unreined, it could be the end of your people."

"Aye," she said in a flat tone.

"You could help me. When this mission is finished—"

"Well... what would you know?" She twisted her face away from his eyes.

He got the cigaret lighted and squinted through the smoke. "What were you doing in The Kraal?"

"I'm nay so sure now that I do love you, Dominic."

"Will you tell me, so I'll know what I have to face?"

She sighed. "Rossala is arming. They are making warcraft, guns, torpedoes—none nuclear, sith we have nay facilities for it, but more than the Terran law allows us. I don't know why, though rumor speaks of sunken Uhunhu. The Sheikh guards his secrets. But there are whispers of freedom. It may or may not be sooth. We'll nay make trouble with the Imperium for fellow Nyanzans, but... we arm ourselves, too, in case Rossala should start again the old wars. I arranged an alliance with The Kraal."

"And if Rossala should not attack you, but revolt against Terra?" asked Flandry. "What would your own re-armed alliance do?"

"I know naught 'bout that. I am but one Nyanzan. Have you nay gained enough?"

She slammed down her 'lung helmet and dove off the edge. He did not see her come up again.

✵ VII ✵

With a whole planetful of exotic sea foods to choose from, the Commander hospitably breakfasted his guest on imported beef-steak. Flandry walked out among morning tide pools, through a gusty salt wind, and waited in grimness and disgruntlement for events to start moving.

He was a conspicuous figure in his iridescent white garments, standing alone on a jut of rock with the surf leaping at his feet. A harpoon gunner could have fired upward from the water and disappeared. Flandry did not take his eyes off the blue and green whitecaps beyond the breakers. His mind dwelt glumly on Tessa

Hoorn...God damn it, he would go home by way of Morvan and spend a week in its pleasure city and put it all on the expense account. What was the use of this struggle to keep a decaying civilization from being eaten alive, if you never got a chance at any of the decadence yourself?

A black shape crossed his field of vision. He poised, warily. The man swam like a seal, but straight into the surf. There were sharp rocks in that cauldron—hold it!—Derek Umbolu beat his way through, grasped the wet stone edge Flandry stood on, and chinned himself up. He pushed back his helmet with a crash audible over the sea-thunder and loomed above Flandry like a basalt cliff. His eyes went downward 30 centimeters to lock with the Terran's, and he snarled:

"What have you done to her?"

"My lady Hoorn?" Flandry asked. "Unfortunately, nothing."

A fist cocked. "You lie, Lubber! I know the lass. I saw her this dawn and she had been weeping."

Flandry smiled lop-sided. "And I am necessarily to blame? Don't you flatter me a bit? She spoke rather well of you, Captain."

A shiver went through the huge body. Derek stepped back one pace; teeth caught at his lip. "Say nay more," he muttered.

"I'd have come looking for you today," said Flandry. "We still have a lot to talk about. Such as the man who tried to kill me last night."

Derek spat. "A pity he didn't succeed!"

"Your father thought otherwise, seeing the attempt was made on his own rock. He was quite indignant."

Derek's eyes narrowed. His nostrils stirred, like an angry bull's, and his head slanted forward. "So you spoke to my father after all, did you, now? I warned you, Impy—"

"We had a friendly sort of talk," said Flandry. "He doesn't believe anything can be gained by shooting men in their sleep."

"I suppose all your own works would stand being refereed?"

Since they would certainly not, Flandry donned a frown and continued: "I'd keep an eye on your father, though. I've seen these dirty little fanaticisms before. Among the first people to be butchered are the native-born who keep enough native sense and honor to treat the Imperial like a fellow-being. You see, such people are too likely to understand that the revolution is really organized by some rival imperialism, and that you can't win a war where your own home is the battleground."

"Arrgh!" A hoarse animal noise, for no words were scornful enough.

"And my would-be assassin is still in business," continued Flandry. "He knows I did talk to your father. Hate me as much as you like, Captain Umbolu, but keep a guard over the old gentleman. Or at least speak to a certain Rossalan whom I don't accuse you of knowing."

For a moment longer the brown eyes blazed against the glacial gray blandness of the Terran's. Then Derek clashed his helmet down and returned to the water.

Flandry sighed. He really should start the formal machinery of investigation, but—He went back to the house with an idea of borrowing some fishing tackle.

Inyanduma, seated at a desk among the inevitable documents of government, gave him a troubled look. "Are you certain that there is a real conspiracy on Nyanza?" he asked. "We've ever had our hotheads, like all others...aye, I've seen other planets, I 'listed for the space Navy in my day and hold a reserve commission."

Flandry sat down and looked at his fingernails. "Then why haven't you reported what you know about Rossala?" he asked softly.

Inyanduma started. "Are you a telepath?"

"No. It'd make things too dull." Flandry lit a fresh cigaret. "I know Rossala is arming, and that your nation is alarmed enough about it to prepare defensive weapons and alliances. Since the Empire would protect you, you must expect the Empire to be kicked off Nyanza."

"Nay," whispered Inyanduma. "We've nay certainty of aught. It's but...we won't bring a horde of detectives, belike a Terran military force, by denouncing our fellow nation...on so little proof.... And yet we must keep some freedom of action, in case—"

"Especially in case Rossala calls on you to join in cutting the Terran apron strings?"

"Nay, nay—"

"Under such circumstances, it would be pathetic." Flandry shook his tongue-clicking head. "It's so amateurishly done that I feel grossly overpaid for my time here. But whoever engineered the conspiracy in the first place is no amateur. He used your parochial loyalties with skill. And he must expect to move soon, before a preoccupied Imperium can find out enough about his arrangements to justify sending in the marines. The resident's assassination is obviously a key action. It was chance I got here the very day that had happened, but someone like me would surely have arrived not many days later, and not been a great deal longer about learning as much as I've done. Of course, if they can kill me it will delay matters for a while, which will be helpful to them; but they don't seem to expect they'll need much time."

Flandry paused, nodded to himself, and carried on. "Ergo, if this affair is not stopped, we can expect Rossala to revolt within a few weeks at the very latest. Rossala will call on the other Nyanzan nations to help—and they've been cleverly maneuvered into arming themselves and setting up a skeleton military organization. If the expert I suspect is behind the revolution, those leaders such as yourself, who demur at the idea, will die and be replaced by more gullible ones. Of course, Nyanza will have been promised outside help: I don't imagine even Derek Umbolu thinks one planet can stand off all Terra's power. Merseia is not too far away. If everything goes smoothly, we'll end up with a nominally independent Nyanza which is actually a Merseian puppet—deep within Terran space. If the attempt fails, well, what's one more radioactive wreck of a world to Merseia?"

There was a stillness.

In the end Inyanduma said grayly: "I don't know but what the hazard you speak of will be better than to call in the Terrans; for in sooth all our nations have broken your law in that we have gathered weapons as you say. The Imperials would nay leave us what self-government we now have."

"They might not be necessary," said Flandry. "Since you do have those weapons, and the City constabulary is a legally armed native force with some nuclear equipment... you could do your own housecleaning. I could supervise the operation, make sure it was thorough, stamp my report to headquarters Fantastically Secret, and that would be the close of the affair."

He stood up. "Think it over," he said.

It was peaceful out on the rock. Flandry's reel hummed, the lure flashed through brilliant air, the surf kittened gigantically with his hook. It did not seem to matter greatly that he got never a nibble. The tide began to rise again, he'd have to go inside or exchange his rod for a trident....

A kayak came over drowned skerries like something alive. Derek Umbolu brought it to Flandry's feet and looked up. His face was sea-wet, which was merciful; Flandry did not want to know whether the giant was crying.

"Blood," croaked Derek. "Blood, and the chairs broken, I could see in the blood how he was dragged out and thrown to the fish."

Hollowness lay in Dominic Flandry's heart. He felt his shoulders slump. "I'm sorry," he said. "Oh, God, I'm sorry."

Words ripped out, flat, hurried, under the ramping tidal noise:

"They center in Rossala, but someone in Uhunhu captains it. I was to seize control here when they rise, if Inyanduma will nay let us help the revolution. I hated the killing of old Bannerji, but it was needful. For now there will be nay effective space traffic control, till they replace him, and in two weeks there will come ships from Merseia with heavy nuclear war-weapons such as we can't make on this planet. The same man who gaffed Bannerji tried for you. He was the only trained assassin in Jairnovaunt— and a neighbor gave you alibi—so I believe none of his whinings that he'd nay touched my father. His name was Mamoud Shufi. Cursed be it till the sun is cold clinkers!"

One great black hand unzipped the kayak cover. The other hand swooped down, pulled out something which dripped, and flung it at the Terran's feet so hard that one dead eye burst from the lopped-off head.

✦ VIII ✦

Elsewhere on Nyanza it growled battle, men speared and shot each other, ships went to the bottom and buildings cracked open like rotten fruit. Where Flandry stood was only turquoise and lace. Perhaps some of the high white clouds banked in the west had a smoky tinge.

A crewman with a portable sonic fathometer nodded. "We're over Uhunhu shoals now, sir."

"Stop the music," said Flandry. The skipper transmitted several orders, he felt the pulse of engines die, the submarine lay quiet. Looking down gray decks past the shark's fin of a conning tower, Flandry saw crewmen gathering in a puzzled, almost resentful way. They had expected to join the fighting, till this Terran directed the ship eastward.

"And now," said Derek Umbolu grimly, "will you have the kindness to say why we steered clear of Rossala?"

Flandry cocked an eyebrow. "Why are you so anxious to kill other men?" he countered.

Derek bristled. "I'm nay afraid to hazard my skin, Impy...like someone I could name!"

"There's more to it than that," said Flandry. He was not sure why he prattled cheap psychology when a monster crouched under his feet. Postponing the moment? He glanced at Tessa Hoorn, who had insisted on coming. "Do you see what I mean, Lightmistress? Do you know why he itches so to loose his harpoon?"

Some of the chill she had shown him in the past week thawed. "Aye," she said. "Belike I do. It's blood guilt enough that we're party to a war 'gainst our own planetmen, without being safe into the bargain."

He wondered how many shared her feelings. Probably no large number. After he and Inyanduma flew to the City and got the Warden to mobilize his constables, a call had gone out for volunteers. The Nyanzan public had only been informed that a dangerous conspiracy had been discovered, centered in Rossala, that the Sheikh had refused the police right of entry, and that therefore a large force would be needed to seize that nation over the resistance of its misguided citizens and occupy it while the Warden's specialists sniffed out the actual plotters. And men had come by the many thousands, from all over the planet.

It was worse, though, for those who knew what really lay behind this police operation.

Flandry mused aloud, "I wonder if you'll ever start feeling that way about your fellowmen, wherever they happen to live?"

"Enough!" rapped Derek Umbolu. "Say why you brought us hither and be done!"

Flandry kindled a cigaret and stared over the rail, into chuckling sun-glittering waves so clear that he could see how the darkness grew with every meter of depth. He said:

"Down there, if he hasn't been warned somehow that I know about him, is the enemy."

"Ai-a!" Tessa Hoorn dropped a hand to her gun; but Flandry saw with an odd little pain how she moved all unthinkingly closer to Derek. "But who would lair in drowned Uhunhu?"

"The name I know him by is A'u," said Flandry. "He isn't human. He can breathe water as well as air—I suppose his home planet must be pretty wet, though I don't know where it is. But it's somewhere in the Merseian Empire, and he, like me, belongs to the second oldest profession. We've played games before now. I flushed him on Conjumar two Earth-years ago: my boys cleaned up his headquarters, and his personal spaceship took a near miss that left it lame and radioactive. But he got away. Not home, his ship wasn't in that good a condition, but away."

Flandry trickled smoke sensuously through his nostrils. It might be the last time. "On the basis of what I've seen here, I'm now certain that friend A'u made for Nyanza, ditched, contacted some of your malcontents, and started cooking revolution. The whole business has his signature, with flourishes. If nothing else, a Nyanzan uprising and Merseian intervention would get him passage home; and he might have inflicted a major defeat on Terra in the process."

A mumbling went through the crewfolk, wrath which was half terror. "Sic semper local patriots," finished Flandry. "I want to be ruddy damn sure of getting A'u, and he has a whole ocean bottom to hide on if he's alarmed, and we'll be too busy setting traps for the Merseian gunrunners due next week to play tag for very long. Otherwise I'd certainly have waited till we could bring a larger force."

"Thirty men 'gainst one poor hunted creature?" scoffed Tessa.

"He's a kind of big creature," said Flandry quietly to her.

He looked at his followers, beautiful and black in the sunlight, with a thousand hues of blue at their backs, a low little wind touching bare skins, and the clean male shapes of weapons. It was too fair a world to gamble down in dead Uhunhu. Flandry knew with wry precision why he was leading this chase—not for courage, nor glory, nor even one more exploit to embroider for some high-prowed yellow-haired bit of Terran fluff. He went because he was an Imperial and if he stayed behind the colonials would laugh at him.

Therefore he took one more drag of smoke, flipped his cigaret parabolically overboard, and murmured: "Be good, Tessa, and I'll bring you back a lollipop. Let's go chilluns."

And snapped down his helmet and dove cleanly over the side.

The water became a world. Overhead was an area of sundazzle, too bright to look on; elsewhere lay cool dusk fading downward into night. The submarine was a basking whale shape...too bad he couldn't just take it down and torpedo A'u, but an unpleasant session with a man arrested in Altla had told him better—A'u expected to be approached only by swimming men.... The roof of sunlight grew smaller as he drove himself toward the bottom, until it was a tiny blinding star and then nothing. There was a silken sense of his own steadily rippling muscles and the sea that slid past them, the growing chill stirred his blood in its million channels, a glance behind showed his bubble-stream like a trail of argent planets, his followers were black lightning bolts through an utterly quiet green twilight. O God, to be a seal!

Dimly now, the weed-grown steeps of Uhunhu rose beneath him, monstrous gray dolmens and menhirs raised by no human hands, sunken a million years ago ... A centuries-drowned ship, the embryo of a new reef ten millennia hence, with a few skulls strewn for fish to nest in, was shockingly raw and new under the leaning walls. Flandry passed it in the silence of a dream.

He did not break that quietude, though his helmet bore voice apparatus. If A'u was still here, A'u must not be alarmed by orders to fan out in a search pattern. Flandry soared close enough to Derek to nod, and the giant waved hands and feet in signals understood by the men. Presently Flandry and Derek were alone in what might once have been a street or perhaps a corridor.

They glided among toppling enormities; now and then one of denser shadow, but it was only a rock or a decapus or a jawbone the size of a portal. Flandry began to feel the cold, deeper than his skin, almost deeper than the silence.

A hand clamped bruisingly on his wrist. He churned to a halt and hung there, head cocked, until the sound that Derek had dimly caught was borne past vibrator and ocean and receiver to his own ears. It was the screaming of a man being killed, but so far and faint it might have been the death agony of a gnat.

Flandry blasphemed eighteen separate gods, kicked himself into motion, and went like a hunting eel through Uhunhu. But Derek passed him and he was almost the last man to reach the fight.

"A'u," he said aloud, uselessly, through the bawl of men and the roil of bloodied waters. He remembered the harpoon rifle slung across his shoulders, unlimbered it, checked the magazine, and wriggled close. Thirty men—no, twenty-nine at the most— a corpse bobbed past, wildly staring through a helmet cracked open—twenty-eight men swirled about one monster. Flandry did not want to hit any of them.

He swam upward, until he looked down on A'u. The great black shape had torpedoed from a dolmen. Fifteen meters long, the wrinkled leather skin of some Arctic golem, the gape of a whale and the boneless arms of an elephant...but with hands, with hands...A'u raged among his hunters. Flandry saw how the legs which served him on land gripped two men in the talons and plucked their limbs off. There was no sound made by the monster's throat, but the puny human jabber was smashed by each flat concussion of the flukes, as if bombs burst.

Flandry nestled the rifle to his shoulder and fired. Recoil sent him backward, end over end. He did not know if his harpoon had joined the score in A'u's tormented flanks. It had to be this way, he thought, explosives would kill the men too under sea pressure and...Blood spurted from a transfixed huge hand. A'u got his back against a monolith, arched his tail, and shot toward the surface. Men sprayed from him like bow water.

Flandry snapped his legs and streaked to meet the thing. The white belly turned toward him, a cliff, a cloud, a dream. He fired once and saw his harpoon bite. Once more! A'u bent double in anguish, spoke blood, somehow sensed the man and plunged at him. Flandry looked down a cave of horrible teeth. He looked into the eyes behind; they were blind with despair. He tried to scramble aside. A'u changed course with a snake's ease. Flandry had a moment to wonder if A'u knew him again.

A man flew from the blood-fog. He fired a harpoon, holding himself steady against its back-thrust. Instead of letting the line trail, to tangle the beast, he grabbed it, was pulled up almost to the side. The gills snapped at him like mouths. He followed the monster, turn for turn through cold deeps, as he sought aim. Finally he shot. An eye went out. A brain was cloven. A'u turned over and died.

Flandry gasped after breath. His helmet rang and buzzed, it was stifling him, he must snatch it off before he choked....Hands caught him. He looked into the victory which was Derek Umbolu's face. "Wait there, wait, Terra man," said a remote godlike calm. "All is done now."

"I, I, I, thanks!" rattled Flandry.

His wind came back to him. He counted the men that gathered, while they rose with all due slowness toward the sun. Six were dead. Cheap enough to get rid of A'u.

If I had been cast away, alone, on the entire world of a hideous race . . . I wonder if I would have had the courage to survive this long.

I wonder if there are some small cubs, on a water planet deep among the Merseian stars, who can't understand why father hasn't come home.

He climbed on deck at last, threw back his helmet and sat down under Tessa Hoorn's anxious gaze. "Give me a cigaret," he said harshly. "And break out something alcoholic."

She wrestled herself to steadiness. "Caught you the monster?" she asked.

"Aye," said Derek.

"We close to didn't," said Flandry. "Our boy Umbolu gets the credit."

"Small enough vengeance for my father," said the flat voice of sorrow.

The submarine's captain saluted the pale man who sat hugging his knees, shivering and drinking smoke. "Word just came in from Rossala, sir," he reported. "The Sheikh has yielded, though he swears he'll protest the outrage to the next Imperial resident. But he'll let the constables occupy his realm and search as they wish."

Search for a number of earnest, well-intentioned young patriots, who'll never again see morning over broad waters. Well—I suppose it all serves the larger good. It must. Our noble homosexual Emperor says so himself.

"Excellent," said Flandry. His glance sought Derek. "Since you saved my life, you've got a reward coming. Your father."

"Hoy?" The big young man trod backward a step.

"He isn't dead," said Flandry. "I talked him into helping me. We faked an assassination. He's probably at home this minute, suffering from an acute case of conscience."

"What?" The roar was like hell's gates breaking down.

Flandry winced. "Pianissimo, please." He waved the snarling, fist-clenching bulk back with his cigaret. "All right, I played a trick on you."

"A trick I could have 'waited from a filthy Impy!" Tessa Hoorn spat at his feet.

"Touch me, brother Umbolu, and I'll arrest you for treason," said Flandry. "Otherwise I'll exercise my discretionary powers and put you on lifetime probation in the custody of some responsible citizen." He grinned wearily. "I think the Lightmistress of Little Skua qualifies."

Derek and Tessa stared at him, and at each other.

Flandry stood up. "Probation is conditional on your getting married," he went on. "I recommend that in choosing a suitable female you look past that noble self-righteousness, stop considering the trivium that she can give you some money, and consider all that you might give her." He glanced at them, saw that their hands were suddenly linked together, and had a brief, private, profane conversation with the Norn of his personal destiny. "That includes heirs," he finished. "I'd like to have Nyanza well populated. When the Long Night comes for Terra, somebody will have to carry on. It might as well be you."

He walked past them, into the cabin, to get away from all the dark young eyes. ✷

A MESSAGE
IN SECRET

⁂

Seen on approach, against crystal darkness and stars crowded into foreign constellations, Altai was beautiful. More than half the northern hemisphere, somewhat less in the south, was polar cap. Snowfields were tinged rosy by the sun Krasna; naked ice shimmered blue and cold green. The tropical belt, steppe and tundra, which covered the remainder, shaded from bronze to tarnished gold, here and there the quicksilver flash of a big lake. Altai was ringed like Saturn, a tawny hoop with subtle rainbow iridescence flung spinning around the equator, three radii out in space. And beyond were two copper-coin moons.

Captain Sir Dominic Flandry, field agent, Naval Intelligence Corps of the Terrestrial Empire, pulled his gaze reluctantly back to the spaceship's bridge. "I see where its name came from," he remarked. Altai meant Golden in the language of the planet's human colonists; or so the Betelgeusean trader who passed on his knowledge electronically to Flandry had insisted. "But Krasna is a misnomer for the sun. It isn't really red to the human eye. Not nearly as much as your star, for instance. More of an orange-yellow, I'd say."

The blue visage of Zalat, skipper of the battered merchant vessel, twisted into the grimace which was his race's equivalent of a shrug. He was moderately humanoid, though only half as tall as a man, stout, hairless, clad in a metal mesh tunic. "I zuppoze it was de, you zay, contrazt." He spoke Terrestrial Anglic with a thick accent, as if to show that the independence of the Betelgeusean System—buffer state between the hostile realms of Terra and Merseia—did not mean isolation from the mainstream of interstellar culture.

Flandry would rather have practiced his Altaian, especially since Zalat's Anglic vocabulary was so small so to limit conversation to platitudes. But he deferred. As the sole passenger on this ship, of alien species at that, with correspondingly special requirements in diet, he depended on the captain's good will. Also, the Betelgeuseans took him at face value. Officially, he was only being sent to re-establish contact between Altai and the rest of mankind. Officially, his mission was so minor that Terra didn't even give him a ship of his own, but left him to negotiate passage as best he might. . . . So, let Zalat chatter.

"After all," continued the master, "Altai was firzt colonized more dan zeven hoondert Terra-years a-pazt: in de verry dawn, you say, of interztellar travel. Little was known about w'at to eggzpect. Krazna muzt have been deprezzingly cold and red, after Zol. Now-to-days, we have more aztronautical zophiztication."

Flandry looked to the blaze of space, stars and stars and stars. He thought that an estimated four million of them, included in that vague sphere called the Terrestrial Empire, was an insignificant portion of this one spiral arm of this one commonplace galaxy. Even if you added the other empires, the sovereign suns like Betelgeuse, the reports of a few explorers who had gone extremely far in the old days, that part of the universe known to man was terrifyingly small. And it would always remain so.

"Just how often do you come here?" he asked, largely to drown out silence.

"About onze a Terra-year," answered Zalat. "However, dere is ot'er merchantz on dis route. I have de fur trade, but Altai alzo produzes gemz, mineralz, hides, variouz organic productz, even dried meatz, w'ich are in zome demand at home. Zo dere is usually a Betelgeusean zhip or two at Ulan Baligh."

"Will you be here long?"

"I hope not. It iz a tediouz plaze for a nonhuman. One pleasure houze for uz haz been eztablizhed, but—" Zalat made another face. "Wid de dizturbanzez going on, fur trapping and caravanz have been much hampered. Lazt time I had to wait a ztandard mont' for a full cargo. Diz time may be worze."

Oh-oh, thought Flandry. But he merely asked aloud: "Since the metals and machinery you bring in exchange are so valuable, I wonder why some Altaians don't acquire spaceships of their own and start trading."

"Dey have not dat kind of zivilization," Zalat replied. "Remember, our people have been coming here for lezz dan a zentury. Before den Altai was izolated, onze de original zhipz had been worn out. Dere was never zo great an interezt among dem in re-eztablizhing galactic contact az would overcome de handicap of poverty in metalz w'ich would have made zpazezship building eggzpenzive for dem. By now, might-be, zome of de younger Altaian malez have zome wizh for zuch an enterprize. But lately de Kha Khan has forbidden any of his zubjectz from leaving de planet, eggzept zome truzted and verry cloze-mout' perzonal reprezentativez in de Betelgeuzean Zyztem. Dis prohibition is might-be one reazon for de inzurrectionz."

"Yeh." Flandry gave the ice fields a hard look. "If it were my planet, I think I'd look around for an enemy to sell it to."

And still I'm going there, he thought. *Talk about your unsung heroes— Though I suppose, the more the Empire cracks and crumbles, the more frantically a few of us have to scurry around patching it. Or else the Long Night could come in our own sacrosanct lifetimes.*

And in this particular instance, his mind ran on, *I have reason to believe that an enemy is trying to buy the planet.*

☼ ▮▮ ☼

Where the Zeya and the Talyma, broad shallow rivers winding southward over the steppes from polar snows, met at Ozero Rurik, the city named Ulan Baligh was long ago founded. It had never been large, and now the only permanent human settlement on Altai had perhaps 20,000 residents. But there was always a ring of encampments around it, tribesmen come to trade or confer or hold rites in the Prophet's Tower. Their tents and trunks walled the landward side of Ulan Baligh, spilled around the primitive spaceport, and raised campfire smoke for many kilometers along the indigo lakeshore.

As the spaceship descended, Captain Flandry was more interested in something less picturesque. Through a magnifying viewport in the after turret, to which he had bribed his way, he saw that monorail tracks encircled the city like spider strands; that unmistakable launchers for heavy missiles squatted on them; that some highly efficient modern military aircraft lazed on grav repulsors in the sky; that barracks and emplacements for an armored brigade were under construction to the west, numerous tanks and beetlecars already prowling on guard; that a squat building in the center of town must house a negagrav generator powerful enough to shield the entire urban area.

That all of this was new.

That none of it came from any factories controlled by Terra.

"But quite probably from our little green chums," he murmured to himself. "A Merseian base here, in the buffer region, outflanking us at Catawrayannis.... Well, it wouldn't be decisive in itself, but it would strengthen their hand quite a bit. And eventually, when their hand looks strong enough, they're going to fight."

He suppressed a tinge of bitterness at his own people, too rich to spend treasure in an open attack on the menace—most of them, even, denying that any menace existed, for what would dare break the Pax Terrestria? After all, he thought wryly, he enjoyed his furloughs Home precisely because Terra was decadent.

But for now, there was work at hand. Intelligence had collected hints in the Betelgeuse region: traders spoke of curious goings-on at some place named Altai; the archives mentioned a colony far off the regular space lanes, not so much lost as overlooked; inquiry produced little more than this, for Betelgeusean civilians like Zalat had no interest in Altaian affairs beyond the current price of angora pelts.

A proper investigation would have required some hundreds of men and several months. Being spread horribly thin over far too many stars, Intelligence was able to ship just one man to Betelgeuse. At the Terran Embassy, Flandry received a slim dossier, a stingy expense account, and orders to find what the devil was behind all this. After which, overworked men and machines forgot about him. They would remember when he reported back, or if he died in some spectacular fashion; otherwise, Altai might well lie obscure for another decade.

Which could be a trifle too long, Flandry thought.

He strolled with elaborate casualness from the turret to his cabin. It must not be suspected on Altai what he had already seen: or, if that information leaked out, it must absolutely not be suspected that he suspected these new installations involved more than suppressing a local rebellion. The Khan had been careless about hiding the evidence, presumably not expecting a Terran investigator. He would certainly not be so careless as to let the investigator take significant information home again.

At his cabin, Flandry dressed with his usual care. According to report, the Altaians were people after his own heart: they liked color on their clothes, in great gobs. He chose a shimmerite blouse, green embroidered vest, purple trousers with gold stripe tucked into tooled-leather half boots, crimson sash and cloak, black beret slanted rakishly over his sleek seal-brown hair. He himself was a tall well-muscled man; his long face bore high cheekbones and straight nose, gray eyes, neat mustache. But then, he patronized Terra's best cosmetic biosculptor.

The spaceship landed at one end of the concrete field. Another Betelgeusean vessel towered opposite, confirming Zalat's claims about the trade. Not precisely brisk—maybe a score of ships per standard year—but continuous, and doubtless by now important to the planet's economy.

As he stepped out the debarkation lock, Flandry felt the exhilaration of a gravity only three-fourths that of Home. But it was quickly lost when the air stung him. Ulan Baligh lay at eleven degrees north latitude. With an axial tilt about like Terra's, a wan dwarf sun, no oceans to moderate the climate, Altai knew seasons almost to the equator. The northern hemisphere was approaching winter. A wind streaking off the pole sheathed Flandry in chill, hooted around his ears, and snatched the beret from his head.

He grabbed it back, swore, and confronted the portmaster with less dignity than he had planned. "Greeting," he said as instructed; "may peace dwell in your yurt. This person is named Dominic Flandry, and ranges Terra, the Empire."

The Altaian blinked narrow black eyes, but otherwise kept his face a mask. It was a wide, rather flat countenance, but not purely mongoloid: hook nose, thick close-cropped beard, light skin bespoke caucasoid admixture as much as the hybrid language. He was short, heavy-set, a wide-brimmed fur hat was tied in place, his leather jacket was lacquered in an intricate design, his pants were of thick felt and his boots fleece-lined. An old-style machine pistol was holstered at his left side, a broad-bladed knife on the right.

"We have not had such visitors—" He paused, collected himself, and bowed. "Be welcome, all guests who come with honest words," he said ritually. "This person is named Pyotr Gutchluk, of the Kha Khan's sworn men." He turned to Zalat. "You and your crew may proceed directly to the yamen. We can handle the formalities later. I must personally conduct so distinguished a . . . a guest to the palace."

He clapped his hands. A couple of servants appeared, men of his own race, similarly dressed and similarly armed. Their eyes glittered, seldom leaving the Terran; the woodenness of their faces must cover an excitement which seethed. Flandry's luggage was loaded on a small electro-truck of antique design. Pyotr Gutchluk said, half inquiringly, "Of course so great an orluk as yourself would prefer a varyak to a tulyak."

"Of course," said Flandry, wishing his education had included those terms.

He discovered that a varyak was a native-made motorcycle. At least, that was the closest Terran word. It was a massive thing on two wheels, smoothly powered from a bank of energy capacitors, a baggage rack aft and a machine-gun mount forward. It was steered with the knees, which touched a crossbar. Other controls were on a manual panel behind the windscreen. An outrigger wheel could be lowered for support when the vehicle was stationary or moving slowly. Pyotr Gutchluk offered a goggled crash helmet from a saddlebag and took off at 200 kilometers an hour.

Flandry, accelerating his own varyak, felt the wind come around the screen, slash his face and nearly drag him from the saddle. He started to slow down. But—*Come now, old chap. Imperial prestige, stiff upper lip,* and so on drearily. Somehow he managed to stay on Gutchluk's tail as they roared into the city.

Ulan Baligh formed a crescent, where the waters of Ozero Rurik cut a bay into the flat shore. Overhead was a deep-blue sky, and the rings. Pale by day, they made a frosty halo above the orange sun. In such a light, the steeply upcurving red tile roofs took on the color of fresh blood. Even the ancient gray stone walls beneath were tinged faint crimson. All the buildings were large, residences holding several families each, commercial ones jammed with tiny shops. The streets were wide, clean-swept, full of nomads and the wind. Gutchluk took an overhead road, suspended from pylons cast like dragons holding the cables in their teeth. It seemed an official passageway, nearly empty save for an occasional varyak patrol.

It also gave a clear view of the palace, standing in walled gardens: a giant version of the other houses but gaudily painted and colonnaded with wooden dragons. The royal residence was, however, overshadowed by the Prophet's Tower. So was everything else.

Flandry understood from vague Betelgeusean descriptions that most of Altai professed a sort of Moslem-Buddhist synthesis, codified centuries ago by the Prophet Subotai. The religion had only this one temple, but that was enough. A sheer two kilometers it reared up into the thin hurried air, as if it would spear a moon. Basically a pagoda, blinding red, it had one blank wall facing north. No, not blank either, but a single flat tablet on which, in a contorted Sino-Cyrillic alphabet, the words of the Prophet stood holy forever. Even Flandry, with scant reverence in his heart, knew a moment's awe. A stupendous will had raised that spire above these plains.

The elevated road swooped downward again. Gutchluk's varyak slammed to a halt outside the palace. Flandry, taller than any man of Altai, was having trouble with his steering bar. He almost crashed into the wrought-bronze gate. He untangled his legs and veered in bare time, a swerve that nearly threw him. Up on the wall, a guard leaned on his portable rocket launcher and laughed. Flandry heard him and swore. He continued the curve, steered a ring around Gutchluk so tight that it could easily have killed them both, slapped down the third wheel and let the cycle slow itself to a halt while he leaped from the saddle and took a bow.

"By the Ice People!" exclaimed Gutchluk. Sweat shone on his face. He wiped it off with a shaky hand. "They breed reckless men on Terra!"

"Oh, no," said Flandry, wishing he dared mop his own wet skin. "A bit demonstrative, perhaps, but never reckless."

Once again he had occasion to thank loathed hours of calisthenics and judo practice for a responsive body. As the gates opened—Gutchluk had used his panel radio to call ahead—Flandry jumped back on his varyak and putt-putted through under the guard's awed gaze.

The garden was rocks, arched bridges, dwarf trees, and mutant lichen. Little that was Terran would grow on Altai. Flandry began to feel the dryness of his own nose and throat. This air snatched moisture from him as greedily as it did heat. He was more grateful for the warmth inside the palace than he wished to admit.

A white-bearded man in a fur-trimmed robe made a deep bow. "The Kha Khan himself bids you welcome, Orluk Flandry," he said. "He will see you at once."

"But the gifts I brought—"

"No matter now, my lord." The chamberlain bowed again, turned and led the way down arched corridors hung with tapestries. It was very silent: servants scurried about whispering, guards with modern blasters stood rigid in dragon-faced leather tunics and goggled helmets, tripods fumed bitter incense. The entire sprawling house seemed to crouch, watchful.

I imagine I have upset them somewhat, thought Flandry. Here they have some cozy little conspiracy—with beings sworn to lay all Terra waste, I suspect—and suddenly a Terran officer drops in, for the first time in five or six hundred years. Yes-s-s.

So what do they do next? It's their move.

☼ **III** ☼

Oleg Yesukai, Kha Khan of All the Tribes, was bigger than most Altaians, with a long sharp face and a stiff reddish beard. He wore gold rings, a robe thickly embroidered, silver trim on his fur cap, but all with an air of impatient concession to tedious custom. The hand which Flandry, kneeling, touched to his brow, was hard and muscular; the gun at the royal waist had seen use. This private audience chamber was curtained in red, its furniture inlaid and grotesquely carved; but it also held an ultramodern Betelgeusean graphone and a desk buried under official papers.

"Be seated," said the Khan. He himself took a low-legged chair and opened a carved-bone cigar box. A smile of sorts bent his mouth. "Now that we've gotten rid of all my damned fool courtiers, we need no longer act as if you were a vassal." He took a crooked purple stogie from the box. "I would offer you one of these, but it might make you ill. In thirty-odd generations, eating Altaian food, we have probably changed our metabolism a bit."

"Your majesty is most gracious." Flandry inhaled a cigaret of his own and relaxed as much as the straightbacked furniture permitted.

Oleg Khan spoke a stockbreeder's pungent obscenity. "Gracious?

My father was an outlaw on the tundra at fifteen." (He meant local years, a third again as long as Terra's. Altai was about one A.U. distant from Krasna, but the sun was less massive than Sol.) "At thirty he had seized Ulan Baligh with 50,000 warriors and deposited old Tuli Khan naked on the artic snows: so as not to shed royal blood, you understand. But he never would live here, and all his sons grew up in the ordu, the encampment, as he had done, practiced war against the Tebtengri as he had known war, and mastered reading, writing, and science to boot. Let us not bother with graciousness, Orluk Flandry. I never had time to learn any."

The Terran waited passive. It seemed to disconcert Oleg, who smoked for a minute in short ferocious drags, then leaned forward and said, "Well, why does your government finally deign to notice us?"

"I had the impression, your majesty," said Flandry in a mild voice, "that the colonists of Altai came this far from Sol in order to escape notice."

"True. True. Don't believe that rat crud in the hero songs. Our ancestors came here because they were weak, not strong. Planets where men could settle at all were rare enough to make each one a prize, and there was little law in those days. By going far and picking a wretched icy desert, a few shiploads of Central Asians avoided having to fight for their home. Nor did they plan to become herdsmen. They tried to farm, but it proved impossible. Too cold and dry, among other things. They could not build an industrial, food-synthesizing society either: not enough heavy metals, fossil fuels, fissionables. This is a low-density planet, you know. Step by step, over generations, with only dim traditions to guide them, they were forced to evolve a nomadic life. And that was suited to Altai; that worked, and their numbers increased. Of course, legends have grown up. Most of my people still believe Terra is some kind of lost utopia and our ancestors were hardy warriors." Oleg's rust-colored eyes narrowed upon Flandry. He stroked his beard. "I've read enough, thought enough, to have a fair idea of what your Empire is and what it can do. So—why this visit, at this exact moment?"

"We are no longer interested in conquest for its own sake, your majesty," said Flandry. True, as far as it went. "And our merchants have avoided this sector for several reasons. It lies far from heartland stars; the Betelgeuseans, close to their own home, can compete on unequal terms; the risk of meeting some prowling warship of our Merseian enemies is unattractive. There has, in short, been no occasion, military or civilian, to search out Altai." He slipped smoothly into prevarication gear. "However, it is not the Emperor's wish that any members of the human family be cut off. At the very least, I bring you his brotherly greetings." (That was subversive. It should have been "fatherly." But Oleg Khan would not take kindly to being patronized.) "At most, if Altai wished to rejoin us, for mutual protection and other benefits, there are many possibilities which could be discussed. An Imperial resident, say, to offer help and advice—"

He let the proposal trail off, since in point of fact a resident's advice tended to be, "I suggest you do thus and so lest I call in the Marines."

The Altaian king surprised him by not getting huffy about sovereign status. Instead, amiable as a tiger, Oleg Yesukai answered: "If you are distressed about our internal difficulties, pray do not be. Nomadism necessarily means tribalism, which usually means feud and war. I already spoke of my father's clan seizing planetary leadership from the Nuru Bator. We in turn have rebellious gurkhans. As you will hear in court, that alliance called the Tebtengri Shamanate is giving us trouble. But such is nothing new in Altain history. Indeed, I have a firmer hold over more of the planet than any Kha Khan since the Prophet's day. In a little while more I shall bring every last clan to heel."

"With the help of imported armament?" Flandry elevated his brows a millimeter. Risky though it was to admit having seen the evidence, it might be still more suspicious not to. And indeed the other man seemed unruffled. Flandry continued, "The Imperium would gladly send a technical mission."

"I do not doubt it." Oleg's response was dry.

"May I respectfully ask what planet supplies the assistance your majesty is now receiving?"

"Your question is impertinent, as well you know. I do not take offense, but I decline to answer." Confidentially: "The old mercantile treaties with Betelgeuse guarantee monopolies in certain exports to their traders. This other race is taking payment in the same articles. I am not bound by oaths sworn by the Nuru Bator dynasty, but at present it would be inexpedient that Betelgeuse discover the facts."

It was a good spur-of-the-moment lie: so good that Flandry hoped Oleg would believe he had fallen for it. He assumed a fatuous Look-Mom-I'm-a-man-of-the-world smirk. "I understand, great Khan. You may rely on Terrestrial discretion."

"I hope so," said Oleg humorously. "Our traditional punishment for spies involves a method to keep them alive for days after they have been flayed."

Flandry's gulp was calculated, but not altogether faked. "It is best to remind your majesty," he said, "just in case some of your less well-educated citizens should act impulsively, that the Imperial Navy is under standing orders to redress any wrong suffered by any Terran national anywhere in the universe."

"Very rightly," said Oleg. His tone made clear his knowledge that that famous rule had become a dead letter, except as an occasional excuse for bombarding some obstreperous world unable to fight back. Between the traders, his own study missions sent to Betelgeuse, and whoever was arming him—the Kha Khan had become as unmercifully well-informed about galactic politics as any Terran aristocrat.

Or Merseian. The realization was chilling. Flandry had perforce gone blind into his assignment. Only now, piece by piece, did he see how big and dangerous it was.

"A sound policy," continued Oleg. "But let us be perfectly frank, Orluk. If you should suffer, let us say, accidental harm in my dominions—and *if* your masters should misinterpret the circumstances, though of course they would not—I should be forced to invoke assistance which is quite readily available."

Merseia isn't far, thought Flandry, *and Intelligence knows they've massed naval units at their closest base. If I want to hoist Terran vintages again, I'd better start acting the fool as never before in a gloriously misspent life.*

Aloud, a hint of bluster: "Betelgeuse has treaties with the Imperium, your majesty. They would not interfere in a purely interhuman dispute!" And then, as if appalled at himself: "But surely there won't be any. The, uh, conversation has, uh, taken an undesirable turn. Most unfortunate, your majesty! I was ah, am interested in, er, unusual human colonies, and it was suggested to me by an archivist that—"

And so on and so on.

Oleg Yesukai grinned.

☼ **IV** ☼

Altai rotated once in 35 hours. The settlers had adapted, and
Flandry was used to postponing sleep. He spent the afternoon
being guided around Ulan Baligh, asking silly questions which
he felt sure his guides would relay to the Khan. The practice of
four or five meals during the long day—his were offered in the
town houses of chieftains belonging to Clan Yesukai—gave him
a chance to build up the role of a young Terran fop who had
wangled this assignment from an uninterested Imperium, simply
for a lark. A visit to one of the joyhouses, operated for transient
nomads, helped reinforce the impression. Also, it was fun.

Emerging after sunset, he saw the Prophet's Tower turned luminous, so that it stood like a bloody lance over brawling, flicker-lit
streets. The tablet wall was white, the words thereon in jet: two
kilometers of precepts for a stern and bitter way of life. "I say,"
he exclaimed, "we haven't toured that yet. Let's go."

The chief guide, a burly gray warrior leathered by decades
of wind and frost, looked uneasy. "We must hasten back to the
palace, Orluk," he said. "A banquet is being prepared."

"Oh, fine. Fine! Though I don't know how much of an orgy I'm
in any shape for after this bout. Eh, what?" Flandry nudged the
man's ribs with an indecent thumb. "Still, a peek inside, really I
must. It's unbelievable, that skyscraper, don't you know."

"We must first cleanse ourselves."

A young man added bluntly: "In no case could it be allowed.
You are not an initiate, and there is no holier spot in all the stars."

"Oh, well, in that case—Mind if I photograph it tomorrow?"

"Yes," said the young man. "It is not forbidden, perhaps, but we
could not be responsible for what the ordinary tribesman who saw
you with your camera might do. None but the Tebtengri would
look on the Tower with anything but reverent eyes."

"Teb—"

"Rebels and heathen, up in the north." The older man touched
brow and lips, a sign against evil. "Magic-workers at Tengri Nor,
traffickers with the Ice People. It is not well to speak of them,
only to exterminate them. Now we must hasten, Orluk."

"Oh, yes. Yes. To be sure. Yes, indeed." Flandry scrambled into
the tulyak, an open motor carriage with a dragon figurehead.

As he was driven to the palace, he weighed what he knew in an uncomforting balance. Something was going on, much bigger than a local war. Oleg Khan had no intention Terra should hear about it. A Terran agent who actually learned a bit of truth would not go home alive; only a well-born idiot could safely be allowed return passage. Whether or not Flandry could convince the Altaians he was that idiot, remained to be seen. It wouldn't be easy, for certainly he must probe deeper.

Furthermore, my lad, if somehow you do manage to swirl your cloak, twiddle your mustache, and gallop off to call an Imperial task force, Oleg may summon his friends. They are obviously not a private gun-selling concern, as he wants me to think; all Altai couldn't produce enough trade goods to pay for that stuff. So, if the friends get here first and decide to protect this military investment of theirs, there's going to be a fight. And with them dug in on the surface, as well as cruising local space, they'll have all the advantages. The Navy won't thank you, lad, if you drag them into a losing campaign.

He kindled a fresh cigaret and wondered miserably why he hadn't told HQ he was down with Twonk's Disease.

The valet assigned to him, at his guest suite in the palace, was a little puzzled by Terran garments. Flandry spent half an hour choosing his own ensemble. At last, much soothed, he followed an honor guard, who carried bared daggers in their hands, to the banquet hall, where he was placed at the Khan's right.

There was no table. A great stone trough stretched the length of the hall, a hundred men sitting cross-legged on either side. Broth, reminiscent of won-ton soup but with a sharp taste, was poured into it from wheeled kettles. When next the Khan signaled, the soup was drained through traps, spigots flushed the trough clean, and even less identifiable solid dishes were shoveled in. Meanwhile cups of hot, powerfully alcoholic herb tea were kept filled, a small orchestra caterwauled on pipes and drums, and there were some fairly spectacular performances by varyak riders, knife dancers, acrobats, and marksmen. At the meal's end, an old tribal bard stood up and chanted lays; a plump and merry little man was summoned from the bazaars downtown to tell his original stories; gifts from the Khan were given every man present; and the affair broke up. Not a word of conversation had been spoken.

Oh, well, I'm sure everyone else had a hilarious time, Flandry grumbled to himself.

Not quite sober, he followed his guards back to his apartment. The valet bade him goodnight and closed the thick fur drapes which served for internal doors.

There was a radiant globe illuminating the room, but it seemed feeble next to the light filling a glazed balcony window. Flandry opened this and looked out in wonder.

Beneath him lay the darkened city. Past twinkling red campfires, Ozero Rurik stretched in blackness and multiple moonshivers, out to an unseen horizon. On his left the Prophet's Tower leaped up, a perpetual flame crowned with unwinking winter-brilliant stars. Both moons were near the full, ruddy discs six and eight times as broad to the eye as Luna, haloed by ice crystals. Their light drenched the plains, turned the Zeya and Talyma into ribbons of mercury. But the rings dominated all else, bridging the southern sky with pale rainbows. Second by second, thin fire-streaks crossed heaven up there, as meteoric particles from that huge double band hurtled into the atmosphere.

Flandry was not much for gaping at landscapes. But this time it took minutes for him to realize how frigid the air was.

He turned back to the comparative warmth of his suite. As he closed the window, a woman entered from the bedroom.

Flandry had expected some such hospitality. He saw that she was taller than most Altaians, with long blue-black hair and lustrous tilted eyes of a greenish hue rare on this planet. Otherwise a veil and a gold-stiffened cloak hid her. She advanced quickly, till she was very near him, and he waited for some token of submission.

Instead, she stood watching him for close to a minute. It grew so still in the room that he heard the wind on the lake. Shadows were thick in the corners, and the dragons and warriors on the tapestries appeared to stir.

Finally, in a low uneven voice, she said: "Orluk, are you indeed a spy from the Mother of Men?"

"Spy?" Flandry thought, horrified, about *agents provocateurs.* "Good cosmos, no! I mean, that is to say, nothing of the sort!"

She laid a hand on his wrist. The fingers were cold, and clasped him with frantic strength. Her other hand slipped the veil aside. He looked upon a broad fair-skinned face, delicately arched nose, full mouth, and firm chin: handsome rather than pretty. She whispered, so fast and fiercely he had trouble following:

"Whatever you are, you must listen! If you are no warrior, then give the word when you go home to those who are. I am Bourtai Ivanskaya of the Tumurji folk, who belonged to the Tebtengri Shamanate. Surely you have heard speak of them, enemies of Oleg, driven into the north but still at war with him. My father was a noyon, a division commander, well known to Juchi Ilyak. He fell at the battle of Rivers Meet, last year, where the Yesukai men took our whole ordu. I was brought here alive, partly as a hostage—" A flare of haughtiness: "As if that could influence my people!—and partly for the Kha Khan's harem. Since then I have gained a little of his confidence. More important, I have my own connection now, the harem is always a center of intrigue, nothing is secret from it for very long, but much which is secret begins there—"

"I know," said Flandry. He was stunned, almost overwhelmed, but could not help adding: "Bedfellows make strange politics."

She blinked incomprehension and plunged on: "I heard today that a Terran envoy was landed. I thought perhaps, perhaps he was come, knowing a little of what Oleg Yesukai readies against the Mother of Men. Or if he does not, he must be told! I found what woman would be lent him, and arranged the substitution of myself. Ask me not how! I have wormed secrets which give me power over more than one harem guard—it is not enough to load them with antisex hormone on such a tour of duty! I had the right. Oleg Khan is my enemy and the enemy of my dead father, all means of revenge are lawful to me. But more, worse, Holy Terra lies in danger. Listen, Terra man—" Flandry awoke. For those few seconds, it had been so fantastic he couldn't react. Like a bad stereodrama, the most ludicrous cliches, he was confronted with a girl (it would be a girl, too, and not simply a disgruntled man!) who babbled her autobiography as prologue to some improbable revelation. Now suddenly he understood that this was real: that melodrama does happen once in a while. And if he got caught playing the hero, any role except comic relief, he was dead.

He drew himself up, fended Bourtai off, and said in haste: "My dear young lady, I have not the slightest competence in these matters. Furthermore, I've heard far more plausible stories from far too many colonial girls hoping for a free ride to Terra. Which, I assure you, is actually not a nice place at all for a little colonial girl without funds. I do not wish to offend local pride, but the idea that a single backward planet could offer any threat to the Imperium would be funny if it were not so yawnworthy. I beg you, spare me."

Bourtai stepped back. The cloak fell open. She wore a translucent gown which revealed a figure somewhat stocky for Terran taste but nonetheless full and supple. He would have enjoyed watching that, except for the uncomprehending pain on her face.

"But, my lord Orluk," she stammered, "I swear to you by the Mother of us both—"

You poor romantic, it cried in him, *what do you think I am, a god? If you're such a yokel you never heard of planting microphones in a guest room, Oleg Khan is not. Shut up before you kill us both!*

Aloud, he got out a delighted guffaw. "Well, by Sirius, I do call this thoughtful. Furnishing me with a beautiful spy atop everything else! But honestly, darling, you can drop the pretense now. Let's play some more adult games, eh, what?"

He reached out for her. She writhed free, ran across the room, dodged his pursuit and almost shouted through swift tears: "No, you fool, you blind brainless cackler, you will listen! You will listen if I must knock you to the floor and tie you up—and tell them, tell when you come home, ask them only to send a real spy and learn for themselves!"

Flandry cornered her. He grabbed both flailing wrists and tried to stop her mouth with a kiss. She brought her forehead hard against his nose. He staggered back, half blind with the pain, and heard her yelling: "It is the Merseians, great greenskinned monsters with long tails, the Merseians, I tell you, who come in secret from a secret landing field. I have seen them myself, walking these halls after dark, I have heard from a girl to whom a drunken orkhon babbled, I have crept like a rat in the walls and listened myself. They are called Merseians, the most terrible enemy your race and mine have yet known, and—"

Flandry sat down on a couch, wiped blood off his mustache, and said weakly: "Never mind that for now. How do we get out of here? Before the guards come to shoot us down, I mean."

✲ V ✲

Bourtai fell silent, and he realized he had spoken in Anglic. He realized further that they wouldn't be shot, except to prevent escape. They would be questioned, gruesomely.

He didn't know if there were lenses as well as microphones in the walls. Nor did he know if the bugs passed information on to some watchful human, or only recorded data for study in the morning. He dared assume nothing but the former.

Springing to his feet, he reached Bourtai in one bound. She reacted with feline speed. A hand, edge on, cracked toward his larynx. He had already dropped his head, and took the blow on the hard top of his skull. His own hands gripped the borders of her cloak and crossed forearms at her throat. Before she could jab him in the solar plexus, he yanked her too close to him. She reached up thumbs, to scoop out his eyeballs. He rolled his head and was merely scratched on the nose. After the last buffet, that hurt. He yipped, but didn't let go. A second later, she went limp in his strangle.

He whirled her around, got an arm lock, and let her sag against him. She stirred. So brief an oxygen starvation had brought no more than a moment's unconsciousness. He buried his face in her dark flowing hair, as if he were a lover. It had a warm, somehow summery smell. He found an ear and breathed softly:

"You little gristlehead, did it ever occur to you that the Khan is suspicious of me? That there must be listeners? Now our forlorn chance is to get out of here. Steal a Betelgeusean spaceship, maybe. First, though, I must pretend I am arresting you, so they won't come here with too much haste and alertness for us. Understand? Can you play the part?"

She grew rigid. He felt her almost invisible nod. The hard young body leaning on him eased into a smoothness of controlled nerve and muscle. He had seldom known a woman this competent in a physical emergency. Unquestionably, Bourtai Ivanskaya had military training.

She was going to need it.

Aloud, Flandry huffed: "Well, I've certainly never heard anything more ridiculous! There aren't any Merseians around here. I checked very carefully before setting out. Wouldn't want to come across them, don't you know, and spend maybe a year in some dreary Merseian jail while the pater negotiated my release. Eh, what? Really now, it's perfect rot, every word." He hemmed and hawed a bit. "I think I'd better turn you in, madam. Come along, now, no tricks!"

He marched her out the door, into a pillared corridor. One end opened on a window, twenty meters above a night-frozen fishpond. The other stretched into dusk, lit by infrequent bracketed lamps. Flandry hustled Bourtai down that side. Presently they came to a downward-sweeping staircase. A pair of sentries, in helmets, leather jackets, guns and knives, stood posted there. One of them aimed and barked: "Halt! What would you?"

"This girl, don't you know," panted Flandry. He nudged Bourtai, who gave some realistic squirmings. "Started to babble all sorts of wild nonsense. Who's in charge here? She thought I'd help her against the Kha Khan. Imagine!"

"What?" A guardsman trod close.

"The Tebtengri will avenge me!" snarled Bourtai. "The Ice People will house in the ruin of this palace!"

Flandry thought she was overacting, but the guards both looked shocked. The nearer one sheathed his blaster. "I shall hold her, Orluk," he said. "Boris, run for the commander."

As he stepped close, Flandry let the girl go. With steel on his pate and stiff leather on his torso, the sentry wasn't very vulnerable. Except—Flandry's right hand rocketed upward. The heel of it struck the guard under the nose. He lurched backward, caromed off the balustrade, and flopped dead on the stairs. The other, half-turned to go, spun about on one booted heel. He snatched for his weapon. Bourtai put a leg behind his ankles and pushed. Down he went, Flandry pounced. They rolled over, clawing for a grip. The guard yelped. Flandry saw Bourtai over his opponent's shoulder. She had taken the belt off the first warrior and circled about with the leather in her hands. Flandry let his enemy get on top. Bourtai put the belt around the man's neck, a knee between his shoulder-blades, and heaved.

Flandry scrambled from below. "Get their blasters," he gasped. "Here, give me one. Quick! We've made more racket than I hoped. Do you know the best way to escape? Lead on, then!"

Bourtai raced barefoot down the steps. Her goldcloth cloak and frail gown streamed behind her, insanely, unfitting for the occasion. Flandry came behind, one flight, two flights.

Boots clattered on marble. Rounding yet another spiral curve, Flandry met a squad of soldiers quick-stepping upward. The leader hailed him: "Do you have the evil woman, Orluk?"

So there had been a continuous listener. Of course, even surrendering Bourtai, Flandry could not save his own skin. Harmless fop or no, he had heard too much.

The squad's eyes registered the girl's blaster even as their chief spoke. Someone yelled. Bourtai fired into the thick of them. Ionic lightning crashed. Flandry dropped. A bolt sizzled where he had been. He fired, wide-beam, the energy too diluted to kill even at this range but scorching four men at once. As their screams lifted, he bounced back to his feet, overleaped the fallen front line, stiff-armed a warrior beyond, and hit the landing.

From here, a bannister curled grandly to the ground floor. Flandry whooped, seated himself, and slid. At the bottom was a sort of lobby, with glass doors opening on the garden. The moons and rings were so bright that no headlights shone from the half-dozen varyaks roaring toward this entrance. Mounted guardsmen, attracted by· the noise of the fight—Flandry stared around. Arched windows flanked the doors, two meters up. He gestured to Bourtai, crouched beneath one and made a stirrup of his hands. She nodded, soared to the sill, broke glass with her gun butt, and fired into the troop. Flandry took shelter behind a column and blasted loose at the remnant of the infantry squad, stumbling down the stairs in pursuit. Their position hopelessly exposed to him, they retreated from sight.

A varyak leaped through the doors. The arms of the soldier aboard it shielded his face against flying glass. Flandry shot before the man had uncovered himself. The varyak, sensitively controlled, veered and went down across the doorway. The next one hurtled over it. The rider balanced himself with a trained body, blazing away at the Terran. Bourtai dropped him from above.

She sprang down unassisted. "I got two more outside," she said. "Another pair are lurking, calling for help—"

"We'll have to chance them. Where are the nearest gates?"

"They will be closed! We cannot burn through the lock before—"

"I'll find a means. Quick, up on this saddle. Slowly, now, out the door behind me. Right the putt-putts of those two men you killed and stand by." Flandry had already dragged a corpse from one varyak (not without an instant's compassionate wondering what the man had been like alive) and set the machine back on its wheels. He sprang to the seat and went full speed out the shattered door.

So far, energy weapons had fulfilled their traditional military function, giving more value to purposeful speed of action than mere numbers. But there was a limit: two people couldn't stave off hundreds for very long. He had to get clear.

Flame sought him. He lacked skill to evade such fire by tricky riding. Instead, he plunged straight down the path, crouched low and hoping he wouldn't be pierced. A bolt burned one leg, slightly but with savage pain. He reached the gloomy, high-arched bridge he wanted. His cycle snorted up and over. Just beyond the hump, he dropped off, relaxing muscles and cushioning himself with an arm in judoka style. Even so, he bumped his nose. For a moment, tears blinded him, and he used bad words. Then the two enemy varyaks followed each other across the bridge. He sprang up on the railing, unseen, and shot both men as they went by.

Vaguely, he heard an uproar elsewhere. One by one, the palace windows lit, until scores of dragon eyes glared into night. Flandry slid down the bridge, disentangled the heaped varyaks, and hailed Bourtai. "Bring the other machines!" She came, riding one and leading two more by tethers to the guide bars. He had felt reasonably sure that would be standard equipment; if these things were commonly used by nomads, there'd be times when a string of pack vehicles was required.

"We take two," he muttered. Here, beneath an overleaning rock, they were a pair of shadows. Moonlight beyond made the garden one fog of coppery light. The outer wall cut that off, brutally black, with merlons raised against Altai's rings like teeth. "The rest, we use to ram down the gates. Can do?"

"Must do!" she said, and set the varyak control panels. "Here. Extra helmets and clothing are always kept in the saddlebags. Put on the helmet, at least. The clothes we can don later."

"We won't need them for a short dash—"

"Do you think the spaceport is not now a-crawl with Yesukai men?"

"Oh, hell," said Flandry.

He buckled on the headgear, snapped down the goggles, and mounted anew. Bourtai ran along the varyak line, flipping main switches. The riderless machines took off. Gravel spurted from their wheels into Flandry's abused face. He followed the girl.

A pair of warriors raced down a cross path briefly stark under the moons and then eaten again by murk. They had not seen their quarry. The household troops must be in one classic confusion, Flandry thought. He had to escape before hysteria faded and systematic hunting was organized.

The palace gates loomed before him, heavy bars screening off a plaza that was death-white in the moon radiance. Flandry saw his varyaks only as meteoric gleams. Sentries atop the wall had a better view. Blasters thundered, machine guns raved, but there were no riders to drop from those saddles.

The first varyak hit with a doomsday clangor. It rebounded in four pieces. Flandry sensed a chunk of red-hot metal buzz past his ear. The next one crashed, and the bars buckled. The third smote and collapsed across a narrow opening. The fourth flung the gates wide. *"Now!"*

At 200 KPH, Bourtai and Flandry made for the gateway. They had a few seconds without fire from the demoralized men above them. Bourtai hit the toppled machines. Her own climbed that pile, took off, and soared halfway across the plaza. Flandry saw her balance herself, precise as a bird, land on two wheels and vanish in an alley beyond the square. Then it was his turn. He wondered fleetingly what the chances of surviving a broken neck were, and hoped he would not. Not with the Khan's interrogation chambers waiting. Whoops, bang, here we go! He knew he couldn't match Bourtai's performance. He slammed down the third wheel in midair. He hit ground with less violence than expected: first-class shock absorbers on this cycle. An instant he teetered, almost rolling over. He came down on his outrigger. Fire spattered off stone behind him. He retracted the extra wheel and gunned his motor.

A glance north, past the Tower toward the spaceport, showed him grav-beam air-boats aloft, a hornet swarm. He had no prayer of hijacking a Betelgeusean ship. Nor was it any use to flee to Zalat in the yamen. Where, then, beneath these unmerciful autumnal stars?

Bourtai was a glimpse in moonlight, half a kilometer ahead of him down a narrow nighted street. He let her take the lead, concentrated grimly on avoiding accidents. It seemed like an eyeblink, and it seemed like forever, before they were out of the city and onto the open steppe.

✴ **VI** ✴

Wind lulled in long grasses, the whispering ran for kilometers, on and on beyond the world's edge, pale yellow-green in a thousand subtle hues rippled by the wind's footsteps. Here and there the spiky red of some frost-nipped bush thrust up; the grasses swirled about it like a sea. High and high overhead, incredibly high, an infinite vault full of wind and deep blue chill, the sky reached. Krasna burned low in the west, dull orange, painting the steppe with ruddy light and fugitive shadows. The rings were an ice bridge to the south; northward the sky had a bleak greenish shimmer which Bourtai said was reflection off an early snowfall.

Flandry crouched in grasses as tall as himself. When he ventured a peek, he saw the airboat that hunted them. It spiraled lazy, but the mathematics guiding it and its cohorts wove a net around this planet. To his eyes, even through binoculars taken from a saddlebag, the boat was so far as to be a mere metallic flash; but he knew it probed for him with telescopes, ferrous detectors, infrared amplifiers.

He would not have believed he could escape the Khan's hundreds of searching craft this long. Two Altaian days, was it? Memory had faded. He knew only a fever dream of bounding north on furious wheels, his skin dried and bleeding from the air; sleeping a few seconds at a time, in the saddle, eating jerked meat from the varyak supplies as he rode, stopping to refill canteens at a waterhole Bourtai had found by signs invisible to him. He knew only how he ached, to the nucleus of his inmost cell, and how his brain was gritty from weariness.

But the plain was unbelievably huge, almost twice the land area of all Terra. The grass was often as high as this, veiling prey from sky-borne eyes. They had driven through several big herds, to break their trail; they had dodged and woven under Bourtai's guidance, and she had a hunter's knowledge of how to confuse pursuit.

Now, though, the chase seemed near its end.

Flandry glanced at the girl. She sat cross-legged, impassive, showing her own exhaustion just by the darkening under her eyes. In stolen leather clothes, hair braided under the crash helmet, she might have been a boy. But the grease smeared on her face for protection had not much affected its haughty good looks. The man hefted his gun. "Think he'll spot us?" he asked. He didn't speak low, but the blowing immensities around reduced all voices to nothing.

"Not yet," she answered. "He is at the extreme detector range, and cannot swoop down at every dubious flicker of instrument readings."

"So . . . ignore him and he'll go away?"

"I fear not." She grew troubled. "They are no fools, the Khan's troopers. I know that search pattern. He and his fellows will circle about, patrolling much the same territory until nightfall. Then, as you know, if we try to ride further, we must turn on the heaters of our varyaks or freeze to death. And that will make us a flame to the infrared spotters."

Flandry rubbed his smooth chin. Altaian garments were ridiculously short on him, so thank all elegant gods for antibeard enzyme! He wished he dared smoke. "What can we do?" he said.

She shrugged. "Stay here. There are well-insulated sleeping bags, which ought to keep us alive if we share a single one. But if the local temperature drops far enough below zero, our own breath and body radiation may betray us."

"How close are we to your friends?"

Bourtai rubbed tired hazel eyes. "I cannot say. They move about, under the Khrebet and along the Kara Gobi fringe. At this time of year they will be drifting southward, so we are not so terribly far from one or another ordu, I suppose. Still, distances are never small on the steppe." After a moment: "If we live the night, we can still not drive to find them. The varyaks' energy cells are nigh exhausted. We shall have to walk."

Flandry glanced at the vehicles, now battered and dusty beyond recognition. Wonderfully durable gadgets, he thought in a vague way. Largely handmade, of course, using small power tools and the care possible in a nonmercantile economy. The radios, though, were short range. . . . No use getting wistful. The first call for Tebtengri help would bring that aircraft overhead down like a swooping falcon.

He eased himself to his back and let his muscles throb. The ground was cold under him. After a moment, Bourtai followed suit, snuggling close in somehow childlike trustfulness.

"If we do not escape, well, such is the space-time pattern," she said, more calmly than he could have managed. "But if we do, what then is your plan, Orluk?"

"Get word to Terra, I suppose. Don't ask me how."

"Will not your friends come avenging when you fail to return?"

"No. The Khan need only tell the Betelgeuseans that I, regrettably, died in some accident or riot or whatever, and will be cremated with full honors. It would not be difficult to fake: a blaster-charred corpse about my size, perhaps, for one human looks much like another to the untrained nonhuman. Word will reach my organization, and naturally some will suspect, but they have so much else to do that the suspicion will not appear strong enough to act on. The most they will do is send another agent like myself. And this time, expecting him, the Khan can fool him: camouflage the new installations, make sure our man talks only to the right people and sees only the right things. What can one man do against a planet?"

"You have done somewhat already."

"But I told you, I caught Oleg by surprise."

"You will do more," she continued serenely. "Can you not, for instance, smuggle a letter out through some Betelgeusean? We can get agents into Ulan Baligh."

"I imagine the same thought has occurred to the Khan. He will make sure no one he is not certain of has any contact with any Betelgeusean, and will search all export material with care."

"Write a letter in the Terran language."

"He can read that himself, if no one else."

"Oh, no." Bourtai raised herself on one elbow. "There is not a human on all Altai except yourself who reads the—what do you call it?—the Anglic. Some Betelgeuseans do, of course, but no Altaian has ever learned; there seemed no pressing reason. Oleg himself reads only Altaian and the principal Betelgeusean language. I know; he mentioned it to me one night recently." She spoke quite coolly of her past year. Flandry gathered that in this culture it was no disgrace to have been a harem slave: fortunes of war.

"Even worse," he said. "I can just see Oleg's agents permitting a document in an unknown alphabet to get out. In fact, from now until whenever they have me dead, I doubt if they will let anything they are not absolutely sure about come near a spaceship, or a spacefarer."

Bourtai sat up straight. Sudden, startling tears blurred her gaze. "But you cannot be helpless!" she cried. "You are from Terra."

He didn't want to disillusion her. "We'll see." Hastily plucking a stalk of grass and chewing it: "This tastes almost like home. Remarkable similarity."

"Oh, but it is of Terran origin." Bourtai's dismay changed mercurially to simple astonishment that he should not know what was so everyday to her. "The first colonists here found the steppe a virtual desert—only sparse plant forms, poisonous to man. All other native life had retreated into the Arctic and Antarctic. Our ancestors mutated what seeds and small animals they had along, created suitable strains, and released them. Terrestroid ecology soon took over the whole unfrozen belt."

Flandry noticed once more that Bourtai's nomadic life had not made her a simple barbarian. Hm, it would be most interesting to see what a true civilization on wheels was like...if he survived, which was dubious.... He was too tired to concentrate. His thoughts drifted off along a pattern of fact and deduction, mostly things he knew already.

Krasna was obviously an old sun, middle Population Two, drifted from the galactic nucleus into this spiral arm. As such, it—and its planets—were poor in the heavier elements, which are formed within the stars, scattered by novae and supernovae, and accumulated in the next stellar generation. Being smaller than Sol, Krasna had matured slowly, a red dwarf through most of its long existence.

Initially, for the first billion years or so, internal heat had made Altai more or less Terrestroid in temperature. Protoplasmic life had evolved in shallow seas, and probably the first crude land forms. But when moltenness and most radioactivity were used up, only the dull sun furnished heat. Altai froze. It happened slowly enough for life to adapt during the long period of change.

And then, while who knew how many megacenturies passed, Altai was ice-bound from pole to pole. An old, old world, so old that one moon had finally spiraled close and shattered to make the rings: so old, indeed, that its sun had completed the first stage of hydrogen burning and moved into the next. From now on, for the next several million years, Krasna would get, hotter and brighter. At last Altai's seas, liquid again, would boil; beyond that, the planet itself would boil, as Krasna became nova; and beyond that the star would be a white dwarf, sinking toward ultimate darkness.

But as yet the process was only begun. Only the tropics had reached a temperature men could endure. Most of the water fled thence and snowed down on the still frigid polar quarters, leaving dry plains where a few plants struggled to re-adapt...and were destroyed by this invading green grass....

Flandry's mind touched the remote future of his own planet, and recoiled. A gelid breeze slid around him. He grew aware how stiff and chilly he was. And the sun not even set!

He groaned back to a sitting position. Bourtai sat calm in her fatalism. Flandry envied her. But it was not in him, to accept the chance of freezing—to walk, if he survived this night, over hundreds of parched kilometers, through cold strengthening hour by autumn hour.

His mind scuttered about, a trapped weasel seeking any bolthole. Fire, fire, my chance of immortality for a fire—*Hoy, there!*

He sprang to his feet, remembered the aircraft, and hit dirt again so fast that he bumped his bruised nose. The girl listened wide-eyed to his streaming, sputtering Anglic. When he had finished, she sketched a reverent sign. "I too pray the Spirit of the Mother that She guide us," said Bourtai.

Flandry skinned his teeth in a grin. "I, uh, wasn't precisely praying, my dear. No, I think I've a plan. Wild, but—now, listen—"

✹ VII ✹

Arghun Tiliksky thrust his face out of that shadow which blurred the ring of cross-legged men, into the scant sunlight trickling through a small window of the kibitka. "It was evil," he declared sharply. "Nothing is more dreaded than a grass fire. And you set one! No luck can come from such a deed."

Flandry studied him. The noyon of the Mangu Tuman was quite young, even for these times when few men of Tebtengri reached great age; and a dashing, gallant warrior, as everyone said and as he had proved in the rescue. But to some extent, Arghun was the local equivalent of a prude.

"The fire was soon put out, wasn't it?" asked the Terran mildly. "I heard from your scout, the Kha Khan's aircraft swarmed there and tossed foam bombs down till the flames were smothered. Not many hectares were burned over."

"In such tasks," said Toghrul Vavilov, Gur-Khan of the tribe, "all Altaians are one." He stroked his beard and traded bland smiles with Flandry: a kindred hypocrite. "Our scout needed but to carry a few foam bombs himself, and no enemy vessel would molest him. He observed them and returned here in peace."

One of the visiting chieftains exclaimed: "Your noyon verges on blasphemy himself, Toghrul. Sir Dominic is from Terra! If a lord of Terra wishes to set a blaze, who dares deny him?"

Flandry felt he ought to blush, but decided not to. "Be that as it may," he said, "I couldn't think of any better plan. Not all the tribal leaders who have come to this—what do you call the meeting?—this kurultai, have heard just what happened. The girl Bourtai and myself were trapped with little power left in our varyaks, and the probability of freezing or starving in a few more days if we were not detected by infra-red that same night. So, soon after dark, I scurried about on foot, setting fires which quickly coalesced into one. The wind swept the flames from us—but the radiation of our varyak heaters was still undetectable against such a background! Since we could not be extremely far as negagrav flight goes from some ordu of the Shamanate, it seemed likely that at least one aerial scout would come near to investigate the fire. Therefore, after a while, we broke radio silence to call for help. Then we ducked and dodged, hunted by the gathering vessels of Oleg, somewhat screened by the heat and smoke...until a flying war party from the Mangu Tuman arrived, beat off the foe, and escaped with us before more of the enemy should arrive."

"And so this council has been called," added Toghrul Vavilov. "The chiefs of all our allied tribes must understand what we now face."

"But the fire—" mumbled Arghun.

Eyes went through gloom to an old man seated under the window. Furs covered frail Juchi Ilyak so thickly that his bald parchment-skinned head looked disembodied. The Shaman stroked a wisp of white beard, blinked eyes that were still sharp, and murmured with a dry little smile: "This is not the time to dispute whether the rights of a man from Holy Terra override the Yassa by which Altai lives. The question seems rather, how shall we all survive in order to raise such legal quibbles at another date?"

Arghun tossed his reddish-black hair and snorted: "Oleg's father, and the whole Nuru Bator dynasty before him, tried to beat down the Tebtengri. But still we hold the northlands. I do not think this will change overnight."

"Oh, but it will," said Flandry in his softest voice. "Unless something is done, it will."

He treated himself to one of the few remaining cigarets and leaned forward so the light would pick out his features, exotic on this planet. He said: "Throughout your history, you have waged war, as you have driven your machines, with chemical power and stored solar energy. A few small, stationary nuclear generators at Ulan Baligh and the mines are all that your way of life demanded. Your economy would not have supported atomic war, even if feuds and boundary disputes were worth it. So you Tebtengri have remained strong enough to hold these subarctic pastures, though all other tribes were to ally against you. Am I right?"

They nodded. He continued: "But now Oleg Khan is getting help from outside. Some of his new toys I have seen with my own eyes. Craft which can fly flourishes around yours, or go beyond the atmosphere to swoop down again; battlecars whose armor your strongest chemical explosives cannot pierce; missiles to devastate so wide an area that no dispersal can save you. As yet, he has not much modern equipment. But more will arrive during the next several months, until he has enough to crush you. And, still worse, he will have allies that are not human."

They stirred uneasily, some of them making signs against witchcraft. Only Juchi the Shaman remained quiet, watching Flandry with impassive eyes. A clay pipe in his hand sent bitter incense toward the roof. "Who are these creatures?" he asked calmly.

"Merseians," said Flandry. "Another imperial race than man— and man stands in the path of their ambitions. For long now we have been locked with them, nominally at peace, actually probing for weaknesses, subverting, assassinating, skirmishing. They have decided Altai would make a useful naval base. Outright invasion would be expensive, especially if Terra noticed and interfered: and we probably would notice, since we watch them so closely. But if the Merseians supply Oleg with just enough help so that he can conquer the whole planet for them—do you see? Once he has done that, the Merseian engineers will arrive; Altaians will dig and die to build fortresses; this entire world will be one impregnable net of strongholds... and then Terra is welcome to learn what has been going on!"

"Does Oleg himself know this?" snapped Toghrul.

Flandry shrugged. "Insufficiently well, I imagine. Like many another puppet ruler, he will live to see the strings his masters have tied on him. But that will be too late. I've watched this sort of thing happen elsewhere.

"In fact," he added, "I've helped bring it about now and then—on Terra's behalf!"

Toghrul entwined nervous fingers. "I believe you," he said. "We have all had glimpses, heard rumors. . . . What is to be done? Can we summon the Terrans?"

"Aye—aye—call the Terrans, warn the Mother of Men—" Flandry felt how passion flared up in the scarred warriors around him. He had gathered that the Tebtengri had no use for Subotai the Prophet but built their own religion around a hard-boiled sort of humanistic pantheism. It grew on him how strong a symbol the ancestral planet was to them.

He didn't want to tell them what Terra was actually like these days. (Or perhaps had always been. He suspected men are only saints and heroes in retrospect.) Indeed, he dare not speak of sottish Emperors, venal nobles, faithless wives, servile commons, to this armed and burning reverence. *But luckily, there's a practical problem at hand.*

"Terra is farther from here than Merseia," he said. "Even our nearest base is more distant than theirs. I don't believe any Merseians are on Altai at this moment, but surely Oleg has at least one swift spaceship at his disposal, to inform his masters if anything should go wrong. Let us get word to Terra, and let Oleg learn this has happened, what do you think he'll do?" Flandry nodded, owlish. "Right, on the first guess! Oleg will send to that nearest Merseian base, where I know a heavy naval force is currently stationed. I doubt very much if the Merseians will write off their investment tamely. No, they will dispatch their ships at once, occupy various points, blast the Tebtengri lands with nuclear bombs, and dig in. It will not be as smooth and thorough a job as they now plan, but it will be effective. By the time a Terran fleet of reasonable size can get here, the Merseians will be fairly well entrenched. The most difficult task in space warfare is to get a strong enemy off a planet firmly held. It may prove impossible. But even if, thanks to our precipitating matters, the Terrans do blast the Merseians loose, Altai will have been made into a radioactive desert."

Silence clapped down. Men stared at each other, and back to Flandry, with a horror he had seen before and which was one of the few things it still hurt him to watch. He went on quickly:

"So the one decent objective for us is to get a secret message out. If Oleg and the Merseians don't suspect Terra knows, they won't hasten their program. It can be Terra, instead, which suddenly arrives in strength, seizes Ulan Baligh, establishes ground emplacements and orbital forts. I know Merseian strategy well enough to predict that, under those circumstances, they won't fight. It isn't worth it, since Altai cannot be used as an aggressive base against them." He should have said *will not*; but let these people make the heartbreaking discovery for themselves, that Terra's only real interest was to preserve a fat status quo.

Arghun sprang to his feet. As he crouched under the low ceiling, primness dropped from him. His young leonine face became a sun, he cried: "And Terra will have us! We will be restored to humankind!"

While the Tebtengri whooped and wept at that understanding, Flandry smoked his cigaret with care. After all, he thought, it needn't corrupt them. Not too much. There would be a small naval base, an Imperial governor, an enforced peace between all tribes. Otherwise they could live as they chose. It wasn't worth Terra's while to proselytize. What freedom the Altaians lost here at home, their young men would regain simply by having access to the stars. Wasn't that so? Wasn't it?

�֍ VIII �֍

Juchi the Shaman, who bound together all these chiefs, spoke in a whisper that pierced: "Let us have silence. We must weigh how this may be done."

Flandry waited till the men had seated themselves. Then he gave them a rueful smile. "That's a good question," he said. "Next question, please."

"The Betelgeuseans—" rumbled Toghrul.

"I doubt that," said another gur-khan. "If I were Oleg the Damned, I would put a guard around every individual Betelgeusean, as well as every spaceship, until all danger has passed. I would inspect every trade article, every fur or hide or smokegem, before it was loaded."

"Or send to Merseia at once," shivered someone else.

"No," said Flandry. "Not that. We can be sure Merseia is not going to take such hazardous action without being fairly sure that Terra has heard of their project. They have too many commitments elsewhere."

"Besides," said Juchi, "Oleg Yesukai will not make himself a laughing stock before them—screaming for help because one fugitive is loose in the Khrebet."

"Anyhow," put in Toghrul, "he knows how impossible it is to smuggle such an appeal out. Those tribes not of the Shamanate may dislike the Yesukai tyranny, but they are still more suspicious of us, who traffic with the Ice Dwellers and scoff at that stupid Prophet. Even supposing one of them *would* agree to brand a hide for us, or slip a letter into a bale of pelts, and even supposing that did get past Oleg's inspectors, the cargo might wait months to be loaded, months more in some Betelgeusean warehouse."

"And we don't have so many months, I suppose, before Oleg overruns you and the Merseians arrive as planned," finished Flandry.

He sat for a while listening to their desperate chewing of impractical schemes. It was hot and stuffy in here. All at once he could take no more. He rose. "I need fresh air, and a chance to think," he said.

Juchi nodded grave dismissal. Arghun jumped up again. "I come too," he said.

"If the Terran desires your company," said Toghrul.

"Indeed, indeed." Flandry's agreement was absent-minded.

He went out the door and down a short ladder. The kibitka where the chiefs met was a large, covered truck, its box fitted out as austere living quarters. On top of it, as on all the bigger, slower vehicles, the flat black plates of a solar-energy collector were tilted to face Krasna and charge an accumulator bank. Such roofs made this wandering town, dispersed across the hills, seem like a flock of futuristic turtles.

The Khrebet was not a high range. Gullied slopes ran up, gray-green with thornbush and yellow with sere grass, to a glacial cap in the north. Downward swept a cold wind, whining about Flandry; he shivered and drew the coat, hastily sewn to his measure, tighter about him. The sky was pale today, the rings low and wan in the south, where the hills emptied into steppe.

As far as Flandry could see, the herds of the Mangu Tuman

spread out under care of varyak-mounted boys. They were not cattle. Terra's higher mammals were hard to raise on other planets; rodents are tougher and more adaptable. The first colonists had brought rabbits along, which they mutated and cross-bred systematically. That ancestor could hardly be recognized in the cow-sized grazing beasts of today, more like giant dun guinea pigs than anything else. There were also separate flocks of bio-engineered ostriches.

Arghun gestured with pride.

"Yonder is the library," he said, "and those children seated nearby are being instructed."

Flandry looked at that kibitka. Of course, given microprint, you could carry thousands of volumes along on your travels; illiterates could never have operated these ground vehicles or the negagrav aircraft watchful overhead. Certain other trucks—including some trains of them—must house arsenals, sickbay, machine tools, small factories for textiles and ceramics. Poorer families might live crowded in a single yurt, a round felt tent on a motor cart; but no one looked hungry or ragged. And it was not an impoverished nation which carried such gleaming missiles on flatbed cars, or operated such a flock of light tanks, or armed every adult. Considering Bourtai, Flandry decided that the entire tribe, male and female, must be a military as well as a social and economic unit. Everybody worked, and everybody fought, and in their system the proceeds were more evenly shared than on Terra.

"Where does your metal come from?" he inquired.

"The grazing lands of every tribe include some mines," said Arghun. "We plan our yearly round so as to spend time there, digging and smelting—just as elsewhere we reap grain planted on the last visit, or tap crude oil from our wells and refine it. What we cannot produce ourselves, we trade with others to get."

"It sounds like a virtuous life," said Flandry.

His slight shudder did not escape Arghun, who hastened to say: "Oh, we have our pleasures, too, feasts, games and sports, the arts, the great fair at Kievka Hill each third year—" He broke off.

Bourtai came walking past a campfire. Flandry could sense her loneliness. Women in this culture were not much inferior to men; she was free to go where she would, and was a heroine for having brought the Terran here. But her family were slain and she was not even given work to do.

She saw the men and ran toward them. "Oh...what has been decided?"

"Nothing yet." Flandry caught her hands. By all hot stars, she was a good-looking wench! His face crinkled its best smile. "I couldn't see going in circles with a lot of men, hairy however well-intentioned, when I might be going in circles with you. So I came out here. And my hopes were granted."

A flush crept up her high flat cheeks. She wasn't used to glibness. Her gaze fluttered downward. "I do not know what to say," she whispered.

"You need say nothing. Only be," he leered.

"No—I am no one. The daughter of a dead man... my dowry long ago plundered.... And you are a Terran! It is not right!"

"Do you think your dowry matters?" said Arghun. His voice cracked.

Flandry threw him a surprised glance. At once the warrior's mask was restored. But for an instant, Flandry had seen why Arghun Tiliksky didn't like him.

He sighed. "Come, we had better return to the kurultai," he said.

He didn't release Bourtai, but tucked her arm under his. She followed mutely along. He could feel her tremble a little, through the heavy garments. The wind off the glacier ruffled a stray lock of dark hair.

As they neared the kibitka of the council, its door opened. Juchi Ilyak stood there, bent beneath his years. The wizened lips opened, and somehow the breath carried across meters of blustering air: "Terran, perhaps there is a way for us. Dare you come with me to the Ice Folk?"

✿ IX ✿

Tengri Nor, the Ghost Lake, lay so far north that Altai's rings were only a pale glimmer, half seen by night on the southern horizon. When Flandry and Juchi stepped from their airboat, it was still day. Krasna was an ember, tinging the snowfields red. But it toppled swiftly, purple shadows glided from drift to drift so fast a man could see them.

Flandry had not often met such quietness. Even in space, there was always the low noise of the machinery that kept you alive. Here, the air seemed to freeze all sound; the tiniest wind blew up fine ice crystals, whirling and glistening above diamond-like snowbanks, and it rippled the waters of Tengri Nor, but he could not hear it. He had no immediate sense of cold on his fur-muffled body, even on his thickly greased face—not in this dry atmosphere—but breathing was a sharpness in his nostrils. He thought he could smell the lake, a chemical pungency, but he wasn't sure. None of his Terran senses were quite to be trusted in this winter place.

He said, and the unexpected loudness was like a gunshot, shocking, so that his question ended in a whisper: "Do they know we are here?"

"Oh, yes. They have their ways. They will meet us soon." Juchi looked northward, past the lake shore to the mountainous ruins. Snow had drifted halfway up those marble walls, white on white, with the final sunlight bleeding across shattered colonnades. Frost from the Shaman's breath began to stiffen his beard.

"I suppose they recognize the markings—know this is a friendly craft—but what if the Kha Khan sent a disguised vessel?"

"That was tried once or twice, years ago. The boats were destroyed by some means, far south of here. The Dwellers have their awareness." Juchi raised his arms and started swaying on his feet. A high-pitched chant came from his lips, he threw back his head and closed his eyes.

Flandry had no idea whether the Shaman was indulging superstition, practicing formal ritual, or doing what was actually necessary to summon the glacier folk. He had been in too many strange places to dogmatize. He waited, his eyes ranging the scene.

Beyond the ruins, westward along the northern lake shore, a forest grew. White slender trees with intricate, oddly geometric branches flashed like icicles, like jewels. Their thin bluish leaves vibrated, it seemed they should tinkle, that all this forest was glass, but Flandry had never been near a wilderness so quiet. Low gray plants carpeted the snow between the gleaming boles. Where a rock thrust up here and there, it was almost buried under such lichenoid growth. In some place less cold and hushed, Flandry would have thought of tropical richness.

The lake itself reached out of sight, pale blue between snow-banks. As evening swept across the waters, Flandry could see against shadow that mists hovered above.

Juchi had told him, quite matter-of-factly, that the protoplasmic life native to Altai had adapted to low temperatures in past ages by synthesizing methanol. A fifty-fifty mixture of this and water remained fluid below minus forty degrees. When it finally must freeze, it did not expand into cell-disrupting ice crystals, but became gradually more slushy. Lower life forms remained functional till about seventy below, Celsius; after that they went dormant. The higher animals, being homeothermic, need not suspend animation till the air reached minus a hundred degrees.

Biological accumulation of alcohol kept the polar lakes and rivers fluid till midwinter. The chief problem of all species was to find minerals, in a world largely glaciated. Bacteria brought up some from below; animals traveled far to lick exposed rock, returned to their forests and contributed heavy atoms when they died. But in general, the Altaian ecology made do without. It had never evolved bones for instance, but had elaborated chitinous and cartilaginous materials beyond anything seen on Terra.

The account had sounded plausible and interesting, in a warm kibitka on a grassy slope, with microtexts at hand to give details. When he stood on million-year-old snow, watching night creep up like smoke through crystal trees and cyclopean ruins, hearing Juchi chant under a huge green sunset sky, Flandry discovered that scientific explanations were but little of the truth.

One of the moons was up. Flandry saw something drift across its copper shield. The objects neared, a flock of white spheres, ranging in diameter from a few centimeters to a giant bigger than the airboat. Tentacles streamed downward from them. Juchi broke off. "Ah," he said. "Aeromedusae. The Dwellers cannot be far."

"What?" Flandry hugged himself. The cold was beginning to be felt now, as it gnawed through fur and leather toward flesh.

"Our name for them. They look primitive, but are actually well evolved, with sense organs and brains. They electrolyze hydrogen metabolically to inflate themselves, breathe backward for propulsion, feed on small game which they shock insensible. The Ice Folk have domesticated them."

Flandry stole a glance at a jagged wall, rearing above gloom to catch a sunbeam and flush rose. "They did more than that, once," he said with pity.

Juchi nodded, oddly little impressed. "I daresay intelligence grew up on Altai in response to worsening conditions—the warming sun." His tone was detached. "It built a high civilization, but the shortage of metals was a handicap, and the steady shrinking of the snow area may have led to a cultural collapse. Yet that is not what the Dwellers themselves claim. They have no sense of loss about their past." He squinted slant eyes in a frown, seeking words. "As nearly as I can understand them, which is not much, they... abandoned something unsuitable... they found better methods."

Two beings came from the forest.

At first glance they were like dwarfish white-furred men. Then you saw details of squat build and rubbery limbs. The feet were long and webbed, expandable to broad snowshoes or foldable to short skis. The hands had three fingers opposing a thumb set in the middle of the wrist. The ears were feathery tufts; fine tendrils waved above each round black eye; sad gray monkey faces peered from a ruff of hair. Their breath did not steam like the humans': their body temperature was well below the Celsius zero. One of them bore a stone lamp in which an alcohol flame wavered. The other had an intricately carved white staff; in an undefinable way, the circling medusa flock seemed to be guided by it.

They came near, halted, and waited. Nothing moved but the low wind, ruffling their fur and streaming the flame. Juchi stood as quiet. Flandry made himself conform, though his teeth wanted to clap in his jaws. He had seen many kinds of life, on worlds more foreign than this. But there was a strangeness here which got under his skin and crawled.

The sun went down. Thin dustless air gave no twilight. Stars blazed forth, pyrotechnic in a sudden blackness. The edge of the rings painted a remote arc. The moon threw cuprous radiance over the snow, shadows into the forest.

A meteor split the sky with noiseless lightning. Juchi seemed to take that as a signal. He began talking. His voice was like ice, toning as it contracted in midnight cold: not altogether a human voice. Flandry began to understand what a Shaman was, and why he presided over the northland tribes. Few men were able to master the Dwellers' language and deal with them. Yet trade and alliance—metal given for organic fuel and curious plastic substances; mutual defense against the Kha Khan's sky raiders— was a large part of the Tebtengri strength.

One of the beings made answer. Juchi turned to Flandry. "I have said who you are and whence you come. They are not surprised. Before I spoke your need, he said their—I do not know just what the word means, but it has something to do with communication—he said they could reach Terra itself, as far as mere distance was concerned, but only through . . . dreams?"

Flandry stiffened. It could be. It could be. How long had men been hunting for some faster-than-light equivalent of radio? A handful of centuries. What was that, compared to the age of the universe? Or even the age of Altai? He realized, not simply intellectually but with his whole organism, how old this planet was. In all that time—

"Telepathy?" he blurted. "I've never heard of telepathy with so great a range!"

"No. Not that, or they would have warned us of this Merseian situation before now. It is nothing that I quite understand." Juchi spoke with care: "He said to me, all the powers they possess look useless in this situation."

Flandry sighed. "I might have known it. That would have been too easy. No chance for heroics."

"They have found means to live, less cumbersome than all those buildings and engines were," said Juchi. "They have been free to think for I know not how many ages. But they have therefore grown weak in sheerly material ways. They help us withstand the aggressions from Ulan Baligh; they can do nothing against the might of Merseia."

Half seen in red moonlight, one of the autochthones spoke.

Juchi: "They do not fear racial death. They know all things must end, and yet nothing ever really ends. However, it would be desirable that their lesser brethren in the ice forests have a few more million years to live, so that they may also evolve toward truth."

Which is a fine, resounding ploy, thought Flandry, *provided it be not the simple fact.*

Juchi: "They, like us, are willing to become clients of the Terrestrial Empire. To them, it means nothing; they will never have enough in common with men to be troubled by any human governors. They know Terra will not gratuitously harm them—whereas Merseia would, if only by provoking that planet-wide battle of space fleets you describe. Therefore, the Cold People will assist us in any way they can, though they know of none at present."

"Do these two speak for their whole race?" asked Flandry dubiously.

"And for the forests and the lakes," said Juchi.

Flandry thought of a life which was all one great organism, and nodded. "If you say so, I'll accept it. But if they can't help—"

Juchi gave an old man's sigh, like wind over the acrid waters. "I had hoped they could. But now—Have you no plan of your own?"

Flandry stood a long time, feeling the chill creep inward. At last he said: "If the only spaceships are at Ulan Baligh, then it seems we must get into the city somehow, to deliver our message. Have these folk any means of secretly contacting a Betelgeusean?"

Juchi inquired. "No," he translated the answer. "Not if the traders are closely guarded, and their awareness tells them that is so."

One of the natives stooped forward a little, above the dull blue fire, so that his face was illuminated. Could as human an emotion as sorrow really be read into those eyes? Words droned. Juchi listened.

"They can get us into the city, undetected, if it be a cold enough night," he said. "The medusae can carry us through the air, actually seeing radar beams and eluding them. And, of course, a medusa is invisible to metal detectors as well as infra-red scopes." The Shaman paused. "But what use is that, Terra man? We ourselves can walk disguised into Ulan Baligh."

"But could we fly—?" Flandry's voice trailed off.

"Not without being stopped by traffic control officers and investigated."

"S-s-so." Flandry raised his face to the glittering sky. He took the moonlight full in his eyes and was briefly dazzled. Tension tingled along his nerves.

"We've debated trying to radio a Betelgeusean ship as it takes off, before it goes into secondary drive." He spoke aloud, slowly, to get the hammering within himself under control. "But you said the Tebtengri have no set powerful enough to broadcast that far, thousands of kilometers. And, of course, we couldn't beamcast, since we couldn't pinpoint the ship at any instant."

"True. In any event, the Khan's aerial patrols would detect our transmission and pounce."

"Suppose a ship, a friendly spaceship, came near this planet without actually landing... could the Ice Dwellers communicate with it?"

Juchi asked; Flandry did not need the translated answer: "No. They have no radio sets at all. Even if they did, their 'casting would be as liable to detection as ours. And did you not say yourself, Orluk, all our messages must be kept secret, right to the moment that the Terran fleet arrives in strength? That Oleg Khan must not even suspect a message has been sent?"

"Well, no harm in asking." Flandry's gaze continued to search upward, till he found Betelgeuse like a torch among the constellations. "Could we *know* there was such a ship in the neighborhood?"

"I daresay it would radio as it approached…notify Ulan Baligh spaceport—" Juchi conferred with the nonhumans. "Yes. We could have men, borne by medusae, stationed unnoticeably far above the city. They could carry receivers. There would be enough beam leakage for them to listen to any conversation between the spaceship and the portmaster. Would that serve?"

Flandry breathed out in a great freezing gust. "It might."

Suddenly, and joyously, he laughed. Perhaps no such sound had ever rung across Tengri Nor. The Dwellers started back, like frightened small animals. Juchi stood in shadow. For that instant, only Captain Dominic Flandry of Imperial Terra had light upon him. He stood with his head raised into the copper moonlight, and laughed like a boy.

"By Heaven," he shouted, "we're going to do it!"

❊ X ❊

An autumn gale came down off the pole. It gathered snow on its way across the steppe, and struck Ulan Baligh near midnight. In minutes, the steep red roofs were lost to sight. Close by a lighted window, a man saw horizontal white streaks, whirling out of darkness and back into darkness. If he went a few meters away, pushing through drifts already knee-high, the light was gone. He stood blind, buffeted by the storm, and heard it rave.

Flandry descended from the upper atmosphere. Its cold had smitten so deep he thought he might never be warm again. In spite of an oxygen tank, his lungs were starving. He saw the blizzard from above as a moon-dappled black blot, the early ice floes on Ozero Rurik dashed to and fro along its southern fringe. A cabling of tentacles meshed him, he sat under a giant balloon rushing downward through the sky. Behind him trailed a flock of other medusae, twisting along air currents he could not feel to avoid radar beams he could not see. Ahead of him was only one, bearing a Dweller huddled against a cake of ice; for what lay below was hell's own sulfurous wind to the native.

Even Flandry felt how much warmer it was, when the snowstorm enclosed him. He crouched forward, squinting into a nothingness that yelled. Once his numbed feet, dangling down, struck a rooftree. The blow came as if from far away. Palely at first, strengthening as he neared, the Prophet's Tower thrust its luminous shaft up and out of sight.

Flandry groped for the nozzle at his shoulder. His destination gave just enough light for him to see through the driven flakes. Another medusa crowded close, bearing a pressure tank of paint. Somehow, Flandry reached across the air between and made the hose fast.

Now, Arctic intelligence, do you understand what I want to do? Can you guide this horse of mine for me?

The wind yammered in his ears. He heard other noises like blasting, the powerful breaths by which his medusa moved itself. Almost, he was battered against the tablet wall. His carrier wobbled in midair, fighting to maintain position. An inlaid letter, big as a house, loomed before him, black against shining white. He aimed his hose and squirted.

Damn! The green jet was flung aside in a flaw of wind. He corrected his aim and saw the paint strike. It remained liquid even at this temperature...no matter, it was sticky enough.... The first tank was quickly used up. Flandry coupled to another. Blue this time. All the Tebtengri had contributed all the squirtable paint they had, every hue in God's rainbow. Flandry could but hope there would be enough.

There was, though he came near fainting from chill and exhaustion before the end of the job. He could not remember ever having so brutal a task. Even so, when the last huge stroke was done, he could not resist adding an exclamation point at the very bottom—three centimeters high.

"Let's go," he whispered. Somehow, the mute Dweller understood and pointed his staff. The medusa flock sprang through the clouds.

Flandry had a moment's glimpse of a military airboat. It had detached itself from the flock hovering above the spaceport, perhaps going off duty. As the medusae broke from the storm into clear moonlight and ringlight, the craft veered. Flandry saw its guns stab energy bolts into the flock, and reached for his own futile blaster. His fingers were wooden, they didn't close....

The medusae, all but his and the Dweller's, whipped about.

They surrounded the patrol boat, laid tentacles fast and clung. It was nearly buried under them. Electric fires crawled, sparks dripped, these creatures could break hydrogen from water. Flandry recalled in a dull part of his mind that a metallic fuselage was a Faraday cage, immune to lightning. But when concentrated electric discharges burned holes, spotwelded control circuits—the boat staggered in midair. The medusae detached themselves. The boat plummeted.

Flandry relaxed and let his creature bear him northward.

✦ **XI** ✦

The town seethed. There had been rioting in the Street of Gunsmiths, and blood still dappled the new-fallen snow. Armed men tramped around palace and spaceport; mobs hooted beyond them. From the lake shore encampments came war music, pipes squealed, gongs crashed, the young men rode their varyaks in breakneck circles and cursed.

Oleg Khan looked out the palace window. "It shall be made good to you," he muttered. "Oh, yes, my people, you shall have satisfaction."

Turning to the Betelgeusean, who had just been fetched, he glared into the blue face. "You have seen?"

"Yes, your majesty." Zalat's Altaian, usually fluent and little accented, grew thick. He was a badly shaken being. Only the. quick arrival of the royal guards had saved his ship from destruction by a thousand shrieking fanatics. "I swear, I, my crew, we had nothing to do with . . . we are innocent as—"

"Of course! Of course!" Oleg Yesukai brought one palm down in an angry slicing motion. "I am not one of those ignorant rodent herders. Every Betelgeusean has been under supervision, every moment since—" He checked himself.

"I have still not understood why," faltered Zalat.

"Was my reason not made clear to you? You know the Terran visitor was killed by Tebtengri operatives, the very day he arrived. It bears out what I have long suspected, those tribes have become religiously xenophobic. Since they doubtless have other agents in the city, who will try to murder your people in turn, it is best all of you be closely guarded, have contact only with men we know are loyal, until I have full control of the situation."

His own words calmed Oleg somewhat. He sat down, stroked his beard and watched Zalat from narrowed eyes. "Your difficulties this morning are regrettable," he continued smoothly. "Because you are outworlders, and the defiling symbols are not in the Altaian alphabet, many people leaped to the conclusion that it was some dirty word in your language. I, of course, know better. I also know from the exact manner in which a patrol craft was lost last night, how this outrage was done: unquestionably by Tebtengri, with the help of the Arctic devil-folk. Such a vile deed would not trouble them in the least; they are not followers of the Prophet. But what puzzles me—I admit this frankly, though confidentially—*why?* A daring, gruelling task ... merely for a wanton insult?"

He glanced back toward the window. From this angle, the crimson Tower looked itself. You had to be on the north to see what had been done: the tablet wall disfigured by more than a kilometer of splashed paint. But from that side, the fantastic desecration was visible across entire horizons.

The Kha Khan doubled a fist. "It shall be repaid them," he said. "This has rallied the orthodox tribes behind me as no other thing imaginable. When their children are boiled before their eyes, the Tebtengri will realize what they have done."

Zalat hesitated. "Your majesty—"

"Yes?" Oleg snarled, as he must at something.

"Those symbols are letters of the Terran alphabet."

"What?"

"I know the Anglic language somewhat," said Zalat. "Many Betelgeuseans do. But how could those Tebtengri ever have learned—"

Oleg, who knew the answer to that, interrupted by seizing the captain's tunic and shaking him. "What does it say?" he cried.

"That's the strangest part, your majesty," stammered Zalat. "It doesn't mean anything. Not that makes sense."

"Well, what sound does it spell, then? Speak before I have your teeth pulled!"

"Mayday," choked Zalat. "Just Mayday, your majesty."

Oleg let him go. For a while there was silence. At last the Khan said: "Is that a Terran word?"

"Well ... it could be. I mean, well, May is the name of a month in the Terran calendar, and Day means 'diurnal period.'" Zalat rubbed his yellow eyes, searching for logic. "I suppose Mayday could mean the first day of May."

Oleg nodded slowly. "That sounds reasonable. The Altaian calendar, which is modified from the ancient Terran, has a similar name for a month of what is locally springtime. Mayday—spring festival day? Perhaps."

He returned to the window and brooded across the city. "It's long until May," he said. "If that was an incitement to ... anything ... it's foredoomed. We are going to break the Tebtengri this very winter. By next spring—" He cleared his throat and finished curtly: "Certain other projects will be well under way."

"How could it be an incitement, anyhow, your majesty?" argued Zalat, emboldened. "Who in Ulan Baligh could read it?"

"True. I can only conjecture, some wild act of defiance—or superstition, magical ritual—" The Khan turned on his heel. "You are leaving shortly, are you not?"

"Yes, your majesty."

"You shall convey a message. No other traders are to come here for a standard year. We will have troubles enough, suppressing the Tebtengri and their aboriginal allies." Oleg shrugged. "In any event, it would be useless for merchants to visit us. War will disrupt the caravans. Afterward—perhaps."

Privately, he doubted it. By summer, the Merseians would have returned and started work on their base. A year from now, Altai would be firmly in their empire, and, under them, the Kha Khan would lead his warriors to battles in the stars, more glorious than any of the hero songs had ever told.

✧ XII ✧

Winter came early to the northlands. Flandry, following the Mangu Tuman in their migratory cycle, saw snow endless across the plains, under a sky like blued steel. The tribe, wagons and herds and people, were a hatful of dust strewn on immensity: here a moving black blot, there a thin smoke-streak vertical in windless air. Krasna hung low in the southeast, a frosty red-gold wheel.

Three folk glided from the main ordu. They were on skis, rifles slung behind their parkas, hands holding tethers which led to a small negagrav tow unit. It flew quickly, so that the skis sang on the thin crisp snow.

Arghun Tiliksky said hard-voiced: "I can appreciate that you and Juchi keep secret the reason for that Tower escapade of yours, five weeks ago. What none of us know, none can reveal if captured. Yet you seem quite blithe about the consequences. Our scouts tell us that infuriated warriors flock to Oleg Khan, that he has pledged to annihilate us this very year. In consequence, all the Tebtengri must remain close together, not spread along the whole Arctic Circle as before—and hereabouts, there is not enough forage under the snow for that many herds. I say to you, the Khan need only wait, and by the end of the season famine will have done half his work for him!"

"Let's hope he plans on that," said Flandry. "Less strenuous than fighting, isn't it?"

Arghun's angry young face turned toward him. The noyon clipped: "I do not share this awe of all things Terran. You are as human as I. In this environment, where you are untrained, you are much more fallible. I warn you plainly, unless you give me good reason to do otherwise, I shall request a kurultai. And at it I will argue that we strike now at Ulan Baligh, try for a decision while we can still count on full bellies."

Bourtai cried aloud, "No! That would be asking for ruin. They outnumber us down there, three or four to one. And I have seen some of the new engines the Merseians brought. It would be butchery!"

"It would be quick." Arghun glared at Flandry. "Well?"

The Terran sighed. He might have expected it. Bourtai was always near him, and Arghun was always near Bourtai, and the officer had spoken surly words before now. He might have known that this invitation to hunt a flock of sataru—mutant ostriches escaped from the herds and gone wild—masked something else. At least it was decent of Arghun to warn him.

"If you don't trust me," he said, "though Lord knows I've fought and bled and frostbitten my nose in your cause—can't you trust Juchi Ilyak? He and the Dwellers know my little scheme; they'll assure you it depends on our hanging back and avoiding battle."

"Juchi grows old," said Arghun. "His mind is feeble as—Hoy, there!"

He yanked a guide line. The negagrav unit purred to a stop and hung in air, halfway up a long slope. His politics dropped from Arghun, he pointed at the snow with a hunting dog's eagerness. "Spoor," he hissed. "We go by muscle power now, to sneak close. The birds can outrun this motor if they hear it. Do you go straight up this hill, Orluk Flandry; Bourtai and I will come around on opposite sides of it—"

The Altaians had slipped their reins and skied noiselessly from him before Flandry quite understood what had happened. Looking down, the Terran saw big splay tracks: a pair of sataru. He started after them. How the deuce did you manage these footsticks, anyway? Waddling across the slope, he tripped himself and went down. His nose clipped a boulder. He sat up, swearing in eighteen languages and Old Martian phonoglyphs.

"This they call fun?" He tottered erect. Snow had gotten under his parka hood. It began to melt, trickling over his ribs in search of a really good place to refreeze. "Great greasy comets," said Flandry, "I might have been sitting in the Everest House with a bucket of champagne, lying to some beautiful wench about my exploits...but no, I had to come out here and do 'em!"

Slowly, he dragged himself up the hill, crouched on its brow, and peered through an unnecessarily cold and thorny bush. No two-legged birds, only a steep slant back down to the plain...wait!

He saw blood and the dismembered avian shapes an instant before the beasts attacked him.

They seemed to rise from weeds and snowdrifts, as if the earth had spewed them. Noiselessly they rushed in, a dozen white scuttering forms big as police dogs. Flandry glimpsed long sharp noses, alert black eyes that hated him, high backs and hairless tails. He yanked his rifle loose and fired. The slug bowled the nearest animal over. It rolled halfway downhill, lay a while, and crawled back to fight some more.

Flandry didn't see it. The next was upon him. He shot it point black. One of its fellows crouched to tear the flesh. But the rest ran on. Flandry took aim at a third. A heavy body landed between his shoulders. He went down, and felt jaws rip his leather coat.

He rolled over, somehow, shielding his face with one arm. His rifle had been torn from him: a beast fumbled it in forepaws almost like hands. He groped for the dagger at his belt. Two of the animals were on him, slashing with chisel teeth. He managed to kick one in the nose. It squealed, bounced away, sprang back with a couple of new arrivals to help.

Someone yelled. It sounded very far off, drowned by Flandry's own heartbeat. The Terran drove his knife into a hairy shoulder. The beast writhed free, leaving him weaponless. Now they were piling on him where he lay. He fought with boots and knees, fists and elbows, in a cloud of kicked-up snow. An animal jumped in the air, came down on his midriff. The wind whooffed out of him. His face-defending arm dropped, and the creature went for his throat.

Arghun came up behind. The Altaian seized the animal by the neck. His free hand flashed steel, he disemboweled it and flung it toward the pack in one expert movement. Several of them fell on the still snarling shape and fed. Arghun booted another exactly behind the ear. It dropped as if poleaxed. One jumped from the rear, to get on his back. He stooped, his right hand made a judo heave, and as the beast soared over his head he ripped its stomach with his knife.

"Up, man!" He hoisted Flandry. The Terran stumbled beside him, while the pack chattered around. Now its outliers began to fall dead: Bourtai had regained the hillcrest and was sniping. The largest of the animals whistled. At that signal, the survivors bounded off. They were lost to view in seconds.

When they had reached Bourtai, Arghun sank down gasping. The girl flew to Flandry. "Are you hurt?" she sobbed.

"Only in my pride—I guess—" He looked past her to the noyon. "Thanks," he said inadequately.

"You are a guest," grunted Arghun. After a moment: "They grow bolder each year. I had never expected to be attacked this near an ordu. Something must be done about them, if we live through the winter."

"What are they?" Flandry shuddered toward relaxation.

"Gurchaku. They range in packs over all the steppes, up into the Khrebet. They will eat anything but prefer meat. Chiefly sataru and other feral animals, but they raid our herds, have killed people—" Arghun looked grim. "They were not as large in my grandfather's day, nor as cunning."

Flandry nodded. "Rats. Which is not an exclamation."

"I know what rats are," said Bourtai. "But the gurchaku—"

"A new genus. Similar things have happened on other colonized planets." Flandry wished for a cigaret. He wished so hard that Bourtai had to remind him before he continued: "Oh, yes. Some of the stowaway rats on your ancestors' ships must have gone into the wilds, as these began to be Terrestrialized. Size was advantageous: helped them keep warm, enabled them to prey on the big animals you were developing. Selection pressure, short generations, genetic drift within a small original population.... Nature is quite capable of forced-draft evolution on her own hook."

He managed a tired grin at Bourtai. "After all," he said, "if a frontier planet has beautiful girls, tradition requires that it have monsters as well."

Her blush was like fire.

They returned to camp in silence. Flandry entered the yurt given him, washed and changed clothes, lay down on his bunk and stared at the ceiling. He reflected bitterly on all the Terran romancing he had ever heard, the High Frontier in general and the dashing adventures of the Intelligence Corps in particular. So what did it amount to? A few nasty moments with men or giant rats that wanted to kill you; stinking leather clothes, wet feet, chilblains and frostbite, unseasoned food, creaking wheels exchanged for squealing runners; temperance, chastity, early rising, weighty speech with tribal elders, not a book he could enjoy or a joke he could understand for light-years. He yawned, rolled over on his stomach, tried to sleep, gave up after a while, and began to wish Arghun's reckless counsel would be accepted. Anything to break this dreariness!

It tapped on the door. He started to his feet, bumped his head on a curved ridgepole, swore, and said: "Come in." The caution of years laid his hand on a blaster.

The short day was near an end, only a red streak above one edge of the world. His lamp picked out Bourtai. She entered, closed the door, and stood unspeaking.

"Why... hullo." Flandry paused. "What brings you here?"

"I came to see if you were indeed well." Her eyes did not meet his.

"Oh? Oh, yes. Yes, of course," he said stupidly. "Kind of you. I mean, uh, shall I make some tea?"

"If you were bitten, it should be tended," said the girl. "Gurchaku bites can be infectious."

"No, thanks, I escaped any actual wounds." Automatically, Flandry added with a smile: "I could wish otherwise, though. So fair a nurse—"

Again he saw the blood rise in her face. Suddenly he understood. He would have realized earlier, had these people not been more reticent than his own. A heavy pulse beat in his throat. "Sit down," he invited.

She lowered herself to the floor. He joined her, sliding a practiced arm over her shoulder. She did not flinch. He let his hand glide lower, till the arm was around her waist. She leaned against him.

"Do you think we will see another springtime?" she asked. Her tone grew steady once more; it was a quite practical question.

"I have one right here with me," he said. His lips brushed her dark hair.

"No one speaks thus in the ordu," she breathed. Quickly: "We are both cut off from our kindred, you by distance and I by death. Let us not remain lonely."

He forced himself to give fair warning: "I shall return to Terra the first chance I get."

"I know," she cried, "but until then—"

His lips found hers.

There was a thump on the door.

"Go away!" Flandry and Bourtai said it together, looked surprised into each other's eyes, and laughed with pleasure. "My lord," called a man's voice, "Toghrul Gur-Khan sends me. A message has been picked up—a Terran spaceship!"

Flandry knocked Bourtai over in his haste to get outside. But even as he ran, he thought with frustration that this job had been hoodooed from the outset.

XIII

Among the thin winds over Ulan Baligh, hidden by sheer height, a warrior sat in the patient arms of a medusa. He breathed oxygen from a tank and rested numbed fingers on a small radio transceiver. After four hours he was relieved; perhaps no other breed of human could have endured so long a watch.

Finally he was rewarded. His earphones crackled with a faint, distorted voice, speaking no language he had ever heard. A return beam gabbled from the spaceport. The man up above gave place to another, who spoke a halting, accented Altaian, doubtless learned from the Betelgeuseans.

The scout of the Tebtengri dared not try any communication of his own. If detected (and the chances were that it would be) such a call would bring a nuclear missile streaking upward from Ulan Baligh. However, his transceiver could amplify and relay what came to it. Medusae elsewhere carried similar sets: a long chain, ending in the ordu of Toghrul Vavilov. Were that re-transmission intercepted by the enemy, no one would be alarmed. They would take it for some freak of reflection off the ionosphere.

The scout's binoculars actually showed him the Terran spaceship as it descended. He whistled in awe at its sleek, armed swiftness. Still, he thought, it was only one vessel, paying a visit to Oleg the Damned, who had carefully disguised all his modern installations. Oleg would be like butter to his guests, they would see what he wished them to see and no more. Presently they would go home again, to report that Altai was a harmless half-barbaric outpost, safely forgettable.

The scout sighed, beat gloved hands together, and wished his relief would soon arrive.

And up near the Arctic Circle, Dominic Flandry turned from Toghrul's receiver. A frosted window framed his head with the early northern night. "That's it," he said. "We'll maintain our radio monitors, but I don't expect to pick up anything else interesting, except the moment when the ship takes off again."

"When will that be?" asked the Gur-Khan.

"In a couple of days, I imagine," said Flandry. "We've got to be ready! All the tribesmen must be alerted, must move out on the plains according to the scheme Juchi and I drew up for you."

Toghrul nodded. Arghun Tiliksky, who had also crowded into the kibitka, demanded: "What scheme is this? Why have I not been told?"

"You didn't need to know," Flandry answered. Blandly: "The warriors of Tebtengri can be moving at top speed, ready for battle, on five minutes' notice, under any conditions whatsoever. Or so you were assuring me in a ten-minute speech one evening last week. Very well, move them, noyon."

Arghun bristled. "And then—"

"You will lead the Mangu Tuman varyak division straight south for 500 kilometers," said Toghrul. "There you will await radio orders. The other tribal forces will be stationed elsewhere; you will doubtless see a few, but strict radio silence is to be maintained between you. The less mobile vehicles will have to stay in this general region, with the women and children maneuvering them."

"And the herds," reminded Flandry. "Don't forget, we can cover quite a large area with all the Tebtengri herds."

"But this is lunacy!" yelped Arghun. "If Oleg knows we're spread out in such a manner, and drives a wedge through—"

"He won't know," said Flandry. "Or if he does, he won't know why: which is what counts. Now, git!"

For a moment Arghun's eyes clashed with his. Then the noyon slapped gauntlets against one thigh, whirled, and departed. It was indeed only a few moments before the night grew loud with varyak motors and lowing battle horns.

When that had faded, Toghrul tugged his beard, looked across the radio, and said to Flandry: "Now can you tell me just what fetched that Terran spaceship here?"

"Why, to inquire more closely about the reported death of me, a Terran citizen, on Altai," grinned Flandry. "At least, if he is not a moron, that is what the captain will tell Oleg. And he will let Oleg convince him it was all a deplorable accident, and he'll take off again."

Toghrul stared, then broke into buffalo laughter. Flandry chimed in. For a while the Gur-Khan of the Mangu Tuman and the field agent of the Imperial Terrestrial Naval Intelligence Corps danced around the kibitka singing about the flowers that bloom in the spring.

Presently Flandry left. There wasn't going to be much sleep for anyone in the next few days. Tonight, though—He rapped eagerly on his own yurt. Silence answered him, the wind and a distant sad mewing of the herds. He scowled and opened the door.

A note lay on his bunk. *My beloved, the alarm signals have blown. Toghrul gave me weapons and a new varyak. My father taught me to ride and shoot as well as any man. It is only fitting that the last of Clan Tumurji go with the warriors.*

Flandry stared at the scrawl for a long while. Finally, "Oh, hell and tiddlywinks," he said, and undressed and went to bed.

❖ XIV ❖

When he woke in the morning, his cart was under way. He emerged to find the whole encampment grinding across the steppe. Toghrul stood to one side, taking a navigational sight on the rings. He greeted Flandry with a gruff: "We should be in our own assigned position tomorrow." A messenger dashed up, something needed the chief's attention, one of the endless emergencies of so big a group on the move. Flandry found himself alone.

By now he had learned not to offer his own unskilled assistance.

He spent the day composing scurrilous limericks about the superiors who had assigned him to this mission. The trek continued noisily through the dark. Next morning there was drifted snow to clear before camp could be made. Flandry discovered that he was at least able to wield a snow shovel. Soon he wished he weren't.

By noon the ordu was settled; not in the compact standardized laagers which offered maximum safety, but straggling over kilometers in a line which brought mutinous grumbling. Toghrul roared down all protest and went back to his kibitka to crouch over the radio. After some hours he summoned Flandry.

"Ship departing," he said. "We've just picked up a routine broadcast warning aircraft from the spaceport area." He frowned. "Can we carry out all our maneuvers while we're still in daylight?"

"It doesn't matter," said Flandry. "Our initial pattern is already set up. Once he spots that from space—and he's pretty sure to, because it's routine to look as long and hard as possible at any doubtful planet—the skipper will hang around out there."

His gray eyes went to a map on the desk before him. The positions of all Tebtengri units had now been radio confirmed. As marked by Toghrul, the ordus lay in a heavy east-and-west line, 500 kilometers long across the winter-white steppe. The more mobile varyak divisions sprawled their bunches to form lines slanting past either end of the stationary one, meeting in the north. He stroked his mustache and waited.

"Spaceship cleared for take off. Stand by. Rise, spaceship!"

As the relayed voice trickled weakly from the receiver, Flandry snatched up a pencil and drew another figure under Toghrul's gaze. "This is the next formation," he said. "Might as well start it now, I think; the ship will have seen the present one in a few minutes."

The Gur-Khan bent over the microphone and rapped: "Varyak divisions of Clans Munlik, Fyodor, Kubilai, Tuli, attention! Drive straight west for 100 kilometers. Belgutai, Bagdarin, Chagatai, Kassar, due east for 100 kilometers. Gleb, Jahangir—"

Flandry rolled his pencil in tightened fingers. As the reports came in, over an endless hour, he marked where each unit had halted. The whole device began to look pathetically crude.

"I have been thinking," said Toghrul after a period of prolonged silence.

"Nasty habit," said Flandry. "Hard to break. Try cold baths and long walks."

"What if Oleg finds out about this?"

"He's pretty sure to discover something is going on. His air scouts will pick up bits of our messages. But only bits, since these are short-range transmissions. I'm depending on our own air cover to keep the enemy from getting too good a look at what we're up to. All Oleg will know is, we're maneuvering around on a large scale." Flandry shrugged. "It would seem most logical to me, if I were him, that the Tebtengri were practicing formations against the day he attacks."

"Which is not far off." Toghrul drummed the desk top.

Flandry drew a figure on his paper. "This one next," he said.

"Yes." Toghrul gave the orders. Afterward: "We can continue through dark, you know. Light bonfires. Send airboats loaded with fuel to the varyak men, so they can do the same."

"That would be well."

"Of course," frowned the chief, "it will consume an unholy amount of fuel. More than we can spare."

"Don't worry about that," said Flandry. "Before the shortage gets acute, your people will be safe, their needs supplied from outside—or they'll be dead, which is still more economical."

The night wore on. Now and then Flandry dozed. He paid scant heed to the sunrise; he had only half completed his job. Sometime later a warrior was shown in. "From Juchi Shaman," he reported, with a clumsy salute. "Airscouts watching the Ozero Rurik area report massing of troops, outrider columns moving northward."

Toghrul smote the desk with one big fist. "Already?" he said.

"It'll take them a few days to get their big push this far," said Flandry, though his guts felt cold at the news. "Longer, if we harry them from the air. All I need is one more day, I think."

"But when can we expect help?" said Toghrul.

"Not for another three or four weeks at the very least," said Flandry. "Word has to reach Catawrayannis Base, its commandant has to patch together a task force which has to get here. Allow a month, plus or minus. Can we retreat that long, holding the enemy off without undue losses to ourselves?"

"We had better," said Toghrul, "or we are done."

✲ XV ✲

Captain Flandry laid the rifle stock to his shoulder. Its plastic felt smooth and uncold, as nearly as his numbed cheek could feel anything. The chill of the metal parts, which would skin any fingers that touched them, bit through his gloves.

Hard to gauge distances in this red half-light, across this whining scud of snow. Hard to guess windage; even trajectories were baffling, on this miserable three-quarter-gee planet.... He decided the opposition wasn't close enough yet, and lowered his gun.

Beside him, crouched in the same lee of a snowbank, the Dweller turned dark eyes upon the man. "I go now?" he asked. His Altaian was even worse than Flandry's, though Juchi himself had been surprised to learn that any of the Ice Folk knew the human tongue.

"I told you no." Flandry's own accent was thickened by the frostbitten puffiness of his lips. "You must cross a hundred meters of open ground to reach those trees. Running, you would be seen and shot before going halfway. Unless we can arrange a distraction—"

He peered again through the murk. Krasna had almost vanished from these polar lands for the winter, but was still not far below the horizon. There were still hours when a surly gleam in the south gave men enough light to see a little distance.

The attacking platoon was so close now that Flandry could make out blurred individuals, outlined against the great vague lake. He could see that they rode a sort of modified varyak, with runners and low-powered negagrav thrust to drive them across the permasnow. It was sheer ill luck that he and his squad had blundered into them. But the past month, or however long, had been that sort of time. Juchi had withdrawn all his people into the depths of the Ice Lands, to live off a few kine slaughtered and frozen while their herds wandered the steppes under slight guard... while a front line of Tebtengri and Dwellers fought a guerrilla war to slow Oleg Khan's advance.... Skulk, shoot, run, hide, bolt your food, snatch a nap in a sleeping bag as dank as yourself, and go forth to skulk again....

Now the rest of Flandry's party lay dead by Tengri Nor. And

he himself, with this one companion, was trapped by a pursuit moving faster on machine than he could afoot.

He gauged his range afresh. Perhaps. He got his sights on a man in the lead and jerked his head at the Dweller, who slipped from him. Then he fired.

The southerner jerked in the saddle, caught at his belly, and slid slowly to the ground. Even in this glum light, his blood was a red shout on the snow. Through the wind, Flandry heard the others yell. They swept into motion, dispersing. He followed them with his sights, aimed at another, squeezed trigger again. A miss. This wasn't enough. He had to furnish a few seconds' diversion, so the Dweller could reach those crystalline trees at his back.

Flandry thumbed his rifle to automatic fire. He popped up, shooting, and called: "My grandmother can lick your grandmother!"

Diving, he sensed more than heard the lead storm that went where he had been. Energy bolts crashed through the air overhead, came down again and sizzled in the snow. He breathed hot steam. Surely that damned Dweller had gotten to the woods now! He fired blind at the inward-rushing enemy. *Come on, someone, pull me out of this mess!—What use is it, anyhow? The little guy babbled about calling through the roots, letting all the forest know—*Through gun-thunder, Flandry heard the first high ringing noise. He raised his eyes in time to see the medusae attack.

They swarmed from above, hundreds upon hundreds, their tentacles full of minor lightning. Some were hit, burst into hydrogen flame, and sought men to burn even as they died. Others snatched warriors from the saddle, lifted them, and dropped them in the mortally cold waters of Tengri Nor. Most went efficiently about a task of electrocution. Flandry had not quite understood what happened before he saw the retreat begin. By the time he had climbed erect, it was a rout.

"Holy hopping hexaflexagons," he mumbled in awe. "Now why can't I do that stunt?"

The Dweller returned, small, furry, rubbery, an unimpressive goblin who said with shyness: "Not enough medusa for do this often. Your friends come. We wait."

"Huh? Oh...you mean a rescue party. Yeh, I suppose some of our units would have seen that flock arrive here and will come to investigate." Flandry stamped his feet, trying to force circulation back. "Nice haul," he said, looking over strewn weapons and vehicles. "I think we got revenge for our squad."

"Dead man just as dead on any side of fight," reproached the Dweller.

Flandry grimaced. "Don't remind me."

He heard the whirr of tow motors. The ski patrol which came around the woods was bigger than he had expected. He recognized Arghun and Bourtai at its head. It came to him, with a shock, that he hadn't spoken to either one, except to say hello-goodbye, since the campaign began. Too busy. That was the trouble with war. Leave out the toil, discipline, discomfort, scant sleep, lousy food, monotony, and combat, and war would be a fine institution.

He strolled to meet the newcomers, as debonairly as possible for a man without cigarets. "Hi," he said.

"Dominic...it was you—" Bourtai seized his hands. "You might have been killed!" she gasped.

"Occupational hazard," said Flandry. "I thought you were in charge of our western division, Arghun."

"No more fighting there," said the noyon. "I am going about gathering our troops."

"What?"

"Have you not heard?" The frank eyes widened. Arghun stood for a moment in the snow, gaping. Then a grin cracked his frozen mustache; he slapped Flandry's back and shouted: "The Terrans have arrived!"

"Huh?" Flandry felt stunned. The blow he had taken—Arghun owned a hefty set of muscles—wait, what had he said?

"Yesterday," chattered the Altaian. "I suppose your portable radio didn't pick up the news, nor anyone in that company you were fighting. Reception is poor in this area. Or maybe they were fanatics. There are some, whom we'll have to dispose of. But that should not be difficult."

He brought himself under control and went on more calmly: "A task force appeared and demanded the surrender of all Yesukai forces as being Merseian clients. The commander at Ulan Baligh yielded without a fight—what could he have done? Oleg Khan tried to rally his men at the front...oh, you should have been listening, the ether was lively last night!...but a couple of Terran spaceships flew up and dropped a demonstration bomb squarely on his headquarters. That was the end of that. The tribesmen of the Khanate are already disengaging and streaming south. Juchi Shaman has a call from the Terran admiral at Ulan Baligh, to come advise him what to do next—oh yes, and bring you along—"

Flandry closed his eyes. He swayed on his feet, so that Bourtai caught him in her arms and cried, "What is it, my dear one?"

"Brandy," he whispered. "Tobacco. India tea. Shrimp mayonnaise, with a bottle of gray Riesling on the side. Air conditioning...." He shook himself. "Sorry. My mind wandered."

He scarcely saw how her lip trembled. Arghun did, gave the Terran a defiant look, and caught the girl's hand in his own. She clung to that like a lost child.

This time Flandry did notice. His mouth twitched upward. "Bless you, my children," he murmured.

"What?" Arghun snapped it in an anger half bewilderment.

"When you get as old and battered as I," said Flandry, "you will realize that no one dies of a broken heart. In fact, it heals with disgusting speed. If you want to name your first-born Dominic, I will be happy to mail a silver spoon, suitably engraved."

"But—" stammered Bourtai. "But—" She gave up and held Arghun's hand more tightly.

The noyon's face burned with blood. He said hastily, seeking impersonal things: "*Now* will you explain your actions, Terra man?"

"Hm?" Flandry blinked. "Oh. Oh, yes. To be sure."

He started walking. The other two kept pace, along the thin blue Lake of Ghosts, under a lacework of icy leaves. The red halfday smoldered toward night. Flandry spoke, with laughter reborn in his voice:

"Our problem was to send a secret message. The most secret possible would, of course, be one which nobody recognized as a message. For instance, Mayday painted on the Prophet's Tower. It looked like gibberish, pure spiteful mischief...but all the city could see it. They'd talk. How they'd talk! Even if no Betelgeuseans happened to be at Ulan Baligh just then, there would soon be some who would certainly hear news so sensational, no matter how closely they were guarded. And the Betelgeuseans in turn would carry the yarn home with them—where the Terrans connected with the Embassy would hear it. And the Terrans would understand!

"You see, Mayday is a very ancient code call on my planet. It means, simply, Help me."

"Oh!" exclaimed Bourtai.

"Oh-ho," said Arghun. He slapped his thigh and his own laughter barked forth, "Yes, I see it now! Thanks, friend, for a joke to tell my grandchildren!"

"A classic," agreed Flandry with his normal modesty. "My corps was bound to send a ship to investigate. Knowing little or nothing, its men would be alert and wary. Oleg's tale of my accidental death, or whatever he told them, would be obvious seafood in view of that first message; but I figured I could trust them to keep their mouths shut, pretend to be taken in by him, until they could learn more. The problem now was, how to inform them exactly what the situation was—without Oleg knowing.

"Of course, you can guess how that was done: by maneuvering the whole Tebtengri Shamanate across the plain, to form Terran letters visible through a telescope. It could only be a short, simple note; but it served."

He filled his lungs with the keen air. Through all his weariness, the magnificence of being alive flowed up into him. He grinned and added, half to himself: "Those were probably the first secret messages ever sent in an alphabet ranging from one to five hundred kilometers tall."

CHRONOLOGY OF TECHNIC CIVILIZATION

✵ COMPILED BY SANDRA MIESEL ✵

The Technic Civilization series sweeps across five millennia and hundreds of light-years of space to chronicle three cycles of history shaping both human and non-human life in our corner of the universe. It begins in the twenty-first century, with recovery from a violent period of global unrest known as the Chaos. New space technologies ease Earth's demand for resources and energy, permitting exploration of the Solar system.

ca. 2055 "The Saturn Game" (*Analog Science Fiction*, hereafter *ASF*, February, 1981)

22nd C The discovery of hyperdrive makes interstellar travel feasible early in the twenty-second century. The Breakup sends humans off to colonize the stars, often to preserve cultural identity or to try a social experiment. A loose government called the Solar Commonwealth is established. Hermes is colonized.

2150 "Wings of Victory" (*ASF*, April, 1972)
The Grand Survey from Earth discovers alien races on Yithri, Merseia, and many other planets.

23rd C   The Polesetechnic League is founded as a mutual
                    protection association of space-faring merchants.
                    Colonization of Aeneas and Altai.

24th C   "The Problem of Pain" (*Fantasy and Science
                    Fiction*, February, 1973)

2376   Nicholas van Rijn born poor on Earth.
                    Colonization of Vixen.

2400   Council of Hiawatha, a futile attempt to reform
                    the League.
                    Colonization of Dennitza.

2406   David Falkayn born noble on Hermes, a
                    breakaway human grand duchy.

2416   "Margin of Profit" (*ASF*, September, 1956) [van
                    Rijn]

                    "How to Be Ethnic in One Easy Lesson" (in *Future
                    Quest*, ed. Roger Elwood, Avon Books, 1974)

                              ✿   ✿   ✿

2423   "The Three-Cornered Wheel" (*ASF*, October, 1963)
                    [Falkayn]

                              ✿   ✿   ✿

stories overlap

2420s   "A Sun Invisible" (*ASF*, April, 1966) [Falkayn]

                    "The Season of Forgiveness" (*Boy's Life*,
                    December, 1973) [set on same planet as "The
                    Three-Cornered Wheel"]

                    The Man Who Counts (Ace Books, 1978 as *War
                    of the Wing-Men*, Ace Books, 1958 from "The
                    Man Who Counts," *ASF*, February–April, 1958)
                    [van Rijn]

                    "Esau" (as "Birthright," *ASF*, February, 1970)
                    [van Rijn]

                    "Hiding Place" (*ASF*, March, 1961) [van Rijn]

✡ ✡ ✡

stories overlap

2430s	"Territory" (*ASF*, June, 1963) [van Rijn]
	"The Trouble Twisters" (as "Trader Team," *ASF*, July–August, 1965) [Falkayn]
	"Day of Burning" (as "Supernova," *ASF*, January, 1967) [Falkayn] Falkayn saves civilization on Merseia, mankind's future foe.
	"The Master Key" (*ASF*, July, 1964) [van Rijn]
	Satan's World (Doubleday, 1969 from *ASF*, May–August, 1968) [van Rijn and Falkayn]
	"A Little Knowledge" (*ASF*, August, 1971)
	The League has become a set of ruthless cartels.

✡ ✡ ✡

2446	"Lodestar" (in *Astounding: The John W. Campbell Memorial Anthology.* ed. Harry Harrison. Random House, 1973) [van Rijn and Falkayn] Rivalries and greed are tearing the League apart. Falkayn marries van Rijn's favorite granddaughter.
2456	*Mirkheim*. (Putnam Books, 1977) [van Rijn and Falkayn] The Babur War involving Hermes gravely wounds the League. Dark days loom.
late 25th C	Falkayn founds a joint human-Ythrian colony on Avalon ruled by the Domain of Ythri. [same planet—renamed—as in "The Problem of Pain."]
26th C	"Wingless" (as "Wingless on Avalon," *Boy's Life*, July, 1973) [Falkayn's grandson]
	"Rescue on Avalon" (in *Children of Infinity.* ed. Roger Elwood. Franklin Watts, 1973) Colonization of Nyanza.
2550	Dissolution of the Polesotechnic League.

27th C	The Time of Troubles brings down the Commonwealth. Earth is sacked twice and left prey to barbarian slave raiders.
ca. 2700	"The Star Plunderer" (*Planet Stories*, hereafter *PS*, September, 1952) Manuel Argos proclaims the Terran Empire with citizenship open to all intelligent species. The Principate phase of the Imperium ultimately brings peace to 100,000 inhabited worlds within a sphere of stars 400 light-years in diameter.
28th C	Colonization of Unan Besar. "Sargasso of Lost Starships" (*PS*, January, 1952) The Empire annexes old colony on Ansa by force.
29th C	*The People of the Wind* (New American Library from *ASF*, February–April, 1973) The Empire's war on another civilized imperium starts its slide towards decadence. A descendant of Falkayn and an ancestor of Flandry cross paths.
30th C	The Covenant of Alfzar, an attempt at détente between Terra and Merseia, fails to achieve peace.
3000	Dominic Flandry born on Earth, illegitimate son of an opera diva and an aristocratic space captain.
3019	*Ensign Flandry* (Chilton, 1966 from shorter version in *Amazing*, hereafter *AMZ*, October, 1966) Flandry's first collision with the Merseians.
3021	*A Circus of Hells* (New American Library, 1970, incorporates "The White King's War," *Galaxy*, hereafter *Gal*, October, 1969) Flandry is a Lieutenant (j.g.).
3022	Degenerate Emperor Josip succeeds weak old Emperor Georgios.
3025	*The Rebel Worlds* (New American Library, 1969)

A military revolt on the frontier world of Aeneas almost starts an age of Barracks Emperors. Flandry is a Lt. Commander, then promoted to Commander.

3027   "Outpost of Empire" (*Gal*, December, 1967) [not Flandry]
The misgoverned Empire continues fraying at its borders.

3028   *The Day of Their Return* (New American Library, 1973) [Aycharaych but not Flandry]
Aftermath of the rebellion on Aeneas.

3032   "Tiger by the Tail" (*PS*, January, 1951) [Flandry]
Flandry is a Captain and averts a barbarian invasion.

3033   "Honorable Enemies" (*Future Combined with Science Fiction Stories*, May, 1951) [Flandry]
Captain Flandry's first brush with enemy agent Aycharaych.

3035   "The Game of Glory" (*Venture*, March, 1958) [Flandry]
Set on Nyanza, Flandry has been knighted.

3037   "A Message in Secret" (as *Mayday Orbit*, Ace Books, 1961 from shorter version, "A Message in Secret," *Fantastic*, December, 1959) [Flandry]
Set on Altai.

3038   "A Plague of Masters" (as *Earthman, Go Home!*, Ace Books, 1961 from "A Plague of Masters," *Fantastic*, December, 1960–January, 1961) [Flandry]
Set on Unan Besar.

3040   "Hunters of the Sky Cave" (as *We Claim These Stars!*, Ace Books, 1959 from shorter version, "A Handful of Stars," *Amz*, June, 1959) [Flandry and Aycharaych]

Set on Vixen.

3041   Interregnum: Josip dies. After three years of civil
                     war, Hans Molitor will rule as sole emperor.

3042   "The Warriors from Nowhere" (as "The
                     Ambassadors of Flesh," *PS*, Summer, 1954)
                     Snapshot of disorders in the war-torn Empire.

3047   *A Knight of Ghosts and Shadows* (New American
                     Library, 1975 from *If*, September/October–
                     November/December, 1974) [Flandry]
                     Set on Dennitza, Flandry meets his illegitimate
                     son and has a final tragic confrontation with
                     Aycharaych.

3054   Emperor Hans dies and is succeeded by his
                     sons, first Dietrich, then Gerhart.

3061   *A Stone in Heaven* (Ace Books, 1979) [Flandry]
                     Vice Admiral Flandry pairs off with the daughter
                     of his first mentor from *Ensign Flandry*.

3064   *The Game of Empire* (Baen Books, 1985)
                     [Flandry]
                     Flandry is a Fleet Admiral, meets his illegitimate
                     daughter Diana.

early 4th   The Terran Empire becomes more rigid and
millennium   tyrannical in its Dominate phase. The Empire
                     and Merseia wear each other out.

mid 4th   The Long Night follows the Fall of the Terran
millennium   Empire. War, piracy, economic collapse, and
                     isolation devastate countless worlds.

3600   "A Tragedy of Errors" (*Gal*, February, 1968)
                     Further fragmentation among surviving human
                     worlds.

3900   "The Night Face" (Ace Books, 1978. as *Let the
                     Spacemen Beware!*, Ace Books, 1963 from shorter

version "A Twelvemonth and a Day," *Fantastic Universe*, January, 1960)
Biological and psychological divergence among surviving humans.

4000   "The Sharing of Flesh" (*Gal*, December, 1968)
Human explorers heal genetic defects and uplift savagery.

7100   "Starfog" (*ASF*, August. 1967)
Revived civilization is expanding. A New Vixen man from the libertarian Commonalty meets descendants of the rebels from Aeneas.

Although Technic Civilization is extinct, another—and perhaps better—turn on the Wheel of Time has begun for our galaxy. The Commonalty must inevitably decline just as the League and Empire did before it. But the Wheel will go on turning as long as there are thinking minds to wonder at the stars.

✼   ✼   ✼

Poul Anderson was consulted about this chart but any errors are my own.